THE HOUSE THAT THAT JACK BUILT

R. Wesley Clement

The House That Jack Built
Copyright © 2024 by R. Wesley Clement

ISBN
978-1-962868-76-1 (Paperback)
978-1-962868-77-8 (eBook)
978-1-962868-75-4 (Hardcover)

The House That Jack Built

TABLE OF CONTENTS

FORWARD

My dad named his construction company after an old English nursery rhyme that I fell asleep to nightly. In the early stages of the terrible twos, protesting with a wail and red face, my mom soothed this tortured soul with the numbing repeated lines of, **The House That Jack Built.** Dad displayed a finger representing each new character as they were introduced. With mom repeating stanzas until the maiden all forlorn was to be wed and dad holding up a whole bunch of fingers, my eyes drooped. (I couldn't see them because I was asleep after all), but I know mom and dad high-fived the success of their nightly ritual. I know this because they were always high-fiving one thing or another, always followed by a shared smile.

The last time I heard that story I was nursing a terrible fever and woke up able to count dads fingers but never able to hear the story again. For my dad, George Whiting, who patterned, planned for, and lived his life following the **Carpenters Creed**; (Measure twice, cut once,) this was but one of many of life's curve balls that would be thrown at our family, In the House That Jack Built.

Other real life characters you will meet either throw some of those curve balls or in some cases catch one on the chin.

Not all of them (measure twice and cut once.)

I am relaying as much of this story as I can vouch for. You will find I am pretty intuitive. However some of the characters passing before your eyes never had occasion to meet mine. For that part of the story I will rely on the memory of others.

CHAPTER ONE

Back when I could still hear, one of the first waking sounds that reached my ears was my dad starting his morning whistling as he entered a room. My sister Sarah would cover her ears and head for a corner but my mom tolerated it. No one in the house had a clue to any possible lyrics but dad's awkward dance moves and body language, along with his, the glass is half full personality, indicated the whistle was coming from a happy place.

I had been deaf a while now but I knew this morning as I watched him bounce around that he had every reason to be happy. This was his last day in a stretch of fifteen years of workdays at Coastal Construction. Dad had showed me the recently printed business cards he would be handing out to everyone who crossed his path. Today was his last day of working for someone else.

As creator, owner, CEO, and working crew-member of a construction company named, **The House That Jack Built,** there would be no turning back after today. The company name was already spelled out and painted on the front doors and rear tailgate of one of two trucks he was picking up this very day. Letterhead, business cards, and advertising would carry the business name as well. When dad showed me his first business card he explained, (as best he could using fingers, body gestures and a rolling of his eyes when he couldn't summon up what he wanted to convey) that what had happened to me was a wake-up call for him and Mom. The company name would be a constant reminder of how quickly life can change and how you need to follow your dreams because life can turn on a dime.

My sister and I were still asleep when mom smiled and delivered a cup of coffee to her husband. She leaned in and gave him a kiss on the forehead. Then the two high-fived. (I told you they did that stuff all the time.) Like most other times following their ritual, words were not spoken. But this morning the high-five was followed by conversation.

"Are you excited?"

George looked up, "I'd be lying if I said no, a little scared too, but yeah definitely excited."

Lane pulled out a chair and sat across from her husband. "Well you've paid your dues. Don't forget fifteen years and half a dozen trade licenses ago you were a little afraid to ask me out on a date." She winked, smiled and finished, "And how has that worked out for you?" She offered another high-five.

George looked into her eyes. He looked at the genuine love being offered and smiled into his coffee. He nodded his head. Fifteen years of being the luckiest guy in the world passed in the time it took to raise the cup to his lips. "We have had a run, haven't we?" He raised his cup in a toast to his beautiful lady. "To you and all you do."

"Right back at you." In one motion she rose, high-fived him, and walked her empty cup to the sink.

George checked his watch. "I'm heading in early, got a breakfast meeting with an applicant who might just might turn out to be my best hire. I'll know for sure when I see how they handle their silverware, and whether they clean up after themselves," he chuckled.

Lane's eyes twinkled, the morning sun just now entering the conversation. "Don't be too hard on the poor guy I remember having to table train you back in the day." George added his own twinkle, "Who said the poor guy is a guy?"

Lane's eyes widened, "Are you serious?"

"School trained and crew tested her paperwork says."

"Is there a picture with that application?"

"Nope, but the name on the app-if you can believe this-is Pleasure." He paused, "Now you wouldn't want me prejudging someone's qualifications with just a picture or a name would you?" George winked.

Lane snapped at him with a dish towel, "Just so my husband's not going to cut his fingers off while someone's unfastening his tool belt," she winked back.

George smiled and held out his two hands showing all his fingers, then moved toward his wife, "You can join me for breakfast if you'd like, but rest assured, you are the only lady who gets to fiddle with my tool belt." He brought his wife into a warm embrace. "Now go get those yahoo's up, I need to hit the John, give them a squeeze, and I am gone."

Lane watched her husband's back moving in a rhythm to the sudden sound of his ever present whistle. She walked down the hallway and opened the door to their daughter's room. "Sarah, time to rise and shine." Sarah groaned and turned her head managing a graveled, "morning."

"Hot water for chocolate is ready and a box of your favorite cereal is on the counter. Those yellow things in a bowl, those are bananas. They say they are good for you." Sarah rolled her half opened eyes.

"Your dad wants to say goodbye, so get up. Oh, and fix a bowl for your brother will you?" Lane stretched and yawned, "I'll wake him up, then I need to take a shower," she closed her daughter's door.

She opened the door to Bobby's room. The shades were tightly drawn. Their son liked the dark except during ThunderStorms. She made her way to his bed, the light from the open doorway helped her avoid several buildings made of Legos on the floor in her pathway. She gently shook her son. He tossed. His dream disturbed. She shook him again, his eyes opened, she signed, "Good morning sleepy head."

CHAPTER TWO

The original founder of Coastal Construction stopped in at the Dunkin Donut shop and picked up four-dozen assorted donuts on this Friday morning. The donuts weren't meant for a celebration, but rather an acknowledgment of effort and truthfully a sad goodbye to a valued employee. Fred Riesling, happily retired, still stopped into his company office several times a week, playing at being busy but having no real responsibility. He had handed over the running of the company to his son Joel, a year ago. With George Whiting overseeing his son's decisions things had gone well, though his son chafed at 'being handled' as he termed it.

Standing in line, Fred observed men and women checking off another workweek, celebrating with a filled pastry or buying a box for their co-workers. Today the donuts were not a celebration for a successful transfer of responsibility. Fred was very concerned with the future of the company with George leaving. The entire twenty five men who made up five separate crews would be dunking their donuts to a man who was leaving the company today, (leaving the company in a lurch most thought.)

While Fred waited for the donuts to be selected, counted, and placed in rectangular boxes, he observed a tired donut employee going through the motions. He might be retired but he could still spot a shirker when he saw one. *Jesus that guy is slow. Christ he's sipping coffee while he's working. He couldn't work for me,* he shook his head. He looked away to study the paper in his hand with the key bullet points he had written about George.

*Five trade licenses. *Never missed a day. *Always brought donuts on Friday. *Always up-beat, whistling whatever tune entered his head. *Never an unkind word spoken. *Improved quality company-wide; the list went on. Fred had a humorous anecdote for each of the positive things he planned to say. Again his mind wandered, *Men liked raw humor. If his own son could only figure out what makes people tick he might actually keep Fred's company from going belly up.*

The donuts reached the counter, the man took another sip of his own brew and smiled at Fred. Fred held his tongue, let out some air, paid, then backed through the door and walked to his company car.

—————————

Just two doors down across the street, George Whiting was sitting at a table with a menu in hand. He glanced up and watched through the window as his boss managed to open the rear door of a Coastal Construction company car and deposit this extra-large order of Friday morning donuts onto the back seat. Fred was a good man George would miss him.

Across the table from George sat Pleasure Hailey Anderson, studying her breakfast choices. George decided on a simple bagel since at least one of the donuts being transported surely must be meant for him.

The waitress arrived and the order was placed. George cleared his throat. "So beyond what I have read on your resume, what else should I know about you that would make me want to hire you as my crew foreman?"

Pleasure Hailey Anderson smiled, "I was about to ask you the same thing, Mr. Whiting. All I have seen is your business card with the name of your company. What is it about you and THE HOUSE THAT JACK BUILT that would make me accept a position?"

"Touché. I like your approach, Pleasure. You can call me George."

Pleasure stopped him right there. "Please call me Hailey. I only listed my given name in case you intended to Google me or check out my credentials in some way." She cleared her throat, "Let me explain." She shook her head slightly, "My father was a smart ass prankster." She widened her eyes, "He thought it would be kinda cute to have a daughter named Pleasure. I had no idea it was weird until I started school. Never ending punchline. My mom was just along for the ride in their marriage so that name became official on my birth certificate." She shook her head, "Funny thing is, my dad, he never called me Pleasure. So Like I said, a smart ass." There's a story regarding my middle name too but I won't bore you." Hailey smiled. "You were about to tell me why I should work for you."

George smiled back and shifted in his seat, "OK Hailey, my company will start off as a single crew. What I didn't put in that career opportunity ad is that within three years I hope to be the busiest construction company in what I hope will cover at least two counties. By then I plan to be running a dozen crews."

Hailey raised her eyebrows, "Your old company is not going to like that competition very much, I'm sure."

George looked to the window at the vacant parking space recently occupied by his old boss and mentor. He shook his head. "Things change, bosses change, the world changes." He nodded his head, determined, "I need a change. I'm hoping to put together like-minded people who want to challenge themselves, to grow with my business."

He cleared his throat. "You haven't met my son. He was struck by an unforeseen illness which for many kids would be life changing. My son inspires me. He's the reason I'm taking a chance on myself. When you meet him you'll understand."

Hailey sat up straight, "I can't wait to meet him." She twisted in her seat. As for me it's two separate stories. I just wasn't prepared for the ending that has brought me to this place." She tapped her chest with a thumb, "I was originally going to be a Dentist." She chuckled, "Who knew? Then my father died, the smart ass, and the money it would take died right along with him. So my first dream died along with my dad." She looked inward, "I did get to college and got through the first two years before meeting a man I thought I was going to spend the rest of my life with." She chuckled again but not with humor, "Hmmph, nobody told him I guess." She straightened. I have boxes in my garage that define my life." She shook away the memories.

"Anyw-a-a-ay, he ended up trying to bed every sleeping beauty he could find. He was a Prince Charming, I'll give him that." She shifted in her seat. "So-o-o, I found myself raising a little boy by myself." She raised her arms in testimony, "I was on welfare for about a year. Lowest point of my life." She bowed but then brightened, "Then-n-n, I read about a program that would train me in a building trade."

She held up hands that had seen physical labor, "I found out I am good with my hands. I would have made a hell of a Dentist," she smiled and winked, showing a beautiful set of teeth. "Sooo world change, life change." She studied George across the table, "You know, I am intrigued by the name of your company." She raised her eyebrows, "Is there a story there?"

The food arrived and conversation was interrupted. George noticed the job applicant handled her cutlery just fine. And when they finished eating, Hailey brushed the crumbs onto her plate, adding the silverware and napkin, making cleanup a breeze.

With a hand shake they came to terms. "See you on Monday," George offered as he left the table then added, "There is a story behind the company name I'll tell you about it sometime.

Hailey was left sitting there watching George walk away with an awkward rhythm to his walk. She picked up the strains of an unidentifiable tune. She rubbed her hands together excited for Monday to arrive.

George turned the ignition and studied himself briefly in the rear view mirror. He set his shoulders readying himself for what promised to be an emotional next two hours. He felt an inner calmness overtake him. He looked at the magnet stuck to the dash. At school Bobby had made a little ceramic house with several characters from the nursery rhyme he'd been subjected to early in life peeking out windows and doors and even the chimney. That boy was a constant inspiration.

George wasn't surprised the parking lot was full when he drove in. He had, after all, seen those boxes of donuts. He exited the company pick-up and on the way to the door removed from the key fob all the plastic additions that had allowed him to stop and shop on his way home over the years. He would attach them to the key fob of his new Ford F-250 Diesel Crew-Cab. He'd be picking up his titanium colored mobile office from the paint shop later this afternoon. A clone of this special order vehicle would be ready in another day or two. He pocketed the magnet, carrying his inspiration into the meeting. He whistled, same as always, well maybe a little bit more animated than normal as he opened the company door. The cheers broke out spontaneously.

George stood in the light from the open door taking it all in. The company secretary, Betty, had put up some balloons. A poster board of pictures of completed building projects sat on a long table. George handed her the truck keys, she gave him a long lingering hug. Wolf whistles and wise guy comments about 'getting a room' emerged from the audience. Donuts and coffee sat on the end of the table. George's eyes misted. He would miss these men. He fingered the magnet in his pocket.

Fred Riesling, the company founder and his son Joel were the only guys wearing ties. They stood to the side talking. The crew members dressed to work, got up and formed a line. George walked that line feeling the strength in the grips of the men he had spent years with. Wise ass comments hid the feelings of respect they had for George. When he had completed the walk he moved to the table to get a coffee and donut. He looked at the pictures of completed projects, mentally removing himself briefly from the buzz of conversation going on around him.

Fred approached, the two shook hands. Fred's left hand rested on George's shoulder. "I'm really going to miss you George. The company is going to miss you even more." He cleared his throat then whispered, "Joel asked me to see if you would reconsider, stay another year or two, with a substantial raise of course. He won't ask you himself, he's too proud." The two men understood without words that half of Joel's problem was exactly that— too proud, too stubborn, and too opinionated.

George took a step back and met Fred's eyes, "I noticed Joel couldn't offer his hand." He smiled then. "It's a kind offer Fred, but the paint is dry on my new trucks so I better get to work and pay for them." He smiled. The two men shook hands once more.

"I don't blame you George, there was a time back in the day when I made the move you're making. I have never regretted it." Fred, done with the easy part, knowing George's response before he asked the question, shrunk slightly. He asked the final question his son wanted asked. "The crew members you hired from us, is there any way you could tell them you changed your mind. They are our best men— after you that is?"

George shook his head and opened his arms, "They approached me Fred, and they are leaving your company even if I don't hire them. I'd be a fool not to take them on." "I told Joel I was sure that was the way it went down, but he's bitter about it anyway."

"I'll talk with your son if you think it would help."

"It's probably better to just let it go. He'll get over it."

Coffee cups were raised, accomplishments praised, funny stories delivered by several crew members, as well as Fred.

Finally a plaque was presented and all the donuts devoured.

By nine am the party was over.

George caught a ride with one of the two men who were also changing jobs today. Another so long, see you Monday morning and George was standing in front of his new gleaming office on wheels. **The House That Jack Built** was painted on the front door on each side of the truck and on the back tailgate. George had to smile, to him the words were so much more than part of a nursery rhyme.

He went into the paint shop and got the keys. He stepped up and entered his new executive suite, making himself comfortable in the President's chair. He put the little magnet on the dash then fiddled with all the bells and whistles that were at his fingertips. Nearly everything was voice activated. A half dozen smartphones could be linked to this main office, allowing him to be on the job even as he was out trying to round up more business. He had programmed his Rolodex of numbers and names when the truck was first delivered so just by opening his mouth he commanded the attention of the mystery lady who seemed to be all knowing: "Call Lane at work." When his wife answered her cell phone, George was astonished to hear his wife's voice exit the eight speakers of his Sony sound system. "Hey honey I'm sitting in my new office and you have never sounded better."

"How did your two meetings go? Do I need to look for a new builder?"

George chuckled. "She's beautiful, she's bright, she's black, and she handled her silverware like a pro. You're gonna love her. I hired her this morning. She has a boy about Bobby's age. I think you should invite them to dinner in the near future."

George's voice lost some of its excitement. "The other meeting was fine except Joel threw me daggers when I left. To be expected I guess."

George mentally shifted gears in his new Ford Diesel. "I'm going to go check out several possible new clients then I'll pick up some chicken to barbecue for tonight. Along with a little wine, a movie or two to occupy the kids, anything else I need to bring home?"

I'll provide all the dessert you need." Her giggle filled the truck. "I'm really proud of you honey, I can't wait to raise a glass with you. See you at home."

Joel Riesling watched George leave, two of his best workers following him out. He could barely contain himself. He tried to make his father understand the significance of what was happening but his father could find no fault with George. Well he knew what this meant. This was going to be an all out war. He hated everything about the man. The remaining crew members were milling about wasting time. Joel shouted, "Get the hell to work, this party is over." Grumbles echoed the men out the door.

Joel went back to hating and remembering why he hated. *Joel had ended up as back-up quarterback on the football squad. Then he lost out as starting pitcher on the baseball team. As if that weren't bad enough he had dated Lane before George ever did. Second fiddle there as well.*

Joel found hope when George joined the military, thinking Lane might see the light with George out of the picture. Hell he might not even come back. Joel sighed. Not only did she remain true to the guy, he came home a damn hero of some kind.

Then his very own father hired George. George gets the girl and Joel gets to listen to that god awful whistle and constant positive attitude for the past fifteen years. He was sitting behind his desk still muttering to himself when his father entered his office.

"This is actually a good thing for you Joel. You're just as capable as George if you apply yourself. This is an opportunity to make this company your own."

"Yeah well, he took my two best men Dad, it's not right." "Listen to me son, those two men worked side by side with George for ten years. They were gone the minute he made the decision to start his own business. Get over it and get over yourself, go drum up some business. Rumor has it, Bill Simpson is going to re-do the clubhouse at the golf course, go feel him out."

Joel got up out of his chair grumbling, "I'm going to check on the crew that's building the house on Parkman road. If I get a chance I'll stop to see Bill. Why don't you call him anyway? You know him. Hell you play golf with him." "I'm retired son and George is gone. You need to take the reins from now on or your very worst fears will keep you awake at night. Not to rehash the past but George getting the better of you on lots of fronts has more to do with you than George."

"I've heard this all before, spare me the tour down memory lane."

Fred shook his head side to side, took a deep breath and left to play golf with Bill Simpson. He would not be picking the man's brain about anything except how to keep his damn head down and finish his swing.

CHAPTER THREE

Joel got in his own company truck, a six year old Toyota Tundra, another source of disagreement with George. When they had decided six years ago on five new trucks, George wanted to buy local, Joel struck what he thought was a better deal fifty miles away. Then the local Ford dealership expanded – moving their location – building a gleaming new office and dealership two miles from Coastal Construction's headquarters. They wouldn't even accept a bid from Coastal Construction and Joel never lived down the embarrassment.

He opened the Styrofoam cooler that was his constant shotgun rider. His three best friends looked up at him. They had become even closer friends since George announced his departure. At first, bottles of good old Jim, Jack, and Evan, helped toast good riddance to George. When reality set in and Joel was going to have to actually run the company they offered a little solace to a bad morning, afternoon, or evening. Half a six pack of coke cans resting on a bed of melting ice, helped sweeten the deal his three friends offered, a quarter sleeve of red solo cups completed this on demand party to go.

Joel gazed at his friends and decided, "A party that's what I need. It's Friday anyway and nothing gets done on Friday," he muttered. He sat up straight and scrolled through his cell phone. He made two calls. He looked up at the blazing sun.

Possible beach party day. He went home to change. An hour later he pulled into an apartment complex in St. Augustine, Florida. The air conditioning in his truck was cooling his face as he raised the red cup to his lips. Jim was in command today – Jack and Evan not offering an opinion – course it was early yet. He spoke to the closed cooler as if Jack and Evan could hear him. "You'll get your day in the sun if this all works out."

He heard a muffled sound and looked up. Myrtle Beech was on the top floor balcony of the four story building waving and shouting something Joel couldn't hear. He watched her mouth move through the windshield. *That's the most sense she's made since I met her,* he chuckled to himself. He raised his cup in salute to his private joke. *She's thinking I'm toasting her, the dizzy bitch. Oh well the things we do when we want to screw.* Joel opened the truck door and the midday heat hit him like a sucker punch. *Whoa, maybe rethink the beach. Maybe dial down Myrtle's thermostat and party at the top of the world.*

Suddenly thinking of the woman on the balcony, *who has a name like Myrtle Beech?* He wiped his receding hair back under his cap and shrugged his shoulders. *Well shit it's too damn hot to work anyway.* He smiled and waved to the balcony. He reached back in the cab, grabbed Jim by the throat, fingered his ball cap, and headed for the Beech.

From above Myrtle viewed a pale white background of scalp appear on an ever decreasing island of brown.

She watched Joel plunk on his greasy ball cap displaying a Daytona Beach logo. She had picked up that damn hat from wherever Joel left it for over a year. The white framing his hairline seemed to be expanding in equal proportion to his waistline. Myrtle didn't need an imagination to see what was happening right before her eyes. She had watched him poke a new hole in his belt at least twice since she met him. His comb over was becoming hilarious. *But don't laugh or comment she had learned.*

When a new wardrobe of jeans and skivvies bearing size 36 on the tags arrived she was smart enough not to make light of this new uniform number. Joel left clothes all over the place and she was expected to keep them laundered and folded. She shook her head, *what is wrong with me?*

Captain of the loser patrol that's me. All this change in just a year of pizza and wing deliveries or the not to be taken lightly drive-thru. Even now as he reached the door to the building her mind wandered. *Take the stairs you lazy ass. It's as if that damn truck were your legs. And Drive-Thru seems to be the man's mantra the few times he had taken her anywhere.*

'I ain't tipping some wide ass scudder for spitting on my food,' *Joel's justification for eating ribs in a parking lot.* She left the balcony, eyebrows raised, gazing up one last time at the clouds dotting a sea of blue. She sighed. *Well at least it's a good beach day.*

The buzzer signaled Elvis was in the house. She breathed in deeply, *Today's the day I just have to tell him about his feet. They're not expanding and contracting like the rest of him, but god the stench.*

—·—•••—·—

In Palm Coast Joel's dad was putting the finishing efforts on two very different nine holes. Bill Sullivan had spent twenty minutes on the range before the round, reinforcing the two areas Fred was trying to improve. Keep your head still and finish your swing. For nine holes Fred kept it together. He looked like he was tracking a deer. It seemed to work. When they stopped for a sandwich after nine holes, Fred actually toasted Bill and paid for lunch. "I think I got this, look at this card. A 45 with two double bogies and those because of the damn water on the par threes." Bill agreed, "I was impressed." Bill didn't go beyond that, he had seen too many nine hole miracles dissolve in the second nine.

By the fifteenth hole a dragged out Fred looked like he had left the golf course and was climbing those apartment stairs his son was avoiding just up the turnpike. It was even worse than that. It seemed his son must have forgotten something in the truck and Fred was forced to climb them once again.

Sweat ran down Fred's chest hairs. His two swing thoughts had deserted him and he found himself flailing at the damn ball. He was looking skyward even before he made contact with the ball and his swing seemed to hit a brick wall a foot after that contact. He was now trying to come to grips with the forty bucks he had lost to Bill with that seven he just penciled in on the fourteenth. He had insisted on the bet. Bill tried to discourage him but Fred just knew today was the day he was going to recoup some of those dollar-a- hole bets he had lost in the last year. Ten bucks a hole he had demanded for the second nine. Even getting a stroke a hole wasn't helping. The two agreed, after Fred put two in the water on the par three fifteenth, to call it a day.

They were sitting in the bar nursing a beer when George Whiting slid into a seat.

"Can I buy you guys another beer?" Fred thought that was an excellent idea. The men chatted and swapped jokes for half an hour, then Fred shook hands and left. He looked back briefly, thinking, *my lazy assed son should be the one about to talk business with Bill. Just like his golf game, there was no easy fix for his son.*

— • •• • •• • —

Joel was staring at the bottom of his solo cup for a third time thinking he might have to get off this couch and invite Jack and Evan to the party when the buzzer sounded. His second cell call had arrived. Myrtle Beech was three beers into a six pack and had just gone into the ladies room to powder her nose. Joel was silently bad mouthing the idiocy of a woman who could never bring herself to simply say she had to take a piss.

He carried that thought to the door.

Franklin Causano jumped back and looked up. At five-fee-tzero inches— in cowboy boots— Franklin could still light up a party. He wielded an oversized head with no neck and a small rectangular mouth half circled by a crazed caterpillar. A fixed shit eating grin showed flawless teeth. It was a grin that hid a past filled with raw emotion.

Franklin was a mongrel. Half white, part black, and a dash of Creole adding a little spice. On the surface Franklin was the perfect foil to Joel's temperament.

Joel dubbed him, 'The Little Train That Could.' And Franklin could. And Franklin would, but in his own time and in his own way.

This afternoon he was dressed in a red flowered muumuu that allowed just the pointed toes of his cowboy boots to protrude. Franklin was wearing a hat that any selfrespecting old time country music fans would recognize it as a Minnie Pearl knock-off. Waiting to be invited in and suspecting the invite would include a wise ass comment about his wardrobe, Franklin kept his smile in place. He was not disappointed.

"How is it that you continue to amaze me little buddy? You own stock in a Goodwill store or what?"

Franklin modeled his way in. "Actually I picked this up in a little shop in the old city. We are going to the beach are we not?"

Joel let out some air from both ends. Franklin held his breath and turned away. Joel spoke, "Re-thinking that idea. It's awful hot. Thought we just might order in and party right here."

Myrtle chose that moment to re-enter the room, "What's that, we're not going to the beach?" she whined, "You promised Joel." With that Myrtle plopped herself on the couch, pouting. "I only get one day off a week you know."

Franklin sat down beside Myrtle and whispered in her ear. Myrtle brightened and giggled.

"What you two whispering about?" Well into becoming shit-faced, every drink adding to the rabbit ears that had Joel thinking someone was always talking about him, making fun of him.

Franklin spoke up, "I was just telling Myrtle since she's already a Beech we could just lay on her for the afternoon."

Joel didn't see the humor, "What's this **we shit** white man, Myrtle's beach is private, he growled."

Franklin with his smile fixed in place opened a hand that had been empty a moment ago. He dangled a baggie. "Then I guess this white sand I brought with me will just have to be spread along my own private little beach."

The baggie was like waving a red flag in front of a bull. The first thought Joel had was, *I could just take the little shits powder and throw him off the balcony.* Then he looked at Myrtle. Then he looked again at the baggie. Then he looked at Franklin. There was something in the little man's eyes that had Joel believing Franklin could see right into his head. Franklin had dazzled Joel from day one with magic tricks, maybe he could read minds as well. He looked back at Myrtle, back at the baggie. He rubbed his chin. *Franklin couldn't hurt Myrtle any. He didn't even know if he really cared for the girl, even as well as she treated him. Her beach had probably been open to the public a long time before Joel found his way here he decided.*

He suddenly smiled, "Franklin," he slurred his speech but it was understandable at least. "You're right. We'll just explore this particular beach together." He stood up. He patted Franklin on the hat. "Be right back. He weaved slightly towards the door. "Let me bring a couple of my friends up from the truck."

— • — • • — • —

George pulled into the driveway of the small house he had built for his family a dozen years ago. He turned off the engine and gazed into the future. He would soon be building a new house for his wife and children. Staring at his present small concrete house he formed a mental template, the lines and the pitches of roof on his planned house emerging.

Son Bobby, a budding architect in his own rite, had made drawings that showed an understanding of the building process. That seemed to be the link that tied father and son these days.

George couldn't sign as well as his wife Lane, or his daughter Sarah, yet father and son seemed to understand one another perfectly. He touched the magnet and imaginary walls appeared laid out as a bright kitchen and breakfast nook. A family room accented with wainscoting held a fireplace and raised mantel for a big screen. Two baths connected to the children's rooms and a spare bedroom, completed downstairs. George pictured a graceful stairway and climbed to a master bedroom and bath with double vanities, walk-in closets, and an open walk-in shower. He looked down at the -soon to be- pool from his home office. From this height he could see the entire patio protected by screening. An outdoor kitchen and changing room with a tiled saltwater pool in the middle would obviously be a family hangout. The new house, twice the square footage of this one, would be costly but by supplying his own labor along with contractor pricing, it was doable. He had already purchased a double lot that looked out over the Inter coastal water-way. He sighed contentedly and opened his eyes.

Bobby was standing there waiting to see the new truck. He opened the door and Bobby climbed in. <u>Have at it</u> he gestured and left the boy to explore.

George grabbed the groceries and entered through the open garage.

CHAPTER FOUR

Monday morning after promising Bobby he could join him later in the day, George treated his new crew to breakfast. The foursome sat around a rectangular table at a small restaurant in Flagler Beach. While they all sipped an after breakfast coffee, George explained the two projects they would be working on today. One was a home renovation. Peter Myers, the most seasoned worker, would take Smiley Dickinson and go there. "You have a material delivery at 9:00 this morning. Pete the blueprints are laid out on the kitchen counter. You'll know what needs doing and the order of things so get started and I'll stop in later. Good news. I have a verbal commitment for the golf club renovation. That project is going to give our company a lot of visibility. Hailey you will head over there and try to come up with an estimate that fits the owner's needs and his budget. I have looked over his plans. We need to figure square footage and material prices. We also need to check the condition of present heating, lighting, and plumbing loads. If we are going to need new permits we need to jump on those. This is a large expansion. We need to do our homework. We can't short change ourselves on our estimate. Chairs scraped in unison and it was off to work.

— • —

Joel had his head in his hands. The party lasted all weekend. He lost track of how it ended up. His work truck was still in the parking lot at Myrtle's apartment complex. The last thing he remembered was Franklin sitting atop a pile of pillows driving him back to his place. Through squinted pained eyes, Joel had watched Franklin's profile. The little man seemed unfazed by the white sand they had snorted.

The same fixed grin that had arrived on Friday wished him well as Joel stumbled away from the car.

Betty knocked on the door of his office. "Your father just called, he's on his way here and he didn't sound happy."

"Didn't I tell you to say I wasn't available today?"

"Joel, your father knows that's code for you being holed up in here with the blinds closed."

Joel stood up, got dizzy and sat right back down. Shit. He attempted to stand again but sat back when the office door opened and his father entered.

His father snapped on the light and moved to the blinds. Joel felt like he was in an interrogation room under a hot light. He covered his eyes. A sudden thought. *I plead the fifth,* he chuckled, *three fifths really, if that helps. OH that hurts.* He held his head. Fred looked down at a son he would like to send back to the manufacturer as inferior material. His voice rose as each word struck like a hammer blow, "What-is-wrong-with your-head! Not a question. I don't mean the hangover you're wearing this minute. I mean the head that's up your ass even when you're sober."

"You're hollering Dad." Joel groaned.

"Yes I'm hollering!" Fred moved around the desk to get a better look at the weekend carnage. "Your mother is the only reason you still have a position here. I'm just on the verge of telling her about your drug use. Even she wouldn't condone that."

"What drug use?"

Fred snorted derisively "I have sized up every conceivable building project this company has done for the past twenty years and I can still read a ruler when I need to. You son, are not measuring up by any standard." He let the words linger. He buzzed Betty for some coffee.

Then he began anew. "George met with Bill Friday afternoon. I'm sitting at the same table watching a million dollar plus renovation disappear before my very eyes at the same time that shit is disappearing right up your nose." Fred shook his head. "An expensive little snort wouldn't you say?" He didn't give Joel the opportunity to even hazard an answer.

Joel had his head back in his hands.

"I'm leaving but I'll be back within the hour so have your ass in and out of the shower and all your shit out of my office." Joel looked up dazed and confused.

"You are going back to work as a crew member. If that doesn't suit you let your fingers do the walking to your next employer." Fred sniffed the air and grimaced.

Joel laid his head down on the desk. The door slammed.

A minute later the door reopened, Betty announcing, "Fred told me to get in here and vacuum out your smell."

'Open the damn windows, his feet smell like an old sheep.' Joel looked up, his face pained. Betty held up her hands, "His words."

⸻●⸻●⸻●⸻

Hailey sat with Bill looking at a drawing of his vision for the club house. She asked him to break down each area, visualize and verbalize the activity. Bill closed his eyes. Then he told Hailey what he saw. Hailey listened, sketching as Bill verbalized his vision. When Bill finished, Hailey held up her work and asked for an hour. When Bill left the room she closed her own eyes, nodding and talking to herself under her breath. Hailey then took charge. She sketched in a half wall.

She added an additional entrance and a built-in glass trophy case. When finished she found Bill chatting away with a member. They returned to the office. Hailey smiled and handed the drawing back to Bill.

He studied the changes. His head moved as he interpreted the plan. A big smile emerged, "Those are great ideas, why didn't I think of them?"

"Sometimes it takes an outsider to see what's right in front of us. Adding an entrance and a half wall right here will keep the in and out traffic moving away from the dining room. Your seated members won't feel like they are eating in a diner. The trophy case will lend more stature to your event winners, A higher profile than just a designated parking space for the club winners I saw coming in."

Bill was having a hard time taking his eyes off this beautiful woman. Breathing in Hailey's subtle perfume he managed, "How long before I can get some hard numbers?"

"Well George is doing some measuring and checking on codes and your energy and plumbing needs. He will look at all that plus what we've come up with. He'll no doubt offer his view as well. But rest assured he'll be right on top of things." The two rose and shook hands. "I'll show the drawings to George at lunch, he's meeting me here. Say, why don't you join us?"

Bill smiled, "I can do that."

George had been busy. After going over the club house, making notes and calling the city code department he spent an hour in his truck calling real-estate agents and contractor friends mining for business. Two potential opportunities had emerged. He needed to share some of the excitement he was feeling.

He checked his watch. Lane would be either vacuuming or getting lunch ready for the kids about now. He instructed—All-Knowing—his name for the voice that left the speaker to dial up his wife. The day was heating up, 85 degrees on the dash readout and climbing. His mobile office was cool though and after this call George would be having lunch with Hailey.

"Why don't you invite her and her son to dinner Wednesday night?"

"I will. Just wanted to keep you in the loop."

"So, a great beginning today. I'm proud of you, love ya babe. By the way Bobby wants to know what time you are picking him up. This kid cracks me up. This morning he wanted to know if there was a way to swear in SIGN language. After I stopped laughing he told me about a kid that's been bugging him and he wants a way to address the situation without punching the kid when school starts back up."

"Well, is there?

"Is there what?"

"A way to swear in SIGN."

"Oh yes, I've been swearing at you for years and you didn't even know it," laughed Lane.

"Did you tell Bobby?"

"Of course not, he'll figure it out on his own. I'm sure he already knows the value of the universal bird. I told him to use his sense of humor. He has to handle it."

"Well, I want some instruction. With this new business I'll have lots of reasons to swear, probably better to do it silently. Tell Bobby to be ready by 3 pm, he can spend the afternoon with me."

"OK, he'll be ready. I'll see you tonight, don't forget to invite Hailey to dinner."

"Ten-four, over and out good buddy."

— • — • • — • • —

The morning wasn't quite as pleasant for Joel. His father returned and made sure Betty's orders had been followed.

Joel found himself still in a dress shirt, slacks and street shoes strapping on a tool belt. The men looked at him oddly as he joined the crew. His head still hurt and he was sweating profusely while muttering to himself. His first task was to carry drywall to the second floor of a new construction. He now understood the complaining he'd been hearing about replacing a broken lift he had sloughed off. He managed to carry one end of the eight foot section and nailed it. On the other end of the eight foot section was Donald Smith doing his part. They finished and went down the flight and a half of stairs to grab another piece. With the lift broken the two men were maneuvering their way up for a third time with what is a very awkward and heavy piece of material. Joel led the way up the stairs. He was four steps from the top of a sixteen step climb when his grip slipped. He tried to readjust but hit the drywall with his shoulder, twisting the piece from Donald's grasp.

Donald, now holding all the weight and downhill to boot, was struck in the chest. He was knocked backward down the eight steps to the landing. He landed awkwardly, striking his head and breaking his arm.

The hollering and shouting that ensued attracted the two remaining crew members who quickly surmised what had happened. The comments an hour earlier surrounding the arrival of Joel, obviously hung over or under the influence, had been summed up as an accident waiting to happen. Neither Joel nor Donald had been wearing a hard hat. An ambulance arrived and carted Donald away. Joel went into full damage control. He texted his father to get over here right away. While he waited he gave the remaining crew members the version they should be conveying. The two crew members felt no loyalty to Joel but they both needed to keep their jobs. And so the truth would be left in the sawdust and debris, left there on the stairs to be stepped upon and pointed to with head shakes and reminders of the danger of not following safety rules and the **Carpenter's Creed.**

CHAPTER FIVE

I lost my hearing when I was two years of age. Just as I was beginning to understand the various nuances of language I contracted the childhood disease of measles. For most kids' measles is manageable. A runny nose and fever followed by a rash that can cover most of the body. I had all those symptoms in spades. I became that rare case. That rare case where more serious side effects occur. For me, Encephalitis, a swelling of the brain occurred. I lost my hearing.

I didn't know it but everyone tells me I am a bright little boy, and within the year my entire family was communicating with me again, in SIGN.

I had been speaking in full sentences before my hearing loss but when the family became comfortable with this new unspoken language I pretty much stopped talking at all. <u>Welcome to my World</u> I signed whenever it seemed fitting.

Mom and sometimes Dad had read to me while I was still in the womb. Later I followed along as Mom or Dad read to me nightly. My favorite story, **The House That Jack Built** involved both Mom and Dad. Dad would count on his fingers and make the sounds of the characters. Soon I would be out like a light. At age two I was reading the story myself with mom helping me break longer words into manageable bites. Mom had introduced the language of Baby Sign, when I was an infant not knowing the future.

Learning for me continued on the page and off after I recovered from the disease. Putting on closed captions for cartoons and children's shows allowed me to get the humor and follow the plot. Mom mastered Sign and taught my big sister Sarah, and me. Dad could manage, but just barely. Still, we understood one another. Now at age eight I can read the written word and the vocabulary of Sign.

Being deaf requires that much of my learning take place in the visual world, not the auditory, so I keep my eyes wide open.

I attend a public school that offers a special needs program. School is closed for vacation so this afternoon I'm going to be riding in Dad's new mobile office continuing to figure out the owner's manual. I love all things mechanical. In my room I create buildings and machines with Legos. In my father's office at home I have learned to read blueprints. I can visualize the plumbing and piping and electrical circuits. "You understand all this?" I noticed the challenge for Dad of making himself understood involved hand movements and exaggerated mouth movements hoping I could lip read. He asked me that question the first time I signed a question that was way too deep for a kid my age. I was confused. "Why wouldn't I? It was then that Dad began involving me in designing our future home. Today he picked me up in the new company truck. I could sense he was watching me from the corner of his eye as I paged through the owner's manual. I could see him smiling to himself. *Dad, limited in his signing ability, seemed thankful when I didn't have to ask a single question. This baby is loaded.*

We drove to the golf course. He left me sitting in the lounge with the owner's manual while he finished up inside. When done we headed to a Dunkin Donut. Before entering the drive thru I tried to sign for a chocolate milk and coconut covered chocolate donut but Dad was having trouble understanding me. Finally I grabbed his notebook and drew a whiskered chocolate donut and a rectangle with the word chocolate. Dad nodded, opened the driver's side window and pulled into the drive thru. "Got it." Phew, I signed, reading Dad's lips.

While we waited in line I studied the dashboard. I had spent a little time in the truck the other afternoon when dad first brought it home so I had a head start. Time, day, and month was displayed. Today was Monday. In two days, Wednesday, -Prince Spaghetti day-our family called it, a possible new friend is coming to dinner, mom said. Dad also tried to tell me about the invitation. Thank goodness for Mom.

I have never played with a black kid but then again a black kid has probably never played with a deaf kid so it's all good.

I spent the afternoon between the two job sites Dad was responsible for and I met Hailey. She is beautiful. Her son Daniel, might become my new friend.

(According to sources in the know) apparently I'm not your average eight year old.

There are some supposed gifts I possess. Mom and Dad have asked questions. Was I gifted from birth? Did the introduction of Baby Sign stimulate some of my brain neurons to be more sensitive? Did the trauma of hearing loss actually strengthen my other senses? Who knows? What they do say is I show an uncanny ability to see the whole and mentally tear it apart, down to its beginning. Even beyond that, without knowing or even exploring the how or why, they tell me I seem able to read body language, even others thoughts as they are forming. For me these things aren't gifts. For me some things just seem obvious.) In school, the ability to read body language has kept me from the clutches of a boy twenty pounds heavier who seems to believe I am his new play toy. I told my parents about the bully.

"Take care of it yourself, use your gifts," Mom told me. Well alrighty then.

The week flew and I'm still in one piece. Tonight Prince Spaghetti. Dad's Mother had made it a tradition along with a salad and garlic bread. Tonight a possible new playmate. That would be better than dessert.

When the doorbell rang, the little light dad had placed above the door lit up. I ran to the door. Hailey, dad's new worker, had apparently received a first lesson from her boss and signed me Hello.

I smiled and shook her hand. It was then that her son Daniel peeked around her skirt and we made eye contact. I 39 judged him to be about my age. I had several black kids in my class but they were older and never played with me. The boy seemed unsure how to begin. I sensed that and simply took his hand and walked him into my room. The rest was easy. I mean really, if you can't get excited about model rockets, a train set and tracks that circle the room, two mini- skyscrapers made from Legos complete with an elevator, and various pieces of construction equipment; then you don't belong in my room. As things turned out we had to be pried to the dinner table.

Sitting there patting my belly I felt good. Everyone else seemed to be happy as well. I watched the body language of the conversation. Comfort food smells and warm smiles drifted over the dinner table. I went to a quiet place in my mind and let the table conversation flow.

Hailey was prompted by mom to describe her first week. "It's the first time I have been given the opportunity to sit with a client and interpret what they envision. I loved every second, Thank you," she toasted dad.

"Don't thank me it was just a business decision," responded dad, but raised his glass anyway.

"Care to expand on what that means, boss man?" questioned mom.

Dad had to smile. "As much as I hate to say this, especially in front of two very capable beautiful women," he raised his glass again in a toast, "it is still a man's world."

The women didn't seem to get it. Dad explained. "Simply put I knew Bill Simpson would listen more closely to a beautiful woman sitting across from him showing him she understands his needs," he winked then, "and then artfully fulfilling those needs."

The women toasted George. Lane responded, "Maybe Bobby gets his – I know what you're thinking before I say it ability— the good old fashioned way— he inherited it." Laughter followed.

I came out of my doze and observed the open mouths and obvious laughter taking place. I loved the language of laughter, the facial gestures and body language from what I could see indicated maybe there might be more play dates with Daniel. I got up out of my seat, went over and hugged my mom. Mom teared up and squeezed me.

Good first date, I thought later as the house emptied of its guests.

With the dinner guests long gone I lay awake in my darkened room. It was thundering and lightning outside. I could see the flashes of light tear at and threaten the edges of my shade. I couldn't hear the thunder but I could feel it. Normally I like the dark but not during a lightning storm. Normally this would be the time I would go into my sister Sarah's room and pull the covers loose from the bottom of her bed, crawl in and hug her feet. My sister has the warmest feet. In the morning when she discovers me I join her at the top and she smooths my hair and hugs me till it's time to get up. Sarah is not home tonight though. With school closed she spent the day and night with one of her friends.

I sighed. There was nothing else to do then except to get up and turn on the lamp. The lightning flashes diminish in the lamplight and I will simply work through the storm. I was told much later in life by my Dad that I didn't so much play with my toys as use them. He told me I was an architect and engineer in the making from day one—self taught.

Earlier today when dad placed the plans Hailey drew up for the golf club renovation on the truck seat I opened it and studied it. The plan had stayed in my head. I could sense the emotion Hailey had put into her effort. Lying there in the light of my lamp, still feeling the roll of thunder in my bones and watching my window shade lighten in concert, I mentally reconstructed the blueprint. Suddenly my eyes widened, *I found a single flaw in her design.* I would share that with dad in the morning. As the storm moved on and the light show lessened I finally gave in.

Mom found me in the morning, still on the rug, tucked tightly in a blanket; a drawing and pencil beside me on the rug.

— • —

In the fourth floor apartment of Myrtle Beech the same storm that kept Bobby Whiting awake had moved north. Joel Riesling was mimicking the storm outside, unleashing a barrage of his own thunder and lightning in a one sided conversation that was both heard and seen by Myrtle and Franklin. They were trying to watch a show in the living room. The two looked at one another. They were witnessing a meltdown of a guy who was losing a lot more than his hair. After ten minutes of ranting, Joel yelled, "Come out here. Turn that damn thing off." They joined him at the kitchen table. A near empty bottle of Evan Williams Whiskey gasped for breath as Joel grabbed it by the neck, emptying the little life left into a glass splashed with Coca Cola. Joel wanted an audience and he did not want the damn TV competing for air time.

"He wrecked my life, and he's going to pay, the son of a bitch." The words slurred but the meaning was clear. Franklin didn't do alcohol. Pot and an occasional snort of cocaine was his emotional medicine of choice and that mostly to make him sociable. Tonight he was doing neither which made this sloppy drunk even harder to bear.

He was beginning to like Myrtle though. "I thought he was gone from the company." Franklin stared across the table at bloodshot eyes that were fighting to focus and stay open.

"Jesus, you heard anything I've said? Does your brain match your shoe size, you friggin dwarf?"

Franklin kept his fixed smile in place. He read from his script not responding to the insult—he heard it though, and sighed. "So how are you going to make him pay for wrecking your life, Joel?"

Joel looked all squirrely like, "You'll know it when you see it little man." He sighed, yawned, rubbed his face trying to focus, and repeated— before laying his head down on the table— "You'll know it when you see it."

Myrtle had remained quiet, busy playing footsie with Franklin out of the sight of Joel. She listened to Joel begin to snore. He was a-gonna for the night now. She reached and took Franklin by the hand. There had to be a way to get this drunken sailor out of her life. She looked Franklin in the eyes, *hmm maybe this little man could help with that.*

Franklin had his own thoughts on this dark and stormy night. *I'll just keep those to myself for now,* he nodded his head and followed Myrtle to her room. Joel snored on.

CHAPTER SIX

Donald Smith, injured on the job by the recklessness of his boss spent a week in the hospital with a concussion. He was left with hospital bills, no promise of a job when he healed and minimal insurance.

Now let's not paint a picture of a man who had his act together before this incident. Donald Smith partied hard, worked hard, had disappointed his fair share of people, but loved his daughter. That being said, on the day of the accident he was straight up sober. And he remembered exactly how he came to be lying at the foot of the stairs. When he was well enough he made his way to the office of Coastal Construction. With a sling holding his arm in place he entered the office of Fred Riesling.

Fred had heard the bitter truth from the two crew members who he swore to secrecy. This morning he was all about damage control. "Come in and sit down, Don. How are you feeling?"

"Well I'd be feeling a little better if your son had found the time to contact me and apologize." Don snorted, "Hell he's looked the other way both times I've seen him." Don eyed Fred. "Not feeling the love, Mr. Riesling."

"I'm sure he's sorry you got hurt. But sit down and let's try to sort this all out. I have your file right here Don." Fred read to himself then looked up, "I've been gone so bear with me while I catch up."

When Fred looked up he was already playing offense. "I'm afraid your time with us is a little spotty. Lots of days you called in sick.

Arrived late on many days. I wasn't in charge in the last year. It seems the only reason you were still employed was George Whiting advocating for you."

Don Smith was rankled, "He knew my story if that's what you're getting at. That piece of paper can't talk but I never missed work because I wanted to. There were reasons, that's all I'm going to say. George knew what they were and supported me. By the way I worked a bunch of weekend days to make up for any time I missed. Is that written down there anywhere?"

Fred didn't comment. "What are you asking for Don, obviously you aren't ready to work?"

"I think my bills should be covered, the insurance only covers a portion. And I need a job. I can read blueprints and schematics. I'm not looking for revenge but I need to work."

Fred needed to think this through. "I tell you what. I'll talk with the crew leaders, see if there is something they could use help with. Leave me a number and I promise I'll get back to you within a couple of days. Fair enough?"

Don looked Fred straight in the eyes. "I still haven't talked with the insurance company, or OSHA. I told them the concussion left me muddled. But Mr. Riesling I remember every part of that day. All I'm looking for is my job back. Think about that when you talk to the crew leaders."

When Joel left the office, Fred hollered to Betty. "Call my son on the job. Get him in here, NOW." ^

Two weeks had passed since George started his new business. He was kidded about the sign on his trucks at nearly every stop. From the lumber yard to the hardware store to coffee and lunch stops, George just kidded back, "You're reading the sign aren't you? That's free advertising. Thank you. Tell your friends we're open for business."

Hailey drove the truck with the number plate bearing the letters NAILIT 2. They had agreed on daily briefings alternating between Starbucks and Dunkin Donuts at 7 am every morning.

Well before that at 5:30 am, George sat at the kitchen table with Lane. His first poured cup allowed the two to compare notes that might have been forgotten during the erratic, sometimes chaotic evenings with their two very busy children. This morning George remembered to tell Lane that Bobby had found a flaw in the blueprint for the golf club renovation. "He was dead on. This kid is special Lane. He walks right into these renderings, like it's an existing structure with doors and windows he can open and close."

Lane had to smile. "In case you haven't noticed he does that with people as well. Did you see how quickly he bonded with Hailey's son? They are best buddies already. They are skyping and Bobby is trying to teach Daniel, Sign. Somehow they are communicating. He wants to sleep over this weekend. He's blossoming before our eyes."

"Has he said any more about how he intends to handle the boy who has been bullying him?" "Nope, he just said he was studying on it."

— · — ● ◆ ● · —

Five hours later, George and his crew were seated in the same little eatery where he had interviewed Hailey. Today George was springing for lunch for the team and was already bearing good news for the company. Menus in front of the five, water glasses filled, side talk competing with conversations in the rest of the room, George tapped his glass with his spoon. "Okay team, before you order I have a couple of things to say. First, the house we're working on should be finished by the end of the week. Good job, it's a quality effort. That being said, I plan to begin the renovation of the Golf club on Monday. Since it's a renovation the only permits we need will be those associated with the enlargement of the foot print. While we're waiting for those we have plenty to do to the existing structure. I didn't anticipate things moving this fast." He smiled. "Two new jobs have surfaced in the last week. We're going to need more help. I am going to start a new crew. This crew will split."

He made eye contact with Pete. "Pete, you will help me interview for a new **NAILIT1** crew. You will be the crew leader." Pete nodded.

"Dick you will sit with Hailey and hire an additional crew for NAILIT2. You will be heading up that crew. Hailey and I will continue to drum up business and be the resource for both crews. Anything you need from permits to materials." George cleared his throat, "On a personal level if we have any down time at all, I will pay you off the books to help me construct my new home. There will be weekend work if you are interested. Ok let's eat and get back to work."

CHAPTER SEVEN

School started back up. So did Arnold.

I didn't tell my parents any more about the abuse I was experiencing at school. They had told me to handle it. I did share ideas with my sister Sarah and we discussed all possible options. My sister is thirteen and a tough little nut. She is a first rate soccer player in her middle school. She knows the older sister of the boy bothering me. This morning when I joined her at the top of her bed, I shared the latest attack. I signed how in the boys' room my head had been forced into the sink and the water turned on. I might not be able to hear but I can read lips. Arnold, who shares the first name of the famous actor from one of my favorite movies, mouthed that line after he had finally released his hand from my neck. He looked me right in the eye. 'I'LL BE BACK.' Then he pointed at the urinal and winked. Sarah thought, cupping her chin,

"Well Bobby he outweighs you by thirty pounds and he's half a foot taller, so fighting him should be your last option."

"I know Sarah but he's got me a little scared. I don't plan to bathe in a urinal."

"You could go to your teacher, they would at least talk with him, warn him maybe. I could talk with his sister, she's not a friend but she seems nice enough."

I shook my head. I rubbed my chin. "Hmm, maybe I could bribe him with one of my toys or give him my lunch money."

"I don't think that's going to work. If he wanted something from you he would have told you by now."

"This is harder to read than one of Dad's blueprints." Suddenly the word blueprints sparked a thought. I snapped my fingers. "That's what I need to do Sarah, I need to figure out his inside. You know, like a blueprint."

Sarah didn't know about blueprints but she knew how smart her little brother was. She took my hand. I lay back on the pillow studying the ceiling but seeing right through the roof, into the morning sky. I felt myself smiling.

—•◦•◦•◦•◦•—

George got a call from the injured Don Smith asking if they could meet. George pulled up outside Don's apartment house. Don was standing in the doorway in bathing trunks and a t-shirt. He immediately climbed into George's office. George watched him struggle to close the door.

"How's that arm Don?"

"Being that it's the arm I hammer with, for right now it's pretty useless."

"You getting any help from Coastal?"

"The old man is back in charge and he's not happy to be back. Looks like he's trying one more time to clean up after his son." He shifted in his seat meeting George's eyes, "So for now everyone is in a cover their own ass mode. Which means I'm getting zilch for my pain and suffering, not to mention a job."

"How can I help?"

"Well first off, I need some advice. If I tell OSHA what really happened, how does that affect me?"

"They might fine Coastal for you guys not wearing hard hats but there was no equipment failure or anything like that so they are not going to do much."

"So Joel being piss-assed hung-over, not fit to work, and dropping the damn drywall doesn't count"

"No way to prove that. They might say it's up to you to refuse to work with a guy in that condition. Is Workers Comp. helping?"

"In the last year most of us were not full timers as you well know." Don's face darkened, "And Joel had us working off the books when he did get busy, so I'm not getting much, about a third of what I was making."

"So I go back to my first question, "How can I help?"

"You know I'm a good worker. It's going to be a month till I'm able to use this arm. Fred said when I can work he'll take me back." Don swallowed, "George I don't want to ever work there again. I heard you were hiring, can you use me? I'll work for minimum until I can do a days' work.

"Hmm." George closed his eyes briefly. "I have an idea. We're in the process of signing contracts on two new jobs. One a renovation the other a new build. Would you be willing to work with a lady I just hired? She will take the lead but you will answer the hundred questions she's going to have. And you will be paid the same wage as my other workers. Does that work for you?"

Don couldn't help himself, he teared up. "Thank you George, you won't regret it."

"How's that little girl of yours doing, by the way?"

"One more operation and she should be able to have a normal life. Thanks for all those times you let me be with her, George. You are a good man."

"Be at Palmetto Golf and Country Club tomorrow at eight.

I'll be there to introduce you to Hailey. You will love her."

Don was whistling when he closed the door of the truck adding a little leg movement to his tune.

George watched him enter his apartment. The poor guy had a rough time over the past year, losing his wife in a car accident and nearly losing his daughter. George sighed. Joel had been running the company at the time and had showed no sympathy. Thinking of Joel's own problems it was hard to have any sympathy, what goes around comes around.

———•••••———

Word travels fast in the construction trade. Chalking a stick for a pool game or bellied up to the bar after work, men talk. The incident at Coastal Construction and the cover up reached everyone's ears. Joel's crew might have to lie on the job but on their own time they were more than willing to separate truth from fiction. Plenty of the regulars had worked with and for Joel over the years, and they had all felt his sharp tongue questioning their intelligence. "Heard the old man had to come back, not surprised."

"He's going to have a smaller company to come back to is what I hear. Cutting back from five crews to four and maybe three before the year is out."

"I heard George is doing good right out of the shoot." 'He's interviewing for another crew as we speak. I'd sure work for him if I could get on."

As the gossip drifted into the other sound bites going on around the room, Joel Riesling and Franklin Causano walked in. Joel blinked in the darkness waiting for his eyes to adjust. He looked to the rear of the place and mumbled something before heading to a bar stool.

Franklin disappeared from view like one of his magic tricks, not relishing an afternoon of Joel wallowing in his misery, crying in his glass. He had agreed to join him when Joel called earlier in the day. Of course that was hours and drinks earlier. Joel was nearly belligerent when he picked Franklin up. Franklin agreed to get in the truck only after Joel apologized, promising to be a good boy. Franklin could sense the good boy was going to go bad when Joel's first look was toward the rear of the bar where men were shooting pool and raising some noise.

Joel, after his eyes adjusted, seemed to study that area of the room before finding his way to a bar stool.

Things started out slow enough. Country music offering up a montage of musical misery loves company to the din. Joel sitting alone, feeling alone. He laid out a line of pretzel sticks like he was designing a building then tore the whole place down. By the time he downed a second then a third dbl. shot of Jack and coke his rabbit ears began to grow. He had built and destroyed three pretzel houses by then.

Franklin was doing magic tricks at a table and had his audience mesmerized.

Joel studied the room as he continued his half spin on the stool. Mouths were moving, laughter and eyes reaching him. The music had moved to a slow waltz. His eyes again found the pool table in the back. Were those fingers pointing at him? Hell these men are talking about me. And laughing. He recognized a couple guys from one of his crews. He nodded. They lowered their eyes. They were talking about him. Joel got up and walked back to where the two pool tables were in use. His antenna was up and his lips had loosened.

Just like kids fighting on a playground when discovered by the teacher, inevitably one would say, he started it. Joel wasn't saying anything just now. He lay flat on his back, shaking his head studying the side pocket where the eight ball had just landed ending the game. Joel hadn't witnessed much of the game. He didn't witness the running of the table.

A new hire of George Whiting's had taken offense to the bad mouthing Joel was spewing about his new boss as he descended to the table. When Joel invaded his space and the spit flying from his lips reached the man's face, only one punch was thrown. A noisy reaction from the men, applause mostly, then things went immediately quiet.

The bartender heard but ignored the whole scene. He actually became a little busy with the buying of a round that followed the knockout.

When he regained consciousness, Joel couldn't even remember who hit him. He lay there blaming George for all this. He finally gathered himself, edging up holding on to the pool table. He took a deep breath. He looked around. His look just dared someone to say something. No one said a word. He straightened his clothes as best he could then slunk out of the bar holding his jaw, mumbling to himself, "That frigging George, he's done it again."

Franklin was already behind the wheel. That fixed grin not revealing if there was mirth beneath it.

— · —◆— · —◆— · —◆— · —

I managed to physically avoid Arnold today. But I kept him in sight. It was time to do a little reconnaissance. I was like a Ninja observing the bully's every move.

Arnold struggled when called upon to read aloud. Hmm. I watched his face go red. I watched kids covering their smiles at Arnold's expense.

I did the math. Given that Arnold outweighs me by thirty pounds and is three inches taller it makes sense that Arnold is occupying that seat for at least a second year. Maybe a third.

At lunch Arnold sat by himself. He seems to study his food, eyeing it closely.

This afternoon the aide in the classroom, Mrs. Tapper, became frustrated with Arnold when he was off task once again. After chastising him and moving away to assist another student she returned. I noticed she stood a distance away from him when she was helping him. Odd. Maybe not. I was close enough to Arnold in that bathroom and even in the overheated classroom to know Arnold had hygiene issues.

I noticed his clothes didn't fit properly and both his shirt and dungarees were stained. I watched a kid who seemed all the time angry. Why had he chosen me to pick on? I had no idea. Maybe he thought a deaf kid couldn't tell on him.

I looked deeper within the blueprint. Could that be a squint? I watched him put his head nearly onto the math page. Then he slammed the book shut. Mrs. Tapper gave up. Arnold put his head down.

Could this boy who stands out with his size and body odor, his lack of school skills, his shabby clothing have a visual problem as well?

I filed all that away and though I couldn't hear myself, I began whistling. I wanted to high five someone like my parents do. By the time the bus let me off at home I had the beginnings of a plan.

CHAPTER EIGHT

The economy was improving, people finding their way to Florida for a hundred reasons. The weather, retirement, a new opportunity, running from their past, illegal immigrants, coming to take care of an elderly parent, and so on and so on.

The building industry was booming as the month of October 2016 began. Flagler County, under populated for its size, offered a world of opportunity for business growth as well as a wonderful place to live. The city of Palm Coast, was beginning to realize the dream that had begun in the 1970's when corporate giant ITT first laid out the future streets and plots of development in a blueprint for the largest planned community in Florida history. The entire planned community was dredged forming a series of canals weaving through the different sections. They eventually found their way to the Inter coastal waterway that runs from north to south through a fair number of states. The blueprint was in place in the 70's but the ebb and flow of the economy, much like one of the sluggish drainage canals, kept the city from taking off.

My dad, George Whiting moved here in 1999. He was going to be a senior in the only high school in the county. His single parent mom moved down here from Maine to assist her aging parents who lived in what was still a pretty rural neighborhood. Dad told me he was not excited about being uprooted but he did love his grandparents who had summered in Maine until recently. I have never been there but dad tells me he wants to go back and visit someday. Dad says once you get off the main roads, Flagler County is pretty similar to being back home in Maine. Except for the lack of hills and mountains of course. Oh yeah and the weather. My great grandfather, (who has since passed and I never got to meet) used to take dad fishing in one of the many man-made canals. My great grandmother taught Dad how to cook those fish. She's gone as well. Dad's dad, my grandfather, (I never met him either) was killed in an industrial accident back when dad still lived in Maine. So since he was stuck here my dad decided to make the best of it. Mom tells me dad is a great athlete. He arrived in the summer of what would be his senior year. When pre-season for football arrived dad signed up. His coaches immediately recognized his talents in the conditioning drills. He finished sprints no worse than third and could throw a football fifty yards in the air with accuracy. Back in Maine he had played quarterback and mentioned it to a coach. The team had a quarterback; Joel Riesling. Dad said he'd play wherever the team could use him. It was pre-season though so the boy deserved a look the coach decided. Mom says dad just showed up at every practice and did what he was instructed to do.

Soon the favored son of a local construction company owner found himself taking fewer and fewer snaps at quarterback.

Dad was oblivious to the animosity building in his team mate and just whistled his way to the starting position. He was passing the coaches office when he heard Joel's father complaining to the coach about his son's demotion. He heard his coach defend his decision. He heard the term work ethic thrown out.

Mom says the two were about the same size, 6' 185 pounds. She had known Joel most of her life. Similarities seemed in her mind to end with their size. She was a cheerleader back then. She had even gone out with Joel as a sophomore but found him lacking.

The word in the hallways and the bleachers and even at the beach was there was a competition going on that wasn't going to end well for Joel.

Their differences became magnified during workouts and pre-season weight room effort. It was George Whiting handling the snaps for the first game. Mom, who didn't even know dad when school started, was now including his name in the cheers. She knew Joel though, he was always hanging around her locker, unbidden. He always had a couple guys hanging off him he was playing to. He began to mimic the strong Maine accent George brought with him. In the locker room it was said Joel put on quite a show. At first his teammates laughed. George though, had the team winning. His teammates began to realize this was Joel's way of fighting for his position.

"Hey he's in the weight room every day getting stronger and faster," one of the big lineman told Joel. "Maybe you might want to consider a different position Joel, he's not going away."

The head coach took Joel aside when he could see the smoke coming from Joel's ears as he watched George coalesce the team under his soft-spoken encouragement and leadership. "Listen Joel, I've been your coach for the past two years. I've always told you nothing is a given, you have to work for it. I told your dad you have as much natural ability as George but he's simply working harder" The coach put his hand on Joel's shoulder, "You show me a can-do attitude, and get to practice on time every day, hit that weight room with a purpose and I'll work you in, give you a chance to get that starting role back. Up to you. For now I'm going to teach you how to play defense."

Too much had come to Joel too easily, both in his private life and in sports up to now. He was just not mentally strong enough, so he took the easy way out and blamed George. His father, who was a self-made man, tried to get through to his son as well. Didn't happen.

George missed his dad, and now his grandad, terribly. He also missed some friends he had played ball in Maine with. Right now though he had a successful football season to occupy his mind. The high school was a little bigger but George took his weight room work ethic into the classroom and fit in easily. He was also enjoying the longer season of day after day sunny mild weather that in Maine would have ended two months ago. When your life is measured in sports seasons the days pass quickly. Suddenly the next season arrived. Basketball season began and once more the year seemed to float from practice to game to homework to sleep to starting all over again. George never even looked up. He just lived it. Once more Lane Starling was cheering him on. She was beginning to take an interest.

If winter ever arrived George didn't feel it and when there was a break between sports George found himself competing again.

He wasn't looking for romance, it just hit him right in the heart. He also had no inkling he was competing for a starting role, in the mind of the same boy at least, for the heart of the head cheerleader. He didn't have to work for this position; he just had to be himself.

For a big strong kid, considered a jock by most of the school, George was really a sensitive studious young man. When the call went out for actors for the senior play, George just thought it would be a fun thing to do. He ended up getting the lead actor role and won the heart of the leading lady.

— •••• —

Lane Starling, was born in South Florida. When her parents grew tired of what was becoming urban sprawl, her Dad opened the first McDonald's in what would later become Palm Coast. What George didn't know was before Lane won his heart she had been seeing Joel Riesling. The first and last time that issue arose was on Flagler Beach the summer they graduated. George had heard rumblings about Joel being upset with him from the moment he had moved here. First it was football, then it was basketball, then the play, then baseball. Now after graduating it seemed woman trouble was in season. George was an easy going guy and let the insults and rumors pass him by. He was comfortable in his own skin. Joel had never confronted him face to face.

He and Lane were on a blanket both deep in separate novels when the sand landed on his book and part of his head. He looked back into the sun just as another scoop struck. This time voices and laughter accompanied the assault. George rolled to one knee to see who was being such a jerk.

Lane was up on her feet already, telling Joel to back off. It was the remark to Lane that brought George to voice. "Joel, don't talk to Lane like that." That was it, George hadn't even raised a pulse, still on one knee. Joel with two older friends who didn't know George thought that was a hilarious comeback.

If he had been alone, Joel would probably have read the warning behind the simple statement. Egged on by his two friends he was now boxed in. "Well Georgie Podgy you gonna kiss the girl and make her cry?"

Lane spoke up, "Joel, just please leave, you are being ridiculous."

"What's ridiculous is you being here with this guy. Look at his farmer's tan for god's sake."

George began to whistle. Not one of his cheery tunes but rather an anthem for action. He stood up. Joel's two friends took a step back, George was a lot bigger standing up. George stopped whistling. "Joel, we're here enjoying the day, I think you need to leave now."

Boxed in, Joel had no alternative but to challenge that statement. He did manage the first verse of Georgie Podgy pudding and pie before George slapped him hard with an open hand, bloodying his nose and adding shades of color to the side of his face. Joel landed on Lane's blanket. That was the extent of it. Joel scrambled back to his feet. With head hanging he stumbled away through the loose sand. George and Lane joined hands. "Thanks for not hurting him badly, George."

George squeezed her hand.

In the fall after graduation, George joined the army. Lane lived at home and traveled to St. Augustine to attend Flagler College. She intended to study Art History and perhaps teach.

In time George was recognized as having the right stuff and selected to challenge himself even further. George was at Fort Benning Georgia rising for day fifty-one of the sixty five day Army Ranger School when the towers came down. After finishing the course George and fellow graduates were sent immediately to Afghanistan to find Bin Laden. When the Taliban refused to give him up the United States declared war. The aim was to dismantle Al-Qaeda and bring Bin Laden to justice. Never had we felt so righteous, thousands had been killed in arguably the most important city in America.

Afghanistan's terrain is forbidding, the weather is wearing, the enemy nearly invisible. George quickly realized the three different training sessions that made up his sixty-five days was something every recruit should have under his belt. The Rangers were used in a number of ways. They worked as their own unit as much as allowed. They had one another's back.

At other times they were loaned out to provide support for the regular troops. George was running point for such a group when they came under fire from a band of Taliban fighters. The squad George was supporting was well trained but out gunned. Someone had to climb out of this valley and get a cell phone signal for air support. Two men were wounded and the other seven pinned down. Pieces of stone nearly as lethal as bullets exploded as bullets struck solid rock. George signaled the squad leader letting his fingers do the talking. The squad leader nodded and George began a dangerous ascent to the top. The squad did their best to lay cover fire on George's signal. He was hit with pieces of broken rock as bullets exploded around him. Cut and bleeding but not seriously wounded he reached the top. A scant five minutes later the enemy was gone. A helicopter gun-ship strafed the higher level George had pinpointed and the squad made their way back to safety. Three militants lay dead among the crevices. George was a reluctant hero. He spent two tours in the mountains of Afghanistan and when his four years were up he came home to a hero's welcome.

Lane had received her teaching degree, and was teaching back in Flagler County. Joel had continued to pursue her. Lane wanted nothing to do with him. Her long letters to her man on a mission continued to motivate George to come home in one piece.

Two months after he returned, the couple made it forever in a wedding ceremony that took place on Flagler Beach. They rented a trailer two streets back from the ocean. The water's edge lured them for weekend morning coffee, long walks, and many moonlight strolls.

Their hopes and dreams were shared among the sound of waves echoing their long term commitment. The sea is forever.

Those early years of struggle, just figuring it all out in a hundred ways from balancing a budget, adding a puppy to test their parenting skills then an attempt at growing vegetables. The yin and yang of grocery shopping, shared household duties, a single vehicle at first, then that first baby.

Fifteen years passed through George's mind as he sat on the lot looking out over the InterCoastal from the cab of his truck. The lot had been cleared and leveled. Half a dozen hardwoods, reminding George of Maine, stood in the new soil. Lane wanted palms in the front, George would have a good view from the lanai and his home office on the second floor of his Oak, two Maples, a White Birch and two others he couldn't name but had shed their leaves so George kept them.

The family was planning a work day with a picnic following this weekend. The plan was to get the footprint laid out with wooden forms. The plumbing pipes and electrical wire conduits would follow. Anything that needed to travel below ground would be added as time allowed.

Next week the concrete will arrive. George invited his two work crews and their families. George insisted they would be on his personal payroll when they worked here. Bobby sat with his dad as he planned the weekend work schedule.

It happened just as planned. The adults sat around a fire. Bag chairs supporting the crew toasting what had been a good day. Card tables remained standing strewn with the remnants of pasta and potato salads, veggie trays and dips, half empty bags of chips, a platter of cooked hot dogs and hamburgers and plastic bottles of soda and water to wash it all down. The workers had been told to bring their own beer.

Colorful coolers marked the owners of the bag chairs and their choice of beverage. The sun going down had moved the chairs and their occupants closer to the fire. Kids were beginning to join the adults at a bonfire as their playground disappeared into the shadows and bats began to flit overhead. An occasional boat floated past on the water. Arms were raised and shouts of 'ahoy there,' followed by laughter and tipped bottles.

George watched his son and how he approached the day. Bobby spent the first part of the day watching the building plans turn into a physical presence. He asked the right questions. In the afternoon he showed he was a leader as well. He had in a natural way taken charge with the other kids.

A simple follow me gesture had the kids walking to a canal that stretched far back into the community. Bobby walked them several hundred yards along the stream then launched a simple stick he had attached a red piece of cloth to. The whole group followed the stick back towards the Intercoastal, waving goodbye as it reached the current. Soon Bobby was helping the other kids launch their own crafts. Daniel trailed every step with a big smile on his face. Bobby gave each kid a chance to be in charge. I couldn't have been more proud of my son. He tickled my heart. The kids played seamlessly, no wrinkles of jealousy or feeling left out. When the other kids left, Bobby walked the perimeter of the work done by the men nodding and seemingly storing new learning. He crawled into my lap, yawned once and promptly fell asleep. A full day for the boy.

I watched my daughter too. Sarah had only one girl near her age attend the picnic. The two girls threw rocks into the canal and kicked a soccer ball back and forth until Lane imposed on the girls to help get the food ready and served. *Yep I'm proud of those two.*

Lane and I were tired but satisfied. We lay in bed comparing our take on the day. "Standing in the footprint of the house I am beginning to see the big picture. It's going to be a big house George."

"Big for a reason honey, you saw how well everyone got along today, I want this house to be the center of our social life. For us and the kids."

"So this will be the house that George built." "Correction, the house George and Lane built, and Bobby and Sarah don't forget And it's no nursery Rhyme." I kissed her on the forehead. "All the interior design, colors, tile, flooring, cabinetry choices, built-in alcoves, everything inside the walls is up to you. We'll have fun making this a real family project."

"It's all coming true George, all those dreams we talked about when we were in that little trailer in Flagler Beach."

"What makes it even better is we have two caring kids that appreciate what they have and show kind hearts." Lane squeezed my hand, sighed, affectionately high fived me and turned off the lamp.

— • —•—•— • —

I was awake in the dark. I revisited my day. Dad has some really good workers and I like their kids. I love the canal and the Intercoastal. It's going to be fun living here.

CHAPTER NINE

Arnold rolled over and nearly hit his little brother in the face with his arm. The morning sun had found its way through the torn shade. A morning breeze wafted the shade in and out like a bellows, there were no curtains to rustle. The double wide trailer sat in an open field just daring the weather to do its damnedest. Water stains colored the ceiling in shapes that changed with every new storm. Below, several well placed plastic containers stood their ground.

This week's forecast suggested a blazing sun would overheat the place by noontime and linger well into the night. This time of year you could bet there would be a 4pm thunderstorm adding to stains on the ceiling. The air conditioner hadn't worked in weeks. Arnold heard his sister holler to get up but didn't respond. He was studying the newest stain above his head that took the shape of what looked like a tootsie roll pop. Arnold lay there tasting it in his head.

When his little brother, knowing he would have the bed to himself, put his feet on his brother's back, Arnold groaned. He turned to the little guy who was now stretching his arms, smiling. Arnold threw his pillow at him and rolled to a sitting position. He reached down to retrieve one of the two pairs of jeans that he owned. He struggled to get them over his hips. He had another pair not yet completely worn through that were even harder to get past his hips.

'You're a growing boy,' his mother told him when he complained.

Arnold wasn't stupid, he realized he was growing but he also realized he had a problem with food. He was too young to make all the possible connections he simply realized food offered a numbing quality to his existence. It was as if he were in an over-lit room that caused his eyes to ache. Food helped him pull the shade. A small closet held three tee-shirts. Arnold sat there studying two of them that should be passed along to his little brother Billy. Arnold stood up. He would settle for the one he had worn to school yesterday and last night to bed. He closed the door behind him and made his way to the kitchen. His cereal bowl was waiting for him. His sister was already seated, slurping up a storm.

"Where's Mom?"

Anna Nicole nodded toward their mother's bedroom whispering, "She says she has a headache. I think she has a new friend in there with her."

Arnold didn't comment but squeezed the box, twisting the face of the character staring at him.

He poured the sugared cereal in the bowl and eyed the skim milk. He held up the carton and complained, "Why does mom buy this stuff, it tastes like chalk and water?" His sister thought to explain his Mother's warped thinking but instead just sighed.

She cleared her throat, and whispered, "I'm not supposed to tell you this but the sister of that deaf kid you've been picking on spoke to me yesterday. She seems nice. Maybe if you lay off I will have a friend."

Arnold snorted, "So the little shit ratted to his sister did he?" How did he do that? Hell he can't even talk. He sucked down the remaining sweetened liquid. He grabbed the cereal box but finding it empty, crushed the life out of the rabbit and tossed it to the floor.

Anna Nicole sighed. She picked up the box and put it in the overflowing trash. "What's he done to piss you off anyway?"

Arnold slumped his shoulders. He rummaged through the food shelf. Finding nothing edible, he turned. "Nothing I guess. I'm just

having fun with him, I wouldn't really hurt him. Not much anyway."
An evil smile appeared.

"Well I think you should just leave him be. You don't need to add
to Mom's worries."

Arnold thought about this for about a second then shrugged and
began to rummage once more. He looked to the bedroom his mother
never seemed able to exit in the morning, "Moms worries!" He found a
box of crackers hidden under a towel. He eyed his sister. "You're hiding
stuff from me!"

Anna Nicole held up her arms feigning innocence. "Francis probably
did it. He's becoming a mini you."

Arnold let a little gas end the conversation and wandered to the
living room to catch a cartoon before he had to catch a bus.

Joel was up early. He and Myrtle had a nasty falling out last night
and it was probably just as well. He had a plan to get back into his
father's good graces and maybe get his office back. Staying away from
Myrtle and Franklin might help him make some needed changes. Part
of him knew his father was right.

Two days ago he called an old business contact. Ironically he'd
heard about a building project at the hospital that was soon to be made
public, at a bar, go figure. He had chuckled at the time. *See dad, I'm
working at the business.* If Joel could bring this off and get them to hire
Coastal Construction to be the main contractor, his father would see
he had made a mistake in judging his son incompetent.

Joel shit, shaved, showered and shampooed. He put on his best suit
and tie, and shined his shoes. He put his truck through a car wash. He
stopped at a diner and had a nice omelet, toast and home-fries. He took

a coffee to go, leaving it black and placed it in his cup-holder. He was early so he sat in his truck thinking about what he would say. He looked at the notes he had prepared, mouthing the words. The sun was already hitting his side window. He turned on the radio. He turned it right back off when he heard a commercial for a new construction company up and running and soliciting business in the area.

That f-ing George Whiting was haunting him in his own vehicle. His three best friends remained in the closed cooler on the floor. Joel intended that they stay there— hidden, unwanted, and unneeded.

But he was early. He checked his watch, early by nearly an hour. He sat there fidgeting, checking himself in the visor mirror. *All fixable* his assessment. He hummed to himself. Out of habit he tried to reach Myrtle but got the message machine. Hearing her voice he realized he was already backtracking, he didn't leave a message.

He sipped the black coffee and grimaced, *why had he left it black he never drank his coffee black.* He placed it back in the cup holder. He looked out at the office building he would be entering. *That's a big building,* he thought. *Big money.* Joel began sweating, purging the poison that had put him to sleep last night.

Suddenly George Whiting passed right by his truck. He had emerged from the hospital building. Joel watched the cadence of George's stride in his side mirror and just knew the son of a bitch was whistling. He had observed that stride and heard that unidentifiable tune for years. He must be competing for the same job. *Son of a bitch*. And the bastard was early just like always. Joel, without thinking (muscle memory I think they call it) invited Jack to join him on the seat. Suddenly riding shotgun the bottle offered a visual command. Joel took the lid off his cup and let Jack smell the coffee and dive right into it.

The coffee was gone when Joel left his vehicle.

Joel left the interview two hours later thinking he'd nailed it. He felt relaxed, answered every question. Just two other firms were being considered, the man said and one had dropped out after the interview.

Back in his truck Joel could already hear the man calling him with the good news. He needed a drink to celebrate. Jack had emptied himself of emotional support but lurking in the shadows old Evan was just full of it. Joel dialed up Myrtle already sliding back into his old life. This time it went directly to voicemail. Maybe Franklin, he'd help him celebrate. His phone just rang and rang. Were his two best friends avoiding him? Joel drank all the way back to his apartment. He changed into his work clothes, checked the time, and changed his mind. Hell it was too late in the day to go to work, he rationalized. He mixed a drink and landed on the couch. He was sound asleep before Evan lost his cool.

A call from the CEO of the company Joel interviewed with did come in and if Joel had not been passed out he would have heard that he needed to call back this afternoon for a final interview.

Fred Riesling got a call during that workday. Fred was invited to come in and sit for the interview his son had not responded to. So in the end Coastal Construction did land a big job but Joel was determined to be an even bigger loser by his father.

George Whiting had in fact sat in for an interview but realized it was too big a job for his fledgling company and begged off. "But keep us in your thoughts," said George upon rising and handing the man his business card. "We'll be ready next time."

— · — · — · —

My plan for helping Arnold was on my mind. It took shape as I sat at my seat gazing out the window. I noticed a bird had done its business on one of the panes of glass. Something clicked. *That's it! Everyone who looks through that window is looking through that same stain. What if my vision was blurred?* Sure now of what needed to be done I went to my sign teacher and told her the whole story of Arnold's actions. She wanted to contact the principal immediately.

I signed, <u>not yet.</u> I had a plan to end the bullying and help Arnold at the same time. <u>If we don't help Arnold he will just go on doing the same thing to someone else.</u> Then I signed what I thought was at the root of the problem. <u>If we help Arnold feel better about himself maybe he'll stop on his own.</u>

———•••••———

And so the school nurse was contacted and an eye exam was administered. To keep Arnold from being singled out the entire class went through the simple eye chart test. Two other students in addition to Arnold would be sporting eyewear in the near future.

I went back to my seat sure this plan could work wishing and hoping I could stay out of Arnold's clutches till the glasses were in place.

———•••••———

If wishes were horses then beggars could ride. Two days later Arnold caught up with me and that childhood nursery rhyme Mom had uttered to me whenever my wishes got too big to handle crossed my mind.

I was standing at the urinal when I heard the boys' room door squeak open. I turned my head and met Arnold's eyes. It was clear from the look he gave me he intended to make good on his earlier threat. I stopped in mid-stream and turned just in time to avoid Arnold's first grasp. I could smell Arnold's body odor as I slid away. I tried to get to the exit. Arnold cut me off. The mirror over the sink brought two Arnolds into view. I watched his chest rise and fall. My eyes surveyed the room. Three bathroom stalls to my left, the exit sign pointed the way. I edged my way away from that exit. Arnold looked confused. I never took my eyes off him. I seemed to be falling into his trap. He smiled suddenly, believing he had me right where he planned to do the dunking.

With an open mouth he roared though I couldn't hear it.

Like a bull to a cape he charged.

Thinking on my feet, even as I moved them, I headed towards an open stall.

Arnold, breathing hard through his open mouth, lunged. All he grabbed was air. His momentum carried him into the bathroom stall where there was no room nor time to stop his momentum. Arnold lost his balance. His arms flailing he struck his head on the toilet. He lay there dazed and panting.

I might be deaf but I do know how to talk, I just choose not to. This moment though needed to be addressed verbally. "Arnold, I'm not afraid of you. I just don't want to fight. If you would like to come to my house to play sometime just tell me."

With that I retreated, snapped off the light and went back to my classroom to let my teacher know Arnold might need some help in the boys' room.

CHAPTER TEN

Victor Thornton moved to Florida for one reason and one reason only-he had to. He got himself in trouble with the law in Pennsylvania where he lived with his mother. His mother and father split when he was just thirteen. He was born and grew up in Erie, Pennsylvania, living with a single mom all the way through high school.

A big kid, Victor played offensive tackle for the high school team and at that anonymous position traveled pretty much under the radar accepted by teammates, but not garnishing much attention from the girls. Off the field he was pretty much a loner, playing video games well into most nights.

Not committed enough to play the sport beyond high school he had approached his studies with the same lack of fervor. College held no attraction. He lived at home off and on after graduation, which mirrored his moving from one job to another.

He began to supplement his sporadic income by selling drugs after seeing how easy it was. Big and looking older than his age, Victor had no trouble getting served in the local bars before reaching legal drinking age. His new career as a drug dealer began innocently enough. He was throwing darts in a dimly lit area of a bar when a student from MercyHurst College joined him at the dart board. One thing led to another. Victor had dabbled in weed for his own use. He had never sold drugs.

"But you know the area, right?" When the student followed up by telling Victor he could get a premium price for any weed he could scare up, Victor took notice. For a while Victor simply linked his own supplier to the college student getting a small finder's fee for each shipment. He continued to go through the motions of trying to find himself. He enrolled in a junior college and promptly flunked out. He moved out of his mother's house only to move back in. At six foot three, two hundred and sixty pounds, he took up a lot of room on the couch. Possibly he could have continued in this manner if his single mother had not met a man and welcomed him to share her home.

By the time the man moved in Victor had moved up the food chain and was now selling drugs out of his newly acquired car.

Wouldn't you know it, his mother had fallen for a cop.

Victor took an immediate dislike to the guy. To be honest, Officer Ralph was wound a little tight. At first it seemed he was trying to be helpful, offering possible job openings to Victor he'd hear about on the street. Officer Ralph created a few job openings himself when he arrested what he termed local riff-raff who used work as a place to hide during the day. To his mind their real work was at night.

Victor began skipping the evening meal when along with the broccoli, he was served up the day's events, unwound like a disappearing ball of yarn; Ralph is always the hero.

Victor moved out again, determined to stay out this time. Things changed when a drug bust landed one of Victor's clients in the clink. Victor decided to get out of Dodge knowing it would just be a matter of time before his name surfaced. He decided to visit his father who years ago had moved to Palm Coast, Florida. *Yeah let's meet the old man. He can't be as bad as mom describes him.* About the time he packed up and left Pennsylvania, his name had in fact been added as a person of interest in the prosecution of one of his customers.

— • ••• • —

Victor moved into a sixth floor penthouse suite his realestate dad used sparingly. His fifty seven year old Father, Tobias, nicknamed in several social circles as the silver fox, preferred to be called Toby. His father sold houses and himself to any lonely woman who would listen.

He let the boy in but spent no time reacquainting himself. He promptly set his son down and explained how he did business. "Look at yourself as a property Victor, one you want to sell me. This monologue predicated how this was all going to go. "Clean up after yourself. I won't come home to a dirty place." He paused for emphasis, "Keep the place clean." Then he began spouting what Victor should do when he wasn't cleaning the place. "Look for a job. No one wants a house that isn't constantly being upgraded, bettered, and made more marketable. Learn the area, find something to do with yourself."

Victor had just arrived and yet his father seemed almost angry.

"There will be no laying around in my place. No slugs living here." Then he offered the first bit of useful information. "I know a guy who's hiring. He'd hire you on my say-so." He then pointed directly at his son. "If you take the job don't let my say-so down; that or a dirty house will send you out of here."

So for two weeks in August of 2016 Victor found himself driving a main thoroughfare in Palm Coast, Belle Terre.

If you visualize the city as an airplane, Belle Terre would be the body stretched out in a north south manner. Belle Terre forms the major artery for the city. Every plane needs wings and in a west to east direction from Route One all the way to the ocean, Palm Harbor Parkway serves as that main wing span.

Victor drove both north and south and east and west. If you keep the plane in the air you look down at endless flight patterns the streets form. Victor drove a number of the smaller east west roadways.

He expanded his search and found a huge tract of new construction in a wooded section on the south side of the city named Seminole Woods. He got lost for a time circling back and around and ending up where he got lost in the first place. Finally recognizing the logic of the layouts and the meaning behind **drive, place, circle** and the like, he eventually found his way back to a main artery. What he hadn't found was a job yet.

An attractive city, Palm Coast, medians lined with trees and shrubbery and main arteries boasting sidewalks. Everything is very clean and modern. In his aimless driving he found nothing that fit his skill set. He drove by lots of fast food places. He stopped in not to seek employment but rather to down a burger or a burrito, or a slice of pizza. *Hell, he thought, I have a year of Junior college. I shouldn't have to do fast food.*

Small medical business parks, real estate offices, banks; Victor kept driving. He had no degrees or special skills so he was really just going through the motions of finding work, stalling for time till the old man forced his hand. As a setting sun began to soften the mood entering his windshield he located the few places that offered nightlife. He drove east over the bridge on route 100 and came face to face with the ocean for the first time.

Gazing out over the Atlantic he nodded his head. *I could get used to this.* The little city of Flagler Beach, iconic by design, stretched out along the ocean's edge. Victor parked his car and walked the wooden sidewalk. Early in the evening people still walked the shore line and he saw a few babes he wouldn't mind sunbathing with.

Victor was sleeping-in these days, so early evening became the time he chose to check out the bars. At five pm it seemed the people in the bars were mostly older people taking advantage of early bird specials and happy hour. He heard accents that indicated many were tourists or transplants like himself. At the periphery of the banter that hung like a cloud of cigarette smoke sat local grizzled growlers who seemingly had season tickets and moved beyond opinion to acceptance.

In Flagler Beach sitting on the upper deck at the Golden Lion, gazing out over the water at people still walking the beach below, all seemingly engaged, Victor was suddenly lonely. He studied the pale ale he was nursing and in it found no future. He saw in the eyes of solitary souls manning their own battle stations what his future might look like. Victor drained his glass, no one acknowledged his leaving, not even the bartender. Victor was merely a bar tab. He had met no one.

Maybe it was time to take up his father's offer to find him a job. Victor was not the ladies' man his father professed to be, his lack of social life as a kid was testament to that.

Back in the condo brushing his teeth in the mirror invited inspection. What would he be bringing to a job? He had been called Abe since adolescence. He had always put the best spin on that nickname he could muster. Sharp shadowed features along with the early need to shave twice a day and a long gangly frame made him appear menacing. He had filled out to a robust 260 pounds but Girls never moved beyond classmates. Waitresses approached without the usual banter, keeping their responses professional. He stroked his five o'clock shadow. He might more easily meet people through a co-worker, he needed a natural connection a workplace might provide.

On his father's say so Victor Thornton was hired as a carpenter apprentice by George Whiting. After a few days on the job, observing and getting a feel for when to add to a conversation and when to just listen he seemed to be accepted by the crew.

He began to join crew members for a beer for the road. He kept his eyes open and his mouth shut. His size prevented anyone from bothering him. He enjoyed watching the crowd from a bar stool where he could turn right or left and ask a question or add to an observation. He played pool. He threw darts. With no one to go home to, Victor stayed and watched the sun recede.

The restaurants and bars emptied for a time. But Victor stayed. Happy hour ended. As the moon rose, diners and new bar patrons appeared. In the taverns younger men now dressed for the evening seemed to emerge from the walls. Then just as that moon showed its full face to join the festivities, gazing down offering no opinion, no judgment, darkness full on; the smell of the place changed.

Perfume drifted in on the night air replacing the smell of sweat and day labor. Softer voices and easy laughter mingled in the raised mugs and cocktail glasses. Victor realized he was still missing out. Victor was lonely.

One late afternoon a very short man dressed in tropical attire entered and walked by Victor. Several voices acknowledged the man's arrival. With what appeared to be a pasted smile on his face, and even in this darkened atmosphere, sporting sunglasses, a straw hat and cowboy boots, oddly he didn't seem out of place. Accompanied by a guy in jeans and work shirt the two found a table near Victor. Victor doing his normal spin couldn't stop glancing toward the table.

What caught his attention at first was how young ladies and young men at tables and on stools at the bar turned, watched, covered their mouths as they whispered. Slowly one after another like they were in a line waiting to pay for their groceries they seemed to gravitate towards this table.

Victor continued to nurse his beer and discreetly watch. He saw money leave the hands of these well-wishers. The small man never appeared to have anything in his hands giving or receiving. Victor was mesmerized.

The man in work clothes appeared to be merely arm candy and eventually drifted toward the bar and took a stool. It was clear to Victor this man had started drinking well before he arrived.

The man carried a look as if he'd had an argument at work or with his best girl. This man spun around on his stool from time to time. With each spin an angrier look darkened his face. His eyes seemed to survey the room.

Victor walked past on his way to the men's room. The man was holding a fistful of pretzel sticks placing them down one after another in the shape of a house. He continued spinning on that stool mumbling to himself as Victor passed.

When Victor returned, the pretzel house had been destroyed and the bartender was standing behind the bar telling the man to pick up the damn pretzels from the floor. The man reluctantly complied.

Victor returned to his seat. He closed his eyes and listened to a heavy metal sound someone had dialed up. He was lost in a guitar riff when he heard raised voices and looked up to see the angry man now in the rear of the bar where a group of men were playing pool. He couldn't see what was going on but suddenly he heard the sound of something hitting the floor. After a moment of silence men began cheering.

Victor watched the little man slip away from the table he had been occupying. Time passed and the bar remained silent. Then the tall man walked past him limping, holding his jaw. Victor watched him leave and turned to an amber ale arriving in front of him. He looked up. 'A drink on the house,' he was told.

CHAPTER ELEVEN

Myrtle Beech worked as manager at a fast food restaurant in Palm Coast. She opened the place two days a week, worked the middle shift on two more and closed one week-end night. For the past year— ever since hooking up with Joel— she had no idea what would be waiting for her upon reaching her apartment. Her private life seemed to mirror the craziness she found daily at work. *How do you just let a year slip by like you pushed the pause button on the damn remote?* She lay a-bed this morning, smells of a sour and recently soused Joel wafting from the sheets. She pushed the playback in her head. *The year she now so desperately wanted to forget started with the wrong sauce on a five wing meal. Those damn kids in the back didn't give a rat's ass what went out the window. They were too busy planning tonight's mischief.*

Just for the record, turn-over at a fast food restaurant rates right up there with a lady of the night plying her trade. In the four years Myrtle had been assistant manager, then manager, she read through a complete novel of job applications. Anyway those thoughts and the smile Joel threw at her as he accepted her apology for the wing order error had put this whole reality show in motion.

Myrtle at age thirty-three had a high school diploma and fifteen years of fast food under her belt. She had worked her way from one joint to another, one ass-hole manager to another, watching how the process broke down depending on the level of incompetence standing in front of her, barking orders.

Her love life mirrored her moves from beef to fish, to Asian cuisine back to beef, and now cooped up with chicken.

In the end it didn't seem to matter the menu, people are people and they want what they want. Myrtle tried classes online, nearly finishing a two year degree in the medical field. But she lay here this morning two promotions ahead of any newbie who could manage an application at Cluck's Chicken Coop.

She hugged her pillow and smelled a trace of the most recent addition to her bed, Franklin. *He seemed to be a mystery. His body wash and cologne smelled of jazz music if you can imagine it. A dark table for two with a flower in a vase. No words, just music. She liked him, she decided. For his part he wasn't offering anything more than magic parlor tricks and mutual satisfaction but she could sense he liked her too.*

She rolled onto her back and spied a cobweb that was visible in the morning sunlight. Just like Joel it had kind of snuck into her room and by the length of the damn thing it had been here awhile and intended permanent residence.

She shook her own cobwebs away and returned to thoughts of Franklin. *He was smart, funny, small in stature but wise in the ways of a woman. He was always quoting some author. She still didn't know what he did for a living but always seemed to have plenty of money and a small stash of what he was now calling Beech sand.*

Joel had left in a huff early this morning. It had gotten pretty nasty last night when she finally broached the subject of his feet. He threw his own insults questioning her intelligence and loose morals. She countered with his approach to fitness and his shrinking hairline. All in all it was probably the most honest conversation since their relationship had begun with a lie.

Back then, Joel in fact had ordered the wrong wing sauce and she let it slide, blaming the back of the house for not paying attention to business. *Looking back, that right there should have put her on guard. I mean hell the guy was making good money. What kind of a man lies over a five dollar wing meal?*

Anyway, he's not welcome back here in his present state, she muttered to herself as she rose to wash the last remnants of the son of a bitch off her body. Her message light was blinking but she ignored it. On her way to the shower she grabbed the sheets and pillow cases and threw them in the wash.

Hair now wrapped in a towel, having continued her mental tirade while scrubbing herself free of the man, Myrtle emerged from the bathroom a woman on a mission. She stalked from room to room looking for anything he might have left. Three tee-shirts, a pair of cargo shorts, and two pairs of stinking socks later, she stuffed all of it into a garbage bag. Then she grabbed the broom and went to work on that damn cobweb, killing a fast moving spider in the process. "THERE!"

——•••••••——

Franklin was thirty miles away when the same sun that highlighted Myrtle's lack of domestic attention peeked into the bedroom window in the large condo building he was renting in the C- section of Palm Coast. The whole city was defined by letters.

Franklin had arrived in Florida as a young teenager from Louisiana. One foster home in rural Louisiana had followed another for the first fourteen years of his life. Then fate stepped in. *Stepped on* he thought in the beginning. Franklin mostly said stuff to himself.

A distant relative emerged, *out of his own need the way Franklin viewed it at first.* Franklin arrived in the sleepy little ocean town of Flagler Beach, Florida in his first ever taxi ride. This followed his first plane ride ever, into Jacksonville.

He traveled down coastal route A-1A marveling at the ocean on his left that emerged at different intervals. Beautiful homes and raised banks of foliage kept the ocean out of sight for vast stretches. The Intercoastal on his right stayed mostly hidden, seemingly embarrassed to be viewed in the same light as the mighty Atlantic Ocean. For a good distance between rural Jacksonville and St. Augustine, he felt like he had entered a vast jungle. Tangled trees, vines, grasses and sharp pointed vegetation defied entrance.

Entering St. Augustine Franklin was up on the seat as the trip across the Bridge of Lions, in St. Augustine had him staring at a flotilla of beautiful sailing vessels plying the Inter coastal waterway. Franklin couldn't take his eyes off the triangles of white that to him represented freedom. With his head on a swivel he had a hundred questions he wanted to ask the taxi driver but kept his lips closed over a grin that might have been a grimace set in stone. *If I ask him something he might ask me something back, then where would I be? Exactly! Just enjoy the ride dummy.*

His uncle on his mother's side— is what they had told him— was claiming his kin when they handed him his ticket and presented him with a small canvas suitcase.

Franklin had never known his mother. He had a history but it was mostly a medical one. Found along with his mother living in squalor, neglected, and malnourished. He was born six weeks early and permanently stunted. Franklin began his long battle with humanity by first battling just to live. He spent two months in the neonatal wing of a hospital in the parish of Claiborne, Louisiana. He survived that and was put in the care of the state.

His first two years there were rocky; he was often reminded on a number of occasions. Sickly and colicky his eyes opened to three different women in as many different foster homes in those first two years.

Then he was returned as damaged goods to the orphanage for three more years.

At age five, small but healthy now, he was picked out of a group of kids and spent three relatively happy years with Mr. and Mrs. Edwards. Actually Mrs. Edwards provided most of the security Franklin felt. Mr. Edwards was gone most of the time.

Franklin was just beginning to trust that all people weren't bad. So of course that couldn't last.

Unbeknownst to Franklin, Mr. Edwards was enjoying the after work drink and company of any woman as miserable as he was.

Finally Ella, as Mrs. Edwards liked to be called, figured it all out and sent Wendal packing. Poor little Franklin ended up not being far behind.

Ella—maybe out of spite who knows— got her groove back on and began experiencing what it was Wendal found so comforting in the arms of another woman.

All the while Franklin was taking shape. Clay forms and hardens in the hands of whosoever turneth the potter's wheel.

By age ten Franklin believed himself to be a permanent resident of the state's social system. He became hardened. The grin he sported twenty-four-seven would have to be chiseled to be removed. It was not a joyful grin, it was more of a grimace that warded off predators. And his eyes glowed. with a chiseled countenance; defiant, daring, determined. With that grin and those eyes, one was reminded of the horror movie doll, **Chucky**.

Four more years would pass before Franklin was given a pass to the outside world.

He was as tall as he was going to get by the time he hit Florida.

He had hardened on the inside as well. Franklin never suffered bullies. In fact no one bothered him in the homes he had lived in.

When he arrived he was introduced to an uncle who was wheelchair bound. Franklin didn't have a clue how this was all going to begin or end. He first thought, *I've been brought here to be a run and fetch servant. How was this going to be any different from the prison he'd just left? At least they did his wash there.*

He was proven wrong on all counts. The two played tippy toe around one another for a week. Franklin did a lot of watching, not saying anything more than required.

On the second Saturday he was living in his uncle's home he was summoned to lunch. "Franklin, you have made yourself nearly invisible for the last week. You are family, you can relax, no one is sending you back." He coughed then laughed, "Heck we even have a housekeeper who will clean up after us. He checked his watch. She'll be here tomorrow." Uncle Paul studied his sandwich, "Any questions I can answer beyond what I just told you?"

Franklin took a bite and chewed. "How did you find me?" A slight breeze waved the palms just off the porch like a magic wand.

Uncle Paul lived two streets back from the Atlantic Ocean half a mile south of the Flagler Beach Pier. Uncle Paul who only recently had become confined to a wheelchair due to a progressive respiratory disease, coughed into his hand. An oxygen tank had just recently been attached to his wheelchair. He grabbed the mouthpiece and took a puff of air. He continued coughing, finally raising his reddened face, rasping, "Those damn chips are beginning to get the best of me Franklin."

He smiled and took as deep a breath as he could manage. "When I found out I am not going to make it to Medicare, I decided to find out who it was I would be leaving all my earthly possessions to."

He wheezed out the next sentence. "I never married. I knew my younger sister had a kid she dumped years ago." He took another oxygen hit. This time his cough quieted. "At least that was what I had been told at the time." He looked across at the sandwich that at the moment was covering Franklin's eyes. "Do you even know that story?" Franklin looked over the top of his sandwich, his mouth full, an orange ring tracing his lips. He shook his head.

"You're fourteen right?"

Franklin nodded, taking a sip of lemonade.

"Well fifteen years ago my sister was sent away because she got herself pregnant and my family felt the need to shame her. She was sent up to Louisiana to a special home for unwed mothers. I was in college at the time and was told none of this." Uncle Paul had to pause for another hit. "I was told at the time she was a runaway and had given you up." He coughed lightly into his hand. "On my mother's death bed she confessed and told me about your existence."

Franklin took another bite of his sandwich.

"Are you ready for this?"

Franklin nodded, biting into a nacho chip.

"She also told me what had happened to my sister." Uncle Paul went red in the face, this time from anger. "That home for unwed mothers' was selling those babies, at least the ones that the mothers didn't want or couldn't keep."

He wheezed again but was determined to finish. "When my sister called and begged to come home my mother said she'd be welcome if she arrived alone." He paused to let that sink in. "My sister went downhill from there." He shook his head. "She did everything she could to get out of there. Even faked a suicide."

Uncle Paul nibbled a bit of sandwich, ignoring those damn chips. The two sat in silence. When Uncle Paul managed to get the bit of bread and meat down he continued.

"While they were evaluating her, she ran. Pregnant and alone." He took a sip of lemonade and coughed again. "She ended up on the street with a low life who took full advantage of the situation. She birthed you in a filthy unheated room." All this came to my mother in a letter your mother later wrote from prison. Uncle Paul fought for a deep breath.

"When it was clear you wouldn't survive without help she dropped you in an emergency room. She loved you Franklin."

Franklin showed no emotion.

Uncle Paul studied those eyes. "Anyway, she was determined to get you back when you were healthy. She relied on this older guy who eventually got Kathleen addicted to drugs."

He looked over at Franklin who had finished his sandwich and was licking orange off his fingers. He was wearing the same look he had arrived with, smudged in orange. *Christ the kid looks like that horror doll. What was his name?* Paul shook the image away and took some more oxygen. "When Kathleen was busted in that filthy apartment, with drugs she hadn't bought or sold, she was incarcerated." A wheeze followed.

"Chance for rehabilitation right?" Happy ending. Your mother gets cleaned up and eventually reclaims you." The red returned to his face.

"Remember she's only sixteen. The state decides they want to put both her and you in state care. Only not in the same place." Uncle Paul stands and spits phlegm over the railing then returned to his wheelchair and his story.

"Alone in a dormitory of other young unwed mothers, not knowing what else to do, she eventually runs again. With nowhere to go she ends up with the same derelict who promises her the moon but delivers more trauma." Uncle Paul threw up his hands and began coughing violently.

Franklin watched all this without a word.

When Uncle Paul was back under control he continued, "So your mother finds herself pregnant again."

Franklin remains still.

"When she confronts the guy he laughs in her face and shrugs his shoulders. 'Not my problem," he says." Uncle Paul studies the quiet young man in front of him.

"You know Franklin, your mother has your eyes. That same intensity." He hesitates then continues. "In that moment of despair, knowing there was no way out, she acted. Your mother stabbed that bastard right through those shrugging shoulders, in the process she nicked his heart."

Nearly done now, Uncle Paul sighed deeply, trying to refill his lungs, "Your mother to this day is in Louisiana Correctional Institute for Women in St Gabriel Louisiana. She is on death row."

Franklin looked at his uncle. "Do you have any cookies for dessert?"

That honest conversation gave Franklin insight to who this man in a wheelchair really was. Franklin decided he would stay. From that day on he became the power behind the van that would transport both the chair and his Uncle down to the beach day after day.

His first time behind the wheel of the conversion van was a hoot. "It's only three miles Franklin, just stuff a couple more pillows under yourself," Uncle Paul laughed then went into a coughing jag. His uncle's body was betraying him but his mind was keen.

Sitting at the beach, across the road a large water tower in the background, watching the waves undulate and the sea birds dip and dive Uncle Paul introduced Franklin to simple magic.

As Franklin sat before him on a blanket, sleight of hand tricks out in the open with only a wheel chair and a blanket as props began to soften the fixed grin. Franklin was offered the tricks behind the magic. It took weeks to turn that hardened fixture to one of genuine mirth and sometimes outright laughter.

Along the way, his uncle pointed out the magic that was not sleight of hand but rather the lulling magic of the beach itself. The first time Franklin laughed out loud Uncle Paul was taken aback by the power and infectiousness of the sound.

The beach became the one place Franklin seemed able to let someone penetrate the wall he had erected. The magic tricks were dissected and digested over and over. Franklin seemed to have a knack for interpreting what his uncle taught him and within the year was putting his own spin and personality into an ever growing arsenal of parlor tricks. When at the beach one sunny afternoon Franklin made one 99 of the many little birds that flit and stagger along the sand appear from what had been empty hands, Uncle Paul applauded and the torch was passed.

Years passed in this same manner and were chronicled by more and more of Uncle Paul's life systems shutting. Franklin learned the way to the emergency room at Flagler Hospital and knew the pharmacist at Walgreens by name.

There finally came a time when Hospice was called and the remaining three weeks were spent cataloging all they had learned from one another. They talked of their first awkward moments both unsure if they could live together. They both agreed it was the beach that had made it all work.

Franklin loved the beach and spent hours wandering up and down the ribbon of sand watching all manner of life emerge with the rising sun from behind dark glasses and under a large floppy hat that softened his features to a passing observer. In the years he spent in his Uncle's home he made the trip from awkward teen to young adult.

Franklin thanked his uncle for homeschooling him. "You saved me from a lot of grief." His uncle had become his best and only friend. He taught Franklin chess and introduced him to the classics in both music and literature.

On his own Franklin learned the solitude of the surfer. He spent hours hundreds of yards off shore not only waiting for the right wave but also just sitting out there looking in at the people on the beach.

His uncle had taught him to drive, well before legal age and they made their way to various beaches and to the pier 100 in town. He would holler from his perch on a surf board then wave to his Uncle sitting alone in his chair reading a beloved book.

His five foot frame never lengthened but he became strong and supple and an excellent swimmer. Being a loner himself Paul would sit on the shoreline in his wheelchair with a blanket on his lap watching life pass by, knowing he was leaving a legacy in this boy who rode the waves. He watched his charge navigate the surf; alone, always alone.

Never without a book, Uncle Paul started early on, sending Franklin into the library with a list of books that featured characters who confronted loneliness in different ways. He remained in the van in the parking spot reading a story of his own, always wondering if this might be his last. He had watched the boy hide his alone-ness by pretending to be shy. Uncle Paul knew better.

Franklin took to the characters he met on the pages who he identified with. He found that loners in literature ran the spectrum from happy to humiliated. Defiant to docile. Evil to envious. Caring to criminal. Sad to sadistic. Like a sponge Franklin soaked up and sifted, filtered and filed away, the mindsets these characters tattooed on his brain. In the process he discovered authors like Charles Dickens who created a character, Miss Havisham, who let heartbreak define her. Albert Camus, in his novel, **The Outsider** showed Franklin that one can be alone even in the midst of a crowd. Some of the stories containing loneliness Franklin read seemed straightforward, like Boo Radley, in **To kill a Mocking Bird.**

Franklin learned that great writing not only entertained him but informed as well. From stories like these and long conversations Franklin began to form his mindset. Coupled with the magic that could change an awkward introduction into a look of amazement and curiosity and finally acceptance, Franklin was left an arsenal of ways to fit in – if he so chose.

When Uncle Paul died, Franklin was alone once again. The characters from his reading all attended the quiet graveside service Paul had requested.

Even as the preacher strung together a host of homilies, Franklin was trying to determine which of these very real characters in his head would define him.

As the first shovel of dirt sounded on the metal casket one of his Uncle's favorite sayings entered Franklin's head quieting Miss Havisham who was pleading her case. A big Shakespeare fan, Uncle Paul was forever quoting the bard. **'Life is a tale told by an idiot, full of sound and fury signifying nothing.'** Those very words would etch the simple concrete marker followed by Uncle Paul's name and one final truism: **I was then I wasn't.**

A week later Uncle Paul's lawyer confirmed what he and his uncle had discussed and agreed to. Franklin could continue to live in the house or take what he wished and rent it out or sell it. He could sell everything he didn't want. Franklin was the only one named and inherited everything. Money had never been a big motivator for Franklin. He had so little of it and his solitary lifestyle now seemed at odds with over two million dollars that was his to do with as he wished. He loved the beach town of Flagler and spent a month walking the beach and driving into town, popping in and out of the small businesses that lined A-1A. He missed his uncle.

One morning, just north of the pier he met a fellow surfer wandering up from the water, a short man as well. They nodded hello. A sudden thought of what might happen if I introduce myself reached Franklin's mind and a line from one of the novels he had read entered his head. 'If? There is no if. There is only what is. What was? What will be.' The quote stayed in his head but the name of the book **The Writing on My Forehead,** exited his mouth and Franklin laughed aloud. That laugh, so much bigger than Franklin, stopped the man in his tracks.

Introductions were made. Franklin explained the name of the book he was thinking about had popped into his mouth unbidden. Jules Croissant studied Franklin briefly then held out his hand. The two wandered to a rooftop bar overlooking the ocean and while comparing notes on wave size and a dozen other surfer details, became instant friends. Jules was married and along with his wife operated a small restaurant a street back from A-1A. Jules did the baking and his wife managed the six table dining room. Franklin learned how Jules and his wife Danni landed in this small beach town.

Franklin began taking his meals at, Au Bleu, Jule's and Danni's inspiration. True to his last name, all entrees were baked in pastry shells Jule's created. The dessert pastries filled with sweetened cheeses or berries were a big hit as well.

After a month watching the couple work in tandem and tasting the creative ideas coming from the kitchen Franklin made a decision. He sat with Jule's and Danni one evening after closing and tossed out his idea. "The empty space immediately to the restaurant's left is for lease. You could double your size with just a wall torn out."

"And what would be on that side of the building, Franklin?" asked Danni.

"What would pair perfectly with your creations?" Franklin did not wait for an answer. "A wine and cheese bar. People could purchase their wine and cheese to take home or bring it to their table. Lots of profit in wine." Jules rubbed his chin. "Who would pay for this addition and who would run it?"

"I would like to invest some of the money I got from my Uncle and there is no one I trust more than you two. I will leave the running of the place in your hands. If it doesn't work out to benefit you, I will take the loss. But I'm not worried I see how hard you two work. And people love wine and cheese. What do you think?"

"Let us talk, Franklin, we will give you a decision in a week."

After helping to get the wine and cheese shop up and running Franklin left the beach to explore the world. His approach to travel would mirror the little birds that seemed to flit, land, and takeoff with no apparent destination. He left his Post office box key with Jule's who promised to forward anything that seemed important. He gave his bank account number to Jules as well. Franklin called exactly once a month fielding questions and offering advice and offering possible solutions for their shared enterprise.

Years of traveling found him visiting most of the civilized world. He spent a spring and summer traveling the USA. He traveled Europe and the Far East. He found he liked the less frequented locations best. There were far fewer questions to answer in the underbellies of the worlds' cities.

He introduced his magic in a hundred different ways. He found he had a way with women even though on the surface he didn't look the part. He discovered Cocaine. Used sparingly, for Franklin, it served as just one more parlor trick the mind could play on itself. Franklin returned from all his travels with some lessons learned. Lesson one: which he had already experienced in literature in the book **To Kill A Mockingbird,** people like to look down on those who don't look like them. What was it the Author, Harper Lee had written? 'You never really understand a person until you consider things from his point of view, until you climb into his skin and walk around in it.'

Another lesson learned: probably already known at some level but rising again and again in his travels, If you have money you can do a whole lot of stuff that should have nothing to do with having money, and still get away with it.

So Franklin Causano at age twenty eight, educated by some very strange forays into darkened corners, was ready to do some exploring in his own backyard. He returned to a relatively innocent part of America.

Palm Coast Florida was still in its infancy while the small city of Flagler Beach to its east, a much older town refused to move in lock-step with the grow at all cost approach visible in the form of high rises up and down the coast.

The new city of Palm Coast seemed to be taking at least some of its cues from Flagler Beach and put some pretty conservative codes in place.

For a while when he returned, Franklin became a fixture on the beach and in the bookshops and the library, continuing to learn a world of lessons from the very best teachers the world could provide. With the exception of Jules and Danni, their little boy Jake and their Irish red setter, Rouge. Franklin remained a loner. Then he decided to try out the new little city just to the west.

CHAPTER TWELVE

Lately Mom and dad have begun walking in the evening from our future home. After supper we load up one of dad's trucks and park in our future driveway. My sister and I tag along usually a few steps behind kicking a stray pine cone as we pretend to play a game of soccer. This was the neighborhood our house was going to be built in. This walking was Mom's idea, "It's a great way to learn the streets, and we might even meet some of our future neighbors."

Dad, always thinking about his new business, insists on carrying business cards and leaving the company truck in our future driveway. "Who knows someone might be needing a builder. They see that sign on the truck, boom." We left the sidewalk to walk onto our someday lawn. <u>Someday a dock might moor a sail boat here.</u> Dad exclaimed all this clumsily with his hands while mom corrected his grammatical mistakes like a teacher red lining an assignment. <u>We will be able to watch dolphins play, fish jump, and watch boats of all size and description pass by. You can sail all the way to St. Augustine or to Daytona Beach.</u> When dad and mom finished and I nodded my understanding, the two high-fived one another.

My sister and I wandered off the sidewalk between houses to gaze at the Intracoastal waterway that will pass right by our lawn.

Back on the street, Sarah, my teacher and mentor, explains that all the street signs in this section begin with the letter C. <u>Be glad you don't live in the F section.</u> She points up to our street sign. Crayfish Circle.

I stare at her. I have no idea what she's trying to tell me. <u>Kids at school tease kids about living in the section where streets begin with the letter F. You know the F word.</u>

I still have no idea what she's going on about. Sarah shakes her head at me like I am a dummy then drops the conversation and we go back to kicking pine-cones. Then out of the blue she SIGNS, <u>Wouldn't it be fun to have a dog.</u> She doesn't wait for an answer; she begins naming the kind of trees we are walking by. Who is this girl? I ask myself.

The Intercoastal waterway runs in front of some of the lots on this street. Other streets have man-made canals as their frontage. All the water from all these canals eventually finds its way to the Intercoastal on its march to the sea. It was cooling down. A constant breeze rode its way from the water moderating the dead calm heat of summer in Florida. The sidewalks were turning dark as we started our way back towards the truck. Streetlights placed only at intersecting streets did not invite evening strolls. We turned on our headlamps as we finished up the last half mile of our walk. The plants and shrubs on the lawns offered no color, just deeper shadow. Sarah Signed me that she could see monster shapes in those shrubs. I peered intently seeing nothing but dark dark.

It was nearly full on dark when we heard the scream. Well I didn't hear it but I reacted when my parent's and Sarah's body language stiffened.

They looked first left then right. I was left literally in the dark with headlights dancing up, down and all around. Sarah took my hand then signed they had just heard a scream. <u>One scream,</u> she signed, <u>a scream of terror.</u> Her eyes widened.

With the waterway so close it could have come from anywhere.

Mom encouraged dad to do something.

He crossed to the nearest residence and rang a bell in a large condo building. I looked up and counted six different levels of light. We remained in the parking lot. Dad looked at six rows of buttons. He chose a button on the first floor. No one answered so he went to row two. A button on floor two lit up. (Sarah later told me all that was said.)

A voice came through a speaker. "What do you want?" The voice did not wait for an answer. "If you're selling something I don't want any. If you're looking for someone, I don't know anyone. If you're looking for a hand-out, I gave at the office. If you're a single dame looking for company then why didn't you say so in the first place." Dad chuckled.

I was out of the loop till my sister could bring me up to speed so I just continued to study the six different balconies.

Dad shrugged. "This is fruitless. That sound could have come from anywhere." He smiled looking at mom, blinding her with his light. "You talk to the guy, you're a dame," he kidded, "you might get a better response than me.

Lane asked the voice if he had heard a scream a minute ago.

The voice of what she determined to be an elderly man indicated he'd heard nothing but the doorbell. His voice became softer. He was talking to a lady after all. "Sorry. It probably came from the water, lots of people on boats out there all hours of the night."

"Well thank you. We heard a scream and we're trying to find where it came from. Sorry to bother you, good night." We returned to the sidewalk. Sarah explained it all to me in the glow of her headlamp.

My parents continued to discuss whether they should call someone. "Too vague I think. We heard one scream. We have no idea from where. Let's call it a night."

I looked back one more time. A man on the top floor was leaning over the balcony looking down. I caught his shadow in the light behind him. He seemed tall to me. He looked like a shadow monster. I shivered.

The man on the sixth floor counted four headlamps. One lamp was facing up. He was too high and it was too dark to be seen clearly but the girl's scream had been heard. From his condo – the source of the scream – the open window that allowed the sound of distress to ride the breeze was now closed. The screamer also now quieted. He watched what appeared to be a family walk away.

We found our way back to Dad's company truck and even without being able to hear I can assure you it was a quiet ride home. We all seemed lost in our own thoughts.

When we arrived home with the drama we had just witnessed, I was reminded of something a little scary that happened to me at school that I needed to tell them about. I went on to give them a shortened version of my escape from Arnold. They looked concerned. <u>I handled it. But now I need your help.</u> I went on to explain what I'd told my teacher. <u>I need you to talk with Arnold's parents. I don't think he has money for glasses. I just know that will fix everything.</u>

Mom and dad shook their heads as if baffled and mystified by my actions.

I read their lips. "He continues to see things that others can't."

"Don't blame me," dad kidded. <u>Bobby we are very proud of you. I'll talk with your teacher irst. She might be able to make this a meeting that will seem less threatening for Arnold's parents. We'll buy his glasses. You may be able to stay out of it.</u>

I nodded. *That would be good, Arnold wouldn't need to know I was involved at all.*

Sarah, my confidant sat in on the conversation. She sat patiently not asking any follow up. She eyed me knowingly though. I would be giving her all the gory details of my encounter with Arnold sometime before breakfast.

CHAPTER THIRTEEN

Victor continued to work. Which kept his father off his back. He made sure he kept the place clean. His father hardly ever showed up and when he did it was just to give the place a once-over and offer one criticism or another. Since that terrible night Victor found his alone time eerily similar to his father's habit of flipping channels. Victor's channels were all in his head however and the flipping involved a flashback sequence that had not ended well. Awake or asleep the flashbacks were unending. Night sweats had joined him in his bed.

At work his mind was occupied by learning to measure, cut, and serve as the grunt at the end of a board or sheet of plywood or dry-wall.

He eventually met the owner George Whiting who seemed genuinely interested in his men. George brought donuts and coffee on Friday mornings and oftentimes donned a hard hat and worked alongside his men. The boss man whistled while he worked. Victor didn't feel the urge to whistle these days.

Victor didn't really enjoy the work. He could do better. He tried to put the idea of buying or selling drugs out of his mind but he continued to see the little man at various bars in the city and in Flagler Beach. Smoothest operator he had ever seen, he decided.

This morning Victor had a lot more than drugs on his mind.

He sat on the balcony of his sixth floor condo on a Saturday morning in mid-September. He was nursing his first cup of coffee after cleaning the unit. He had made no friends in the condo building, and had no idea who might be occupying the other units. He had no idea if anyone in the building had heard the scream. It was a big building. Just as well. For the time being it seemed all the worry remained in his own head. The graveled voice of the singer Ray Lamontagne put words and music to what he was feeling. Oh yeah he had both <u>trouble and worry.</u>

Thinking of trouble His father came to mind. He usually checked in at least once a week to make sure Victor was 'doing the chores', as he called them. Wiping his finger across one appliance or piece of furniture or another. 'The old white glove test,' he called it. *Probably he'll be here today* Victor thought earlier as he lay abed but awake, a million things running through his head, none good.

He looked at his clothing strewn everywhere around the room. The place had a dead air smell. He yawned, got up, and lumbered out into the kitchen where he put on a pot of coffee, his massive upper frame naked, rising from orange and green boxers. Twenty minutes later the noise of the vacuum was just leaving his ears. Actually that sound muffled the other sound that was there without being plugged into a wall; one scream that could change his life.

He was sweating profusely as he opened the glass door leading to the balcony. Still clad in just his boxers, sweat glistening on his hairy shoulders, he leaned over the balcony holding his coffee.

He looked down onto the tops of the palms. The fronds rustled in the breeze. In his mind he could still see four lights walking away from the building in the near dark. One of them seemed to have guessed the scream had come from the top floor. His head slumped with the memory. Below, the parking lot was half full of vehicles, most wearing various shades of gray or silver, gleaming in the morning sun. His eyes caught movement. A tropical style hat and a colorful shirt appeared, walking towards a car. When the car door opened the man looked around then up. Victor stood back from the railing, but not before he recognized the short man in dark glasses he had seen doing magic tricks and selling drugs in bars around the city. Victor's eyes widened. Does he live here?

CHAPTER FOURTEEN

Newly hired by George Whiting and already promoted, Hailey and her son Daniel arrived home from an evening trip to an ice cream Shoppe. Daniel had been selected as student of the week in his elementary school. Hailey attended the school assembly, having been informed of her son's honor. She sat in the Principal's office waiting for the program to begin. She stood off to the side out of view when all the good things she believed about her son exited the mouth of his teacher. She had joined her son on stage and given him a big hug.

Now tonight she honored him in their own special ritual of smothering good happenings in ice-cream. Daniel went in to shower and Hailey was left listening to the water running and Daniel singing. With the bathroom door open his special smell mixed with ivory soap joined her in the living room.

They had experienced a lot of good happenings lately. She sat there counting her blessings and mentally tallying the who and the how surrounding their good fortune. One image appeared in strong focus—George Whiting. There are good people in the world and there are special people, George was special. She couldn't help but smile. My God was she developing a crush on her boss? Her face became heated with the revelation. She took a deep breath. Daniel hollered. He had soap in his eyes. Hailey rushed in to assist. The little guy was getting so independent any need for mom was savored. "I'm right here."

CHAPTER FIFTEEN

Joel, having slept his way through the early hours of a workday refused to respond to the message light that he surmised carried anger from his father. He rubbed his grizzly whiskers three days in the making. There was a cut on his right hand that had been poorly bandaged and stopped bleeding on its own during the night. Blood stained his pillow and sheet. He felt like he'd allowed Franklin to do one of his magic tricks while walking on his head. He sat on the edge of the bed in the darkened room trying to make sense of yesterday. *My god it was yesterday wasn't it?* He was woozy. He remembered Franklin. Just the effort of that one thought had him gasping, feeling nauseous. He lay back down. When his head cleared he vaguely recalled meeting a girl. He rubbed his head like a magic eight ball summoning memory from the beginning. *Already a beer in his belly, several drinks, alone in his truck before picking up Franklin. Franklin ragging on him to behave. Introducing himself to a girl in the bar. The afternoon was a blur. He rubbed his head, still dizzy.* If he remembered correctly the word *cocaine came up which took the party to Franklin's Condo.* He held his head once more. Oh yeah Cocaine came up. He remembered *snorting some of Franklin's white sand and following up with a chaser of Beam.* Somewhere in his frog brain *a glass was shattered.* How and why that happened was a mystery, but now studying his hand obviously he'd been cut.

He remembered waking in the night. *Hugging the floor in his own apartment.* Somehow he'd made it into his bed. He sniffed and smelled then saw the vomit on the rug. "Aww man, I didn't remember that," he uttered as the stink had him retching.

He lay back breathing heavily, discouraging any discharge. He looked to his right and checked the radio alarm, the numbers were fuzzy but accurate and silent. That effort hurt his head. He closed his eyes. He awoke. *The numbers on the clock had moved so he must be alive Christ it was after noon time.*

He felt chunks of vomit in his throat. How in hell had a complete day disappeared? He moved and groaned, he was lame all over. He remembered that feeling from the fight he'd lost in that bar. A sour smell continued to rise over the bedside. Avoiding the splatter he rolled off the bed. He limped to the bathroom, put his mouth under the faucet and gargled away some residue of chips and what might have been Beef Jerky and pizza. He could still taste alcohol. He rinsed the cut which seemed to have stopped bleeding. He studied his bloodshot eyes in the mirror. He looked like an old man for Christ's sake. Gray whiskers seemed to be taking up permanent residence. A double chin was emerging as the repository of a general top down melting of his physical self. The song, **Man in the mirror** reached inside his head as he studied this stranger looking back at him.

He held his head again, still slightly dizzy. His breathing was shallow. He looked down at what was clearly another gathering place for his melting flesh. As much as he hated to admit it, Myrtle was right. Franklin was right. Even his father was right.

Standing here in all his glory was a complete failure. His belly was reaching for the floor hiding his waistband and his stinking feet. He looked again at the unexplained cut on his hand.

Can a man have an intervention with himself? Suddenly Joel felt all that failure well up and his knees buckled. He found himself on his knees vomiting bile of regret down the toilet and sobbing aloud. *His circle of friends engulfed him, each looking him straight in the eye voicing the transgression that had hurt them or himself.*

When he rose, eyes wet, sweating and breathing deeply, he viewed an empty shell. He looked to the mirror once more and gritted his teeth, hating the look of truth. The words of his old football coach added his two cents. *'You are a talented kid, you just need to believe in yourself.'*

Joel took a deep breath like he was about to plunge down a ski slope to what end he didn't know. He lathered his face and the razor made its first slalom. Like snow outside a coal mine his dirty gray whiskers marked the path he had been following, a path that would lead straight into a tree.

Each stroke of the razor revealed more truth. *Well* he thought as he rubbed his clean shaven face, *I look more human even if I can't claim to feel like one.* The thought of an empty shell sunk in. He took another deep breath and entered the shower. He turned the knob to scald and tried to hide in the steam. He set his shoulders and began to wash the old Joel down the drain. He scrubbed away with a vengeance. As his washcloth tortured his body parts the stinging hot water added to his self-punishment. He remained head down watching failure, regret, arrogance and ego all enter the drain. It was cold water that motivated him to take the next step. He turned off the water and remained in the small enclosure, a prison cell of his own making, shivering. He wept. He remained in his confessional.

Much later wrapped in a towel, the air conditioning kicking on raising another shiver, he moved about the kitchen.

His reflection from the toaster revealed the ugly truth once more. His towel slipped and he left it lying on the floor. The naked truth stalked his kitchen. He nearly chuckled at his nakedness. He found humor in being naked cracking two eggs into a bowl. A pot of water began to steam. He placed two spoonfuls of coffee into a cup. He stirred a squirt of water into the eggs and beat the crap out of them. The pot of water began boiling. He removed the pot, replacing it with a frying pan. He placed a pat of butter in the pan and poured his coffee.

Remembering that morning in his truck when he blew any chance of rejoining his father's company, he would drink this bitter brew black. *Beat yourself up Joel you deserve it* he thought as the coffee reached his throat. Oddly the taste seemed to reinforce all the things he put into himself that in the end simply brought him despair. *This is what rock bottom tastes like.* The toast popped and once again he viewed his image. He looked himself dead in the eye in the reflection of the toaster. He raised his right hand as if testifying before the court.

"I promise today will be day one of a different Joel Riesling." He toasted nothing and everything. He put the eggs on to cook. He checked his watch. He went to the calendar and wrote the number <u>I</u> beside the date. He suddenly found himself humming. He would go this very day— day one— to his father and ask to be a member of the crew. It wasn't too late. He set his shoulders once again. After a breakfast that filled him but he could not taste he set about cleaning up the aftermath in the bedroom. He wrestled all the bedding into the washer. When he closed his door wearing a clean denim work shirt and khaki pants, a working man's uniform, he was still humming. His final thought, *George, is this why you whistle?*

Two weeks went by and in the mundane pace of getting up and going to school or work— or in Joel Riesling's case trying to find work— the sun came up and the sun went down. Joel, following a ritual that convinced him he was on the right path still had not convinced his father to give him another shot. In his new humble beginning he began doing one day at a time day labor by calling contractors he knew. He managed to stay sober and avoided calling Franklin. He continued to hum through his disappointment. He called Myrtle but was only reaching the message machine.

CHAPTER SIXTEEN

Florida offers an abundance of sunny days year round. In the ever growing swamps, marshes and nearly impenetrable foliage that sits just off the road. Weather does a number on anything that has crawled there to die. A body of any kind landing in one of these areas is discovered only by a gathering of turkey buzzards or sheer happenstance.

It took the early days of autumn for a small population of people to come to the realization that one of their own was missing. It was the owner of a bar that first brought it to light. "Hey Dee-Dee, I haven't seen Nona for a while. I thought you two were best buds?"

"I've tried to call her but she's not answering. I've left a dozen messages. Maybe she went back to that loser you barred from here. Maybe she moved back home. All I know is she isn't answering my messages."

"I don't know about any of that but I liked the kid. She asked me for a job. Is anyone else missing her?"

The girl thought for a moment. "Now that you mention it I guess we aren't the only ones she's not talking to. Her sister called to ask if I had seen her. She didn't seem worried though. Nona, as you well know, is a free spirit."

CHAPTER SEVENTEEN

Not all was doom and gloom during those weeks of day after day good weather. Arnold arrived a week after our altercation in the bathroom wearing glasses, sporting a new pair of jeans and a bright new tee-shirt. Even more amazing, he didn't smell up the classroom. Along with his new glasses and better hygiene he was wearing a smile. The school principal had been candid with Arnold's mother. Forced to get sober for the first meeting she had ever attended for her son, she walked headlong into four ladies intent on offering one of two possible outcomes for today's meeting. She had obviously listened— at least in the short term.

A week later people's attention turned to a different mother. Mother Nature. Hurricane season is said to start at the beginning of June. Potential storms in the Atlantic originate in the simplest of ways. It had been a quiet season. A warm summer. School had started back up in August. About the only excitement in the air was that other season that arrives every four years, a political season. A Presidential election. The chatter on the left and right was non-stop.

But the chatter returned to the weather towards the end of September. From a tropical wave southeast of the Cape Verde Islands on September 25, dubbed Invest 97L, a storm with the future name Matthew, was spawned.

The State of Florida yawned; been there done that. At first the updates seemed designed to add a bit of drama to weather reports. Mundane weather forecasts that generally show seven smiley faces of sun week after week. You might see a bit of gray beard in the form of a thunderstorm dimming a smiley face but they are wham bam thank you ma'am downpours accompanied by sight and sound.

If it storms in Flagler County during the rainy season it means it's 4pm. you can set your clock to it. Those 4pm. Thundershowers chase beach goers to bars, roofers to the bowels of construction projects and send golfers scrambling into cart barns with the sound of an air horn. Thirty minutes later the sun is shining. No news there.

So thru the early and mid-part of the month Clinton vs. Trump was still clogging the airways.

For a number of years the east coast of Florida had pretty much escaped a major hurricane.

Then from three days of churning and nourishing itself in an overheated ocean, tropical storm Matthew was born - given a name - not usually a good sign but we could hope the babe would perish in infancy. This baby however was fed a formula that had it growing twenty-four-seven. As it gained strength it came under closer scrutiny. Matthew moved up in the food chain becoming the top story on the weather portion of the local news up and down the state. Once Matthew became a category five hurricane even the national news started showing the frenzied speck in the south Atlantic.

Donald Trump and Hillary Clinton became the second lead. Matthew's strength ebbed slightly and the State of Florida and the gulf region collectively sighed. Then just like the election cycle things heated up.

Matthew hammered the Bahamas as a category 3 Hurricane and suddenly the air waves were tossing out spaghetti shaped possible tracks the storm might take as it moved ever closer to the tip of Florida.

People on both sides of Florida began to worry. Eeniemeenie-minee-mo, which way would Matthew choose to go? The East coast rather than the Gulf of Mexico began to loom in the cross hairs. When it was clear that the East Coast was the target, Flagler County entered its path. Coastal Flagler and the Intercoastal that parallels it were asked to evacuate.

C-Section of Palm Coast with the Intercoastal waterway running the length of it was an area where evacuation was recommended before the storm hit.

———◆◆◆◆◆———

Franklin closed and locked the door to his fourth floor Condo in the heart of the evacuation zone. This was the first time since moving here he'd been asked to evacuate. Having moved into Palm Coast after selling his Uncle's house in Flagler Beach and going off to see the world, Franklin was now a resident with a different view of a different body of water, the Intercoastal.

While throwing clothes in his duffle bag, on the spur of the moment he decided his planned trip should be an extended one. He needed to get away from Joel and Myrtle, at least for a while. Joel's actions worried him and Myrtle, well he was pretty sure she was not his soul mate. A good friend, yes that was it.

Time to shake things up. He discovered he still had the old canvas suitcase. A hundred memories filled his head. He packed to be away for a while. Several books he'd been meaning to read joined his luggage. Suddenly his uncle and the story of his mother filled his head. *Hmm just a thought.* He called Jules and made financial arrangements. The thought didn't leave him. Franklin had not been back to his home state since being summoned to Florida.

Though not terribly curious about his mother he might at least find out if she was still alive.

Ahead of the storm he left Interstate 95 in Jacksonville and headed west on Route 10. With a coffee warming his knees he turned on the radio to hear what he would be missing. The latest weather report had the storm predicted to hug the coastline making a mess of anything in its path. Franklin turned off the radio and returned to a plan he was devising on the fly. Hell thought Franklin *I could stay right on this route and end up at that other ocean.* He chuckled, he'd actually spent a bit of time in Nevada and California. "Seen the sights and reached new heights," he sung aloud, nodding to the past memories and one recent one. The recent one was the reason Franklin wasn't taking Joel's calls. Franklin had recently witnessed a complete meltdown of his friend.

The evacuation couldn't have come at a better time if he was being honest. Franklin thought back to that afternoon. *He found when Joel arrived to pick him up he had been drinking. Franklin insisted on chauffeuring. They entered a bar in Flagler Beach. Joel, two dance steps from a stagger seemed to think he knew the girl who was dancing by herself to a mostly empty room. Joel joined her on the floor and the two danced separately together. When the song ended Joel took her hand and brought her to the table. She was in a similar condition as Joel. She introduced herself as Nona. Joel said he had seen her somewhere before. She struggled with where that could have been then suggested maybe at Cluck's Chicken Coop in town. She had worked there a couple of times. Joel snapped his fingers. 'That's where I have seen you. Small world.' Franklin had remained silent.*

A couple of drinks later the girl agreed to come back to Joel's apartment to party. Franklin drove. With Willie demanding <u>whiskey for his men and beer for his horses</u> the two-some managed to join right in. Franklin, not a big drinker, suggested a little beech sand and the party moved to Franklin's Condo.

That afternoon with Joel and the young woman, Nona, who seemed intent on drinking and snorting away her pain, had ended with Joel passing out after cutting his hand rather badly on a whiskey glass he slammed onto the kitchen table.

The girl, seated opposite panicked at the sight of all that blood. She exited quickly to the bathroom and immediately became sick. Franklin wrapped Joel's hand in paper towels. Joel lay his head on the table.

With eyes glistening, breathing heavily from too much drink, her shirt splattered with blood, Nona charged out of the bathroom reeling towards the door.

Franklin tried to reason with her, offering her a ride but she refused and stumbled away.

A half hour later Joel came back to life with Franklin lightly slapping him awake at the table. Franklin took him to his apartment and left him the door. He was still belligerent and Franklin had heard enough.

Franklin went to Jule's and Danni's restaurant for an evening meal. He shared the story of the afternoon with Jules and decided in the retelling to no longer hang out with Joel. The needless debacle in the bar and that afternoon signaled Joel seemed intent on drinking and drugging himself to death. Franklin fingered the little plastic packet in his pocket. That was causing problems as well. He certainly didn't need the drugs or the money. He opened the car window enough to let the grains catch the wind. He determined Cocaine would not be a passenger on this trip. *Time to grow up, Franklin.*

Being short enough to curl up in the backseat at a rest stop was a plus in Franklin's mind. He had plenty of cash so there was no credit card trail. He could get his meals in drive-thru. So for all practical purposes Franklin went off the grid. *I like that,* thought Franklin. Joel had left messages but Franklin was going to let some time pass. *Maybe a long time. As far as Myrtle, well he hadn't really made any decisions. It was clear she was fond of him. Again, friend seemed to nail his relationship with Myrtle.* He'd give that some thought on this trip but he would not be answering any cell phones he'd intentionally left his in the Condo. He had made plans to call Jules on occasion from a pay phone.

Two hours later into all this thinking he took an exit paid in cash for a fill up and exited his vehicle to use the restroom.

Sporting sunglasses, cargo shorts, sandals, a silk tee shirt and a Tommy Bahama straw hat pulled low, he entered and looked for the restroom sign. On his way he spotted a girl hanging at the long row of coffee choices. She's a bit young, his first thought. Franklin went to the bathroom. The girl was still there when he came out.

Walking to the coffee area, he studied her. She was cradling a backpack like a baby. She seemed to be wrestling with a decision. He poured a coffee to go. He approached where she was leaning against the counter. When he spoke she turned, her eyes took him in and they widened.

"It looks like you could use a cup of that coffee. Go ahead I'm buying." The girl didn't answer but nodded her head slowly in thanks and poured a cup. Franklin smiled, a real smile. *The best laid plans of mice and men* he thought to himself as he put the lid on a dark roast. *I have always traveled alone, but like Uncle Paul advised, maybe it's time to broaden my horizons.*

After she doctored her coffee he took both to the counter and on the way grabbed two pastries which brought Jules and Danni to mind. *Would they approve? He thought they would.* He did not speak to the girl until he'd paid and was out the door. She followed. When he reached his car which was parked on the side where no cameras were visible he placed his coffee on the roof and turned to hand the girl her coffee and choice of pastry. "Raspberry or Cream Cheese, your choice."

The girl, two inches taller and ten years younger than Franklin studied him for a moment and decided he was harmless. "Raspberry is my favorite but I'm so hungry it doesn't matter. Thank you by the way."

"Get in. Let's talk about your past and your future. I hate to drink my coffee alone." He smiled then. A softer smile. One he had discovered at Flagler beach.

The girl shrugged and slowly moved to the passenger side where a leaning Franklin had already pushed the door open. They settled and sipped. Both seemed to be studying the gray concrete wall that could have been a movie screen. Franklin innocently probed, finding out the girl had arrived by hitch with a trucker who turned out to be an "ucker." The girl explained this new term by suggesting she was not ready to drop the f-bomb on a stranger who might be a traveling preacher or something.

Franklin laughed aloud. Franklin's laughter was a lot deeper than one would imagine given his size. That too seemed intriguing to the girl. She laughed aloud as well.

"I'm not a preacher, just a traveling salesman taking a roadtrip to wherever I end up." Franklin looked across into a pair of liquid blue eyes that belonged on someone much older. He suddenly felt a dose of honesty here would go a long way in keeping the girl in the passenger seat. He began a monologue. "If you have been following the news at all you know parts of Florida are being evacuated ahead of Hurricane Matthew. I am actually one of those fleeing the storm. I am a salesman though. Don't laugh. A used car salesman. You know, the guy to avoid at all costs."

When Breanna opened her mouth to respond Franklin held up his finger. "So this is when you might want to make your exit. Especially if you're looking for a good deal." Franklin winked and laughed again. His laughter was just infectious. Breanna sat back in the seat smiling, fully relaxed.

"An honest used car salesman, I am having a good day," she toasted. Her lips parted, showing a dazzling smile. "She sipped her coffee then bit into the Danish. She chewed slowly, savoring the flavors. The sun felt good on her shoulders. The air conditioning cooled and soothed her. She offered her hand, "I'm Breanna and I am not a used car person nor am I looking for a car." The building wall in front of them remained blank except for a lottery sign promising a new beginning starts here. If she stayed in this car they would be filming their own movie moving forward.

Franklin took her hand and introduced himself as himself, Franklin Causano. "Where are you headed, Breanna?"

"Texas I think, at least I hadn't gotten beyond there on the map. Wide open spaces. Anywhere away from Florida." She took on a serious look. "Bad-bad break-up Franklin. Threats and all that goes with it." She thought for a moment, "Kinda like the storm that's about to hit Florida, my storm just landed earlier."

Franklin nodded. "No circle of friends or family you could call on, to help you through it?" She looked inward,

"That was a big part of the problem. That guy— that's what my parent's labeled him— THAT GUY—turned out to be a control freak and it kept getting worse and worse. Their concern followed me all the way down the coast; every time they called." She shifted her weight. "My family is back in Massachusetts. They would love to see my smiling face so they could add amen to the sermon I was given when I started seeing—THAT GUY— in the first place."

She sipped and silently gargled her brew. Her body language kept pace with the conversation. "In the here and now I never made a single friend outside the workplace since coming down here." She looked across at Franklin, "Well now, maybe one."

Franklin nodded his head, "Where you coming from in Florida?"

"Palm Coast, a little city half an hour below St. Augustine."

Franklin nearly choked on the remainder of his coffee. Probably ought to keep a little distance here, thought Franklin. "I know Palm Coast, I live just below it in Daytona Beach. What did you do for work?"

"A fast food restaurant was my last job. A place called **Clucks Chicken Coop,** have you heard of it?" Franklin was glad his coffee and pastry were gone, he would have choked for sure. Myrtle Beech was the manager there. His eyes behind the glasses glazed over. What just happened here? He asked himself.

The two talked for a few more minutes. Breanna excused herself to the restroom. The car had turned its back on the blank wall and was pointed in the direction of a possible new future as Breanna climbed back into the passenger seat.

———•••••—•—

For what seemed like 48 hours the storm rode the waves and the coastline north toward Flagler and St. Johns County. On October 6, 2016 Hurricane Matthew took up fleeting residence. Acting like a surfer who refuses to come to land, Matthew aimed the edge of its board in such a way as to kick up storm surge that ended up doing most of the damage. Picture a giant bite out of an apple. Matthew's wind and storm surge gnashed its teeth and devoured great chunks of beaches along route A-1A in Volusia, Flagler, St. John, and Duval Counties. A mile of route A-1A was removed to the center line in one bite in Flagler Beach. With the taste of asphalt hard to digest, Matthew picked its teeth on wooden walkovers, left them splintered hanging in mid-air like exhibits in a modern art show. Matthew chewed great chunks out of the beaches all along the eastern side of Florida. In central and northern Florida, Daytona Beach to MarineLand. St Augustine to Anastasia Island in Duval, County. The Intercoastal swelled and flooded with the surge, ocean sized waves flooding hundreds of homes along A-1A.

———•••••—•—

Two days after Matthew left Flagler County, moving north just off the coastline, it finally made landfall in South Carolina as a category one hurricane. Exhausted by the efforts of chewing, swallowing, and expending asphalt, homes, and millions of gallons of water, it purged itself, drowning an area termed the Low Country. So much for Southern Hospitality.

In Flagler county and surely throughout eastern coastal Florida, the need for new roofs and repairs from beach-side to ten miles inland pushed new construction projects to the back burner.

George formed three additional crews using temporary labor. He put one of his original team members on every roof or repair job. Along A-1A near Marine Land and to the north, houses had flooded to the second story. Most of the homes on the Intercoastal side of A-1A in northern Flagler and St. Johns County received structural damage that sprouted twenty foot high piles of furniture, appliances, wall board, windows and everything in between at intervals of fifty feet along A-1A.

It was at the end of the day a week after the storm that Dan, one of George's crew leaders called George. "Guess who was standing in line with the day laborers when I showed up to hire a crew for next week?"

George, having no idea, let the answer linger in silence until Dan caught on. "It was Joel Riesling. I didn't recognize him at first. He looked like a new man. He approached me and insisted you would want him to be hired. So I did. Was that okay? He did a good day's work. I'll say that for him." Dan thought for a minute. "He kinda reminded me of you George." Again George was at a loss, he remained silent. Dan caught on once again. "He hummed the whole day through, kinda reminded me of you and your whistle."

"Well fine then, I don't have a problem with that. Keep him on as long as he does what you ask. I might get around to your crew in the next several days. I'll check him out." Then it was down to business. "We have two dozen people calling every day for new roofs. I'm spending most of my days talking with the insurance companies for these people. We have a whole list of potential clients who need major construction as well. It's too much of a good thing during a bad time for people."

When dad got home I was waiting for him. <u>Dad that boy Arnold lost his home. The wind peeled off his roof and everything inside is ruined. Can we help him?</u>" Dad did his best to answer me. I mostly read his lips. "<u>That the kid who bullied you. You helped him once. Now you want to help him again?</u>" Now he needs my help in another way. He has a sister in Sarah's class too.

Dad seemed to have a lot on his mind. He didn't give me the answer I wanted. <u>Bobby my crews are right out straight. I've got six crews working twelve hour shifts.</u> I looked down, disappointed. I walked away already thinking. There had to be a way.

The city of Palm Coast contracted for help to cut up and transport downed trees, limbs, and damaged foliage that covered sidewalks, lawns and back yards. Golf courses experienced scores of downed trees and scattered branches and limbs. Some of the trees uprooted across power lines and protruded onto roadways. Some toppled backward into the undergrowth.

Restoring power was job one. A power company crew was cutting up a tall pine that had fallen onto a street downing a power line. This remote part of the city was one of the last to be reached. The top of the tree extended twenty-five feet into the jungle. With the street cleared and the line repaired the crew gathered at the water cooler, sweating.

Two guys lit up a smoke. The top part of the pine tree joined the thick undergrowth off the roadway. As it happened one of the crew members needed relief. Excusing himself he walked along the path the tree had created into the Jungle. As he emptied himself, sighing, mentally counting the seconds of his effort while letting his flow dance back and forth across a pine bough, he studied his surroundings. All this overtime, he was a happy man. He breathed deeply, filling his nostrils with fresh pine scent. Just a man and his pride.

He caught the faint odor of something dead. He looked a little deeper into the jungle as he waggled the last drops. *Hmm. A piece of clothing visible beneath one of the branches.* He finished and zipped up. Curious but not concerned, he took the two steps needed to get a better view. He saw what looked like a piece of colorful shirt protruding from beneath the tree. Odd. He took another half step. The smell intensified. A decomposed hand was barely visible in the greenery and pine needles. He jumped back and hollered. Within minutes, noises that publicly announce and accompany one calamity or another, headed towards a long stretch of woods in the area of the city named Seminole Woods.

The death was first announced simply as that, a death; possibly storm related. There was no identification on the body. Its location was strange but cause of death would be determined by an autopsy. That was the extent of the news report. In The News Journal and later two weekly publications, the Tribune and the Observer, the same information was repeated. No new news to report. ^ Storm clean up, closed beaches, washed out roads in Flagler Beach, a visit from the Governor, and neighbors sharing war stories of where they were when the hurricane hit dominated conversation and newspaper space.

Oh yeah, let's not forget the upcoming election. Meanwhile in the morgue, an unclaimed badly decomposed young woman lay in a darkened drawer.

CHAPTER EIGHTEEN

The results of the autopsy came back on the woman who now occupied drawer 13 since being discovered in the tangled under-growth. The autopsy revealed only two things for certain— much like the wording on Franklin's uncle Paul's tombstone— the woman had lived and the woman had died. Decomposition and attentive scavengers had removed her stomach, both eyes, and most of the skin on her face and torso. Her height and approximate age were determined from what remained. One finger, less chewed than the rest offered up the only hope that what remained might supply an identifying fingerprint; nope not enough.

When they had all the information they were likely to get, the Sheriff's office reached out to the media to ask for the public's help. From the skull a composite sketch was configured along with an approximate height and a possible age range.

— • — • — • — • —

Unfortunately news programs were not a steady diet for those closest to Nona and what turned out to be a pretty good likeness of the dead girl went unseen for the month of November.

— • — • — • — • —

What was taking up everyone's attention in early November of 2016 was continued cleanup and the election for president. Everyone had an opinion. In the bars where construction workers assembled in the late afternoons and evenings the talking heads out shouted one another from rectangular screens. The latest reveal, many times offered up with no supporting data, encouraged heated arguments. And so it went, from argument to disbelief to denial.

In what was shaping up in the minds of the Sheriff's office as a homicide, one additional piece of evidence had been found on the girl's clothing. A blood stain that did not match the victim. It was analyzed and filed away for future reference.

More than a month after Nona's disappearance her sister had called the Sheriff's office. All the sister could offer was that Nona had not been in touch with friends or family. Was that unusual she was asked?

"Not really," the dispatcher was told.

"Do you want to come in and file a formal missing persons' report?" Having been down this road with her sister before, her sister said, "Mmmhhm, maybe we'll just give it another week or so, I'll get back to you."

More time passed with no contact from her sister. Finally Nona's sister and a friend entered the Flagler County Sheriff's office. They had hardly opened their mouths to ask the question, when on a bulletin board staring them directly in the eyes - an artist's rendition of Nona Ashby. With mouths agape while pointing fingers at the poster, they were ushered into a detective's office.

Clean up had been ongoing since the storm hit. George and Hailey visited a dozen sites a day. Blue tarps covered what was not repaired. Both Shingles and Roof tiles were arriving daily. They picked up additional renovation work with nearly every roofing job. The renovations would have to be done at a later date George told his new clients - roofs come first.

Joel had proved to be a steady reliable worker and this morning George was about to do something he thought would never happen. He was going to ask Joel if he wanted a full time job. His former secretary at Coastal Construction, Betty, had also left him a message to call. Funny how things happen. George was contemplating opening a real office in a fixed place. The company was so busy George and Hailey couldn't handle all the calls. George returned Betty's call. Betty wanted out of Coastal Construction. She had worked for Fred for twenty years but it wasn't the same since Fred had been forced back on the job.

"He hates being back and it shows. He never ever sniped at me before." She began sobbing. "George I'm fifty seven years old and I still need to work. Can you use an old hasbeen?"

"Betty it's like we're traveling the same cosmic path here, I have been trying to figure out how to go about setting up an office. Who gets to tell Fred?"

"He won't be surprised. It might just be the motivation he needs to either wake up or close up. I can start in two weeks. I'll tell Fred today. Let me know if I can help in any way."

George, whistling as he waited for the call to connect, told Lane the news. Lane was pleased but seemed a bit stressed.

It had been a rough time for the schools since the hurricane. Whole families had been evacuated before the storm and some with water and roof damage would not return until repairs were made.

The rancor of the election both before and after had seeped into the schools as well. "Right about now George I'd like a job on one of those roofs. I could look up at blue skies, breathe deep and the only chatter would be one of those damn nail guns."

"I hear you. Hell, crew members are chirping their politics up on those roofs waving their arms and nearly coming to blows when they are on the ground. I had to lay down the law. The best thing that could happen for this country would be for the Satellites and Cables to go silent for a month or two. Let us get our feet back under us as a city and a country. So you want a job?"

Lane chuckled, "No, I guess I'm good here. You'll be lucky to have Betty though, that woman has good common sense."

The airwaves went silent for a moment. "I have one more surprise to throw at you, tell me what you think." He paused for effect. "I'm going to hire Joel on full time. He's been working hard. He seems sober and he could really help us expand if he's willing to lose the ego." George could imagine Lane absorbing all this a half dozen miles away.

A moment of silence while this all sunk in and then Lane made an observation. "George, I'm not sure who influences who in this family." She chuckled, "Does Bobby's sense of justice and compassion come from you or is that boy rubbing off on you. Either way I leave it to you. I haven't seen nor spoken to Joel since before we got married."

George nodded to himself. "OK I got this. I have some questions that need answering but given the right answers I'd like to hire him."

"Don't need my permission. I love you, see you at home." Another pause. "By the way, When Bobby tugs on your sleeve tonight— well— just keep an open mind." One more bit of dead air. "You're going to leave me guessing?"

"Yup. See you tonight."

— • — • —

George and Hailey met and discussed Joel. "Hailey, I want you to be part of this interview. Joel will need to know you are his boss as well."

"I'm good with that. You do the talking, I'll just listen."

"Listen close, I'll be asking your opinion when it's over."

They drove together to the job site where Joel was working. When George asked Joel to join him in the truck, Joel thought the worst.

Hailey was sitting in the back seat. George introduced Joel. Reaching back to shake her hand, Joel noted a beautiful smiling woman dressed as if to do a day's work in a denim shirt and dungarees, looking him dead in the eye. Hailey wore her hair short, cut close to the shape of her skull. Her eyes studied him even as their hands met. Joel had to take a deep breath. He turned back and settled himself waiting for the ax to drop.

"I have been hearing good things about your efforts Joel," offered a smiling George Whiting. "You have even offered advice when asked that has been well received by Dan." Joel nodded but didn't speak. The air of tension was about to smooth.

"Look, we both know how capable you are. And we both know that we have never seen eye to eye for a hundred reasons that don't matter."

Joel silently agreed with that assessment.

"I'm considering you for a full-time position with this company."

Joel sat up straight.

"You should know up front that Betty is leaving your Father's company. She starts with us in two weeks." Joel who had vowed to himself that he was going to turn his life around saw this as a life line. Hearing the words he would never in a thousand years have thought of as good news, his eyes moistened. He sat up a little straighter, breathed deeply, still he couldn't speak.

"Just think about it. Hailey and I are going to look at all aspects of what this would mean for the company. If it makes sense we'd love to have you aboard. As you have seen, the hurricane is opening new doors for us to grow. Joel, you could be back in a leadership position within a few months."

Joel cleared his throat, "What kind of a commitment do you need from me?"

"Just continue being the capable guy Dan tells me he's seeing doing the job every day. Be positive. Keep things light. Be on time, on task."

Joel met George's eyes, "That's what I say to myself every morning in the toaster." He chuckled. "Private joke." He fidgeted, "Anyway so far it's working. My goal is to have my father take me back to run the company." This would be a good opportunity for him to see that I'm serious." He offered George his hand.

Hailey met George's eyes in the mirror and nodded.

"Hailey and I are here to answer any questions you have. There is a crew leader on each job. I'll leave you on Dan's crew in the short term but in a few weeks if this is working for all of us you'll have your own crew and we'll go from there. Any questions right now?"

"No questions. Just thank you George, I won't let you down." He turned once more in his seat. "It was nice meeting you, Hailey. I'll see you two around I'm sure." In the back seat Hailey studied the back of the head of her boss.

— • — • — • —

Myrtle Beech checked her messages. Three calls had come in from Joel. She went to the refrigerator and grabbed a beer. She settled into a cane chair on the balcony and decided to at least listen to what had him so worked up. Her voice mail had piled up. It had in fact chirped three times in the last hour.

*Myrtle this is Joel and I am stone cold sober so if you can believe that go to my next voice mail.

Myrtle was curious, at least. Joel wasn't ranting on and on about some perceived wrong he'd been done. He did sound different. She went to the next voice message.

*Myrtle I am being offered a full time job with George Whiting. And I'm done drinking and feeling sorry for myself. Go to the next message for the very best part.

Myrtle chuckled, at least his sense of humor was coming back.

*Myrtle, I'd like to ask you out on a real sit- in- a- restaurant-and-talk- date. I know I've been a selfish, wallow in my own misery kind of guy. But let me show you I can change. I already have. No drinking for me again, ever. Please call me back.

Myrtle sat back and sighed. She closed her eyes and looked back over the year. *Started out just a fun time. Then as Joel's problems in his job increased so did his drinking and lack of attention to his health, loss of laughter, and nastiness toward her. What had attracted her to him in the first place? It was the crazy sense of humor she had just witnessed in three messages rather than one. Could she believe him? And what about the wild card in all this, Franklin? What did she really think of him? One thing for certain if Joel wasn't drinking he wouldn't want Franklin hanging around with his beech sand covering the table.* Myrtle returned to earth and thought aloud, "Lots to think about before I call back." *Where is Franklin anyway?*

- · - — ◆ — · · — · -

Franklin and Breanna were still on the road. They stopped in nearly every town and immediately looked for the Chamber of Commerce. Reading the brochures that touted local businesses and places to visit, they sipped their coffee deciding, then bopped from place to place. This educational tour eventually found its way to New Orleans and they spent an entire week there. The conversations, stops for coffee and gas and change of drivers was like a chess game unfolding. They shared a room with two single beds and so far there had been no sleep walking. Just two people sharing a room. Franklin who as a young man had never spent much time thinking about girls, they had kind of fallen into his lap. His magic and his white sand attracted mostly short term liaisons. With Breanna he was operating for the first time without the white sand and he was just starting to introduce Breanna to his magic.

As for Breanna she was just enjoying not having someone hitting on her, literally or sexually. Franklin had her laughing when he began magic tricks. A candy bar appeared out of thin air. A flower emerged from behind her ear; she was thoroughly enjoying herself. Franklin used his magic and his love of literature to tell her the story of the time he had spent with his Uncle and how those conversations had unconsciously led to this trip.

Today they started their trip toward the place Franklin's mother was in prison. Franklin, who had always traveled alone, was enjoying this bright eyed, obviously capable, young woman. Breanna was driving. She placed her cup of coffee in a center holder, Franklin cradling his. The warmth of the cup lightly touching the inside of his thighs suddenly aroused him. *Out with it Franklin,* he said to himself. "Breanna I'm not going to pretend I haven't grown fond of you and that you don't turn me on. The question is what are we going to do about it?"

Breanna smiled, turning her head, "I wondered when we'd get around to that topic. To be honest I thought you would have issued an ultimatum before now." She looked back to the road. Franklin opened his mouth to say something. *Whatever comes out,* the only thought in his head.

Breanna filled the void. "I'm not a kid, and I don't kid myself. Let's begin with a simple night of dancing. I love to dance. The guy I was with, he hated to dance. Do you like to dance, Franklin?" Franklin, who had never danced in his life, decided in the moment, "Actually I think I would."

"Then let's start there."

CHAPTER NINETEEN

George arrived home in the late afternoon. Days end arriving earlier, the setting sun blinding him as he turned into his drive. To his right Lane was sitting in a bag chair on the lawn. She turned and hoisted a beer in his direction then pointed to a cooler at her feet. George smiled back and nodded. Near the cooler Bobby was bent down with his back to George, his sister on her knees facing him. George took all this in even as he opened the truck door and stepped down on the concrete. His family awaiting his arrival brought a smile and his trademark whistle to his lips.

He wandered onto the grass like a thirsty man in the desert seeking an oasis. All that love awaiting his arrival. He put his hand on the back of Lane's chair and looked down. Bobby and Sarah were cuddling a ball of curly fur; Sarah talking as if to a doll. George's whistle evaporated on his lips. He had no words. He grabbed the bag chair that was still in its canvas holder on the ground and still not focused, set it up next to his wife and plunked himself down. Someone had some explaining to do.

Bobby looked up and smiled. Isn't she sweet Dad?

George returned the smile but said nothing.

Sarah took over, "We got this puppy from Mrs. Oulan, one of my teachers. Her husband is being transferred. They can't take the puppy with them, it's a really expensive dog Dad she's a Wheaten Terrier she doesn't shed and almost never barks." Her run on sentence completed and her sales pitch finished, she turned back to the puppy. All that

Knowledge thought George with no clue to the responsibility that makes up all that is not being voiced.

I signed, She doesn't bark. Kind of like me dad.

Dad choked on his beer. The bottle suddenly spouting foam. He laughed aloud in spite of himself as beer dribbled onto his shirt.

We all cracked up. Mom took a swallow of her beer and clinked her bottle against dads. "To the good times we'll have walking this new family member."

Feeling ganged up on dad could manage only a weak response, "So it's a done deal."

Mom pointed down to us two kids obviously in love already. "I would say it's a done deal. I didn't know Sarah had agreed to have the dog brought over before we talked, though. When Bobby saw that puppy scramble across the lawn it was pretty much over Rover in my mind."

Dad sighed, "I don't lose my easy chair do I?"

Mom loved this man.

We knew we had achieved victory and ran across the lawn with the puppy nipping at our heels. Away from us dad shifted gears, the puppy already in his rear view. "I hired Joel today. I think it will turn out to be a good move." Mom raised her bottle once more. "To second chances. You are one of a kind George."

Speaking of second chances, Joel showered and changed into jeans and a t-shirt. He had stopped into a Wal Mart and found a foot powder, if as good as advertised should take care of at least one of Myrtle's pet peeves. He dressed his feet and put on a new pair of sandals. He decided to go in person to see Myrtle. It might be harder for her to dismiss him in person. He looked at his reflection in the toaster for good luck. If this all worked out he might be able to face a real mirror once again. He was fifteen pounds lighter and his three former side-kicks no longer rode shotgun, though the cooler with cans of diet coke remained.

Hoping to catch Myrtle at home in St. Augustine and drive to dinner together, when he arrived Myrtle wasn't home. Possibly working a middle or late shift. He decided chicken for dinner sounded like a plan. Changing his routine right down to new ways to get there from here he drove south on Route One into Palm Coast listening to a station he had never dialed up before.

"New-new-new everything old shall become new." Joel sang these made up words to some jazzy instrumental on this brand new station.

He pulled into the parking lot at Clucks Chicken Coop and parked. He sat there for a moment. He had made up his mind. *No more eating in his vehicle,* another of Myrtles complaints. The cab was clear of wrappers and red cups.

He entered and as his eyes adjusted he saw Myrtle at the front counter placing freshly baked cookies in a glass case. He had eaten his fair share of those at Myrtles' apt. She looked up. Joel sucked in his already receding gut and put up both hands. "Can I have a minute?"

Myrtle looked around. She eyed the clock. The dinner rush was over. She sized him up like the first impression of a job applicant, taking in all the physical changes in a glance. She directed Joel to a booth in the back. "Want a coke? Just give me a minute."

Joel took that as a good sign. He nodded, "diet coke please."

Joel studied the businesses outside the window as he waited for Myrtle to join him. Coastal Construction had helped develop this part of the city that sat just off the main thoroughfare. He had been someone to look up to to back when that was going on. He sighed, *that was then this is now.* Then he pumped himself back up. *New-new-new* he hummed silently

Myrtle placed the drink in front of him then slid into the booth across the table. She sipped her beverage not saying a word.

Joel sipped his slowly, drawing it out as if gaining strength from the liquid. He swallowed and cleared his throat. He met Myrtle's eyes. "I'm here to say I'm sorry. Truly sorry. Sorry for the way I have treated you these past few months. Truth is, it was me I was mad at and took it out on you." Myrtle nodded. She heard the words.

Joel pointed to the new look he was sporting, I'm brand new on the inside as well Myrtle. I really have stopped drinking. Would you consider giving me a second chance?"

Myrtle said nothing.

Just then a smiling recent hire stopped at their booth. She bowed. "Welcome to Cluck's Chicken Coop." She handed Joel a cellophane wrapped-chicken shaped-chocolate covered mint.

Myrtle smiled and thanked the girl. Myrtle followed her with her eyes. "You know that girl right there has left for a different job twice, and yet here she is. My role here seems to be all about second and even third chances." She sighed, watching the girl. "Why would I hire her back, you might ask?"

Joel listened.

"Well Joel, she knows the job and when she's here she does a good job. It takes time, money, and energy to train someone new. So second chances, I'm all about that."

Joel thought he understood where Myrtle was going with this. He smiled. "So how about a second chance for this guy who wants to rejoin your company?"

Myrtle took his hand and winked. "You want to fill out a new application."

Joel laughed out loud. "Let's just start out with a new verbal contract-discussed over dinner- maybe tomorrow night if you aren't working. And we won't be eating in the truck." Myrtle had to chuckle, then she turned serious. "I have a funeral to attend at four pm." She saddened for a moment but did not explain. "I'll be home by six." Absently she checked her watch. Let's shoot for six-thirty." "That will work." Joel squirmed as he asked one final question. "What about Franklin?"

——•——••——•——

The body of Nona Ashby was finally released to her parents who lived in Ormond Beach, Florida. The afternoon of the funeral, former classmates entered the church after stubbing out their cigarettes on the walkway. Bunched in a group on the lawn they had spent the last twenty minutes hugging and holding on to one another. Nona had reached the ripe old age of Twenty-one. Three years after graduating high school with what promised to be a bright future, the Sheriff's Department of Flagler County along with State Police detectives were attempting to piece the girl's life together since leaving school.

The group of friends in attendance showed at some point in her life she would have been missed much earlier.

This afternoon Detective Sergeant Errol Monroe stood at the back of the church while services were being conducted. He had not approached any of the young people as yet. He stood apart taking in the scene. In his interview with the girl's parents, they seemed oblivious to who their daughter had become since leaving home in the summer after high school. He had her graduation picture and several snapshots in a file sitting in the passenger seat of his unmarked vehicle.

The ceremony was brief but poignant. Several friends offered testimony to what a wonderful friend Nona had been. Lots of white tissues raised and lowered in cadence with the words and guitar solo that ended with people filing out after passing Nona's closed casket. The young people gathered outside and lit up, tissues still in use, hugs sprouting spontaneously.

Detective Monroe hung back. He watched each person walk past the casket. First the kids, then a woman in her thirties if he had to guess. She placed something on top of the closed casket.

Detective Monroe, the last to file past nodded to the grieving parents. He noted a cellophane wrapped chocolate chicken on top of the closed casket.

Detective Errol Monroe walked to the exit. The knot of young people had grown larger. The lady who had placed the chocolate chicken, a past teacher maybe, was now in the middle of a group hug. The group was swaying in cadence.

The woman spoke quietly to the group.

He waited until the group dispersed. Cigarettes reappeared as the kids waved to one another and headed to the parking lot. He casually walked over and introduced himself to the lady. "So you knew the girl. Can you help me get to know who she was?"

"I'm not sure anyone knows these kids, really. But she did work for me for six months. Two separate times actually."

"Where was that?"

"Clucks Chicken Coop in Palm Coast. I'm the Manager there." She held out her hand. "I'm Myrtle Beech."

—-—◆-◆◆-◆—-—

Many miles west, Franklin and Breanna had reached the city of St. Gabriel, Louisiana. It was near dinner time when they pulled into a Holiday Inn Express. They had taken a circuitous in no hurry route that allowed them to spend two nights in Baton Rouge. The dancing was over and Franklin must have been light on his feet. On the second night in a room with two single beds Breanna left hers, crawled in and snuggled up to Franklin. Franklin opened his eyes in the dark and that dissolving fixed grin became a big smile. It had been quite a journey. Franklin, feeling Breanna's warm body, suddenly thought of his uncle who shared proverb after proverb in his day to day conversations: *patience has its own rewards* was one of his favorites. He nodded to the memory of Uncle Paul and turned to face the warmth.

The atmosphere in the car changed. They made their way to the small city on the eastern bank of the Mississippi with Breanna resting her hand on Franklin's shoulder. A squeeze here, a playful rustling of hair, then a light kiss on the side of his face moved them through the countryside. On the stops for food or fuel, Breanna filled the coffee cups as Franklin filled the gas tank. Franklin's grin was no longer cast in concrete, it was pliable and offered up laughter. Breanna seemed to be thoroughly enjoying this adventure as much as Franklin. When she wasn't hugging or offering 159 affection to Franklin she was hugging her own knees and smiling out the window.

They checked in, dropped their bags and left the hotel immediately, to walk the streets. This might be the last fun part in this particular town. Franklin wasn't sure what meeting his mother would mean to him. They sat sharing coffee and conversation in a small sidewalk cafe. Breanna asked Franklin how he planned to approach his mother.

"Well first I have to make an appointment, I doubt they do walk-ins."

Breanna nodded. "I mean when you actually meet her, what are you going to say?"

Franklin who had thought about this ever since making the decision to come here, chuckled, "I have absolutely no idea."

CHAPTER TWENTY

George was reading the News Journal. A family was being featured as having lost their roof in the storm and no insurance. The family was pictured, all staring at what used to be their roof. **A Go Fund Me** campaign was being started.

Lane delivered George's coffee and read briefly over his shoulder. "You should help them, George, send a crew out for a day. Probably all it would take by the looks. It's a small house."

"Dammit Lane, you prick my conscience when I'm thinking the same thing and trying to talk myself out of it."

Lane sat across from him after pouring herself a cup. She sipped. She frowned. She got up and returned to read over George's shoulder. "That last name. I've seen or heard that name before. Hmm. I think that's the boy Bobby had problems with."

George looked down at the article then up. "I'll be damned."

"You're right. Here read this."

Lane took the paper and began reading aloud the part that George must be referring to. "A local teacher said one of her students started the ball rolling by donating ten dollars and challenging his classmates to make a pledge. Two other classes joined in and things kind of snowballed from there."

"That boy can't take no for an answer. Get that kid up, I need a hug."

I was still half asleep and bleary eyed when Sarah and I joined them at the table. Little Teddi followed, nudging between first mine then Sarah's legs. Dad showed us the article. We simply smiled. Sarah yawned and said, "So it worked."

I signed, <u>So are you going to help Dad? We have nearly enough for a roof.</u>

Dad called the puppy and took her in his lap. Nuzzling the little ball of fur he assured us kids he would look into what was required. We high-fived, (that stuff rubs off you know) and went our separate ways.

Dad returned to the paper.

He always checks the police log to see if any of his crew members might be missing work for whatever reason. His crew was growing and that always upped the odds and opportunity for a screw up. He noted the Sheriff's department was seeking assistance in the murder of a young person recently identified as Nona Ashby.

It was believed the girl disappeared sometime during September. If anyone had witnessed or heard anything out of the ordinary around that time were encouraged to contact the Sheriff's office.

George's mind immediately filled with the scream the family had heard on that evening in September. It had not been an ordinary scream. Probably nothing to do with any of this. But George had his instincts. He was about to holler to Lane but she was in the shower. Instead he checked his watch. He was late. *I'll talk to her tonight.*

⸺•⸺•⸺•⸺

Myrtle rolled over, hitting a leg that was already becoming familiar once again. She turned onto her back and studied the ceiling, the morning light just beginning to lighten the shade. Enough light to see that damn spider was trying to make a comeback. She had brushed him off her ceiling weeks ago. She thought she'd killed him. Second chance Myrtle. It seemed even the spiders figured they could talk, walk, or crawl their way back into her life.

Well Damn! She jumped out of bed so fast Joel awoke with a start. "What the hell, someone breaking in or what?" Myrtle was in tears rushing from the room, "It's that damn spider, he's back," she hollered on her way to a broom. In the next instant she was standing on the bed, trampling Joel in the process, the broom swishing the length of the ceiling like it was going to whisk her away even as her tears flowed and she breathed great gulps of air through her mouth.

Joel groaned aloud, "Holy shit Myrtle what's going on?" With the spider dead and the cobweb imprisoned in the bristles, Myrtle threw the broom into the corner and collapsed into Joel's arms, wailing like a newborn. Joel hugged and comforted her as best he could.

When she finally settled, Joel asked her if she could talk about it.

"I was just feeling sorry for myself I guess. And sorry for that poor girl." she sighed long and loud. "They found her murdered. Thrown out like trash." Wiping her eyes on the sheet and breathing deeply she slowly settled. She spoke quietly. "She worked for me twice, you know. She was a nice girl, smart, funny. A little crazy maybe but a good kid."

She pushed up to Joel's back. "That detective told me he thinks she was raped and strangled." She shifted, pushing herself further into his warmth. "Joel, who could do something like that?" The short sentences Myrtle was throwing out like sifting through what clothes needed washing, all landed on Joel.

Joel had met a lot of men who, given the right or wrong circumstances were capable of going over the edge. He didn't voice that belief. He just continued to hug Myrtle and let her purge. He was working on a crew right now that included guys who partied too much every afternoon and evening. Joel, now a teetotaler, still accompanied some of the guys on occasion and imagined his old self in action. "Myrtle no one in their right mind could do something like you described. I'm sorry for what you are feeling." Myrtle rolled right over the top of Joel and into his arms, her eyes still glistening, "Joel, I really like you a lot more now that you aren't drinking."

Joel needed to lighten the mood. He stuck a foot outside the blanket. "How about my feet, you like my feet. I'm not drinking and my feet aren't stinking."

Myrtle laughed, "Seems some second chances might work out." She grabbed the dangling foot and leg and hugged their way back under the covers.

—•—•—•—•—•—

Victor was restless all night long in and out of his blankets. Sheets wet with night sweat. It had been this way since what he termed-the accident. There were still parts of that night he hadn't come to grips with. Awake, he forced himself to play detective. He studied the ceiling looking for construction flaws. Now that he was learning the trade he seemed to examine things more closely. All the while he was trying to figure out how had the girl gotten here in the first place? After disposing of the body he had tried to figure out if one of the cars in the parking lot was hers. He watched from the balcony at every opportunity as cars left the lot. He put pieces of paper beneath a wheel of every car and within the week determined she hadn't arrived in her own car. Trying to figure out how she got to the building was a question in and of itself.

At night lying in the dark trying to summon sleep his mind revisited the sequence of events. *He had arrived alone back to his unit after a couple shots and beer chasers at a bar in the European Village— a quaint rectangle of small businesses with apartments above. He fully intended on returning later for pizza and a beer at Mezzaluna's, just five minutes from his Condo. She had literally stumbled into his arms when the elevator doors opened.*

She was obviously drunk and upset. She collapsed against him. That initial warmth triggered his next action. Without thinking he gathered her in his arms and pushed the button to his floor. Holding the girl against him he became aroused. As the elevator rose Victor didn't have a thought in his head. But the girl did feel warm in his arms. When the doors opened he practically carried her to his unit. Inside he leaned back against the door holding the girl up and against him. With her weight folded in his arms the warmth reaching his loins she began to stimulate him further.

He carried her to his room and laid her down. He noticed a red stain on her blouse and shorts. The stain was still wet. A little rubbed off onto his shirt. The girl was out like a light. He went into the kitchen and opened a beer. His heart was beating in his ears. He sat at the kitchen table as early evening brought shadows, nursing one beer then one more.

He wrestled with himself. The girl in his bed stayed in his head. He fondled himself. Was he about to jump off a cliff? Pacing now, the liquor and beers he had consumed seemed to be holding sway. Victor reentered the bedroom. The girl stirred but was surely in for the night. The good angel suggested letting her sleep it off and then getting her home. Victor was not usually rash. Slow moving and slow thinking had always been his style. He sat on the edge of the bed. Football had help shape him. One play then a huddle; controlled. He began stroking the girl's hair. The bad angel emerged. Victor fought the impulse. It was warm in here. Clearing his throat he got up and opened the bedroom window.

Immediately the curtains began to rustle.

His heart was pounding now. He looked out over the Inter coastal. A boat moved silently in the breeze, lights shining from its bow. Dark was descending. Victor turned to the girl, she appeared beautiful lying there. The shadows seemed to soften what his mind was suggesting.

He sat back down on the bed. He stroked her cheeks. He spoke softly to her about nothing. Impulsively he touched her arms, they were warm to the touch. He took a deep breath. He ran his hand the length of her legs. Heart racing he brushed the fabric covering her breast. He squeezed lightly. The girl stirred and moaned but didn't wake. Aroused, Victor, still without a plan, an angel on each broad shoulder, decided. He moved his hands downward, raising her t-shirt and rubbing her warm belly. Frog brain now asking for control, and aroused, his breathing deepened. A light sheen of sweat appeared on his brow. He had never been in this situation. The girl moving and sighing added sound and movement to Victor's own stirrings. He began removing her clothes. He took off her sandals. In a dazed trance he placed them one after the other on the floor as if she would step into them and disappear.

He paused, one last effort by the good angel reminding him his next move was crossing a line. He nodded acknowledging that but then gave himself permission. Victor wrestled off her shorts. Clad now in her panties and t-shirt he rolled her on to her back. She stirred but did not wake. He slid her top over her head. He stared at the firm body lying there. Her flat stomach moving with each breath. Dark descending, the scene slightly altered with each passing minute. His heart was a drumbeat. Breathing through his nose, mouth closed tightly as if about to dive into a cold body of water, he took the plunge. He quickly finished undressing the girl. She lay there in the half light, the curtains stirring in concert with the rising and falling of her breasts.

He removed his own clothing. The girl in her sleep had turned onto her side. He lay down beside her. His front to her back. The girl stirred and moaned, not waking, perhaps dreaming. Her body warmth against his own naked skin eliminated any going back. Victor probed and fumbled and found his way. He was moaning and just eliminating a premature release when the girl woke.

She raised her head slightly as if she'd heard a noise. When her other senses arrived her body stiffened. Her head was pointed away from Victor. There was a moment of utter silence. She slowly turned her head as she tried to wrap her mind around what was happening. Their eyes met in the near darkness. Her eyes widened. She uttered one terrified scream before Victor clamped his hand over her mouth and brought the pillow into play. He kept whispering "calm down, calm down," even as he kept the pillow over her face. Victor straddled her. The girl's violent struggle continued but was no match for the offensive lineman.

Staring at himself in the mirror these weeks later, his ever thinning face wet from shaving foam, dark circles around his eyes seemed to be taking up permanent residence. *Who are you?* He silently asked his reflection. He didn't see himself as a rapist and killer so in his own mind he wasn't. *It was an accident.* The girl was dead though. *And he had hidden her body.* She was found by poor shit luck.

The whole situation was shit on a stick for that matter. I have to stop thinking about this, *Christ I'm falling away.* Victor worked daily on a construction crew and he'd made sure he kept his nose clean. His father hadn't mentioned the missing throw rug Victor used to wrap the body. Victor disposed of it at a work-site dumpster. He had promptly bought a new one. *No need to give dear old dad another reason to complain.*

He gathered the stained and sweated sheets, tossing them into the wash. He poured in the detergent and pushed the start button. The sound of water entering the machine seemed to trigger his own need to clean things up. *How did the girl get here and how did she get into the building? How do I go about finding that out?*

His new boss was teaching Victor as much about life as he was carpentry. The golden rule of carpentry and life for that matter was shared daily. 'Measure twice. Cut once.' Usually adding, 'and if you still aren't sure, measure again or ask for help.' Every day that line would get repeated at some point. Even in the bars after work if guys were discussing their latest breakup or screw-up, the Carpenter's creed would be tossed about. 'Don't do anything stupid till you've followed the Carpenters Golden Rule.'

Victor wasn't religious but lately a different Golden Rule seemed to be haunting him. He began to think of hell and damnation. He was sweating again. He checked the clock. It was time to get ready for work. Clean shaven he entered the shower, a long cold shower this morning. His mind still wandering, he found himself dressed and entering the elevator. When the door opened for some reason he glanced up. *Shit!* Why hadn't it registered before? He was staring directly into a security camera. He looked away and began to sweat once more. Another more damaging thought followed, *if her arrival was recorded he too would show up. Maybe twice. There would be no recording of her leaving the building on her own.* Victor left the building with the thought that he needed to measure *twice and cut once.*

— • — • — • —

This very same morning in Louisiana, Franklin and Breanna were sharing a bathroom. Breanna showered first and was now fixing her face while Franklin sat on the bed observing, listening to the new noises in his life. Breanna walked by him smelling like a flower. Franklin took his turn standing under the hot spray thinking of the loners he'd read about under his Uncle's watch. He had pretty much given up the idea that he would ever welcome someone into his life long term. *I guess I better broaden my reading horizons and include some stories with more than one character.* Last night Breanna had asked to accompany him on his visit to his mother. Somehow that made this morning easier. As the soap washed its way down the drain Franklin with eyes closed sighed with satisfaction. Breanna had made the entire trip easier. Some of the stops they made he would never have made alone. How long this relationship would go on or how far it might take them he didn't know but Franklin right now was a willing passenger. He turned off the shower and began toweling himself.

Breanna, fresh as a daisy, turned to face him. Franklin felt something like joy overtake him— if that was the proper word. If it wasn't joy he had no idea what to call it. Time for complete honesty Franklin determined. He put on a robe and took her hand moving to the side of the bed. "Sit down, I have a confession to make, Breanna."

Breanna frowned at the serious look on Franklin's face. "I am not a used car salesman."

Breanna's mouth opened to respond.

Franklin held up a hand, "There's more. I don't live in Daytona Beach. I live in the same city you do, Palm Coast." He sighed, the truth seeping from his bones.

"And, I know your old boss, Myrtle. I have even partied with her." He waited two beats. "But that was all before I met you." He took her hand, "Truth is I'm part owner of a little restaurant and wine and cheese bar in Flagler Beach." Still keeping with the truth he continued, "I have sold and used drugs in the past. I don't want any secrets between us. If what I'm feeling for you has legs then it has to be based on total honesty."

Breanna looked deep into Franklin's eyes. "Well that was quite a mouthful Franklin. Why did you think you had to reinvent yourself for me?"

"Because I have been a loner and I never let anyone in before. And if things hadn't worked out, who I really am and what I do would have been nobody's business, including you."

Breanna gathered Franklin in her arms, "Well I'm glad I matter enough to find the real Franklin."

They breakfasted in an I-Hop and lingered, "stalling," Breanna kiddingly scolded.

"Okay let's do this," said a somber Franklin as if off to do battle.

CHAPTER TWENTY-ONE

The season of holidays arrived. Thanksgiving brought families together and George gave his crews a rare four days off-with a twist. He invited the five crews and their families to join him on the weekend for a cookout and work day on his new house. With the demands after the hurricane, very little had moved forward from the concrete pad and the basic underground plumbing. He offered cash money to anyone who wanted to put in a days' work.

All of George's crews and their families showed up.

Lane cooked up a big pot of beans, made a coleslaw, and with Sarah and Bobby's help whipped up a triple batch of biscuits. The little dog Teddi, ignored, stayed underfoot when she wasn't chasing a squirrel.

Most of the wives had reached out and brought their own favorite casserole or dessert. A nine o'clock coffee and George's famous donut run had kicked things off. Four hours of work later twenty men carrying, placing, and mortaring, finite definition was beginning to shape George's dream. Time to eat. The kids were fed first. As the adults sat down to eat, the kids explored the rising walls peeking out of what would become windows and doors. George sat just at the edge of conversation satisfied with just about everything in his life.

Lane brought him a plate and sat with him. Suddenly one of the kids screamed. It was just part of kids playing hide and seek, but George's memory was triggered.

"Lane do you remember that night we heard a scream and couldn't figure out where it was coming from?"

"Of course I do, why?"

"Well a while back I saw in the paper a girl disappeared around that time and her body was found weeks later. You don't suppose there is a connection?"

"I have no idea. Why is that on your mind?"

"I meant to bring it up to you when I read the article but then it slipped my mind. Anyway the Sheriff's department asked for the public's help. Even something a person might not think is important might be the clue they are looking for. So do you think I should contact them? I mean it was around the same time frame."

"George, as usual I would say follow your instincts they have served you well up till now."

George sighed, "It's probably nothing," he rubbed his thumb over his index finger, ruminating. "It's like a tiny splinter in your finger. You ignore it and over time it festers."

Lane chuckled, "I've seen some of those splinters George, go introduce yourself to the sheriff."

George nodded. He'd go first thing on Monday morning.

Hailey found her way to a bag chair beside George and sat down. "Lane is a good cook George, this has actually been fun. I know my boy is enjoying himself. You picked a beautiful spot for your home."

"It is nice here and I hope when it's done these get-togethers continue without the labor part. What about you Hailey, you going to build something permanent or remain flexible, preparing for your next move?"

"It all depends, I guess. *In that instant a dozen scenarios ran through Hailey's mind. George Whiting was in at least half those scenarios.* I mean I feel like all my plants are in flower pots right now. I can choose the spot that gives them the best light. If I put those plants in the ground I want to make sure there's light and sun and enough moisture to keep them in full bloom." She pointed out her son running around with Bobby and the new puppy, smiling and squealing with delight not a care in the world. "Things look promising here though, I'll say that much."

"Well I know you'll make the right decision for you and Daniel."

As the afternoon progressed George made contact with each of the crew members. Joel showed up with a good looking woman on his arm. He introduced Myrtle Beech. George thought he had seen her before and asked.

"I'm a manager at Cluck's Chicken Coop, you might have seen me there."

George snapped his fingers, "Best chicken in town, my kids love the boneless wing meals. Pleased to meet you Myrtle."

"Ask for me when you come in again, I'll give you some coupons," smiled Myrtle.

George shook her hand, "I'll do that. See you two later." George continued his rounds and eventually found his way to Victor Thornton who was carrying a cement block in each hand passing them up a ladder. George offered his hand. "I haven't really had the opportunity to talk with you. How do you like the job?"

Victor, seemingly nervous, was sweating. He took a deep breath, dusted his hands and the two men shook. "It's ok. I'm learning a lot so that's all good. I'm liking the overtime." He looked away toward the Intercoastal, "This is going to be a pretty spot, Mr. Whiting."

"Your Dad sold me this lot. He lives somewhere in this section. He said it was quiet and peaceful here and showed me the lot when it was still covered with trees and scrub. Smart man, your father."

"Yeah he's that. I'm actually a neighbor. I'm living in dad's high rise apartment around the corner till I get my feet under me."

"Really. I knew your dad owned a Condo but didn't know which one. My wife and I and my kids walk this neighborhood on occasion.

"Well if you know my dad then you know he likes to be on top of things, so I'm on the top floor."

George chuckled, but his mind immediately located the building and again it filled with that evening not so long ago. He had it on the tip of his tongue to ask Victor about that night but instead finished his greeting, "Well neighbor, glad to have you on my crew." He shook Victor's hand once again and moved on.

At home that evening the family shared their day. My sister and I had tag-teamed the attention of our new puppy. We reported that with all the excitement of the day Teddi had done pretty well. Our friends had all fallen in love with the little girl. I gave two thumbs up to the work performed today. I did have something else on my mind but kept it to myself.

So on the surface all seemed right with the world. Later, well after bedtime had claimed its rightful place, I went to my sister's room and joined her at the top. Teddi slept curled in a laundry basket in the corner.

<u>Why are you here so early Bobby, it's not morning? I snapped on the lamp. I met one of Dad's worker's today. I didn't like him. He was</u>

acting funny. He kept watching everybody. He was sweating. He gave me the willies.

When did that happen?

I was using the toilet Dad had set up and Teddi was outside. I heard him growling. When I opened the door this big guy was just standing there. I thought he was waiting to use the toilet, but he just stood there. He didn't move out of our way, he just kept looking back toward the men working. He was shaking. When he finally looked down he reached down to pat Teddi. She didn't like him. She kept growling.

When he finally realized Teddi wasn't going to let him pat her, he walked away. I got this feeling. Like his blue print wasn't right. Something is wrong with that guy.

Which one was he? I served lunch to every worker there.

The biggest one. I snapped off the lamp and went back to my room. I didn't sleep well, imagining giant robots trying to run me down. I was at the bottom of Sarah's bed hugging her feet before midnight.

Monday morning George parked and shut down his rig. He had called the Sheriff's office on Sunday and made an appointment to see the Sheriff.

Franklin and Breanna made the trip to the prison and were now back in Palm Coast. All that Uncle Paul had predicted was a reality. Franklin's mother, still in her forties could be mistaken for a seventy year old. Folded over, onto, and into herself, like un-ironed laundry, her skin the color of unkempt bed linen. Her eyes refused to focus and her slackened facial muscles could not contain the drool that stained her gown.

Five minutes, that was all Franklin could take. Her wheelchair had been placed in a shadowed corner, an unintended metaphor for the lack of any meaningful light in her life. Breanna squeezed Franklin's hand and for five full minutes not a single word was spoken. Franklin thought of Miss Havisham who had exiled herself to a life of loneliness. His own mother though had not asked for any of this. She had simply not followed the house rules. Her very own family had cast her out. Franklin touched the cold hands of his mother then drew her lap blanket up to cover those hands. Franklin reached for Breanna's hand, his eyes wet. They turned and left.

Now back from the road trip and living in his Condo with Breanna, the two spent time getting to know one another in a more normal, less cramped fashion. They had their first disagreement and found middle ground— Franklin kidded he liked the making up part best. They began to give one another space after having spent weeks together in a car. Breanna liked some evening television dramas but hated the evening news. Franklin didn't care much for television beyond the news. Ever the reader he introduced Breanna to quiet evenings with no television. A quick study, he intuited what kind of book Breanna might enjoy from her choice of television shows.

The two went to the library together and suddenly a whole new world of entertainment was introduced. Breanna had read assigned books in school but mostly with the idea of passing tests associated with the reading.

Franklin introduced her to ordinary people from other cultures and times in history whose lives could have mirrored their own except for the circumstances they found themselves in. Just in the last week it was Breanna's lamp clicking off last.

Franklin also introduced Breanna to Jules and his family.

Breanna fell right in love with their little boy, Jake and their dog Rouge.

Franklin and Jules this morning sat at a table sipping coffee while the women and little Jake laughed and giggled in the kitchen. "Don't touch anything in there," kidded Jules loudly. The women ignored him. "So you would like to train Breanna to manage the wine and cheese side. Hey it's your end of the business and I'm sure it would be one less headache for Danni. They seem to be getting on, as the Brits would say." Jules laughed, "I'm just happy for you Franklin, I've never seen you in such high spirits." Franklin sipped his coffee, then looked up. He clinked Jule's cup.

"For the first time in my life I feel responsible for someone, not to someone. When I visited my mother and saw what her life turned out to be I determined I wasn't going to die alone. My Uncle Paul had no one either, until me and he was ill when we met. I'm going to break the mold." He clinked his friend's cup once more, "She melts my heart Jules."

CHAPTER TWENTY-TWO

Sheriff Oliver Rodriguez was a veteran cop from New York. It seems most Sheriff's come to the job after a prior career in law, the military, or the criminal justice system. Sheriff Rodriguez had been part of all three.

An over achiever and the first in his family of eight to attend college he joined his college ROTC program and entered the military as a second lieutenant. He never saw combat but obtained his degree in law with Uncle Sam paying the dime. He worked with an outfit overseas that was just beginning to try to understand the new face of America's enemy. He made sure the law was not being completely thrown under the bus as investigations unfolded. When ten years had passed in the blink of an eye, Oliver Rodriguez left his active role in the military and worked as a prosecutor in the state's attorney's office. He stayed with the military in a reserve capacity and gained his pension.

Still a young man but not enjoying his prosecutor role he joined the NYPD in the role of an intelligence officer. He was part of the investigation of 9/11 and his heart would never heal from what he witnessed. He married late and had a young daughter and a loving wife.

In 2010 he made the decision to move south and enjoy life watching his daughter grow up. His daughter was now thirteen and a very good athlete. He was thoroughly enjoying her soccer skills.

That was not enough to fill his days however and in the election of 2016 he threw his hat in the ring for Sheriff of Flagler County. He had met a lot of people just by being involved with youth sports and when he voiced the idea of a run for Sheriff a good number of people thought he offered a refreshing change. Two prior Sheriff's had run into hot water with their constituents. One a Republican the other a Democrat, so Oliver Rodriguez ran as an independent and surprised everyone when he emerged a narrow winner.

George sat across from the Sheriff and after comparing notes on their daughter's chances of winning an upcoming soccer tournament, like the carpenter he was, George laid the foundation for his visit. When he finished he didn't wait around to discuss possibilities. He simply rose, shook the Sheriff's hand and went back to work.

Sheriff Rodriguez buzzed his secretary and asked to have the lead detective on the murder case located and sent to his office. The no nonsense presentation by George Whiting invited a closer inspection. Sheriff Rodriguez was new to this role but he saw immediately that solving this case would cement the publics' opinion that they had made a good decision.

— · —◆—◆—◆—·· —

Franklin and Breanna returned from a workday at the wine and cheese section of Jules restaurant on a cold wet December night. Sharing an umbrella, they rushed to their unit not pausing at the rectangular kiosk of mailboxes the building shared.

An hour later Victor Thornton arrived from an evening at a pizzeria in the European village. He had the remaining seven pieces of a specialty pizza in a box. He didn't seem to have much appetite lately. He would gnaw on the remainder all week he determined.

The rain had ended and Victor stopped to gather his mail. As he turned to leave the kiosk the message with a sheriff's office logo met his eyes. Victor read the typed message. **All unit owners or renters are being asked to contact the Sheriff's office regarding a crime that might have happened in your area. Please contact the Sheriff's office at 386-333-8888.**

Victor looked around. The wind was blowing, the rain beginning again as a steady drizzle. He took a deep breath. His heart began beating furiously, as unsettled as the gloomy night. He ripped the message from the wall. Taking another deep breath he looked around and entered his building.

Sitting in the dark with the message fresh in his mind, he realized he had to get his hands on that surveillance tape if it still existed. Using his father's computer he had done some online research of surveillance systems. The length of time security tapes are stored varies greatly. Victor did the math. Ninety days seemed to be the longest time tapes were generally stored by businesses. Some companies sent old surveillance tapes to off-site places like a cloud. Some just erased tapes every forty-eight hours. This was a residential building so most likely the tapes would be erased in a timely manner. If kept for ninety days he had maybe two weeks to get his hands on that tape if it still existed. Was the Sheriff's department requesting those surveillance tapes? The name and phone number of the company monitoring the building was on a printed calendar in his unit. *How to proceed.* He decided to sleep on it. The next morning he called his father.

"You didn't lose your job did you son?"

"Well good morning to you too Dad. No I did not lose my job. But I might have lost something personal a while ago, and thought maybe you could help."

"Ok what's up?"

"Well not long after I moved in here I met a girl." Stopping, then dragging the story out so it didn't seem concocted. "One thing led to another and we started seeing one another. Sorry Dad but I stupidly lent her a key." He sighed heavily. "And now I'm realizing an expensive ring mom bought me is missing--- has been missing actually. I thought at first maybe I misplaced it or left it somewhere. Now, I'm pretty sure the girl came here while I was gone." He let that sink in.

"I never wear the ring on the job. I found some other stuff out of place. I thought back then maybe you had come here looking for something. So I've been thinking if she came here while I was gone she would show up on a surveillance tape. I see we have cameras on every floor at 184 the elevator. I'm sorry about the key. But I have it back now." One more beat then, "So could you help me get those tapes? If she's on them I can confront her. I know she has my ring dad."

"I'm pretty busy here, you're sure she came in and took it huh?"

"I know she did Dad. She was always admiring the little diamonds on the sides."

"Ok let me make a call, I'll have someone call you."

"Thanks Dad."

"You can thank me by keeping that job."

Victor hung up shaking his head. His father always had to have the last word. He breathed deeply. *Well at least, hopefully I can eliminate that threat.* Victor dressed for work. Sweating profusely.

— · ● ·· ● ·· ● ·· —

At 11:00 am Franklin and Breanna left the condo. There was a sheriff's office SUV parked in the street. Franklin made eye contact. The deputy nodded. Two more days passed.

The buzzer in Franklin's unit sounded. Breanna was home Franklin was doing some errands. Detective Errol Monroe asked if he could come up.

They sat on the sofa. Breanna offered coffee insisting Franklin should be home momentarily. In the meantime the detective gathered from what the girl told him she was not living here during the time frame he was here to ask about. He sat back sipping his coffee. On a whim he showed the girl the snapshot he had of the girl.

Breanna was taken aback. "Oh my god, I worked with her for a short time at Cluck's Chicken Coop. I had no idea she was dead." Breanna was clearly upset.

"When was the last time you saw her?"

"Just before I quit, that would have been in August. She came into the place one day to pick up her last check. To be honest she didn't look very good. Like she had been partying quite a bit." Breanna shook her head, "Oh my God I can't believe it."

Franklin opened the door, catching the last part of Breanna's sentence. He saw a man framed in the light coming from the balcony. His breath caught. "What can't you believe, Breanna?" He moved to be in position to see the man's face. The detective rose and offered his badge, his name, and his hand.

Detective Monroe noted the slightness of stature but was even more transfixed with the intensity of the man's eyes and smile. Franklin again asked Breanna what it was she couldn't believe.

"This girl I worked with in that chicken place, she's been found dead. Murdered."

Detective Monroe filled in the blanks and handed the photo to Franklin.

"She disappeared around the time someone reported hearing a scream from near here."

Franklin saw the afternoon in question pass before his eyes and the girl stumbling out of his unit. What had happened to her after she left he had no clue but he knew he and Joel had nothing to do with it. He needed to be real careful in his answer. He needed to talk with Joel.

"What time was that scream?"

"Around dark I think, so between seven and eight I'd say," answered the detective.

"I wasn't here. I had taken a sick friend home much earlier that afternoon."

"Do you recognize the girl in the picture?"

"Breanna, you say she worked at Cluck's Chicken Coop?" Breanna nodded.

"I might have seen her in the past. I can't be sure but yes I think I have seen her."

Detective Monroe rose. "Well thank you for your time. If you hear any of the residents talking after I speak with them or you hear something that might help, please call this number." He handed them his card and left.

Breanna began pacing. "I need to talk with Myrtle. She treated me well. She needs to know I had no idea Nona was killed or I would have been in touch."

Franklin took her hand. "We'll go together. Myrtle doesn't know we're a two-some. And you're right Myrtle is a good person. We'll go tomorrow."

That evening Joel's cell rang. Joel checked the number, it was long lost Franklin. *Maybe he's heard I stopped drinking.*

"Hey Franklin, long time no hear. Did you discover one of the many messages I've sent."

"I was out of town with no cell phone for a while Joel. Anyway, I'd like to get together for a drink. I have some news you need to be aware of."

"I'm not drinking these days but if you want to buy me a coke it works for me. I have some news myself."

"You still live in the same place?"

"I do."

"I'll pick you up in an hour."

The two men caught up on small talk. Joel revealed that he and Myrtle were trying to make a go of it. Franklin toasted that announcement. He told Joel about his trip to Louisiana and how he'd found a girl from this very town who had worked for Myrtle. Joel raised his coke skyward.

"Small world huh?"

Franklin got serious, "The world grows even smaller with what I have to tell you. Do you recall the afternoon we met a girl in a bar?" Joel looked befuddled.

"It was back in the summer." When the light didn't seem to come on, Franklin added, "You had met her before. At Cluck's Chicken Coop."

"Ok. To be honest I don't remember much about the whole summer. Why is that important?"

"Myrtle hasn't told you about one of her workers being killed?"

Joel frowned, "She attended a funeral a while ago. We had just started seeing one another again. I remember she was pretty upset. She said the funeral was for one of her workers but we didn't get into who. I wouldn't have known the girl anyway."

Franklin nodded his head, "That's just it Joel, we both met the girl."

"What the hell are you talking about?"

"I'm talking about an afternoon months ago when we met a girl named Nona in a bar and took her to your place and then mine."

Joel's eyes widened as that afternoon came to mind, though not clearly. "That's the girl who got killed?"

"Exactly the girl who got killed. And now there are detectives talking to the residents in my area about a scream someone heard. Possibly from my building, that evening."

"Ok, but I still don't follow. After we got to your place I passed out. I woke up back in my apartment with a gash in my hand and a hangover that turned out to be a lifesaver."

Franklin filled in the blanks. "That girl had no transportation when she left. She panicked when you cut your hand on the broken glass and blood spurted everywhere. She threw up, then bolted. She was not in any condition to walk very far." He let that sink in. "I slapped you awake and packed you up shortly after she left and brought you home. I didn't see her anywhere along the way. Now, I'm thinking maybe she got picked up by someone who took advantage of her and killed her."

"Ok, say you're right. I still don't see what that has to do with us."

"Nothing except we might have been the last two guys to see her alive. We need to go to that detective and tell him what we know."

After bringing Joel up to speed Franklin asked Joel to call Myrtle. Breanna wants to speak with her anyway. We should explain to both of them what we know before we speak to anyone else. Breanna needs to know why I wasn't completely honest with that detective. We have nothing to hide."

The two ladies sounded like prosecutors in their questioning but in the end were satisfied their men were telling the truth. "That afternoon changed a lot of things for both of us," offered Joel.

Franklin nodded, squeezing Breanna's hand, "I didn't realize it at the time, and if I hadn't met Breanna maybe I would have continued beating myself up as well." Breanna gave him a bright smile.

"But I'm a changed man."

"So what's your next step?" Asked Myrtle.

Franklin removed the card he'd been given. "I'm going to leave a message for Detective Monroe that I have information regarding the girl's disappearance."

"You know he's not going to take your first evasive answer very well don't you?" suggested Breanna.

"Oh indeed I do. But that can't be helped now. If our time line helps solve this it will all be worth it."

CHAPTER TWENTY-THREE

Joel was at work the next day when his cell rang. Joel, the new crew leader, was in the process of installing yet another roof. He nodded his head. When George Whiting appeared a half hour later and shouted up the ladder to Joel, Joel told the men to take a break.

Victor the second worker descending the ladder, saw a brown sedan park behind his boss's truck. By the time he hit the ground the passenger door was open and the little man Victor had seen in local bars and recently leaving his building walked right up to Joel and the two shook hands. In that moment Victor put two and two together. His eyes widened. Hell Joel was the other guy he had seen in the bar that day. It had been a drunken Joel spinning on that bar stool then lying on the floor and stumbling past him holding his jaw. He had changed some, lost weight and looked healthier but it was him alright.

The men walked away from the building talking quietly. The driver of the sedan approached the three men. He shook hands with both George and Joel. Soon Joel left in his pickup, the sedan following. The little man was back in the passenger seat, his hat barely visible.

George took over signaling everyone back to work. Victor was left to climb back up that ladder sweating and worrying over what in hell just happened.

⸻ ⋆ ⸻

When Victor got home he spotted that same car in the parking lot next to Joel's pick-up. He immediately called his Dad. "Any luck with those tapes?"

"I have been up to my eyeballs in business, son. I'll try to get to it tomorrow. You can always call them. You have their number on the calendar."

Victor sighed, trying not to show how anxious he was feeling. "No, if you can do it tomorrow that's soon enough."

— • — • — • —

Two floors below Detective Monroe was reviewing his notes. "Ok, I think I have all this down. Let's go over it one more time. You will probably both have to come in and write out a statement anyway but if what you are telling me is true we have a starting point at least."

Joel began with the innocent meeting in the bar and how it ended in Franklin's Condo.

Detective Monroe interrupted, "So Franklin, the reason you didn't give me this information yesterday was that you three left Joel's apartment and came to your Condo to add Cocaine to the party?"

Franklin nodded his head.

"And you didn't wish to share that with me?"

Franklin nodded once more. "Yes sir, that's right but you need to know those days are over."

"Franklin I could try to jam you up, but my greater concern is finding out what happened to that young girl. So tell me again what happened after the girl left your unit?"

"I rousted Joel as quickly as I could, which took a little time. Then I brought him back to his place. I did not see the girl anywhere along the way. I didn't give it any thought at the time. Then I drove around a while and ended up at my business in Flagler Beach. I talked with my business partner and had an evening meal. I got back to my place around nine pm."

Detective Monroe closed his notebook. "Ok I'll hold off on those statements for a day or two. If anything else comes to mind, call me. I'll be in touch if I think of anything as well." He was half way out the door when he did think of something. "Would you both be willing to give us a blood and DNA sample? Just to have on file." The two men nodded. "Stop by the Sheriff's office, I'll leave your names. We have a lab we work with."

—————

Detective Monroe briefed the Sheriff on his conversation with the two men. "So what is your gut telling you Detective?"

"I think they are telling the truth. But the truth doesn't always set you free now does it? Right now they are the last two to see the girl alive. I didn't tell them we have a blood type from the girl's clothing. They are coming in to give a blood and DNA sample so we'll see."

Sheriff Rodriguez pondered. "If she was in that condo building there could be surveillance tape, correct?"

"It was a while ago but it's worth checking. I'll get right on that."

—————

Victor's father finally called Flagler County Surveillance, he talked with a temporary worker who had no idea how to check on past video.

"My son had a valuable ring stolen, I can make it worth your while to find me that tape."

—·——◆——·—

Along A-1A and in Palm Coast, piles of debris had been trucked away and giant rectangles of blue tarps covering damaged roofs were no longer competing with the blanket of blue sky that dominated December.

George and his crews were working six day weeks now. With Christmas arriving within the week he planned to give his men another four day weekend. Christmas fell on a Sunday this year so George sent out an invitation for his men. Spend Saturday and Christmas day with your families then work two days on my house, with appropriate lunchtime cookouts and an evening party on Tuesday.

Christmas was a hot topic for Sarah, she had been promised her first smartphone and a data package she would control herself. "You're ready, you have been a very responsible kid."

I kidded that I should be getting a phone as well. <u>Of course all I could do is text and play video games, but I'd take that.</u> What I got was a surprise. For weeks a long rectangular package had me guessing and wheedling, lifting and handling, and visibly frustrated. I who could normally see the inner workings of things was drawing a blank.

Christmas morning after a rare all in attendance bacon and egg breakfast, the family gathered in front of the tree. It was Sarah's year to play Santa. She began by giving mom a small square present. Mom opened the box to find a black bracelet made of rubber of some sort. On its face was a shiny rectangular surface. When she touched the face a message immediately appeared. 'Take me for a walk' lit up the screen. Mom, who was still pale after a bout with the flu, coughed into a tissue. She had missed the last two days of school and even now said she felt just north of miserable. She had heard about these fitness bracelets but had never used one. Sarah couldn't contain herself as she explained how it all worked and how she had registered her mom and set up a fitness account where the bracelet could interact with a computer. Mom mustered a smile. "You couldn't have given me a better present. I can't wait to go for a walk can you George?"

Even as dad was being handed an identical package. He sighed, "Does this thing register climbing a ladder and swinging a hammer? I sure hope so." "I guess you'll find out," squeaked Mom.

"Thank you Sarah," thank you Bobby. Dad gave us both a big hug.

Sarah got her smartphone and jumped for joy. She managed to postpone her first text until completing her Santa duties. She pulled the last big package from under the tree. Several presents remained but Sarah had been briefed on the order of things.

I tugged at the colorful paper. A plain brown carton continued to hide my present. I snipped tape. Styrofoam emerged as the carton was opened. Beneath that was a metal case of some kind. I unsnapped the locks and suddenly my eyes went wide. Inside was a Telescope! *How in the world did they know this is exactly what I wanted?*

As if reading my mind, mom signed. <u>Your Dad and I watch how you seem to look right into things and figure stuff out. There is no better place on earth to figure things out than the sky above. We will continue to learn a lot about the world from you son.</u> The physical effort it took mom to get all that through to me had her sinking deep into the couch cushion.

I noticed how exhausted she seemed but was too excited to comment.

I hugged both mom and dad and sat back down knowing there was more to follow. A pair of jeans and two t-shirts later I got several books on astronomy. As quickly as I could I grabbed the case and disappeared into my room, I had some studying to do. The rest of Christmas day went well, as you can imagine.

Monday at 8:00 am George's cell rang. He was on his way out the door to pick up donuts and continued to his truck even as he answered. It was Joel. "I apologize George but I'm not going to be able to help with your house today, something has come up. Hopefully I'll be at work on Wednesday."

"Is everything all right?"

"I think so. Just a misunderstanding I need to explain."

"Well if you need help with anything let me know."

"Will do. And as soon as I know more I'll fill you in." George was left wondering if the detective showing up at the work site the other day had anything to do with this. He sure hoped it didn't.

I spent all of Christmas day exploring what this new telescope could do. I found it could be adjusted to bring earth bound objects into view as well. Last night me and Sarah looked at the stars but also looked at houses on our block. We giggled at seeing Mr. Amoros down the street in his kitchen wearing his yellow Bob the Builder pajamas. Sarah looked at me and Signed <u>who knew?</u> Then we both laughed.

This was a whole new world, above and below. This morning I carefully packed it in its hardened case. Already in my mind I could see the little strips of wood we had raced previously in the canal bobbing up and down, rapidly 198 disappearing in the Intercoastal. But this time with the telescope we would be able to track them for a much longer distance.

------◆------

Hailey packed a cooler with juice boxes, bottled water, and a bottle of Pinot Grigio, George had given her for Christmas. The five hundred dollar bonus was appreciated as well. She couldn't get this man off her mind. She tried to rationalize this as simply professional respect and gratitude she was feeling. But hearts don't lie. She called her son and got him into the shower. They had shared the nicest Christmas ever. Hailey had much to be thankful for. But again, hearts don't lie.

—·—◆—◆—◆—·—

Victor spent Christmas day with his dad and his Dad's latest playmate. The woman was maybe five years older than Victor. He watched his father ignore the woman's comments as he punched through the TV channels as alone with himself as he'd be on a surfboard. Victor realized he had been ignored as well since arriving. Victor really needed to have a conversation. As much as his father seemed disappointed in him, Victor did not like lying to him.

Victor presented his father with a bottle of expensive Bourbon.

His father accepted the bourbon and covered up his callousness with a half-hearted offer. "You can continue to stay a while longer, though if it goes into the spring you can expect to be charged rent." The two had never really had a meaningful conversation. He'd received orders and vague threats of being thrown out, all the while his father flipped through channels, the TV acting as strobe light, never making eye contact with his son.

Christmas offered no breakthrough. Several times during the day he tried to confide in his father. Holding a glass of bourbon in one hand and manning a remote in the other his father flipped channels ignoring both him and the woman who prattled on about nothing.

Obviously his father could multi-task however; he had heard him. He eventually turned to his son. "I'll get that damn tape first thing tomorrow." Then he turned his head the other way and provided an acceptable answer to at least one of the questions the woman at his side had posted. Then he turned back to sipping and flipping.

Joel called Franklin with the news that his blood type showed up on the girl's clothing.

"Of course it did. When that glass shattered during one of your rants, you waved your bleeding hand like it was a flag. There was blood everywhere. It was on me as well. We can explain that."

"Well we'll need to. That detective wants me at the station first thing tomorrow morning."

"Do you want me with you?"

"That might help, him hearing it from both of us."

It didn't help at all. Joel was placed under arrest. Franklin was warned not to leave town. He might be a material witness. For all we know you two might have acted together.

On Wednesday morning Victor called George's secretary. He would not be at work today; he had an appointment. He did not elaborate. His appointment consisted of finally gaining access to security footage his father had arranged. He was allowed to view the tapes in private.

There was an old man managing the security office this morning. "Those tapes are getting pretty popular. You're the second one asking for em." Victor raised his eyes. "The kid who works the night shift said someone paid him to see them. He wouldn't say who or how much he got. What's it worth to you?"

Victor opened his mouth without any idea what he was going to say.

The old man held up his hand. "I'm just kidding, I'd lose my job. I think it's going to cost that kid his job if anyone finds out."

Victor's hands were sweating as he was led into a small office where a TV monitor sat on a desk. Victor was given instructions and left alone. The tape sped forward.

Small numbers indicating date and time sped past on the lower part of the screen. Victor re-lived that day, and in his mind just like the blur on the screen, his life since that day had been out of focus. He found the day. He found the hour. He watched the elevator open. In his mind he could see the girl just about to step forward when he collected her in his arms. The tape showed his back but his body completely kept the girl from view. He sighed with relief. Halfway home.

He fast forwarded once more. He watched the time stamp. Just as the time frame that would show him removing a rug, neared; the tape went black. He fast forwarded. He rewound. Nothing. The next visual was stamped 8:00 am the following morning.

Victor was left guessing. He repeated the process. Same result. Is there a schedule? Does the company change these tapes manually? Victor was afraid to ask. Someone had viewed the tape, but who and for what reason?

He left with one answer but many questions left unanswered. He returned to his Condo. He spent the rest of the day parroting his father, drinking Christmas bourbon and flipping channels. In a restless night bathed in sweat he flipped among various endings for all this; not a smiling Emoji in the bunch.

CHAPTER TWENTY-FOUR

Joel too spent nearly a week of restless nights in the Flagler County Jail. Myrtle stopped in every other day trying to reassure him. She told him Franklin was trying to solve the case. "Don't give up. We believe in you."

On the morning of day five he stood in front of a judge and was granted bail. His father put up fifty-thousand dollars after spending two hours the day before talking with his son. Joel assured his father he was innocent and had stopped drinking the day the girl disappeared.

George Whiting at Joel's behest assured his father that Joel had been sober and at work every day since he'd been hired. Father and son and their lawyer left the courthouse together. Joel's father blamed his son's association with Franklin for this mess and if Joel wanted his father's help he was to avoid Franklin at all costs.

—————•◆•————

Franklin hadn't given up though. He talked through all that had gone on that afternoon, with Breanna. "There are only two explanations that make any sense," summarized Franklin. "One, the girl was picked up shortly after leaving the building or two, she didn't leave the building. At least not then."

Breanna agreed. "So what can we do?"

"Well we can try to view the security tapes for that afternoon and evening. That might be a start."

"Hasn't the Sheriff's department already done that?"

"No idea. That detective isn't speaking to me anymore. He says I might be a witness. He obviously doesn't believe our story. For that matter he thinks Joel and I might both be guilty."

Breanna hmmed aloud and postulated, "What are the odds that a drunken girl, here in a residential community, would not be noticed stumbling down the street? She didn't call anyone to pick her up that you know of, right?"

Franklin didn't think so. "She was in no condition to call. I never saw a cell phone."

Franklin this is as confusing as some of your magic tricks.

"Yeah, well I know how my magic works. This is beyond that," mulled Franklin rubbing his chin. "Which leaves me to believe option two needs to be explored. I am going to get a list of the tenants. And I'm going to ask for those tapes."

"Myrtle says she believes you and Joel. She wants to help. She told Joel you are trying to find out what happened.

She's picking me up for lunch then we're going together to see Joel. He's staying with his dad. I'll run all this by both of them."

Breanna stood on the balcony watching Franklin leave. He waved up at her. She loved this man. Watching his car make its way out of the parking lot she was reminded of the journey that car had taken, covering much more than miles. Two lifetimes had merged in the front seat amid sandwich wrappers and paper cups. She nodded, yes she loved this man.

She was still musing when another individual entered the parking lot. Even from the fourth floor this guy looked tall. She didn't remember ever seeing him before. Just then Myrtle's car entered the parking lot and Breanna went inside to finish getting dressed. ^

George Whiting had a business to run. He served as a character witness when Joel asked to post bond. He left the courthouse before the hearing finished but assumed Joel would be granted bail.

George, and Fred Riesling, his former boss, had met before entering the courthouse. After nervous small talk Fred simply asked George what he thought. "I have known Joel in a different way than you Fred. He can be petty and self absorbed, but physically violent I've never seen that in him."

Fred sighed, "I agree, but what a mess."

"It's that alright. So you have a lawyer?"

"Oh yes. Probably a private investigator as well real soon. What a mess." Fred shook his head from side to side.

"Listen George, there's something else I'd like to discuss." George could hear the emotion in the something else to follow.

"I want to sell you my business." He held up a hand.

"Now before you answer listen to the whole proposal." The terms were so generous George left the meeting not wondering would he accept the proposal but rather mulling the possibilities. As he sat at a table waiting to have lunch with Hailey he mentally enlarged his office space in his future home. *Could what he had always dreamed of doing become a possibility? Could he work from home designing energy efficient homes powered strictly with solar? Could one of his crews begin building these solar homes on speculation and if successful build an entire neighborhood?* His napkin was covered in numbers and lines when Hailey joined him at the table.

"Looks like you've done a days' work there, boss." George smiled. "Hailey I think you are about to get another promotion." George explained the possible merger and the very important new role Hailey would be asked to play.

She leaned over the table and kissed George on the forehead. "Looks like more than one dream coming true at this table George."

George looked up. He didn't have his son's ability to look right into people so he simply smiled. "I have to give Fred an answer within the week. What do you think? Can we handle it?"

"Oh yes I do George, I don't think there's anything we can't handle, together?"

When George got home he sat Lane down and excitedly explained Fred's proposal. Lane listened but didn't show the normal encouragement.

"If you think it's too much too soon I can beg off." "No George, I'm sure you've measured twice. I'm just tired I guess. Lately when I get home I have been napping before our evening walks. I'm sure the kids have mentioned it."

"Actually since that puppy arrived, followed by a cell phone and a telescope, any conversations we have surround one of the three. Any aches or pains?"

"Some, but really just all the time tired. I can't seem to shake this flu. I'm not sleeping well either. I'm sure it's nothing.'

"Well make an appointment for a physical anyway. It's not like you to be tired."

Lane made an appointment.

During the two weeks Lane waited for her appointment February slipped into March.

⸻ ⬩•⬩ ⸻

Franklin secured the list and a brief description of the tenants. Fifteen tenants rented as couples and he immediately dismissed them as being anything more than possible witnesses. *I'm sure they have been interviewed by now,* he thought. Nine older women lived by themselves. Not very likely they were involved but they might have heard something. Eight men also rented as singles. He'd scrutinize them. In addition to Franklin two other younger people were listed as tenants. Both of them, women. In the end he decided his best chance to uncover anything new was to view those tapes. Tomorrow he had an appointment.'

⸻ ⬩•⬩ ⸻

Joel, now out on bail, went back to work for George. While disappointed his father had decided to sell the firm, for the first time in his life, Joel understood what he had put his parents through. His mother served dinner at the same time every night. She had done that for the forty years she had been a married woman. Since coming back home wearing an ankle monitor he had stayed pretty close to home after work. For the first time in years he had the time and took the time to get to know his mom. Fred was not an easy man to live with. Joel had experienced that when he joined the firm. But his mother, she was unflappable. She did her own hair and nails. She hated high fashion and loved to cook. Tonight's meal with vegetables from the farmer's market and organic chicken from a whole foods store was served up as a crock-pot creation. Fresh organic bakery bread lay in its own little basket awaiting natural butter. Joel reached across and claimed a slice. His mother met his eyes. The reassuring look and the fresh healthy smells surrounding him had Joel believing maybe he could get out of this mess.

Fred grabbed his own slice and buttered. His eyes met Joel's and he began. "I hired a private eye today. He's going to want to come by tomorrow and hear your story." Joel nodded. "I'll be right here after work unless Mom needs me to do something."

Mrs. Riesling summoned the bowls and served up dinner. Later Joel and his mother took an evening walk. She took her son's hand. Once again she met his eyes, smiled and nodded.

— • — ◆ •◆• — • —

Victor was stymied. He met with the detective. He assumed the man had viewed the tape so did not dispute being home that evening. He knew he was not recognizable entering the elevator on the tape in the afternoon. He lied and said he came home just after 8 pm.

"You didn't hear or see anything out of the ordinary that evening?"

"No sir, I came home from work and never left again until the following morning."

"I noticed you signed a request to review the video tape from your security company."

"Yes sir, I thought a former girlfriend might have entered my apartment when I wasn't home and removed a ring I had been given. I checked the tapes. Obviously I was wrong and must have lost the ring somewhere."

That had ended the interview.

Victor wasn't sure if the detective believed him. He hadn't asked for the girl's name so he must have.

Victor remained stymied. Where did the missing hours of tape go? Obviously the detective didn't have them. He could not reasonably go down that road any further. He was still not sleeping well and still losing weight. He really needed to talk with his father about this. He stood on the scale. A buck ninety five, not since Jr. High School had he seen those numbers.

—·—◆—◆—·—

On the other side of town I hadn't been sleeping well either. I was worried about mom. Something was wrong with her. I hadn't poked and probed but I could still see right through mom's eyes, right into her soul. Tonight for instance at dinner. Her smile seemed forced. Her hands were not as animated when she answered me. When my sister Sarah announced she was going to run spring track mom simply listened without comment. Dad wasn't home for dinner. He was taking over another business, coming home lately, after the sun had set. I need to talk to him. Tonight Sarah surprised me. She joined me in my bed. I wasn't fully asleep and she startled me when she snapped my lamp on.

We sat up, our backs against the headboard. <u>I heard mom and dad talking. Mom thinks dad should let Hailey be more involved in the business. She sounded scared. She said, 'I need you more than the business needs you right now.' Dad said, 'let's see what those tests turn up.' What tests is he talking about?</u>

I told Sarah what I was feeling regarding mom. I'm scared. I think Mom is sick.

CHAPTER TWENTY-FIVE

It's often stated that the wheels of justice spin slowly. In the case of a murdered girl left to rot in tangled undergrowth, the tires seemed to have rotted off those wheels.

Detective Errol Monroe had enough to charge Joel Riesling, but his gut was telling him there was more to this story. He asked the Sheriff and County Attorney for more time.

He reviewed the tapes once again. The elevator door opens around the time Franklin suggested the girl left his condo. The tape showed the back of a man entering. No more elevator activity for an hour. The tape shows the back of an old lady entering with a bag of groceries. Nothing else. All routine comings and goings till a gap in the surveillance tapes loses hours of coverage. The tape was either erased, missing, or for some unknown reason did not record. The company seemed to have no idea how or why that happened. Errol Monroe didn't like coincidences. What was he missing? The District attorney seemed bent on taking Joel Riesling to trial on a second degree murder charge using the blood evidence.

Lane made it through the day at school and entered her Doctors office. After the normal wait, during which she thumbed through the latest People magazine counting her blessings as a normal person. She was greeted by the doctor herself. She ushered Lane into her office. "I agree with you this flu shouldn't be lasting this long. Let's take some blood tests and do a complete physical. At your age this doesn't sound normal."

"Well thank you for taking this seriously. I have never felt so dragged out in my life." She teared up. "I'm not even taking proper interest in my kids. And my husband he's essentially working two jobs and building a house and all I do is whine. Doctor Sebbia, you need to figure out what's wrong and fix it."

— • — • — • —

Victor's father came to his condo on the first day of spring 2017. He was waiting for his son to come home from work. He did a walk through. His son seemed to be making an effort to keep the place clean. He opened some windows to get rid of the stale air. He opened the glass doors to both the front and back balconies. During his inspection he noted a new 6x6 rug in the hallway. He shook his head, *Victor should know by now a good real estate man misses nothing.* He poured himself a drink and sat down. He turned on the TV and began flipping channels. The world seemed to be one big conspiracy theory. The Russians hacked the election. Donald Trump touted fake news. The choice for the Supreme Court had both parties at one another's throat. Promises were being made. Investigations into illegal wiretaps filled the airwaves.

Mr. Thornton flipping madly couldn't seem to get away from conspiracies. He finally found a channel that wasn't in commercial or in denial.

A movie was playing – he couldn't remember the name – but he loved Jack Nicholson. He couldn't stand Tom Cruise. Jack was just about to utter that famous line: 'You want the truth? You can't handle the truth.' When reinforcement of exactly what he was thinking hit Tobias Thornton's ears he promptly turned off the set and began pacing and thinking.

So what is the truth Victor? His son seemed to be in turmoil. He looked older and smaller every time he laid eyes on him. His nails were bitten down to the quick and were those gray hairs emerging the last time he saw his son? One thing he knew for sure. It wasn't a ring his son was looking for on those tapes. He mulled in his mind what he had seen on that tape. He hadn't believed his son for a minute when he concocted that story.

He raised a glass to himself. Nope you can't put much past a good Real-estate man.

So unbeknownst to Victor, dear old dad took a look at those tapes before his son. He bribed the temporary worker not to record his comings and goings. The kid didn't care anyway. He was playing some stupid game on his smartphone. He obviously could give a shit what was done with the tapes. When Mr. Thornton viewed his son carrying a rug out of his Condo his first thought was maybe Victor had been sick or had stained the rug in some way. Was Victor so afraid of his father he'd try to get rid of the rug and replace it thinking I wouldn't notice? He chuckled to himself, a good real estate agent notices everything. What was Victor really looking for on these tapes? The only time Victor appeared on the tape he was coming or going and the only thing unusual was Victor carrying out a rug.

Mr. Thornton erased that segment showing his son carrying a bulky rug out of the building, and later returning.

—•••—

Victor was into the seventh hour of work in a ten hour day. He had a new crew leader. He wondered what had happened to his old boss, Joel, but no one seemed to know for sure. The gossip at the other end of the sheetrock being carried to a future living room suddenly added weight to the trip. "I heard he's been arrested and is out on bail and the boss has him doing other things."

Victor had to ask, "What did he do?"

"Word is he killed a woman and buried her in the woods. All drug related I hear."

Victor nearly dropped his end of the drywall.

At the end of his shift Victor sought comfort and memory loss on the deck of The Golden Lion. He hardly spoke to his fellow worker he had invited to join him. The Atlantic Ocean shimmering in the late afternoon light mirrored the golden glow of his craft brew. Two liquids, both seemingly capable of drowning a man's sorrows. He studied his glass. Eventually his co-worker, up and left.

Victor sat there through two beers and an approaching dusk. Looming darkness as murky as his thoughts brought him home. When he turned the key to his condo the first light to reach his eyes was from the TV. *Had he left it on?* Channels moving like waves washing the beach. He was about to speak when suddenly the TV went dark.

His father's voice split the darkness, "Tell me Victor, what have you gotten yourself into?" ^

Detective Monroe loved puzzles. This evening he was at his kitchen table halfway through a 1000 piece puzzle. Tied up sailboats at a marina in the glow of a rising sun, its theme. While his mind tried to match up colors and shapes his inner mind went over the pieces of the murder case that didn't seem to fit.

His doorbell rang. He looked through the glass at the side of the door. That young man Franklin and his girlfriend Breanna were standing there; Franklin was nervously twirling a straw hat. Detective Monroe opened the door and welcomed them to his home. Breanna was immediately drawn to the puzzle. Detective Monroe could use all the help he could get.

He pulled out a chair. "Go ahead young lady, I can use the help." He turned to Franklin. "Franklin, you appear to have a lot on your mind. Maybe you and I could sit in the living room. Can I get either one of you something to drink?" Breanna shook her head no and lowered herself to the table. She seemed focused on solving at least one puzzle tonight.

"Go ahead Franklin I'll leave you two to your business."

The two sat and after a brief silence Franklin began. "The private detective Joel's dad hired came to see me. He thinks their only defense is going to be to implicate me in the girl's death. 'Raise reasonable doubt,' is what he said." Franklin paused to let that sink in. "Detective Monroe, neither myself nor Joel had anything to do with that girl getting murdered. I need your help."

"What kind of help?"

"We need to solve this thing."

"The District Attorney seems to think we have done that."

"Yeah, well what do you think?"

"I'm paid to follow the evidence trail. Right now that leads to your friend's door."

Franklin raised a finger, "Actually it starts outside my door. Have you viewed the tapes?"

"I have. The tape does show you escorting Joel out of your apartment. Which proves nothing by the way. We're missing the part about you coming home around nine."

"How is that possible?"

"There are hours' worth of tape missing. Some of the time frame you are telling me this all happened in is gone." Franklin opened his mouth to ask how that was possible.

Detective Monroe was ready with an answer. "That is a mystery I am still pursuing. Right now what we see is you and your friend leaving the building. We do not see the girl leaving, or you coming home at nine."

Franklin frowned and rubbed his chin. "Someone in this building had that tape erased."

"I have interviewed every tenant in the building. They all seem to have an alibi. Which unfortunately leads right back to your Condo. And remember from our standpoint that girl could still have been in your condo when you took Joel home. You can bet that private detective is going to raise that theory. Joel's passed out drunk. They are going to argue that maybe you did something to that girl while Joel was passed out. Then you hid her body until you could get back there. There's their reasonable doubt."

Franklin was agitated. "Why is that piece of security tape missing? Look Detective I know you don't need to do any more digging but I see you like puzzles. This whole thing is a puzzle and right now there is a piece missing. I swear to you Joel and I did not harm that girl. I think your missing piece is somewhere in my building."

Detective Monroe rose and shook Franklin's hand. "I have to say I've never had a possible witness or co-defendant come to my home before. I'll do what I can. Personally, I believe you."

Breanna left the table, pointing out a pattern she had discovered which had filled an entire section.

Detective Monroe ushered them out. But rather than returning to the table he went into the living room and snapped off the light. He did some of his best thinking in the dark.

—··—●—●—●—··—

Poor Lane Whiting had her own mystery going. The tests did nothing to pin down why she was feeling so poorly. She made an appointment with her school principal, she simply could not manage a full day right now.

So a week later on a rare rainy spring morning in Florida, Lane sat at her computer nursing a cup of tea, honey, and lemon. Coffee had lost its taste over the past month. She began googling her symptoms. The Principal had suggested a leave of absence and Lane had reluctantly agreed.

George told her to give up her job entirely. The business was growing and maybe it was time for her to slow down and focus on her health.

Lane, scrolling websites like she was preparing a lesson plan, matched symptoms being described with her own. She had written down all the ways she was feeling miserable. She listed dates and symptoms. She had noted she was sleeping longer hours but not feeling energized by them. Her muscles ached for no reason. Her joints felt stiff and sore. She traced the beginning of all this to her bout with the flu. The one constant in how she felt was a listlessness that did not subside.

She typed in each symptom in turn, hitting search, looking for a common enemy. There were lots of enemies to choose from. She came away with a better understanding of why her doctor hadn't made a definitive diagnosis.

George called. "How are you this morning honey?"

Right now her nose was running. She sniffed, "Same as what seems like forever."

"I'm sorry honey. I have a meeting in front of the planning board tonight. If you need me to bring anything home before the meeting let me know. Fred had started getting permits for a new planned community before he sold me the business and its run into a snag. So, I have inherited some angry citizens who do not want this development in their backyard. I'll be late."

"We'll be fine. The kids will be here. I'll leave something in the fridge."

"Don't bother. Hailey and I will grab something before the meeting."

After hanging up, Lane blew her nose and went back to her search.

CHAPTER TWENTY-SIX

Vacation week arrived with both Sarah and Bobby expressing big plans. Bobby wanted to spend two nights with Hailey's son. Sarah was going to have a friend in for the two nights Bobby would be gone. Sarah promised Bobby she would help her mom do housework. Lately the two had subtly begun doing dishes, straightening their rooms and making their beds.

As for Lane, she was still feeling miserable. The tests had come back negative for lymphoma, or any of the diseases Lane had googled. She had a follow up appointment this afternoon.

The door-bell rang. Hailey and her son Daniel stood smiling and talking softly to one another as Lane opened the door.

"Hi Hailey." She looked at Daniel flanking his mother, "you're growing like a weed Daniel, come on in. Bobby should be ready, go get him."

When Daniel left the room, Lane took Hailey's hand. "As you can see I'm a mess. Tests haven't come up with anything. I appreciate you letting Bobby spend a couple of days. I can barely manage to dress myself."

"I'm so sorry, Lane. If I can do anything else just ask. George is giving me the entire week off to be with Daniel. Bobby can stay for as long as you like."

"Thanks if I'm not feeling better I just might take you up on that. Sarah and Bobby have been cooking and cleaning and doing the wash." She shook her head in despair, "I have never felt so useless."

The boys came into the room with Bobby's backpack and a duffel full of who knows what.

Mom hugged me tightly. I looked deep into her eyes. <u>When I get back we'll figure this out Mom.</u>

Lane's eyes watered. She hugged her son once more ferociously. When the door closed she went in to shower. She had a million questions for her doctor.

— · ◆ · —

Victor was at work but his mind wasn't exactly on task. He nearly hit a co-worker with a hammer he dropped from a second floor rafter. When his boss heard the men arguing he confronted the men. "Vic is out of control. He's screwing up the plywood cuts and he's a danger to himself and the rest of us."

Dick, the crew boss, listened. He looked Victor in the eye. Bags under bloodshot eyes and what appeared to be a new nervous twitch he had not observed before, prompted his next line. "I don't normally take sides Victor, but it's clear you aren't ready to work. Go on home I'll have George call you. You can explain whatever you need to explain to him."

Victor didn't argue. He went to his Condo but it was not to rest. Rather he relived the first meaningful conversation he'd had with his father. The question his dad had posed: 'What have you gotten yourself into Victor?' That opened the floodgates.

Victor broke down and told his father everything. Mr. Thornton left the TV off. There was no need to be flipping channels, a real live drama was taking place in his own living room. 'Just let me handle it,' his father advised after watching his son melt down. 'I already have actually.' Victor still didn't know what his father meant by that. And his father had not explained.

Mr. Thornton knew that at some point the authorities would be leaning on that temporary security worker he had bribed. If push came to shove the kid would give him up in a heartbeat. He needed to assure that didn't happen. He told his son none of this. He did tell his son that he would probably be interviewed again. Victor just might need to come up with a past girlfriend who could possibly have taken his ring. 'Do you even have a girlfriend, past or present? If not, you might want to get one. One who will like you enough to lie for you.'

Victor attempted to follow his father's advice. He began frequenting a number of bars in the area. Insecure when it came to girls he spent more time drinking than trying to attract a girlfriend.

But maybe last night without trying he'd hit the jackpot. His shakiness at work today and the red in his eyes had many fathers, liquor and worry were only two of them.

Pearl Crosby, an extremely long and leggy girl had actually picked him out of the line-up at the bar. "You look like you could use a friend." She hauled a bewildered Victor onto the dance floor. She wrapped her long arms around his neck and immediately introduced him to a slow dance using a body that showed no quit.

Tall and regally thin, Victor himself six-three found the girl meeting him straight in the eye with just the barest tilt to her chin.

Trading names and a handshake she ushered him to a table. Two beers interrupted by every slow song, moved Victor from bewildered to bewitched. After another beer, the party moved to the back parking lot and Pearl's car. Pearl literally took control of Victor by grabbing his junk and offering to relieve him of his stress. Do you have a place of your own he was asked?

Back in Victor's condo she remained the teacher with a curriculum she needed to work through. So Victor had started the day in no condition to work.

He took a deep breath. He would be seeing her tonight. If things worked out she just might become his ally and his alibi. He closed his eyes for a well needed nap.

⸺⸺◆⸺⸺

Hailey's son Daniel and overnight friend Bobby played quietly outside Hailey's apartment. She peeked out the window as her son took his eyes away from the telescope and covered his mouth in laughter. The angle of the scope indicated it was not the heavens that was causing the mirth. Bobby's dad was coming for dinner. Hailey went back to preparing an evening meal she hoped would please George.

A sense of guilt tempered her happiness. She thought the world of Lane, George's wife and their family was precious. She sighed and hugged herself. *Dammit Hailey why can't you get the thought of you and George together out of your mind.* Maybe she should change jobs. The two of them were together day after day and that was not helping her deny her feelings. But this job was an opportunity for a successful career in what is normally a man's trade. Just then her son shrieked with laughter. She checked the roast in the oven.

I just have to remember what I'm risking and stay strong. She nodded, yes just stay strong.

⸺⸺◆⸺⸺

Joel got the news that his case would be going to the grand jury. If indicted he'd be going on trial for murder in the second degree in the fall. Some lesser charges might be tacked on if they could be proved. He was at Myrtle's apartment tonight and they were watching an episode of dateline. Joel hated the show but Myrtle seemed fascinated by the seemingly endless ways what was advertised as true love could end. During intermission Joel broke the news he had received earlier.

"What's your defense going to be?"

"The only defense I have is Franklin. And my lawyer wants to implicate him to raise doubt in the jury's mind. I don't want to do that. Hell, Franklin's my only friend in all this. Except for you Myrtle."

"What has your private eye found?"

"Nothing more than we already know which is pretty much nothing."

Myrtle wanted to ease Joel's mind but there was really nothing to say. Besides, the show was about to continue.

Their relationship seemed to be withstanding the stress and Joel couldn't be kinder. Still Myrtle couldn't get the murdered girl out of her mind. Maybe she could get one of her workers, one she could trust, to poke around a little. What were they hearing on the street?

She closed her eyes and did an inventory of her workers. There was one girl, a recent hire but one who had worked in nearly every fast food establishment in Palm Coast and beyond. She came to Cluck's with a solid resume. She was in her last year at Daytona State College. She seemed extremely sociable but capable. She told Myrtle she had known Nona. Partied with her even. She appeared to have an active social life but was always on time and task at work. Yes, Myrtle would talk with Pearl Crosby.

— · —◆— ·· —◆— ·· —◆— · —

Franklin and Breanna were inseparable. Never had either been this happy. Franklin was only marginally concerned he would be charged in the death of the girl but he remained Joel's only witness. Franklin was determined to figure all this out. Like his magic tricks, on the surface the truth evaded even the most discerning eyes. If the trick could be slowed down and dissected step by step the truth would become obvious. The two sat at the kitchen table in Franklin's condo. Franklin had a notebook and pencil sitting on the table between them. "Ok let's start at the beginning, Breanna. You write down what I remember. We will add what the detective told us."

George arrived at Hailey's at six pm. The boys followed him inside. They were sent to wash their hands and returned to a feast. Daniel was being taught sign by Bobby. The two boys silently tried to communicate while George described his day.

"It went pretty well. Just one incident. You remember Victor, one of our more recent hires? He obviously must have partied too hard last night. Dick had to send him home. Doesn't want him back till I talk with him, safety issue he said."

The conversation continued both verbal and by gesture. The boys' eyes widened as a lemon meringue pie was placed in front of them. Hailey held up a finger, "I'll just serve this hard working man first if you two boys don't mind."

The smile she gave dad lit up the room and wasn't lost on this mind reading kid who missed nothing. I showed no reaction but decided in the minute I was too full for pie.

I rubbed my belly indicating I was too full for dessert.

"Maybe later," suggested Hailey. <u>Maybe not,</u> I signed. I rubbed my belly, but I think she caught my meaning.

Daniel wolfed down his pie and the boys went to Daniel's bedroom but not before I made a production of hugging dad.

George got home a little after nine. Lane was already asleep.

I spent a restless night wrestling with what I thought was happening. Maybe I was just imagining things. I love Hailey and Daniel. I won't have the opportunity to join Sarah at the top of her bed for another night. Too much to think about.

Instead I focused my mind on our home under construction. I mentally went through the blueprints flipping pages like counting sheep. I fell asleep tallying the two by eight studs dad was using to super insulate the inside walls. I think we will need to order more.

• — • ◆ • — • ◆ • — •

When Victor opened up, Mr. Thornton realized he had no idea the seriousness of his son's crime. Christ, he had destroyed evidence in a murder investigation.

He attempted to reach the temporary worker he had bribed but the young man had since moved on. *How long before an investigator finds him and leans on him? Just how far can I go with this before I'm charged with obstruction?* Channels flicked past him on screen. Lies and half-truths continued to dominate the news cycle. Just dial up your flavor of the month and gorge yourself. He was starting to mirror his son's problem in getting to sleep.

Christ he hadn't built a career just to watch it crash down around his ears. Stupid, stupid, Victor. Maybe he should tell his son to move out.

Mr. Thornton's work was taking a hit as well. Lately he just didn't want to hear what some of his prospective buyers had to say. Today he hung up on a lady who, in his estimation, just needed to get out of the house and was going to waste his time looking at a property she had no intention of buying. The channels continued to evade his interest as his mind, like a wheel of fortune game, kept stopping at tilt. *Damn you son.*

━━━━◆━━━━

The temporary security worker Mr. Thornton was trying to find was just one of thousands of kids three years out of high school who had left their home states with few skills that were marketable. You see them on the sidewalks of cities hunkered down filling out applications for a dollar store, a deli, or a fast food restaurant. This particular young man was in plain sight. He had filled out an application and was heading in for a final interview at Cluck's Chicken Coop.

Myrtle looked at the work history the young man provided on the application. He graduated from Lubbock Texas High School in 2013. His job history included a Car Wash in Texas. He had a year of Junior college, also in Texas. No degree. Since moving to Florida he had worked at a McDonald's for six months. His reason for leaving that job was a disagreement with management. He had worked as a waiter on the beach. And finally as a temporary worker at a security company. Myrtle looked him in the eye. "You realize this job is part time, right?"

"I thought it was a full time position."

"When you worked at McDonald's, was that full time?"

"No, it was sometimes twenty, sometimes twenty five hours a week." He added, "With no benefits."

"Well that's pretty standard for the food industry. It is what we're offering as well. And you and I both know if something better surfaces, you'll be gone like one of those greasy burgers you used to flip." Bellamy had to smile at that.

"So what do you think, do you want to work?" She held up her hand. "Before you answer that let me give you the conditions of your employment. Number one: No cell phone anywhere in this building when you are on duty. Number two: Come to work on time clear eyed and ready to work." Myrtle raised her voice and maintained direct eye contact with Bellamy Tyrone Curtis. "NUMBER THREE: NO CELL PHONE ANYWHERE IN THIS BUILDING WHEN YOU ARE ON DUTY!" She widened her eyes and softened her voice, "The reason one and three are the same you might ask? Because this is the only time I'll repeat myself on this issue. If you bring a cell phone onto these premises you can expect to be terminated immediately. Consider you have already been told twice."

She raised her eyes and pointed a finger to the sky, "one more thing, No alcohol or drugs at any time. Non- negotiable."

Bellamy Tyrone Curtis, taking all this in, nodded his understanding and agreement.

Myrtle tidied things up. She splayed her fingers, "So help me out here Bellamy, first quiz. What is it that will get you gone?"

Bellamy stood. He ticked off the offenses that would keep chicken out of his diet.

"I'm a good worker, just tell me when I can start training."

Myrtle smiled for the first time. "Why don't you come on Wednesday at four o'clock? That's a quiet time. I'm just finishing up some training with another worker. You'll like her. Her name is Pearl."

CHAPTER TWENTY-SEVEN

Sarah Whiting was on the attack. She received a pass in front of a defender at mid-field. Her friend Winona was on her right, staying just onside. Sarah feinted left then left footed the pass to Winona. Winona moved on the goalie and let loose with a booming kick from twenty yards, shoulder height and into the extreme right corner of the net. SCORE!

In the stands George Whiting and Sheriff Rodriguez high fived one another as the whistle blew. Game Over! As the girls went through their rituals, George spoke up. "Do you really think Joel Riesling is guilty of murder?"

"Why do you ask?"

"Sheriff, I have known Joel for twenty years. We haven't always been the best of friends but I don't think he's capable of such a thing."

The sheriff, here in uniform, re-set his hat. "I can't go into detail but everything we have points to him. He may have had help. I can tell you he was quite drunk on that day. He's admitted to that. He's going to trial that much I know. It's not my call. The state seems to think they have enough to convict him."

George shook his head; he had nothing to add, just a gut feeling.

When dad and Sarah got home I was putting the finishing touches on a peanut butter and jelly sandwich. I held up the jar which was now empty. <u>We'll find something for ourselves. Where's Mom?</u> I pointed to my parent's bedroom.

"You rustle something up Sarah, I'll go see how your mom is feeling."

The bedroom was in half-light, the shades drawn, allowing just enough light for George to see a raised mound of bedding. He went over to his side of the bed and turned on the lamp. He kicked off his shoes and laid down, moving himself to the warmth of Lane's back.

Lane stirred and spoke huskily. "Hi honey, sorry about dinner. I can't seem to get out of bed."

George put his arm around her, drawing himself closer to her warmth, fitting himself to her outline. "I'm so sorry this is happening. I like to think I can fix everything and I can't even help my wife."

Lane sighed, "I've about exhausted all the possibilities. I have an appointment with a natural healer on Friday. I'll try anything now." Silence overtook the room, what was left to say?

George changed the conversation. "Sarah won her game today. That puts them in the district final." He hugged his wife from behind. "She could have scored the game winner but passed off to her friend Winona, she took an assist instead." He sighed, "We have a very unselfish daughter, honey." George squeezed her tighter. "On a different front, Joel is going on trial soon. They actually think he killed that girl."

Lane managed, "You never know about people. I don't think he would do something like that but who knows anything anymore," she sighed long and loud.

George nodded his agreement to that assessment of life in general and closed his eyes.

Two hours later Sarah knocked on the bedroom door. She spoke to the darkness. "Bobby is taking a shower then I'll tuck him in. He has his homework done and I'm going to my room to study. I cleaned up the kitchen. Dad, you have a bowl of beef stew in the refrigerator. Love you guys, goodnight."

George mumbled his thanks to Sarah. Lane was sound asleep. George undressed and slipped under the covers; he was soon asleep for the night as well.

I made my way to Sarah's room and once again surprised her by coming to the top of the bed well before midnight.

Sarah snapped on the lamp.

<u>I have had this on my mind. I need to ask you what you think.</u> I went on to explain what I was sensing about Hailey and dad.

Sarah signed, <u>Did you get any vibrations from dad that he's even aware that Hailey might be hot for him?</u>

<u>Dad loves everyone. I might be wrong anyway but I had to tell someone.</u> I furrowed my brow and squinted my eyes. <u>What does hot even mean?</u>

Sarah chuckled and hugged me. <u>Hit the foot of the bed and get some sleep I'll keep my eyes open this weekend when we have another work session at the house.</u>

~~~~~

Franklin and Breanna left their notes regarding the murder on the kitchen table with their coffee. During breakfast they reviewed them.

This morning after Franklin left to do some banking Breanna took the notes out to the balcony. The sun had not hit here on the west side
~~~~~

as yet. A cool breeze was moving the palm leaves in the trees that circled the perimeter of the parking lot. The notes pulsated, pages not blowing away but suddenly gaining oxygen. Breanna placed her cup on the pile as she selected a page and reviewed all they knew. Every owners name, age and description had been checked off.

The fresh air cleared Breanna's mind as well. Suddenly the memory of the big man Breanna had observed leaving the building came back to mind. She looked back at the descriptions. This man was not among them. Not sure if this was a Eureka moment or not Breanna immediately wrote what she remembered of the man onto the page.

— • — • — • — • — • —

Lane went to see a natural healer. After reclining, eyes closed on a couch and describing her symptoms: her aches, lethargy, and general run down feeling, then she opened her eyes. The lady took her hand. "Walk me back through your days. Let each ache tell their story. Believe it or not they wish to be heard. Close your eyes. Who arrived first?"

Lane's first thought was this lady is wacked.

But the strength of the woman's grasp and the warmth of her hand was comforting. Lane closed her eyes once more. *She found she did recall the aches that caused her to miss dinners. And the tiredness that sent her to bed early. She recalled the joint pain that caused her to miss her daughter's games. She remembered visualizing Bobby outside her window playing with Daniel. The squeals of laughter from his friend and the joyful yapping of Teddi brought a smile to her face even as she had laid there in misery. She thought back to her visit with her principal where she had spoken of the host of ailments that forced her to cut back and then finally leave her job entirely. When she arrived mentally back at the beginning. It was clear this had all started with the flu around Christmas.* Lane opened her eyes and retold the story aloud.

The healer spoke. "Your journey is one I hear daily. The world has changed. The air and water and food carry new challenges to our well-being. Traditional medicine is making huge strides in treating disease. The one thing it cannot replace however is knowledge of our own body. I cannot tell you why you suffer Mrs. Whiting but I can propose a way to fight back."

She had Lane's full attention.

"First you must take this assault on your body personally. Then you must arm yourself with knowledge." She handed Lane several pages. "What I will leave you with today is a series of questions you should pose to yourself. Search for those answers and write them out in long hand."

Lane looked at her quizzically.

"Yes in long hand. Using your different senses as you pursue the enemy helps you get to know them. That is how you will defeat them."

Lane was starting to believe this woman might be onto something.

"When you have done that, come back and I will help you develop a plan. Within the month if you answer the questions honestly, we will write a holistic prescription for your health."

Lane closed the door already glad she had met this woman.

On the ride home Lane thought, *No more invasive tests that had revealed nothing. No more hour-long waits reading People magazine or dated issues of Time.* She could still feel the strong hand of support this woman was offering. She entered traffic on a cloudless day that seemed to hold promise of many cloudless days to come.

— · — ◆ — ◆ — · —

Myrtle and Joel began to skirt the elephant in the room— the upcoming trial. Their eyes barely met these days as they talked of their workdays. After sharing a meal while watching the local then national news and then entering the world of evening television fare, Joel usually left to sleep at his parent's home. They erected a wall as solid as the concrete one's Joel erected at work. Joel did ask Myrtle to join him on Sunday to work at his boss's house.

"Bring a bowl of Coleslaw or some of your famous wings. If you want to show up just in time to eat, that's okay too. I realize it's your day off."

"Actually I have two new employees scheduled to work on Sunday afternoon so I will probably stop there for at least a while. Put me down for wings. I'll get there if things are running smoothly at work."

—◆◆◆◆◆—

Victor continued to see Pearl and after learning she was employed at Cluck's Chicken Coop, he was taking an occasional meal there. On Friday he came in for a take-out lunch and Pearl introduced him to her boss, Myrtle.

Looking out the serving window, Bellamy Tyrone Curtis did not have a clue he was viewing the son of the man who paid him to look at the surveillance tapes at his old job. Bellamy also did not know that more than eight hours of those tapes were now missing. He had taken a shine to Pearl though, and looked a possible rival for her affection up and down.

Myrtle noticed. She gave him a look and Bellamy disappeared.

Bellamy thought himself pretty clever and in his mind he had this job figured out in short order. Once he had the cook times down and the order of putting the meals together he and Pearl found time to kid around and get to know one another. Bellamy was a big kidder. He kept the crew in stitches. He looked forward to Sunday when the two would be working the same shift again. In checking the schedule for the week which was posted on a whiteboard he saw that Myrtle wasn't on the schedule for Sunday. You didn't kid around much when Myrtle was on duty. The assistant manager, Juan, scheduled for Sunday was as young as Bellamy and flirted with all the girls.

Bellamy had grown up in Texas and from day one had made friends easily. Black, White, Hispanic, Russian. He had dated at least one girl from about every ethnic group. The vibe he was getting from Pearl indicated she was color blind as well.

Meanwhile in the front of the house Pearl wandered over to Victor while he was waiting and handed him a chocolate covered chicken shaped mint. She noted him in profile, appearing to be even thinner in the short time she'd known him. She walked him to a booth and took a sip of his drink.

Victor asked her if she was scheduled for Sunday.

"I am. Eleven till six, what's up?"

"Nothing really. Just going to work at my boss's place on Sunday and they are having a cookout at the end of the day. We won't eat till six-thirty or so. Are you interested? Tub of brewski's floating on ice. Table full of good food."

"Hell yeah!"

CHAPTER TWENTY-EIGHT

Lane began by reading the laundry list of questions posed by her natural healer. Food, exercise, life balance, spirituality –in whatever form – and a host of lesser queries. She took stock of what she valued in life and things she would gladly discard. She took special notice of her children and what she was feeding them. She noted habits both personal and family. For a solid week she searched the internet for possible connections. She compared her findings and took notes.

Finally armed with a boatload of information she sat down to answer the questions. She came to realize as her hand floated over the paper and the words seemed to materialize magically, the power she had over most of what happened regarding herself and her family. If changes needed to be made in her own life and by extension her family, they started with her.

Sunday morning when the children came to the table. Organic cereal replaced the comfort food that had dominated the table in the past. Fresh fruit thinly sliced, adorned the cereal.

I was the first to react. <u>What happened to my Chocolate Fruit Loops?</u>

Sarah wasn't far behind. Who leggo my Eggo? She asked only half kiddingly.

Mom was ready for us. She had her lesson plan all rehearsed.

Since Sarah understood Sign as well as she did, mom used it.

<u>Kid's I need your help. A lifetime of less than healthy choices surrounding food is part of what I need to fix to begin feeling better. I can't do it alone. Will you give me a month? I'm going to be making lots of other changes as well. Some you may like some you may not. Will you give your tired old mother the benefit of the doubt for one month?</u> She walked around the table ruffling our hair. <u>Remember back when I was a wave of energy and fun to be around. That's what I'm shooting for. Team effort.</u> She offered her palm. We both high fived her.

Dad entered just as mom finished. He was about to raise his own questions when Sarah piped up. "Don't ask, Dad just go with the flow."

—•—•—•—•—

{And so a Sunday of new beginnings, chance meetings, and overheard conversations, perhaps a tipping point in this story takes place in the soon to be, House That Jack Built.}

The afternoon began at 1pm. After a light lunch a five hour day would be devoted to the inside of the house.

The shell was completed. Doors and windows in, tile on the roof. Rough plumbing and electricity at the curb. HVAC all plumbed in. The house had been painted with its first coat. A watering system for the future lawn had little red flags indicating their location.

I walked around with Daniel. We both wore small construction helmets. I showed Daniel the punch list dad had created for the construction from start to finish. Together we checked off as completed: Grading and site prep., Foundation, Framing, Doors and windows, Roofing, first coat of paint over stucco, rough electrical, plumbing and HVAC.

With a pencil behind my ear I pointed out each of these features to Daniel as we made our way around and through the building. Some of the men noticed and kidded dad that he was soon to be replaced. Dad shook his head in agreement.

Joel and Victor were working on the same project today. They were insulating the inside walls. The rolls of aluminum foil backed insulation were stacked in the garage. The two men were measuring and cutting strips from those rolls while two other men were carrying and stapling those strips to the studs.

This was the first time the two men had occasion to talk beyond a head nod or something work related. Victor had heard about Joel being charged with murder and felt terribly guilty.

Joel asked Victor how he liked the construction business.

"Measure twice, cut once, that's my new philosophy," voiced Victor in response.

Joel laughed, "Well you have the religion down pat I see. If I still drank, I'd offer up a toast later." Then he got serious, "I'm sure you have heard the stories. Just so you know I won't be slitting your throat anytime soon with this box knife."

Victor was left speechless.

It was at this moment that Daniel and I entered the garage. We stood back and watched the two men work. I explained to Daniel what they were doing. I noticed that even on this cooler than normal Sunday the tall thin man I had questions about was sweating profusely, his arm pits darkened. He seemed thinner than I remembered. His hands shook when he was making his cuts. The memory of him outside the Porta-Potty entered my head. We were about to move on and continue our inspections.

When Joel recognized me as George's son, Daniel signed me. I looked up.

Joel asked us two boys if we would like to help. I couldn't hear but I could read lips. Soon we were measuring and cutting strips of insulation. I kept watching the tall thin man out of the corner of my eye. He didn't introduce himself or say anything but he was clearly uncomfortable. Something was off with this guy. Sarah wandered over and asked for a volunteer to help grill the meat. The man seemed eager to be doing something else.

———•••••———

Meantime at Cluck's Chicken Coop Bellamy and Pearl were three hours into a quiet Sunday shift. They were at a back table in the back of the kitchen where employees took their lunch or gravitated like black flies to eat a food order that didn't make it out the serving window.

Pearl dipped a celery stick in ranch sauce while Bellamy chewed on a wing bathed in a super-hot chili pepper sauce. His eyes watered and he gasped before quickly slurping his Mountain Dew.

Pearl laughed, "You do take to a challenge Bellamy."

Two veteran crew members were high-fiving one another and laughing at Bellamy's distress. The assistant manager Juan watched and laughed as well.

In a strained husky voice, Bellamy's eyes still watering, he responded, "Now I know. Try everything at least once, then you know."

The co-workers returned to their stations, Pearl remained.

Bellamy seemed to want to try something else at least once. He fidgeted with his drink straw, twisting it this way and that. Pearl eyed his actions. Bellamy finally threw out a challenge of his own. "Would you go out with a black guy?"

Pearl smiled, "It depends on who the black guy is. Do you have a friend you want to introduce me to, Bellamy?"

Bellamy squirmed, "What if the black guy was me?"

"Well I'm kinda seeing someone right now."

"I saw him here the other day. He's tall. So are you locked in?"

"Not necessarily, I'm still trying to figure him out. We haven't talked about getting serious."

"Then I'm asking. Will you go out with me? There's a new night spot on the beach, Flaming Torches, Mexican food."

Pearl took a last bite of her celery stick. "Hold that thought. Let me give this guy another week. Right now he's still a mystery to me. I'll get back to you. Fair enough?" Bellamy smiled and nodded.

Myrtle popped in shortly after three pm. It was quiet. She invited Pearl to sit with her and quizzed her knowledge of the menu. Pearl had done her homework.

Myrtle then went to the back of the house and asked Bellamy to give the cook times for various chicken dishes.

Bellamy just had to ask, "Why do we need to know cook times when everything has its own timer?"

Myrtle had heard this question dozens of times. She had a stock answer. "Just checking your chicken IQ, Bellamy, I need to know my workers are sharper than the bird in the fryer."

Bellamy chuckled and pointed to number one fryer where a crew member was dropping twenty-four floured pieces.

"Well those birds right there, they need to tan up for four minutes. Just a little lighter than me," he pointed to his forearms.

Myrtle had to smile.

"You want fries with that bird Miss Myrtle, that's three and a half minutes gone from your day."

Myrtle laughed, "Bellamy you certainly have a way with words. You are a smooth operator, you are. Well I've got a party to go to, carry on young man."

Bellamy saluted, winked and flashed a big smile. Myrtle just shook her head.

Myrtle arrived at the future home of George and Lane Whiting at 4:45 pm. She waved to Joel and brought the platter of uncooked wings to the table. Lane welcomed her and put the wings on ice.

Pearl arrived at that same residence at 6:15pm. The workers and their spouses or girlfriends were standing around drinking beer by this time. Smoke was rising from a gas grill loaded with hotdog and hamburgers, turkey burgers, and wings.

Sarah had enlisted Victor to help with the cooking. Victor spotted Pearl. He waved her over.

Myrtle joined them at the grill. "Hey Pearl, I didn't realize you were headed here. I thought I recognized Victor, though."

Pearl, completely unaware of all the potential storm clouds gathering, shrugged, "Small world I guess. Hey Victor I'd have one of those beers if you're offering."

Hailey was in conversation with Lane. "George tells me you have found someone who might be able to help you get well. That sounds encouraging."

Lane explained in a light manner, "It starts with those turkey burgers on the grill." Hailey looked at her quizzically.

Lane chuckled, "If you really want to know I'll gladly tell you all about it."

I had dad in tow and walked him through what I had learned today. Daniel and Teddi tagged along.

Sarah, placed in charge of the food, announced everything was now ready.

Bag chairs surrounded the folding card tables of food. Dad found his way back to one of them and before sitting down raised his beer in salute to all they had accomplished today. "I have contracted out for the finished work. We have too much of our own work to do now, so thank all you guys." He saluted once more. "We'll have another gathering when this place is done. Hopefully within the next six to eight weeks. Now let's eat and drink."

Still standing he found his way to Lane and Hailey who were deep in conversation. He gave his wife a big hug. "I can't wait to share this place with you honey."

Hailey excused herself to go find and feed her son.

Myrtle and Joel sat off to the side watching George and Lane hug. "Look how happy they are. I'd like some of that," said Myrtle.

"If I get through all this I'd like to offer some of that, God willing," uttered Joel.

Myrtle sighed. "I know you're trying Joel."

Victor completed his chore as chef. He and Pearl chowed down on baked beans, burgers, chicken wings, coleslaw and a roll. All washed down with a cold beer.

Pearl asked, "Who is the guy with Myrtle?"

"Joel is Myrtle's boyfriend. He heads my crew." Small talk ended.

For something to say, Victor told Pearl Joel seemed to be in big trouble.

Pearl's eyes widened. "What kind of trouble?" Victor suddenly realized he probably shouldn't have said anything. Pearl was waiting for him to continue.

Like plowing into a main dish you don't recognize but you might be allergic to, it was too late now.

He lowered his voice, "I think he's going on trial for murdering some girl."

Pearl's eyes widened further, "So why is Myrtle still with him?"

"I have no idea. The whole thing is a mess."

"When did this happen?"

Victor was suddenly wary. "I, I, don't really know much about it. Sometime in the fall I think."

"Who found her? Where did they find her?" Pearl wanted answers.

Victor should not have started this conversation. He wanted to stuff something in his mouth besides his foot. His voice lowered still further, "They found her body in a secluded area, that's all I know, really." Victor was beginning to sweat.

Pearl studied Myrtle from a distance. "From the short time I've known her I would say Myrtle doesn't put up with any bullshit. She's a straight shooter. If she's still with him she must think he's innocent. So what's the evidence?"

Victor was squirming inside, He looked left then right, "I'm hearing Joel's blood was found on the girl's clothing." Victor then stuffed his mouth with a roll.

"Hmm." Pearl continued to eat but glanced at Myrtle and Joel occasionally.

Two bag chairs away I watched this large man sweat. I caught enough of the conversation by reading lips to know the man was in trouble with the truth. What truth? I wondered. I went back to eating. I'll figure this all out if I see enough of the man. I needed to talk to my father about all this.

— • — • — • — • —

Just up around the corner on the fourth floor, Franklin and Breanna were sitting on their back balcony sipping a medium priced Malbec. Breanna had closed the wine and cheese portion of the restaurant in Flagler Beach at 6pm. Franklin looked over the top of his wine glass at Breanna and raised a toast. Breanna was becoming quite the little Oenophile, bringing home wines from different regions of the world. Franklin's palette was experiencing different cheeses as well. This early evening a plate of whole grain crackers, grapes and an imported Asiago cheese set before them.

Franklin's world had changed since becoming involved with Breanna. The happiness she brought him, their ease with one another, had worked to soften Franklin's frozen smile. He no longer resembled Chucky from the horror film, a look carried since adolescence that had kept the curious and hostile at bay. Always there had been a part of his heart undernourished.

His Uncle had thawed it out and now Breanna caused it to heat up and beat with abandon. Franklin no longer felt threatened. For the first time in his life he had someone to care for. The new permanent grin that put a twinkle in his eyes was genuine and engaging.

Breanna went inside. She returned with their notes and plunked them down in front of Franklin.

Franklin looked up and sighed, "I think we have about exhausted those, Breanna."

Breanna raised her glass. "I might have one more lead in all this. It came to me this morning. I have been thinking about it all day at work." She went on to explain seeing the tall man leaving the building. A man who did not fit the descriptions of any of the tenants.

Franklin put down his wine glass and popped a grape.

CHAPTER TWENTY-NINE

Dad sat in his home office, mom and I sat beside him. We viewed pictures of the studded and insulated inside walls. When dad began speaking, mom Signed, *It's like they have always been there. But we know how this all began.* One photo after another preserved in plastic like chapter headings, told the story. Clearing the lot, the digging, shaping, rough plumbing, and electrical pipes. <u>Bobby you were here when the men put up the concrete walls and within a week the roof rafters.</u> I pointed to the next photo.

<u>Those roof tiles didn't get up there by themselves.</u> I flipped a plastic sleeve. <u>The doors and windows are all there in this one.</u>

Dad spoke aloud. "Read my lips Bobby, now the hard part begins. You two, along with Sarah when we can capture her, are going to be making most of the decisions." He pointed to a dozen catalogs sitting on the office couch. "The three of you are going to decide what each room will look like. The moldings and trims, built in cabinets, wainscoting, rounded corners, pocket doors, floors, access doors to the pool and lanai. The cabinetry in the kitchen and baths. Are you getting the idea?"

I got most of it.

"That's not all. Paint, window dressings, new and replacement furniture. Paintings and room decorations. I will take care of designing my office and will get the furniture for that. The rest is up to you guys." He finally took a breath, "I have hired out for the finished carpentry" He turned to mom. "I have a designer you can call. They will have ideas as well but I want this to be your house so get busy you two.

Go and find your sister, Bobby." Later that night Sarah and I discussed the last work session and decided not to say anything about their suspicions of Hailey to their dad. She spent most of the day talking with Mom. They seem to like one another.

I nodded, we agreed on that much. I also shared my growing concerns about the tall man and told Sarah I planned to talk to dad about it.

———◆———

Joel went to a court hearing with his lawyer. Joel's lawyer asked for a continuance. The Judge agreed. The trial would start in October. Secretly the Judge was pleased. The damn air conditioning in the courthouse didn't work right half the time. The courthouse was fairly new so the reasons given for the problem didn't hold much weight with the judge. He didn't feel like sweating his ass off for two weeks midsummer though, so October it was. Who knows maybe he could end this thing without the need for a trial. The judge invited the two attorney's into chambers. Joel was left cooling his heels in the corridor.

On the drive back to his lawyer's office it was very quiet in the car. When they were seated in the lawyer's office, he started by offering Joel a cup of coffee and his opening line.

"Joel, we need to talk."

Joel shook away the offer of coffee.

"The investigator hasn't found out anything we didn't already know. We are left with your blood on the victim. The state prosecutor has an offer. Actually the judge suggested the idea."

Joel studied the man's eyes. He had seen this look a dozen times or more when working for his father's company. **This project is not going forward was** always the bottom line. He waited for the shoe to drop.

"If you plead guilty to involuntary manslaughter, the state will recommend five years in prison. No trial just a hearing, with the judge imposing sentence."

"So you are recommending I take this plea?"

"It's your decision. All I can do is give you my professional advice."

"I am not going to admit to a crime I didn't commit. That's my answer."

—••••••—

Franklin was not allowed to have any contact with Joel. He was going to be called as a witness by the state. He was still not sure he wouldn't be charged as an accessory or used as part of an alternative defense. He had told the truth in his deposition which left him open to the whims of the prosecution and the defense. He and Breanna wanted to see the security tapes again but the State had them in their possession.

Franklin contacted the detective who had been to see him. This morning Detective Earl Monroe joined him at a new little donut shop in Flagler Beach named Swillerbees that Breanna had discovered. The donuts were incredible and the coffee was hot and distinctive. Detective Monroe lent an attentive ear but nothing was resolved.

The parting words from the detective made things crystal clear. "If you can come up with something that gives us a legitimate suspect I'll investigate. My boss is not going to let me try to raise reasonable doubt. The state is satisfied they have their man."

An hour later, after a ride north on A1A, the ocean soothing and clearing his mind Franklin was back on his Condo balcony offering Breanna a fresh donut. While Breanna munched on a pumpkin spice donut, Franklin gave her the Reader's Digest version of his conversation with Detective Monroe. "No one else is going to clear Joel."

Breanna listened as Franklin then offered up the beginning of his plan. "First off, I need to find out who this big guy you saw is. Where does he stay in the building? Where does he work?"

Breanna described the clothing she remembered. "He was dressed to do physical labor. A denim shirt unbuttoned and untucked over a tan tee shirt. Dungarees, work boots. He might just have been visiting. This could be another dead end you realize."

"It's the first new bit of information we have. I am going to follow him if he's still here and leaves from here tomorrow morning."

"Be careful Franklin. He's a big guy I don't want you to get hurt."

Franklin hocus-pocused his hands, "With my magic ability, he won't even see me."

"Breanna laughed. "Well I'll nose around the building. See if I can figure out what floor he's staying on at least."

—·—◆—◆·◆—◆·—◆·—

When Victor emerged from the building and closed the door to his car the very next morning, Franklin raised his head. He'd been sitting in his own car for an hour sipping coffee, waiting. He saw a very tall thin man in work clothes, just as Breanna described. He followed Victor at a distance. It was 6:30 am, nighttime grudgingly giving way to another sunny day. Headlights still reached into the shadows.

Victor turned onto Palm Coast Parkway heading west then took a left turn onto Colbert Lane. He drove the length of the road then turned left onto Route 100 towards Flagler Beach.

Driving over the Intercoastal Bridge Franklin was treated to an early morning sun beginning its day bathing in the Atlantic Ocean.

Victor continued to the intersection of Route A1A, he turned right. The damaged and hastily repaired part of this scenic roadway just south of the little city of Flagler Beach devastated by Hurricane Matthew was open again. On the left with the sand dunes and foliage washed away the ocean feigned innocence, offering up a calm gentle moistening of the remaining beach, much as a mother cat washes her young with her tongue.

The Sun with its face washed and about to deliver a full head of orange pink hair stretched and yawned, opening its mouth. A pink tongue emerged from a light cloud cover. Shadows began to disappear in a beam of natures' flashlight like one of Franklin's magic tricks.

Victor oblivious to the man tailing him, yawned along with the sun. Restful sleep had continued to evade him. He sighed as he turned right then pulled into a half constructed two tenant condo building being erected two streets back from the ocean.

A single vehicle was parked on the side of the street. Joel's truck. He pulled in directly behind. He sat there a moment remembering the big boss's stern warning when he'd reached him. 'Don't bring your problems to work Victor. That's the only reminder you'll be getting from me.' Franklin following a hundred yards behind, drove past Victor without staring. He pulled off. He watched him in his rear view mirror as Victor sat there behind the wheel. Finally Victor got out and crossed the road. Franklin noticed the vehicle just beyond Victors. The truck still bore Joel's father's company logo on the hood. Franklin straightened. *Was Joel working with this guy?*

— • — • — • — • —

Hailey studied her eyes in the mirror. To her mind they were her best feature. Though she had to admit she kept herself looking pretty good on all fronts.

"So Why, George?" she asked the mirror. *Cause you can't have him dummy,* the mirror answered silently. To the mirror she made a vow. "I am going to move on before I make a damn fool of myself. George loves his wife and family." She took a deep breath, finished with her make-up and went in to wake her son. The mirror reflected the body language of someone who just made a very unconvincing vow.

—·—•—••—•—·—

Franklin returned to the Condo. Breanna was gone, left to open the wine and cheese shop. Lately she was getting lessons on how to make crepes. The thoughts of fruit filled crepes mingled with the smell of Breanna that filled the condo, Franklin smiled. He added the aroma of fresh coffee then moved to the balcony nursing a second more thoughtful cup than early this morning. He had a lot to think about. He needed to talk to Myrtle.

—·—•—••—•—·—

Cluck's Chicken Coop opened at ten-thirty. Myrtle was early, putting a truck delivery away then doing paperwork. Her mind took a break and she thought of her new employees. *She liked Pearl, she was a quick study and seemed serious.* She could hear her just behind her mini office talking to Abby who was providing her first day of training on preparing salad base. She finished her paperwork and joined the two girls. "How is she doing Abby?" "She's a fast learner. I haven't had to repeat myself." Pearl looked at Myrtle and smiled, "She's a good teacher, boss."

Myrtle asked Abby to go and ready the front of the house for opening.

When Abby left, Myrtle suggested to Pearl that if she liked the work and was serious about it she would consider training her as a crew leader then fast track her to an assistant management position.

"You are a year or two older than most of the workers and it's clear to me, people listen to you. So if you're interested. I can give you an extra five hours a week that we'll use for training. There is a manual that will echo the training I give you. In a month or two I would be willing to send you to corporate, to take a test that certifies you. You pass the test, you'll return with a four dollar an hour raise. Abby is going to college full time next year or she would be getting this offer."

Pearl liked the idea and agreed immediately. The two shook hands. As an afterthought Myrtle added, "Say Pearl, why don't you join my boyfriend and I for dinner some night. I didn't get the opportunity to introduce you the other day."

Pearl nodded her head.

"Okay," announced Myrtle, "let's open up this Coop."

When the doors opened Franklin was the first customer of the day.

Myrtle huddled with Franklin for an hour.

—•—◆—••—◆—•—

A day later Myrtle was at work when Franklin called.

"Did you tell Joel what I saw?"

"Of course I did," said Myrtle. Joel's going to see if his boss George can help narrow things down."

"I hope so. I think I've done about all I can do unless I get some more information. Breanna hasn't had any luck asking other tenants. I do know this guy has a girlfriend. Now that I know who I'm looking at I think I've seen them leaving the building together."

"Is the girl arriving there by herself or is the guy bringing her?

"Good question. They left in his car but I don't know if she drove there. That's something else to figure out. Thanks Myrtle."

CHAPTER THIRTY

Pearl admired the management skills Myrtle used to run a successful business. The Owner of Cluck's Chicken Coop owned a dozen other franchises and was seldom on site. Hiring and firing and running the business day to day was left to Myrtle. Pearl had been hired a short time ago and was already training for a possible assistant manager's position. She was sporting a new management collar shirt and ball cap with a little metal chicken when she entered the building.

Bellamy worked in the back, the cooking part of the restaurant. He had heard rumors that Pearl was being promoted but had not worked with her. Bellamy noted her new wardrobe and fist bumped her offering congratulations. He still had hopes of that maybe in the future date.

Pearl, who had been trained on the sale and customer relations part of the business, was now learning the proper cooking times and placement of the food on the in house plates and to-go boxes. This area was termed back of the house.

The team of four working in the back didn't have time to socialize during the busy middle part of the day or during the evening rush. The morning assistant manager was working the front. Pearl was on the serving line sporting an apron.

Customers began entering the restaurant while others pulled up to drive-thru usually by eleven am. A steady stream of activity for the next three hours saw most workers with heads down and hands moving. It would be 2:30pm before everyone came up for air.

In the back a food table where employees took their break or if working a full shift eat their meal had several cartons of food that were placed there when an order got screwed up. Management tried to keep these mistakes to a minimum since that was profit being consumed.

Myrtle had held a meeting with all employees two days ago on this very subject. She used terminology she had picked up from her boyfriend Joel to explain how to cut down on the waste. She even used the carpenter's creed in her opening statement. "If a carpenter cuts a board too short for the work he's doing, can it be fixed?" She waited for an answer. No one spoke.

"No it can't be fixed, but possibly it can be used somewhere else— eventually."

She moved along the tables and booths making sure no one was checking a phone for messages. This was a voluntary meeting so the employees were off the clock and phones were allowed but were not to be used during the meeting. "With food, a mistake is pretty much forever. Shelf life for a five wing meal and the fries that go with it is what?" She looked at a raised hand that answered correctly. "That's right, fifteen minutes. The owner of this business has a razor thin margin of profit. When a meal ends up on this back table that means somebody failed to read the order correctly or they didn't remove the food from the grill or the fryer on time. Or for you people in the front of the house, possibly putting the wrong order out the window."

She continued moving making sure eyes were following. "My boss has been good about you guys eating the mistakes. But it's been happening way too often in all his business establishments."

She held up a slip of paper. "I just received this memo several days ago. There is a new bottom line." She tapped her chest. "My manager's salary is going to be reflected by his monthly profit and loss reports."

Myrtle went back to the space in the front that allowed her to meet everyone's eyes. "So since every screw-up has the potential to affect my salary we are going to do things differently. My assistants have been briefed on this." She dragged the next line out, "So   if you screw up an order, the assistant manager on duty is going to note the meal involved as well as who screwed up on a shift report." The room squirmed a bit.

"For the time being, the messed up orders will be placed in a container in the office, not on the back table. No more free meals. If taking ownership doesn't get you to measure twice and cut once, different measures will be taken, up to and including dismissal."

She had everyone's attention. "I will review these shift reports every time I work." Myrtle smiled for the first time. "Individually I love all of you but this is my salary we're talking about."

The smile disappeared. "In some cases this could mean your job. It goes right back to the interview we held when you were hired." She met eyes up and down the tables. "Come to work prepared to work your shift with your game face on." She raised her arms. "Now for those of you scheduled to work let's get to work."

——-•••••••——-

A day later Pearl was part of the back of the house crew. The four mistakes sitting in the container in the office came from two separate employees. One was an order that did not get to the right customer in drive-thru.

The three others were caused by Bellamy and his social skills. He did in fact get along with everyone and he was constantly wise cracking and thoroughly enjoying their responses. Pearl watched, removed the mistakes and noted them on the shift report. Twice she had tried in a nice way to tell Bellamy to tend to business.

When things quieted she asked him to join her in the office. She asked the other assistant manager on duty to be there. She pointed down at the wing meal with the wrong sauce. Then she lifted the salad with the tomatoes and cucumbers that had specifically been ordered with no tomatoes and cucumbers. Finally she opened the carton of twenty boneless wings that were overcooked.

Bellamy looked a little sheepish. "We were really busy." He tried to socialize his way out of this.

"What were the numbers Pearl? I bet we had three five hundred dollar hours."

"If you really want to know those numbers I'll get them for you. But those three meals laying there won't be part of the numbers, will they?"

"You sound like Myrtle right now," Bellamy tried to kid. The other assistant manager, Juan, spoke up. "Myrtle told me that each mistake takes up to four sales to cover."

"So," offered Pearl, not missing a beat, "sixteen of the meals we sold just disappeared, Bellamy. Do you follow that?"

Bellamy said nothing.

Pearl showed him where she had entered his name beside the three meals. "I haven't looked at any of the other shift logs Bellamy but I hope for your sake you aren't listed on any of them."

Bellamy squirmed, knowing well his past transgressions. "Can't you cut me a little slack Pearl, that damn salad could have been saved." He pleaded, "I thought we were friends. Your new shirt and hat change that?"

Pearl steeled her eyes. "Nope it didn't but I have a job to do just like you do. And I'm going to do mine." Pearl thought that would be the end of it.

A little later Bellamy returned to the office where Pearl was counting the tills for the shift change. Pearl really didn't have time for any more discussion.

Bellamy started.

Pearl put up her hand. "No more Bellamy." She met his eyes. "By the way we can't go any further in a relationship either. Now that I am in management I can't be seeing an employee socially. That's another rule Myrtle shared."

The environment darkened, a different side of Bellamy emerged. His voice changed, deepened, he began shaking. "My name there three times probably gets me gone Pearl. I think you should consider erasing it. I need this job."

Pearl noted the tone, "I'm sorry Bellamy but I can't. I'm just following orders. Don't be upset with me."

Bellamy's true personality emerged in the form of a smart ass comment, "It's you with the eraser. Wouldn't take but a second."

Pearl shook her head, "Not going to happen Bellamy." They eyed one another.

Bellamy went rigid. He whipped off his apron, throwing it in Pearl's direction. Sputtering to no one in particular he headed for the back door. He turned, "Don't think I'm going to forget this Pearl. You'll see me around." The back door slammed.

Several employees gathered. "We heard him threaten you Pearl." Pearl shrugged, "Oh he was just angry in the minute. It's fine."

When Myrtle arrived she seemed distracted. Pearl let the incident with Bellamy sit.

She finally caught up with her in the hour before the shift change. "I need to tell you what happened with Bellamy." They sat in a corner booth. Pearl explained the situation and Bellamy's sudden departure. Myrtle just listened. "I had a lot on my mind I guess. I didn't even realize he was on shift." Then she nodded. "I'm not surprised he bolted. He's a nice kid but way too social. His name is on every shift report he worked. He probably figured when I saw today's report I was going to send him packing anyway." She sighed. Did he threaten you?"

"Nah, I don't think so. He was angry that I wouldn't erase his name and that I wouldn't be able to see him socially now that I'm management. It was all too much for him I guess."

Myrtle nodded again. She raised her brow. "You were considering that?" Pearl shrugged.

Myrtle put on her game face. "Well for the last hour of your shift, go through the applications on my desk and schedule some interviews for Friday afternoon." She made to get up and leave the booth.

Pearl had noticed a difference in Myrtle today. "Are you okay, you seem to be somewhere else?"

Myrtle considered for a moment then decided. She continued out of the booth. "Let me get you a soft drink. I need to share something with someone but promise me this won't go any further."

With the Styrofoam cup of Mountain Dew sitting in front of Pearl, Myrtle looked out the window as if gathering her thoughts from the white puffy clouds that appeared. "You probably saw me with my boyfriend Joel at the cook out. You haven't met him. I'm sure you heard the story though, right?"

Pearl nodded.

"Well I've seen him at his worst and I don't believe he would ever hurt anyone." She shifted gears, "Anyway Joel has this friend. Actually he's my friend too. This friend was with him on the day the girl disappeared. Did you know she once worked here for me?"

Pearl shook her head.

"So Joel's friend, he's going to be called by the state to testify that he and Joel were with the girl on that day. Since he's a witness the state says he can't have any contact with Joel. So this friend is trying to find out what really happened on his own. He came to see me the other day. He's found a possible new suspect. The problem is the state thinks that Joel did it and won't give him any help. So now I'm the go between for Joel and our friend. Are you following all this?"

Pearl nodded.

Myrtle lowered her voice even further. "Here's the part you can't talk about. It may be a dead end anyway. Joel's friend followed this guy to work the other morning and the man parked right behind Joel's truck." Myrtle nodded her head. "Weird right?"

Pearl was totally confused. She didn't know whether to nod or shake her head. She just sat there.

"Anyway that's kind of where it's been left at the moment. We're stymied. I told Joel but he has no idea who we might be talking about. There are a lot of men coming and going on his crew. And he changes crews as well. Franklin is going to try to get a better description. All he saw was a tall guy. It was early morning when he followed the guy."

Myrtle sighed, "Joel is depressed but determined. They are offering him a plea deal but he's not going to take it. He says he's innocent and I believe him."

Myrtle sighed again, "Stressful times." She sighed and got up to go back to work.

Pearl remained seated. And I thought I had problems. Three hours later those little problems Pearl was thinking about, well they got magnified tenfold.

CHAPTER THIRTY-ONE

Bellamy, fuming, left Cluck's and went directly to a sports bar off Palm Coast Parkway. He found an empty booth just at the end of the bar. Golf was dominating the two big screens and Bellamy absolutely hated golf. He sat there by himself. He ordered, received, and sat nursing a beer feeling sorry for himself. Studying the liquid in his glass between sips it was revealed that all women were bitches. He toasted this revelation, his half-filled glass raised to the air. A waitress seeing the gesture assumed Bellamy wanted another and promptly delivered it to his table along with some peanuts. All smiles, the girl offered, "Would you like me to take that glass for you sir?"

Bellamy who hadn't knowingly ordered another beer, looked at the remaining amber and shook his head. Anger from earlier resurfacing. "Are you stupid or what?"

The girl with no clue why Bellamy would say something like that to her, said nothing. Her face betrayed her though.

Bellamy softened, "I was just toasting you ladies. I haven't finished this one yet." Then he smiled, "I'll take those peanuts though," then he winked, "so it wasn't a wasted trip." The girl turned on her heel.

"By the way, could you change the channel? I hate golf." Bellamy, alone once again, began pondering payback. His job was gone. Any chance with Pearl was over. Right in this minute he'd love to screw with Pearl's head, the self righteous bitch. He signaled for another beer. This time the waitress ignored him. All bitches for sure.

He was about to go to the bar and complain. He stood up. He saw a guy walk to the bar and sit down. Damned if it wasn't Pearl's boyfriend. A thought struck him. *Hmm maybe payback comes early this year. Let me think this through.* Bellamy had seen enough drama to know that rumors can start with just a nugget of truth.

He turned and grabbed his nearly empty glass and the peanuts and walked to the bar. He sat down beside Victor. He nodded hello to the glance Victor gave him and took a long swallow, finishing his beer.

Looking at the mirror behind the bar he spoke straight ahead. "I have seen you with Pearl."

Victor looked his way. "Are you speaking to me?"

"Yeah, you're with Pearl, right? I've seen you at the chicken place."

Victor took a pull on his beer, "Yup that's me, what about it?"

"Oh nothing." Bellamy asked the bartender for another beer. He nursed it, finding his way. Then he spoke. "None of my business really." He took another swallow. Victor looked his way.

"I mean it's probably innocent as hell. Just kidding around probably."

Victor turned in his seat.

Bellamy, facing a full audience of attention, finished up. "Don't take offense but if she was my girl I'd be pissed."

Victor's face darkened, his voice rose, "I think you better spell this out for me buddy, I don't like what you're saying."

"Ok. Ok. Only since you ask." Bellamy took another drink. "Pearl has been coming on to an assistant manager who works there. I just left there." He returned to his beer. Neither man spoke.

Bellamy broke the silence. "One guy to another I thought you might want to know that's all." Like the lyrics of a song you just can't get out of your head Bellamy spoke the chorus, "She'll deny it but all us workers, we see it." Bellamy waited a couple of beats allowing Victor to replay the song in his head.

"Anyway I got to get going. Just a heads up that's all." Bellamy slid off the stool and left Victor with a dozen peanuts and as many questions.

⸻ ● ⸺ ● ⸻

Franklin and Breanna sitting on their balcony witnessed a car come barrel assing into the parking lot tires squealing.

Victor, who had been imagining the worst for the past hour and a half while fueling those thoughts with alcohol, slammed his car door and weaved towards the front entrance.

Franklin immediately went to the elevator and punched the down button. When the elevator door opened Franklin managed to get off and walk away in a different direction just as Victor reached the lobby. Franklin waited then turned back around to watch the lights as they moved upward. The elevator stopped on floor six.

Another hour passed. Franklin and Breanna spent that hour trying to figure out their next move since they had narrowed their mystery man to the top floor. A different car came squealing into the parking lot. This time it was a young woman. She too seemed on a mission.

"I think that might be the girl I've seen with that guy."

"Let me go this time." Breanna rushed to the elevator and pushed the down button. Not as quick as Franklin, she was still in the elevator when Pearl reached the lobby and they met face to face. Neither spoke. Breanna remained in the lobby as Pearl closed the door and pushed the button to floor six.

Breanna, back on the balcony reported that the girl did not look happy.

—·—••—◆—••—·—

Two floors above Victor was getting an earful from a girl who didn't appreciate being called at work and accused of being a slut and a whore. It had been a short conversation on the phone with Pearl hanging up; but not before telling Victor she was coming over to set the record straight and pick up a sweater she had left.

"So you believed that little prick without even talking to me." Pearl shook her head. "I knew you were insecure but this is ridiculous."

Victor, feeling the full effects of the two whiskeys and beer chasers he guzzled at the bar and a double-double shot he poured from his father's stash since getting home, was having trouble focusing. He managed, "I'm sorry Pearl. I should have known better."

"That's the best you can do." Pearl began looking for the sweater.

"Can't you give me another chance?" Victor slurred. He was hanging his head, two droopy unfocused red eyes blinking rapidly." He reached deeper. "You are the first girl I have ever really cared about."

Pearl didn't seem convinced. "Where did you put my sweater?"

"Please Pearl he sputtered," trying to rise but failing. He continued, "I do trust you." He managed to get to his feet. His body language mimicking his frog brain he wavered then staggered. He held up one finger, eyes not focusing. "Listen, I'll prove it." Somehow he managed to get in front of Pearl. He whispered with a finger over his lips, "I'll tell you something no one else knows."

Pearl didn't bite.

"It's about Myrtle's boyfriend." He looked at Pearl. He had her attention now. He needed to focus his mind. "I do trust you and love you." He reached out for her once again. He was feeling the full effects of his drinking and nearly vomited.

Pearl repulsed, moved away.

Victor took two deep breaths trying to clear his head. Hesitating, not sure of what he wanted to say.

Pearl spoke. "Give it up Victor." She continued her search. Victor touched her shoulder.

Pearl turned exasperated, "Ok Victor, what about Myrtle's boyfriend?"

Victor focused, spoke quietly, his mouth slack, "I saw something."

"You saw something Victor?" Pearl eyed the drunken fool. "Well that clears up everything!" Pearl felt along the couch and located her sweater under a cushion. She turned and was about to leave.

Victor struggled to gather his thoughts. "I, I, mean on the day that girl was killed."

Pearl shook her head from side to side. This was all ridiculous. "How did you see something Victor? I thought they found her in the woods?" She didn't even want an answer, moving towards the door as she spoke.

Victor managed, "It didn't happen in the woods. It happened here. In this building!"

In spite of herself Pearl was interested. She turned her head back around.

Victor, frog brain in control continued in a slurred voice, "Please Pearl, sit down, let me explain. He was struggling trying to create in the moment. "I was on the balcony. It was just getting dark." Pearl in spite of herself sat down.

His lips puffed with the effort he was making. "I thought I heard something."

Pearl was losing her patience.

"I looked down and saw someone lugging something in a blanket out of the building." That one complete sentence was all he could manage before closing his eyes. He slumped back into the couch.

Pearl began to rise.

Victor felt the movement and opened his eyes and his mouth. "The guy looked around like he was nervous, he looked right up at me." Victor wasn't feeling well and had to grab his head. Three deep breaths later he continued, "I didn't know Joel at the time."

Pearl's ears took that name in. She remembered a recent conversation with Myrtle.

One final burst then Victor sunk back into the cushion. "When I started working with him I realized he was the guy I saw that night." He opened his eyes as wide as he could manage. "It might have been that girl."

Pearl pounced all over that. "What makes you think it was the girl? And why haven't you told anyone?"

Victor sighed, "I didn't know what was in the rug." Then I didn't want to get involved. I still don't." He belched and reached for Pearl's hand. "I'm only telling you this so you know how much I love and trust you." He reached deep for sincerity. He searched for her eyes. "You can't tell anyone."

Pearl allowed Victor to take her hand.

"I'm really sorry Pearl." His eyes half closed summoning real tears. "I didn't think someone would just come up to me at a bar and spread lies like that." He bristled, "When I see him again he's dead meat."

"Forget about Bellamy, Victor." She stared him straight in those blurred eyes. "You do realize you are breaking the law yourself, don't you? God. Victor you might be a witness to a murder."

She offered up another scenario, "They could charge you for withholding information. And what about Myrtle? She might be dating a murderer."

Victor sighed aloud. A slowly deflating balloon. He belched more air. He melted into the cushion. The liquor in his system was making one last run at taking over his brain.

Pearl began talking to herself aloud. "Myrtle believes he's innocent. Someone has to warn her." Pearl removed her hand from Victor's.

Victor's eyes, struggling to focus, snapped open. He was already regretting his decision. He began wringing his hands, stammering, "Well we-we can't, I-I can't, I shouldn't have said anything." His frog brain was in free fall. 'They-They have enough evidence anyway." Somehow he found his next line. "They charged him, didn't they?" Victor was in distress, he tried to hug her.

Pearl shrugged him away. "You have to tell someone Victor." Then she took him by both arms and looked at him. "Or I don't know you at all." Seconds elapsed. "If you don't say something I'm going to."

Victor, his brain absorbing this new threat as fatal, began to panic.

"Bu-Buutt Pearl." He suddenly felt like vomiting. He tried to breathe but a tightness in his chest had him gasping. Spots appeared in front of his eyes. He nodded forward.

Pearl her mouth set, seemed to be waiting for a response.

Victor looked into her eyes. Resolve rested there. There was no way out. The red in his eyes suddenly glowed a different shade. He slowly nodded his head in unison. He had reached an agreement, not with Pearl but rather himself. Resignation.

Alcohol continued to cloud his thought process. He was panicking on the inside but he'd been down this road before.

He reached for a hug. His father entered his mind. Thoughts as fleeting as flipped channels offered added confusion to the fog. Victor wrapped his arms around Pearl.

Thinking Victor was in submission she hugged him back. Victor's squeeze intensified.

Pearl couldn't get her breath. Victor began crying silently into Pearl's hair even as he continued to squeeze.

Pearl began melting into nothingness. She tried desperately to free herself. She was a strong girl.

The vise tightened. Her efforts produced squeaks from the leather cushions. Victor was not letting up.

She squirmed, tried to scream. There was no air. No window open to betray even the one feeble squeaky noise that barely made it past her lips. It all happened so fast. Total darkness descended.

Victor lay for a long time on the sofa with Pearl on top of him, his legs and arms wrapped and locked. Neither had closed their eyes.

Later from the edge of the dimly lit parking lot a quiet pair of eyes witnessed a rug being carried from the building by a shadow monster.

CHAPTER THIRTY-TWO

Two nights ago in the driveway of our new house mom grilled organic turkey burgers paired with a fresh salad. After eating, Sarah and I played outside while mom thumbed through her vision of a color scheme for the kitchen, family room and downstairs bath. We had Teddi chasing a ball till he saw something else to chase. That rabbit took one look at us kids, then spied Teddi. He perked up its ears and bolted. Teddi tensed then took off after it. Sarah hollered to come back but Teddi paid no attention. Sarah immediately ran in to tell mom and dad.

I ran after Teddi.

It was getting dark. Mr. Rabbit zigged and zagged from sidewalk to foliage and back to the sidewalk.

I tried to keep Teddi in sight. I reached the parking lot of a large building and stopped to catch my breath. I couldn't see either Teddi or the rabbit.

Mr. Rabbit came back into view hopping between automobiles, Teddi following. Teddi was hot on the heels of Mr. Rabbit and it seemed like they were just playing tag, appearing then disappearing from view.

Suddenly a long shadow stretched out over the parking lot. The shadow was carrying something over its shoulder. When the shadow shrunk and became a man he stopped behind a parked car. I hugged a Palm tree and watched. Teddi and the rabbit continued their game. I know Teddi was barking because I could see his jaws moving.

When the man reached the rear of the car he fumbled in his pocket for keys. The trunk opened and a light melted the darkness. The man looked back over his shoulder. I saw his face, I thought I recognized him. The man shifted what looked like a rug from his shoulder to his arms.

Teddi appeared, zigging when he should have been zagging and ran into the shadow man's legs. The man reacted by nearly dropping the rug. The man was one of dad's workers. The one I didn't care for. The man kicked at Teddi. Then I knew for sure. Teddi retreated barking. The man looked around then but I stayed hidden.

Teddi made his way back onto the sidewalk and I followed. Teddi was done in, tough work chasing rabbits. Mom and Dad and Sarah were making their way down the sidewalk to find us.

I'm not sure why I didn't tell my parents about the shadow man. I was confused about it. All the way back everyone was scolding Teddi and I didn't really know what it all meant anyway.

After the excitement, back in our old house, routine set in. Mom and Dad sat across from one another at the kitchen table sipping wine. Magazines and brochures littered the table, the new house their main topic. We did our homework, Teddi was asleep on a rug. We took showers and went to bed.

The part of the excitement not shared at the time remained in my head. I laid awake.

My sister and I had not discussed the strange man who worked for dad since observing him at the company workday. Nothing much had happened on that day. Daniel and I had spent most of the day in hard hats inspecting the job. But I couldn't get what I had seen tonight out of my mind. I should be able to figure this out. I mean I can read blueprints. There was something strange about that rug. There was something in that rug. I played it again in my mind. *A big man and a strong man, but he seemed to buckle when he shifted the load and placed the rug in the trunk. I need to talk to Sarah, maybe dad too. Morning will be soon enough.*

Dad was beginning to whistle again, a direct result of mom seeming to be feeling better. Whether it was her taking charge of her health issue or the change in what we were all eating? Didn't matter. She was up in the morning with dad, and awake when he came home. She was even getting dressed and putting on make-up. I heard the news through my sister. Mom was not going back to work as a teacher. I asked her about it.

<u>I have decided to focus on our family and my health. I'm going to teach in a different way.</u> I liked that idea.

Sarah and I were still in bed when my parents had the following conversation.

"Well I told you a while back to stop working so hard. What are you going to do? I don't see you hanging around the house all day."

Mom finished chewing her granola. "You are right about that. One thing I am going to do is start a blog."

"What in hell is a blog?"

"It's me writing on the computer. It can be through Facebook or some other online site. I am going to start writing about how we deal with bad things that happen to us. I got the idea when I was researching with that natural healer. I am going to do research then offer advice on different ways to face life's challenges. It is going to be inspirational. At least I hope it is, a once a week message. At least that is my intent."

"Well let me be the first to react. I have a problem and I don't know how to handle it."

Mom eyed him warily, wondering if dad was making light of her announcement.

"I'm not kidding. It's Joel. He came to me. Here's the problem." Dad explained how Joel thought one of the men on his crew might have some information about the girl who was murdered. He didn't know which crew member it was and he didn't even know if the guy had any real information but it was his last best hope. Joel was hoping I could do some digging. He's asking for addresses, phone numbers, and references for every crew member. Remember I move guys from crew to crew on a daily basis based on the skill required on that job for that day. We're talking about fifty guys. I told him I'd consider it but it would take time. Betty is right out straight."

"Well George, that was quite a mouthful. My short answer is anything you can do to help Joel is the thing to do. Now that being said, here is where I might really be able to help. I'm not working. I would be glad to come into the office and gather that information for you."

Dad smiled. "That's a great idea and then I can take you to lunch." Dad smiled again. Win-win.

Mom returned the smile. "See how this problem solving can work."

Dad got up and put water in his cup, placing it in the sink. He began whistling. "I'll see you at the office."

CHAPTER THIRTY-THREE

Lane opened the door to her husband's new office. Betty was working at her desk. "Hey Betty. Did George tell you I would be in?"

Betty nodded. "Lane, it's so good to hear that you're feeling better. George told me all you have been through. He loves you a lot, girl. I knew you were feeling better though." Lane cocked her head in a how did you know that manner?

Betty, who was a bit of a mind reader herself responded, "You can imagine how quiet it has been around here without George's whistle. George is whistling again. That's how I knew." She laughed aloud. "I have the employee folders in a pile on George's desk, so have at it. Would you like a cup of coffee?"

Lane held up a thermos of herbal tea. "Nope. I have one of the reasons for feeling better right here with me." She slid into George's chair and began looking through the files. She had no real idea what she was looking for but had been at it an hour when Hailey entered the office. She seemed surprised to see Lane at George's desk.

"Hey Hailey I'm glad you popped in. Maybe you can help me here. I'm trying to narrow down who might have been on Joel's crew a week ago."

Hailey looked at her quizzically. Then she frowned. That was followed by a look that was unreadable. As she pulled up a chair she suddenly brightened.

"You look like you're feeling better." The frown reappeared when she voiced, "I'm surprised George didn't ask me to do this. I'm the one who would know how to find what you're looking for."

"He was just giving me something productive to do with my time I guess."

Hailey sat down and slowly began to relax. She would run her concerns by George when she saw him. Hailey began by explaining how crews were divided. "We usually have a set crew of men working a job unless we need someone with a special talent. Or if we're behind on a job and want to lend a hand to the project. Some guys are better at finishing carpenters than others. So those would be times when we might move people around."

She organized the folders in piles according to which foreman they normally worked with. She then turned back to Lane. "Do you have a specific date in mind? Every night the job foreman lets George and I know what they are going to be doing the next day. If they are going to need something or someone special they would put that in an email. George and I both see the emails but I am the one who moves workers around."

Lane thought that made sense. She looked at the note George had given her. The date and day of the week was listed. She gave that information to Hailey.

Hailey went to her computer. "I could search this on my smart phone but, since I'm here." She opened the folder. "Okay, on that date Joel's crew was larger than normal. His regular crew of four plus three others." She explained. The job was a little behind so we sent three extra men to do drywall in the two units. Besides Joel there were seven men who would have been working putting up drywall."

"Can you help me pull those men's files?"

"Certainly. Do you mind telling me what we're looking for?"

Lane placed her hands on the arms of the office chair. "George says we may be helping Joel. That's all I really know."

Hailey was beginning to fume. She tried to mask her feelings. "Well let's get to it. Always good to keep the boss happy," Hailey said with a tight little smile. Hailey felt left out. *Why hadn't George come to her with this? She would be the one to know how to gather the information.* Her face and furtive movements revealed frustration.

Lane observed Hailey's body language. *Hmm. Something has set her off.*

Lane called George. She was feeling stronger and energized for a while now. As the new house entered the finished work stage they had brought the grill and stored it in the garage. The family was spending more and more time there in the evening. The house was already becoming a home. "Hailey is helping me out. I should have something tonight.

Why don't you pick up some fresh fish at Flagler Fish Market and I will Panko it up. You can grill it with some fresh carrots and asparagus. We'll foil up some sliced red potatoes, onions and fresh Parmesan cheese."

"Will do. That sounds delicious. I'll meet you and the kids at the new house around six. Love ya."

Lane checked her watch. "I would say lunch is a no go." George agreed.

• — • ◆ • • ◆ • — •

Myrtle had arrived early to put away stock and get the business open. Abby arrived within the hour. Pearl was late. Myrtle checked her watch, fifteen minutes late to be exact. *Had she made a mistake with this girl?* "Go ahead and make the salads, Abby, we'll continue training Pearl another time. Another half hour passed before Myrtle dialed Pearl's cell phone. It rang but then went to voicemail. Myrtle left a message. "Pearl we were expecting you an hour ago. Please let me know if you won't be here for your shift. I'll have to call someone in."

Juan, an assistant manager, showed up for his shift and Myrtle told him Pearl hadn't come in or called. "I'm surprised, she seemed really excited about the promotion." Juan cupped his chin. "Is this her first shift since she had trouble with that boy the other day?"

Myrtle nodded. "Why?"

"Well she was mad as hell at someone when she left that day. I think it might have been Bellamy. She was screaming over the phone and I heard his name in the conversation a couple of times. She stormed out of here."

Myrtle became all business. "Well check the list of people not working and see if you can get someone to come in. I'll deal with this later."

— ❖ ❖ ❖ —

George was having lunch with Hailey the day after Lane had asked her to help. She seemed distant, but George had learned a long time ago not to probe. To his mind it was like the hunting he'd done with his grandfather. **'You are the tree George, when the prey want to make themselves known to you they will. Be patient.'**

The two sat looking over menus. Hailey had said nothing since sitting down. They ordered. Still nothing. The food arrived.

Enough with the patience, thought George, "Thanks for helping my wife with that search. Between the two of you I have what I need." Pretty innocent opener.

Hailey took a breath. She looked directly at George, shook her head, but said nothing.

George eyed his garden salad, "Good looking salad, I'm glad you suggested the place."

"Em hmm."

To hell with his grandfather. George did not want to spend the next thirty minutes in silence. He thought, *at least I can sign with my son.* "What's troubling you Hailey?"

It all came out in a gully washer. Hailey's eyes began leaking even before she opened her mouth. "I thought we were on the same team, George." George watched the flood in amazement.

"I come into the office and find Lane doing my job. I have no idea what she's looking for or why." Hailey used her napkin to wipe away tears. "Has Bobby told you something? Are you going to fire me George?" She continued to unravel.

George would have used words if he had any.

"I'm worn out George. I see your house going up and your business growing and your perfect family and in the end there's no place for me." Hailey had the napkin covering most of her face. George found his voice.

"I don't pretend to understand women. Everything you just said is true in one way or another." Then he added with emphasis, "Except the part about firing you." George shook his head, baffled. "And what's Bobby got to do with anything?" He shook his head, "I'm going back to work and when you can tell me what you mean by any and all of this I'll listen. For now this conversation is like a board with a knot hole in it that we need to discard."

He stood up, threw his napkin and a twenty dollar bill on the table. "Take the rest of the day off."

Hailey sat there with a damp napkin on her lap realizing she had just had an emotional breakdown. She sat at the table long after George left. She spun the drink straw in her iced tea, stirring up all kinds of stuff. *All these feelings she had for George were never going to be reciprocated. They couldn't be. And George was blind to her feelings. Why wouldn't he be? Christ I'm a mess.* She didn't take the afternoon off, she went to talk with maybe the one person who would understand.

Franklin had not seen the girl at the condo for several days. It was possible she arrived without Franklin seeing her but he had been pretty much watching. The man had not appeared from his Condo either and his vehicle wasn't in the lot. Maybe they left on a trip together. Franklin and Breanna both kept watch when they weren't at work. Nothing seemed to be happening. Franklin called Myrtle. "Any news on who this guy might be?"

Myrtle sounded distressed, "George told Joel he would call when he has something. That's where it was left."

"Myrtle, your voice sounds a little harsh. I've heard that voice before when you were having trouble with Joel. Is everything ok?"

"Just the usual employee problems, sorry Franklin but I have had to pull a double the last couple of days."

When George arrived from work, Lane asked him to draw up a bag chair. "Hailey came to see me."

George was about to ask why when a different topic was raised by his children. Sarah and Teddi had moved from throwing a ball to practicing fetch the stick.

I came over to talk to dad. I wasn't sure where to begin. I decided to remind dad how I sometimes could see through a problem like a blueprint. Dad acknowledged his son's insight had been valuable. <u>Well there's something wrong with one of your workers. The other night when Teddi chased that rabbit, I saw a man put something in the trunk of a car. Dad he was like a shadow monster. I was scared.</u>

<u>Who are we talking about?</u>

<u>He's really tall and nervous looking. He sweats a lot. I think he must live in that big building.</u>

George immediately thought of Victor Thornton. That was a name in the folder he had brought home as well. He lived in his father's condo. <u>So what are you telling me?</u>

<u>I don't know dad, just that he's weird I guess. He tried to kick Teddi. He's not a good person.</u>

<u>Ok son I'll keep my eyes open.</u>

Supper was delicious. We kids retreated once more to the lawn while mom and dad sat in bag chairs sipping an after dinner wine. I ran over and Signed to watch Teddi's latest trick. Teddi rolled over when I made a circle with the stick he was holding. Parent applause. We wandered away chasing our puppy.

George had the folder on his lap. He remembered what Bobby had told him earlier. Victor had been acting strangely at work. George remembered Joel telling him a friend had followed the worker in question from a Condo building in the C section. George decided tomorrow he would call Victor's father.

When George got home he checked his email. There was a message from Hailey. One of the workers had not shown up for the past two days. She thought George should know. Victor Thornton had not been at work. Did George want her to try to reach him?

This is getting weird, thought George. George e-mailed back. He'd take care of it. When George returned to the living room Lane had one more bit of news.

"George, Hailey confided in me. She's agreed to resign if you want her to."

George's eyes widened. "What? We had a really weird lunch. She cried her eyes out and I have no idea why?"

"George, for a smart man you are pretty dense." George, the woman is in love with you. She asked me to forgive her."

George's eyes bugged out, "She told you that?!"

"She did and she is going to do her best to get over you. She loves our family and wouldn't do anything to hurt us." George was left speechless.

Lane smiled. "I hugged her and held her and told her to get in line. Everybody has always loved George, I told her."

George appeared exasperated, "You don't think I encouraged any of this do you?"

Lane took George's hand. "Of course not." She looked him in the eyes. She smiled. "Actually I'm a little flattered that I have the man who would grace the cover of Carpenter's Quarterly, if there were such a publication."

George took a deep breath. "So, should I keep her on?" "Of course you should. Hailey may be a little sheepish around you for a few days but that will fade."

CHAPTER THIRTY-FOUR

Victor came to a final decision shortly after he made it back to his condo on foot. He was shaken to the core. He showered, trying to remove the self-disgust from his body. Had he forgotten anything? In his mind he had loved Pearl. He began to cry. With water cascading down and his eyes squeezed tight, segments of what happened just hours ago emerged. *Laying there till his mind cleared. His body cramping. Pearls' warmth melting away. The physical effort of getting Pearl down six floors using the stairs to avoid the camera. It was nighttime dark when he made it to the parking lot. He stayed in the shadows as best he could while making his way to Pearl's car. He had just opened the trunk when that damn little dog had him nearly dropping Pearl. He had slammed the trunk and heart racing, made it to the roadway.* When the shower turned cold he stepped out and wrapped himself in a towel. In bed his head banging against the head-board again and again, Victor began to cry once more. The movie continued as if being shown in installments.

He traveled west on Palm Coast Parkway. The first two lights he passed through were green. The third light moved from red to green keeping him moving. A major intersection loomed ahead. When the left turning arrow lit, his decision was made. Old Kings Road south was a two lane road Victor drove quite often on his way to or from some of the jobs.

Suddenly blue flashing lights screamed in his rear view. Victor swallowed hard and pulled to the side of the road. Two cruisers were upon him in seconds. He lowered his head. Caught.

The cruisers blew by him headed for wherever. Victor took a deep breath, he hadn't been found out. He felt a warmth between his legs, he had wet himself.

He got himself under control and pulled back onto the darkened roadway. A fully rounded moon was just now rising above the treeline.

Remembering a biking and hiking trail just up ahead— Graham Swamp, he turned into the small dirt parking lot. There were no other vehicles. He got out, closed the door and looked up directly into the face of the man in the moon. A sour sweat smell mixed with the odor of urine reached his nostrils.

His eyes remained two black holes. He took a deep breath remembering those fifty yard sprints at the end of practice he hated so much; and his coach's words: 'You'll thank me in the second half, men.' Well this wasn't the second half, this was game over if he didn't get this done. He removed Pearl's body, hoisting the rug over his shoulder and in the moonlight followed the path. The rutted well worn path challenged every step, the moon appeared only fleetingly as the jungle swallowed him whole. Night sounds real and imagined entered his head. He didn't really have a destination; he just knew somewhere out here he had to leave Pearl's body.

The jungle was as solid as a barricade. The moon light entered through small breaks in the blackness. A tree rose on his left. The moon sitting on a middle branch, watching. A break in the jungle to the tree's right. He stopped. He worked his way to the back of a large thick plant. He laid Pearl on the ground and tried to think.

His breath was ragged from exertion, trauma, and earlier drinking. OK then. One more fifty yard sprint. He rolled Pearl's body from the rug directly under the dense foliage. He took the rug with him, he would leave it in a construction dumpster. She was bound to be found here within days but he would be gone later tonight.

He stood. Several bats dive bombed him, scaring the bejeesus out of him. He nearly wet himself again. He ended that threat by relieving himself. Back on the pathway he found his way back to Pearl's car.

His mind demanded a break. He slowly got dressed. Absently he threw just the barest of clothing into a duffle bag. He toyed with the idea of leaving a message for his father. Then he decided what a perfect message to his father would look like. He closed the door on his past and headed toward an unknown future.

He sat a full five minutes in the Condo parking lot before starting the engine. *His mind jumped from what at any other time might be a comment on —what a lovely evening this is — to the last time he watched a* **Forty-Eight Hours** *murder mystery trying to figure out who dunnit? Then he drove. Drove, drove, drove, thinking—thinking— thinking. Just as he had left his home in Pennsylvania it was now time to land somewhere else. It was only a matter of time before the girl would be missed. His bosses would be calling about his absence from work. It was public knowledge he had been seeing the girl.* He banged his hand against the steering wheel over and over. *And his father- Christ his father- he'd go bonkers.* Nearing Jacksonville, heading north, light traffic, with no one challenging a lane change or the speed he was traveling, the movie in his head, as if he'd left the room to get popcorn, started again.

After depositing the body he had arrived back in Palm Coast after twenty miles of oblivion wrestling with how best to get rid of Pearl's car. A mile from his condo, he saw a sign, **Home For Sale By Owner.** *It was deserted. Something registered.*

Something his father had told him in one of his rare moments of sharing, complaining really, about a lost sale. **'Home For Sale By Owner** *is a fool's errand. Unless you get lucky you'll still be the owner a year from now.' Victor drove past slowly. No one was living here. There was a big lock on the front door. He backed into the driveway. With the number plate on the back, Pearl's car would be hiding in plain sight.*

As the sign announcing **Georgia On Your Mind** welcomed him to the Peach state. The last six hours had left Victor's mind, empty and limp with exertion. He pulled off the highway into a business closed for the night and slept. When he awoke he got back on the highway and opened his window. He flipped the piece of plastic off into the bushes.

The next morning George called Victor's father. "I thought you should know Victor hasn't been to work for two days. He's not here this morning either. Something seems to be going on that you might want to check on. Just a heads up. Have him call me. We need to talk."

Mr. Thornton hung up and finished dressing. His eyes were a mess. He was beginning to look his age for Christ sake. He found one of the buttons on his dress shirt broken. He removed it and threw it on the bed. Damn laundry people. Damn Victor. *Damn it all to hell. He was going to give him a dressing down and send him packing.*

His hands shook he was so angry. He couldn't get his Windsor knot to balance and in a fit of anger ripped it off. He changed shirts, throwing on a tropical print. Deciding in the moment, *frig it. I'm taking the day off myself. I'd probably lose a half dozen clients if I went in today. Damn that Victor.*

When he arrived at the condo, a speech and anger all playing out in his head he was greeted by silence. He opened the blinds. He raised the window to clear the stale air and looked around. Nearly all remnants of Victor were gone. Some clothes had been left but little else. There was food in the refrigerator and nothing else. He saw that the replacement rug was gone. *Now why in hell would he take that with him?* He began to think of self-preservation. He had still not found the kid in security he had bribed. *If Victor were gone for good maybe now that wouldn't matter.*

He called the buildings management to arrange a change of locks. *He won't be parking his ass here again.* Tobias Thornton needed to think.

To think, he needed to be flipping channels. He looked for the remote and couldn't find it anywhere. He always left it in the same place. He left in a fit of rage not having settled anything in his mind. *Damn you Victor.*

Myrtle had the number Bellamy put on his application. She called. Bellamy answered. "Have you seen or heard from Pearl since your little flare up?"

"Can't say I have. Why? She saying I've been bothering her?"

"I am just trying to reach her, that's all. So you have no idea where she might be?"

"I can't have nothing to do with her, ain't that right Miss Myrtle? Her being management and all."

"Bellamy, you made your own misery. Anyway good luck wherever you land." Myrtle disconnected.

She turned to Juan. "Bellamy says he hasn't seen or heard from her. I don't have a number for Victor but Joel could get it. I'll try Joel and have him call me back. Something odd in all this." She put on her game face and went out front to open for business.

After the busy lunch crowd had come and gone Myrtle took a diet coke to a booth and sat down. She dialed Joel's number. She told him what she needed and he said he'd try to get the number immediately. Ten minutes later he called back with Victor's cell number. She dialed but got a busy signal.

Across town George was meeting with Joel. George was dialing Victor just as Myrtle was trying to reach him. George got voicemail. Myrtle got a busy signal. George told Joel what he had learned. Victor was obviously the tall man Joel's friend had tailed from the Condo building.

"You know he hasn't been to work for three days. Your friend may have a reason to call that detective back. I'm going to call the Sheriff. See if I can light a new fire under him." The two men rose.

George offered his hand. "I know you would never hurt someone like that Joel."

Joel, who had developed a nervous tic in his left eye, shook George's hand. His eyes misted. He stood and headed back to work. George remained seated watching this quickly aging man shuffle out the door. He dialed the Sheriff on his private line.

Detective Monroe was summoned to the Sheriff's office. The two men shook hands. The detective pulled up a chair as the Sheriff took a seat behind his desk. "I got a call from a friend. You met him I believe. George Whiting, the building contractor."

Detective Monroe nodded.

"Well to make a long story short he continues to think we have the wrong guy and he's suggesting a man who works on his crew as someone who might have more information on this. His name is Victor Thornton. Supposedly he lives in the Same Condo building the girl disappeared from."

Detective Monroe looked at his notes. "I interviewed him early on. Nothing stood out. He said he wasn't home at the time."

"Well, Mr. Whiting says this Victor works for him and has not been coming to work. He also said his son, Bobby who is a good judge of people according to George, thinks the man is very strange. I met the kid at a soccer game. He's deaf. He also seems very bright.

He told his father he recently saw the man carrying something heavy wrapped in a blanket. The boy called him a shadow man. He placed the blanket in the trunk of a car. George's family is building a home right down the street from this Condo building and apparently their little dog nearly ran into the man in the parking lot."

Detective Monroe nodded again, "I have a message from one of the state's reluctant witnesses, Franklin Causano. In his message he mentions this same guy, Victor. You want me to re-interview this Victor, squeeze him a little?"

"I suggest you bring him to the Sheriff's office, squeeze him here. Squeeze him a lot. It's probably nothing but it seems this Victor character is on a lot of people's radar."

CHAPTER THIRTY-FIVE

Detective Monroe returned Franklin's call. He would meet him at his condo in an hour. Franklin, armed with new information, was hopeful. He ushered the detective into the kitchen. The table was stacked with the results of his own investigation. Breanna offered the detective some coffee. The three sat eyeing one another.

Franklin started. "Is there any way we can get those tapes back? We have discovered a resident of this building who seems to have escaped notice. Until now. Breanna and I remember seeing on the tape someone entering the elevator around the time the girl left this condo. Now we know who he is. The image isn't perfect but we think it was him entering that elevator. The timing fits the time that girl would be leaving. He might know something. He doesn't appear to be around. It's all very strange."

Detective Monroe nodded. He checked his notes. Victor had assured him he was not home until later that evening. Things had been missed. How much could he share with these two? "Anything else?"

"That's all we know."

"You two might be onto something and the Sheriff has asked me to talk with the man. I can't reveal what we know but I agree something doesn't pass the smell test. I'm going up to visit him now. He lives in his father's condo on the sixth floor."

"He's not there, I can tell you that much. His car is not in the parking lot. Like I said, hasn't been there for the last couple of days."

"I have his father's name and number. I need to get into that Condo anyway. If it makes sense to look at those tapes again we'll get them. Thanks for all your help. Now let me do my job. No more investigating, you two."

Detective Monroe went to the sixth floor. When summoned the building manager found new locks on the door, the building manager didn't have a key, and anyway shouldn't he get permission to enter. The detective dialed the number for Victor's father. Mr. Thornton answered, "Beach side Realty, Tobias Thornton here, how can I help you?"

———•••••———

Alice Diamond lived alone in a small house in the E-section of Palm Coast. She was eighty three years old and nearly blind. A year ago she had taken in a boarder who lived in the other bedroom. The boarder was helpful in a hundred ways. Household chores were done, meals prepared, food shopping completed. And the myriad of appointments an eighty three year old is subjected to, were faithfully met.

All by way of Pearl Crosby. She charged the girl no rent and gave her use of her old 1999 Saturn. This morning Alice was worried. The girl hadn't been home for the past three nights. The girl worked various shifts at a chicken place but had been faithful about meeting the old lady's needs.

Something was wrong. She couldn't see well enough to dial but she had memorized the location of 911 on the phone pad of her wall phone. The dispatcher seemed sympathetic but told her that was not the number to call unless it was an emergency.

Alice was nobody's fool. You don't survive eighty three years without learning to think on your feet. "Why, I can't catch my breath right now, I'm so upset. I feel like I'm going to faint. You probably should send someone." The dispatcher knew she was being had. But the old lady's plea was on tape.

"What was that address Ma'am we'll get someone right over there?"

While the paramedic checked her vitals Alice Diamond got to tell her story. Soon there was a sheriff's deputy ambling up to the door. "Something bad has happened to the girl, I just know it."

"We'll check it out Mrs. Diamond. Can you describe the vehicle for me?"

———•————•••••————•———

The spring of 2017 in Florida had been hot and dry. Burn bans began popping up all over the state. At one time there were wild fires burning. Palm Coast had been lucky. Experiencing only little flare-ups that were quickly squelched. Two weeks after Pearl was killed and her body placed beneath that Palmetto patch she remained missing. Bellamy was eventually called in for questioning. Detective Monroe sat across from the young man with a sheaf of papers in front of him.

"I'm told you had an argument with the girl just before she disappeared. Is that correct?"

Bellamy had seen all the cop shows. He said nothing.

"The girl was heard arguing over the phone just before she left work on the day she disappeared. The girl spoke your name in an angry manner. I have witnesses to that. "Were you on the other end of that call?" Some of those cop shows were repeats. Bellamy said nothing.

Detective Monroe decided to take a different tack. "Look, we're not trying to jam you up here. We're simply trying to find the girl. Let's try it this way. When was the last time you saw Pearl?"

Bellamy mulled this over. No harm here. There were witnesses anyway. He answered with emphasis, "THE LAST TIME I SAW PEARL WAS THE DAY I LEFT THE CHICKEN COOP FOR GOOD!"

"Word at the coop is you were sweet on her. Is that correct?"

Bellamy considered the question. He saw no harm in it. "I liked Pearl but she couldn't go out with me no-way. Cause she was management."

"Were you upset by that? You lost your job that day didn't you?"

Realizing his coworkers had witnessed his out-burst he wasn't revealing anything by answering.

"Listen man, I was angry when I left. I'll admit that. But I had no contact with the girl after that door hit me in the ass. I told Myrtle all that. She sayin something different?" Bellamy shifted in his seat. "You ask me, that tall skinny geeky guy she was seeing, he's the one you ought to be grillin."

A little light came on in detective Monroe's eyes. "You've met Pearl's boyfriend?"

Bellamy had committed a faux pas. Suddenly Bellamy was thinking back to those cop shows. *Say nothing or tell your version of the truth. You deny what they can prove they'll catch you up like a spider web.*

Not knowing what Detective Monroe had maybe heard from Victor, Bellamy was left with a dilemma. He cleared his throat.

"Actually I did see him come into a bar the same day I got done at the Coop. He was throwing em' down. He might have recognized me from the chicken place. He was pretty upset." Bellamy's new version of the truth slid out like a greasy burger. "He talked to himself for a while and slid down the bar. He started asking me about, was Pearl flirting with the guys working there?" Bellamy was on a roll and the real truth didn't matter. "When I left he was still throwing them down and cussing out Pearl."

"Did he threaten her?"

"He was pretty upset. What's his story?"

Detective Monroe had seen a cop show or two himself. He was not going to tell Bellamy anything. "Victor is staying quiet about it all right now."

— • — • — • —

That deserted house. The one **For Sale By Owner**. It was Mother's day when the man and his wife took a ride down from Jacksonville to check on it. Left in the estate of his wife's mother the couple had simply tried to unload it as cheaply as possible. They traveled down on route A1A and stopped at The Mellow Mushroom for lunch. An hour later they pulled into their driveway. A Gold Saturn was sitting up next to the garage facing the road. The Phinney's got out of their vehicle and checked the premises. Elwood Phinney called the Sheriff's office while Mrs. Phinney opened windows, airing the place out. A deputy arrived, checked the license plate and called it in. The vehicle was registered to an Alice Diamond.

Hardly anybody works on Mother's day so the report on the 1999 Gold Saturn lay on the desk of a Sergeant until the next day.

The next day the four cruisers, lights flashing, arrived at the Phinney residence which brought people out of their houses. One of Mr. Phinney's neighbors, Mr. Snowden,- the one directly across the street-when asked by Sheriff's detective Monroe, remembered the night his living room curtains lit up.

He chuckled as he remembered to the sheriff's detective. "Oh shit I said to myself." Then he had to explain. "I was sitting there naked in the dark, like I do." He added, "I was alone." He blushed then. He covered it by checking his watch.

"Musta' been 9:45 or so." He checked his watch again as if triggering his next line. "Who's stopping in this late?" He pointed back towards his house.

"Martha was in bed ah-course. That woman is in bed before it's dark under the table." He had an audience now and played it out like a crime show.

"So I peeked out the curtain and I see this car has backed into that yard across the street." He waited to be prompted.

"Did you see anyone exit the vehicle?"

"It was awful dark that night."

He stopped as if the story had ended. Then he lit up.

"Of course, I still got my eyes. My legs ain't worth crap but I can still see all I can't do." Detective Monroe found himself chuckling. This man needed to tell his story his way. "So what did you see?"

The old man rubbed his whiskered chin. "Wellll," he dragged out, "I seen this tall skinny fella.

"What was he doing?"

"Wellll, first he just stood there kinda like he was thinking things over."

"Then what did he do?" Detective Monroe realized he was the straight man in this story.

Mr. Snowden's chin seemed to be the crystal ball that revealed the truth. He began to rub it vigorously. "He took off his shirt."

"His shirt?" questioned Detective Monroe.

"Yup. Then that fella leaned right back into that car and using that shirt he wiped it down. First inside then out." Two sentences strung together now that was progress. Thought the detective.

And then unprompted, Mr. Snowden started back up,

"Then that fella he looked up and down the street and all around and trotted on down the street." he pointed the direction. "That way."

Edward Snowden remembered something else, his fingers opening and closing over his chin, "Maybe important maybe not."

After a three second pause, "There was a full moon that night spot lighting him."

Detective Monroe noted that information. "You didn't think it all looked suspicious?"

Edward Snowden hmphhed, shook his head almost appearing angry at such a question. "Course I did."

"But you never called anyone?"

Edward Snowden, age Seventy six, snorted at that.

"Course I called someone." Another drum roll. "I called my son."

"Your son. And what did he tell you to do?"

"He's a smartass he is. **Edward Snowden Junior,**" the old man shook his head raising his voice at the thought of his son. "He's all knowing, that one." Edward senior continued to shake his head. "Wise ass told me why don't I get a job at Walmart if I want to work security. 'Mind your own business Pop,' he tells me, "so that's what I did." He looked around at all the activity. "So much for all he knows."

So weeks after the girl disappeared they finally had the car she'd been driving. The description fit Victor Thornton who was also missing. Detective Monroe was trying to keep the two cases separate. Somehow though Victor Thornton kept squirreling himself into both. Detective Monroe asked for a meeting with the Sheriff.

Thank the lord for bored adolescents. Not really, but the deputy couldn't help but think that, as he was ushering two boys to his cruiser. He was also silently thanking them. Two boys on a bike. A path into the woods. An adventure in mind. Doesn't anyone read anymore?

A burn ban had been in effect in Palm Coast for over three weeks. Even without the signs, some lit up and strategically placed, common sense would tell you don't light a match in the woods.

Well these two yahoos had it in mind to build a little fire, roast a hot dog on a stick and sip on their energy drinks after a trek into Graham Swamp. There were others using the trail going in so the boys waited for their return trip before dropping their bikes within a quarter mile of the entrance.

Billy led the way. Carrying a nap-sack they left the trail near a big tree and a patch of dense Palmetto that hid the trail from passersby. Billy and buddy Randy scraped raw a spot that was covered in pine straw, dead leaves, and general debris. They began to gather small sticks and dead limbs.

They sat down to sip on their drinks before taking that fatal step— striking that match. Billy remarked that they were like two hunters lost in the wilderness.

"Yeah we got to keep our strength up or we'll never find our way out of here," added Randy. The two boys laid back, hands behind their heads studying the sky. After a minute of nothingness Billy turned over onto his stomach and looked directly at the decomposed body of Pearl Crosby.

In an odd twist of fate the very cruisers who had barreled past Victor on Old Kings Road that night of the full moon were the first to arrive, lights flashing and sirens wailing.

CHAPTER THIRTY-SIX

The news of a body found in a swamp hit the airwaves like the wildfires that were plaguing Florida. Sheriff Oliver Rodriguez and Detective Monroe rode together to the crime scene. A news chopper was already making passes over the area. One news van was in the dirt parking lot on site and they passed another as they approached with light and sound.

The two boys sat in the back seat of a cruiser already planning on exaggerating their find. The find was Pearl Crosby, though no one could tell it was her from what lay beneath the Palmetto. The body was clothed and sunken into the little bit of flesh that remained. One clue. A shirt with Cluck's Chicken Coop logo above the pocket on the left. The face was gone. Eyes, ears, nose, all missing. Long blond hair shaped in a pony-tail a possible clue to gender, resting on a bone white skull, resting on the red collar shirt. Black pants that had been gnawed or pecked through showed signs of white bone. Pretty gruesome scene for anyone, much less two twelve year olds.

The scene however seemed to be bothering the adults more than the two boys. Billy and Randy were on their smartphones texting about their adventure. When the deputy checking on them saw fingers flying he confiscated the phones and shook his head in amazement. *Was I thinking about thanking them, hell I should arrest them.*

Detective Monroe, standing off to the side after viewing the body that had been rolled out from beneath the palmetto told his boss, in his mind there was no doubt it was the missing girl. "That's two young women in the span of a few months discarded, like tossed out trash from a McDonald's drive thru.

"One name surfaces in both cases. Victor Thornton. Now he's missing. Sheriff, I'd like to put out an alert for Victor Thornton as a person of interest."

"We'll do that immediately. Also let's go back over those surveillance tapes again as well. I want you to re-interview anyone and everyone who had access to those tapes. Someone is holding information back. And let's take a look at any surveillance tapes for the last month. If Victor Thornton is responsible for this latest murder he might turn up on one. I'm going to alert the District Attorney to what we have. Do we have a serial killer on our hands?"

"I am tending to believe what Franklin Causano has been telling us from the beginning. Neither Joel Riesling nor he had anything to do with the disappearance of Nona Ashby."

— • — •• — •• — •• — • —

Two weeks later the Daytona Beach News Journal announced that the trial of Joel Riesling charged in the death of Nona Ashby was being removed from the docket. Charges had not been dropped but it was certainly looking like someone else committed the murder. Joel Riesling refused to comment for the story.

His lawyer did reiterate that his client was not surprised, since he had maintained his innocence all along.

A second article offered a possible link between the murders of two young women in the last year. A person of interest in the latest murder has been named; Victor Thornton, who it's believed was dating Pearl Crosby, the latest murder victim. While it's not known if there was any relationship between Victor Thornton and the first murder victim, Nona Ashby, it is known that the girl disappeared from the same condo building where Victor Thornton was staying at the time. The Sheriff's office has not released any of the evidence collected from the crime scene or from their search of the residence of Victor Thornton. He is a person of interest is all they will say.

⸺•⸺⬥⸺•⸺

George Whiting read both these articles with a little inside knowledge and more than a little trepidation. It was only a matter of time before Victor Thornton would be found. Found and brought back here to possibly stand trial for at least one of the murders. In a bedroom, probably his daughter's, son Bobby was still asleep. He shook his head. The boy was an eyewitness to Victor Thornton carrying what was most probably the body of Pearl Crosby and watching Victor put it in the trunk of Pearl's car. He had already been interviewed by Detective Monroe here at the kitchen table with George and Lane present. Bobby's description and attention to detail left little to the imagination.

⸺•⸺⬥⸺•⸺

A block away Tobias Thornton was literally losing his hair.

He had lots on his mind. His son's whereabouts was the least of his worries. He read the two articles in this morning's paper and realized his own future was in serious jeopardy. Palm Coast is a small town in many ways. True the population of the city had grown tremendously in the past twelve years but it still had a small town feel. The young people have their own communication network and by now even without today's headlines these kids probably knew more about the two girls and what happened than the Sheriff's Department.

Mr. Thornton had stopped trying to find the young man who had given him unfettered access to those security tapes after Victor disappeared.

Recently he was contacted by an anonymous someone claiming to have knowledge of his time spent with the tapes. Time that had not been duly recorded but witnessed nevertheless. That information could only have come from the young man himself. *Was this message from him?* In his hand Tobias had the number he was to call at 8:00 pm tonight to meet with the voice who left the message regarding those security tapes. There was one added bit of information on the message that brought a quiver to Tobias's spine. 'Didn't realize you were Victor's father.' To make matters even worse, that damn detective wanted to see him again this afternoon. 'New information he wanted to share,' was what he told the elder Thornton.

CHAPTER THIRTY-SEVEN

It was June hot and sticky. The rainy season had set in. Those four o'clock showers would soon find their cadence and deliver the light and sound show that marked the time of year as well as any holiday listed on a calendar. On this afternoon the clouds had been building up for the past hour. Tobias Thornton closed the door to his 2015 Mercedes E class sedan. The heat hit him like a shock wave. He entered the Sheriff's office feeling like a shoe was about to fall. The receptionist led him to a small conference room and asked if he'd like coffee or perhaps some ice water. Tobias chose water. He was jacked up enough as it was. He sat. The water was delivered. He sat. He sipped. He studied the clock. He sat. He sipped some more. The clock continued its sixty second attempt at explaining time. He began counting with his eyes closed to sixty then snapping them open to see how close he'd come to silently, blindly, catching the clock in a lie. *Was this waiting part of the detectives' attempt to unsettle him? Well dammit it was working.*

He got up and studied the bulletin board that had a map of the county laid out with streets and roads. He began to look at the streets and roads where he had sold a house in the past. He was up to fifteen properties when the door opened. Detective Monroe shook his hand and thanked him for coming in. He apologized for keeping him waiting. Mr. Thornton looked once more at the clock. It was 4:32pm. He heard thunder. Shortly he saw a flash of lightning then another drum roll of noise.

Detective Monroe began, "I called you in because we believe your son was spotted in North Carolina. Do you know of anyone he might know in that State? Where he might be headed?"

Mr. Thornton was glad to be able to honestly and calmly say, "I have no idea, unless he's on his way back to Pennsylvania."

"Well if he is, he's taking his old sweet time about it. He's been gone for a while now. He's been staying with someone. No idea who that could be?"

"Detective I set my eyes on my son for the first time in years just a few months back. I offered him a place to stay, found him a job and that was the extent of it. If my son is guilty of these crimes I'm reading about, I pray he turns himself in and gets the help he needs."

"We have looked at those security tapes again. From the day the first victim disappeared. Your son lied to me about not being in the building that afternoon. We know he shows up entering the elevator around the time a witness says the girl left a condo on the fourth floor. We further believe your son somehow tampered with the security footage." He waited a beat. "We know he viewed it." Detective Monroe continued. "We are trying to find the young man who worked as a temporary employee at that time. We think Victor might have bribed him and destroyed a crucial piece of evidence."

Detective Monroe knew he had the man feeling anxious so he shifted gears to the disappearance of the second girl. "On the day we believe a girl by the name of Pearl Crosby disappeared, the security footage in your building shows your son arriving home mid-afternoon."

He waited, watching if Mr. Thornton had a response.

When it didn't come he followed up. "A little over an hour later the victim, Pearl Crosby, shows up entering the elevator. This time there is no tape missing. Pearl Crosby is not seen leaving. Not an hour later, five hours later, not ever."

"Well my life has entered the toilet over all this. People are discovering I'm the father of a potential murderer. Not getting a lot of calls to show houses these days, Detective." He sighed, "So the sooner this all ends the better. If my son contacts me I will try to get him to turn himself in. That's the best I can do."

"Well thanks for coming in." He handed Mr. Thornton a card. "If anything or anyone or anyplace comes to mind give me a call."

Tobias rose and slowly left the office. He attempted to run back to his car through a gully washer. He slipped as he tore his door open and banged his knee on the door edge. *Jesus!* He had trouble catching his breath.

Wet to the bone he looked in the lighted mirror on his sunshade. *Jesus!* His normally well-groomed self was in disarray. *Shit-a-goddamn.* He had a sudden glimpse of a character from <u>The Walking Dead.</u> *Jesus!*

Sitting behind the wheel, rain pounding down too hard to drive, he let the wipers dance while his mind flashed and banged along with the storm that would be gone out to sea in another ten minutes. *And this is going to be the easy part of my day. Jesus!*

From a window in the sheriff's office, detective Monroe watched the man in the pretty green Mercedes sitting there. *I hope I've given him something to think about.*

—•◆◆◆◆•—

Three miles away in the spare bedroom of a friend he'd met at a party shortly after first arriving in Palm Coast, Bellamy sat on the edge of the bed listening to his room-mate throw out a little thunder, matching the noise outside.

"Mama says you've got to fork over some rent money Bellamy, if you're gonna stay here."

"I know, Treat. I'm gonna have me a whole bunch of money pretty soon now." Thunder rolled, lightning flashed.

Treat Johnson looked skeptically at Bellamy. "You gonna rob a bank? Knock over a liquor store?" He angled his jaw. "Mama is BB gun serious Bellamy, she's gonna sting your ass if you don't have some rent money by Friday." That statement brought the rain.

"You tell your Mama, Bellamy always pays his way." The pounding on the tin roof seemed to spark Bellamy's next line. "Tell her, come Friday dark time she'll be taxing her brain counting out twenty dollar bills. She gonna mark me, **Paid In Full** come Friday night. Now get outta here I got some thinking to do."

—•—•—•—•—

The house that George built with love, sweat and tears was ninety-five percent finished. It was Thursday evening. George had sent the crews home early which kinda becomes a way of doing business during the rainy season. They were on the job at 6:00 am working under artificial light these days, so the hours were still being put in. George captured Lane and suggested a ride and a walk through. The kids and the dog were in their rooms.

Lane hollered, "be right back." They grabbed an umbrella and off they went.

George skirted the ever present worry on his mind as they parked in the garage. Beginning the tour as prospective buyers, kidding each other on what great ideas the builder had incorporated, they entered each room and nodded with satisfaction. Lightning and thunder accompanied them on their tour. The tour ended back in the kitchen.

"We did good George."

George found these little escapes from the kids was doing wonders to rekindle what had kinda gone to sleep during Lane's illness.

"Your personal touch is what makes it, Lane. The color scheme and that hickory flooring. And the contrasting tile. Magic." George took Lane's hand.

The kitchen appliances were all up and running. Stools stood sentinel at the bar. Lane took one. George went to the refrigerator and brought back a beer for himself and a plastic cup of organic wine for Lane. Lane took a sip. The two toasted the house, the wine, and the good things in their life.

"Don't forget health George, it all starts with that." Seeing the now radiant lady sitting across from him, George raised his beer once more. Outside the storm seemed a million miles away.

"Joel's friend certainly knows good wine George, when are we going to meet him?

"Actually I asked Joel to invite him and his fiancé to a little party before the big party. Now that Joel's trial is in doubt, the two are able to communicate. I thought breaking this place in with just a few guests would be appropriate. Just a simple barbecue." He took Lane's hand, "Test your new stamina before going all out party time. I've invited Hailey, the Sheriff and his wife as well."

Lane touched her cup against George's bottle. "That's a good idea. I am feeling good though. I have most of my strength back and I have never been happier. Reaching my goals. The kids are doing super as well."

George looked over the bar at his wife then at the matching bracelets that now monitored their daily activity. Lane had made a mission of reaching twenty thousand steps a day.

They compared them before retiring each night. "Well babe I know I can't keep up with you, and now we wear the evidence to prove it."

Lane chuckled.

George switched gears and brought up the elephant in the room. "If they find this guy are you worried about how testifying at a trial is going to affect Bobby?"

Lane thought a moment. "First of all it might never happen. They haven't caught the guy yet. If it comes to that time I have no doubt Bobby will leave the courtroom mesmerized.

We both witnessed his statement. The kid is outer worldly for his age."

"You're probably right but a good defense lawyer is going to try to unsettle him. Scare him even if they can."

"Well it's not going to happen this summer so I say let the boy be a boy and enjoy his vacation time."

At 8:50 pm. Bellamy circled the WalMart parking lot. He drove up and down every row. The parking lot was packed as usual. He decided it was safe. The parking lot was still steaming from afternoon and evening on and off showers. The parking lot lights above cast an eerie glow bouncing off the wet vehicles. He drove to the row on the far left. He pulled in facing a hedge of shrubbery. He left his parking lights on. He had described his car during the cell phone call. Within minutes a green Mercedes pulled up beside him. Bellamy recognized the logo on the side of the car. He took a deep breath and got out of his vehicle. He walked to the passenger side of the Mercedes. The Window slid down.

Mr. Thornton did not smile. "Get in."

Bellamy sat down in the passenger seat. Some old song was playing. Bellamy didn't recognize the song or the artist. Mr. Thornton turned down the sound. "So you would like me to pay for your silence, is that correct?"

Bellamy scared to death on the inside, nodded.

Mr. Thornton reminded Bellamy he had paid him once. Then followed with, "What do you think you know young man?"

Bellamy cleared his throat and ticked off on his fingers all that he thought he knew. "I know your son is wanted for killing Pearl. I know he's wanted for possibly killing some other girl. I know you paid me to look at them tapes and not put your name in the book."

Mr. Thornton, as if negotiating the sale of a house and wanting a quick turnover of the property, tried to get Bellamy to see the flaws in the building. "Everything you know or think you know really doesn't have anything to do with me."

"No offense man, but then why am I sitting in a Walmart parking lot in your car?"

Tobias Thornton took a breath, "Because even though you know nothing, rumors could hurt my business. I'm here to end those rumors." Mr. Thornton reached into his jacket. Bellamy's eyes widened.

When Mr. Thornton removed his hand an envelope landed on Bellamy's lap. Bellamy took a deep breath.

"This is a one-time offer young man." He looked straight into Bellamy's eyes "Take it and disappear. I mean really disappear. Or you just might find yourself joining those two unfortunate young women."

"How much in that envelope?"

"Just the right amount. Trust me, just the right amount. You did your homework, **Bellamy**."

Hearing his name, Bellamy's eyes widened once more.

"I did my own studying as well." Mr. Thornton winked.

Bellamy fidgeted.

"Yes, I know who you are and I know where you have been staying." He let that sink in.

"They say Texas is nice this time of year. You're from there aren't you? You have family back there?" Mr. Thornton twisted in his seat to directly face the boy. "Truth is you don't know enough about any of this to be forced to come back here. To talk to anyone." He patted the envelope.

"Call this my one good deed of the year. Take what's in that envelope and be gone." Mr. Thornton darkened his voice, "I have everything to lose, and consequently nothing to lose. If you catch my meaning."

All those smart ass answer words evaded Bellamy's tongue and he simply nodded.

Mr. Thornton had one more exit line. He reached back into his jacket. This time he came out with a handgun.

"See Bellamy this was going to end one way or another tonight. Now be on your way."

As if on cue the rain resumed. A downpour. Mr. Thornton sat mesmerized as the wipers moved across the windshield. Left, right, left, right, left, right. His mind shut down even as he turned the radio volume back up. *'If you're ever going to see a rainbow you gotta stand a little rain'* the words mirrored his very thoughts. He glanced as red tail lights, quickly receding, symbolized an exit sign. A way out of all this.

— · — ● ● ● — · —

Bellamy was on his way to Texas shortly after midnight. $800 dollars in the black after giving Mama her due. "Way too much drama in this town anyway," he said aloud to his rear view mirror as he headed north on Route One.

—◆—◆—◆—

As Franklin and Breanna sat watching the sound and light show and thinking aloud, Franklin's door-bell rang outside the building. Joel hadn't been to Franklin's place since that fateful afternoon. Two minutes later Joel buzzed the apt. Just behind him was Myrtle.

Franklin put out his hand. "Come in, we were just talking about you two."

Joel placed a rack of diet coke on the counter. Breanna spoke up. "Grab those cans and show them to the patio Franklin, I'll bring glasses and ice."

Seated and properly introduced to Myrtle, Breanna opened and poured the soft drinks.

Joel announced, "before I forget you two, you're invited to my Boss's home this Sunday. George told me Lane loves the wine you gave me to give him."

Small talk dominated for the first fifteen minutes. Like two boxers circling the ring they finally got down to business.

"Have you heard any more about being brought to trial?" Joel shook his head. "My lawyer thinks they know they have no case now that Victor Thornton is on the run. That's the good news. If and when they find him they still have to prove he's guilty. Until that happens I'm not completely off the hook."

Franklin had his chin cupped in his hands. "I've been thinking about that missing tape." He suddenly brought a playing card from who knows where and placed it on the patio table. "Everything is explainable if you slow things down and really pay attention."

Franklin sipped his coke and another card appeared. His audience chuckled. "I still think that tape is the key. Did Victor erase it? Your own lawyer and that detective have doubts that he did. He signed in and signed out. I don't think he would even know how to erase it."

"Well I know the detective is trying to find the kid who was working as a temp at the time. No one seems able to locate that boy. They have a name. How hard should it be to find a kid with a name like that?" He looked at Brianna "I thought I had a strange name. Can you believe a name like, Bellamy?"

Myrtle sat up straight. "Did you say Bellamy?" She stood up and went to the balcony. She turned back around. "I had a young man named Bellamy working at the coop. He knew Pearl. Could that be who we're looking for?"

Franklin already had a pen and pencil. "Do you know where he lives?"

"I have an address. I'll check it out in the morning. I have his phone number too. You know this is getting stranger and stranger."

Franklin said, "You have my number, call me. I'll let detective Monroe know. We're old puzzle pals now aren't we Breanna?"

Joel wasn't drinking these days so the evening ended before the 11:00 0'clock news came on.

CHAPTER THIRTY-EIGHT

Some things went as planned during the summer of 2017. Our house was finished. The National Weather service predicted a very active hurricane season but Florida did not appear in the cross hairs early on. I turned nine. Sarah turned fourteen.

There were some surprises. Franklin and Breanna made plans to get married. Joel and Myrtle became engaged. Though Joel wouldn't commit to marriage until his name was cleared. Hailey met a practicing attorney who she met when the man contracted with the company to build a smaller house. The poor man's wife had died of cancer and he couldn't bear to face the walls she had painted. One thing led to another and Hailey began seeing the man socially. Cookouts that brought all four couples together expanded to include various restaurants in town and at the beach.

I turned as brown as a tree nut while my friend Daniel was already brown, we looked like twins. We were inseparable.

We learned to swim in our new pool.

Mom and Hailey hung out around the pool whenever Hailey could get a day off. Every evening for sure they were there. They were becoming best friends like me and Daniel. Sarah and her phone were best friends. When she wasn't texting she was playing summer soccer texting or learning to surf with a real best friend, the Sheriff's daughter.

Mom did make her read a couple of books that would be required reading during her freshman year. When she complained to dad he just offered up the Carpenter's Creed he lived by, Measure twice cut once. My sister just shook her head.

— • — • — • —

Tobias Thornton took up praying that summer. Every night. Not a prayer in any traditional sense but he prayed. Perhaps it was less a prayer than a demand.

The news and drama of the girl's death had died down even as the afternoon storms increased in ferocity. The economy was continuing to grow. Tobias's business had picked back up. Tonight as he flipped channels nursing a good bourbon half way gone, and two thirds through three hundred channels – just as he did every night – he would suddenly turn off the television.

Alone in the dark he sipped then put his drink down. With his hands clasped thus began his prayer: "Die tonight. You stupid bastard Victor, wherever you are, die tonight." He felt around for his drink, took another sip, put it back down and recited the second stanza: "Stay gone Bellamy you little black prick. If you know what's good for you, stay gone." He had recited this mantra for forty-seven nights now and it seemed to be working. Finished now, with the TV back on, his remote replaced, his run through the channels continued. A drained glass gave way to the sound of sucking ice. Same routine every night.

The Condo was up for sale and he might have a buyer. *A good sign. Moving on.* A new woman had entered his life, a fifty year old widow. He stood and raised his empty glass. Tonight he would treat himself. He managed to pour a fourth bourbon not spilling a drop. He toasted the future.

— • — • — • —

Bellamy was back in Texas that summer. He kept a low profile and was a week from taking a test to work for a local delivery firm. He had held several menial jobs, none with the needed hours to sustain him, so was nearly out of the money he'd been given to be gone.

He was curious about what was going on in Palm Coast, Florida though, wondering if Pearl's killer had been found. The hot Texas winds sweeping dust from one spot to another like a poor housekeeper, were swirling outside the window of a little eatery that served very good Mexican food. It was soon to be dark. He bit into a taco. Bellamy realized he was bored. He looked at the study materials he'd been given. He took another bite of the taco. *I could pass this test in my sleep.* He put the booklet down. He managed a gulp or two and on a whim picked up his cell phone.

(In life there are things you know, things you don't know much about, and things in which you don't have a remnant of clue. Bellamy was about to get caught up in what was behind door number three.)

He dialed the number for Cluck's Chicken Coop. The thing he didn't have a clue about was Myrtle's relationship with the accused murderer of Nona Ashby, the first victim. Joel.

Myrtle, working the night shift answered. "Cluck's Chicken Coop, this is Myrtle, how can I help you?"

"Hey Myrtle this is a blast from the past. Remember me?" Myrtle, knowing Joel and Franklin and the detective would love to get their hands on this guy, took a deep breath. "Of course I remember you Bellamy. The gang here still laughs about the sense of humor you brought to the place. What's up?"

"I was just thinking about Pearl. Wondering if her killer, Victor, ever got caught?"

"No, he's still on the run. Where are you by the way? You haven't been in for a while. Not still mad I hope. I have been known to give second chances if you're interested?"

Bellamy, getting positive vibes, opened up a little more. "Nah, I'm not mad. I'm back home in Texas about to be offered a good job with a delivery company. Full time Myrtle. Pretty sure I'll get hired." Then he had a thought. "Say, you wouldn't offer me a positive recommendation, would you? It would guarantee me that job."

Myrtle shaking her head in disbelief had to move her mouth away from the receiver. She fist pumped the air. "Of course I would Bellamy, you bring a lot of ability with you. Just need to tone down your <u>Saturday Night Live</u> act." Then she chuckled.

On the other end Bellamy laughed aloud. "You are so right about that. I'm learning to watch my mouth, you taught me that." Bellamy proceeded to read the name and address and fax number of the company that was on his study materials. "I'll get that right out Bellamy, you'll be hearing from me real soon."

After hanging up she dialed Joel. "You are not going to believe," she began. When the business quieted down she retreated to the office and typed up a recommendation for Bellamy. It was a glowing report. Myrtle surely wanted Bellamy to get that position.

— • — • — • —

Joel called Franklin. Franklin called Detective Monroe. They all planned to meet tomorrow afternoon at Franklin's Condo.

— • — • — • —

Fifteen hundred miles to the north Victor Thornton was on the Kennebec River in rural Maine. A week ago Victor had sold his car at a used car lot housed on a man's lawn outside Dunn, North Carolina. He gave the car one last look as he gathered the single suit case of necessaries and hit the road. Like links in a chain, a series of rides found Victor in Northern Virginia. He wandered into the restroom at a truck stop.

Men standing at a urinal don't normally converse. Eyes stare straight ahead like being part of a police line-up. Victor, slumped and disheveled, was studying the wall above the porcelain looking for flaws in the construction he now understood a little after working the trade. A voice reached him.

"You drive a rig?"

Victor, not thinking the question was directed at him, stared straight ahead mentally playing foreman. *Whoever did the finished work on the drywall in here hadn't completely hidden the nailing. Poor job of taping.*

"If you're looking for work I'm hiring." The voice echoed off the ceiling and wall of urinals.

Victor finished up, waggled, zipped, and moved to the sink.

Suddenly a guy with a big grin and a friendly face stood at the adjoining sink. He looked into the wall mirror. The man spoke to the mirror. "Hey, I don't mean to be a pest but you look like you're carrying the world on your shoulders." The man didn't wait for a response. "Do you need work?" I'm looking for drivers. The pays good. You're home every weekend."

Victor didn't know if he was looking opportunity in the face or he was hearing the world's oddest pick up line. The man washed his hands and face, slicked down his hair and rubbed his hands vigorously under the hand dryer. He approached Victor with his hand outstretched.

"My name is Troy Dunphy. I'm part owner of a trucking company up in Maine. I lost two drivers last week. That's why I'm driving. I thought I was done with all that." He continued, "I'm just heading back up there from a trip to Georgia. I am seriously looking for an honest man." He met Victor's eyes, "You look like an honest man." Like gears being shifted in an eighteen wheeler with a manual transmission, Troy Dunphy shifted once more. Victor still had not spoken but straightened a little.

"I have driven trucks for over twenty years. Do you know how many of these restrooms I've washed my hands in? He sighed, "I can't run my business from the cab of a truck."

Victor remained silent.

"Look I can tell you're running to or away from somewhere. If you're interested and you're not an ax murderer I can have you nearly trained by the time we hit the Kittery Bridge" He smiled.

Victor turned his head, catching himself in the mirror. He thought of his father flipping channels back in the condo. He thought fleetingly of his own actions in the past year. *A ride in a rig didn't sound that bad.*

Troy finally got to a gear that could make for smooth travel.

"So at least you get a ride, we talk, and if things work out by the time we're in Maine I'll know whether to offer you a job."

Victor finally spoke. Maybe things could work out. "Mr. Dunphy, you've got yourself a rider. I don't know how to drive a big truck but I'm willing to learn." Victor watched from the passenger seat how this big rig rode high above the road and how smaller vehicles melted away in its path. Troy was a beacon of good natured-ness (so unlike his own father). Two stops along the way saw Troy making deliveries and picking up part of a load that would land in Maine.

I can do this, Victor constantly reminded himself as the miles passed and his understanding of the trucking business, delivered by the soft spoken man driving, grew with the accumulation of mileposts.

Victor crossed that bridge into Maine. He had been picked up and delivered, landing in a small town in central Maine. Hired and now renting a room in a house. He received his commercial license on his first try.

He weighed seventy pounds less than he had a year ago. His new Maine picture license sporting a full beard looked nothing like the man on any databases shared by law enforcement. He was now using his middle name as his first, Arthur. Indeed it seemed he was now Arthur Victor Thornton.

In a strange bit of fate, in truth, that was how he had been named on his birth certificate. Called Victor since birth however and enrolled in school using that name he had been an alias his whole life. Getting a social security number and his new license had been a breeze. A new beginning. He was soon to make his first out-of- state truck run.

Today though, he was white water rafting. Troy Dunphy, his new boss, used rafting trips as a way to amplify the team work necessary to run a successful company. Victor was sitting with a group of six other employees, a rafting guide in the stern, the men dipping their oars when directed. A spray of cold water hit his face, he took a deep breath. For the first time since leaving his father's condo that breath felt free and clear. Just maybe this could all work out. He took a deep breath of that fresh air.

Around the next turn though the water suddenly turned violent. The water rushed into and over boulders while the guide shouted orders. The water had turned white.

"Men on the left pull hard. Men on the right push your paddles away. The raft skirted the boulder and landed in a whirlpool of foaming water. Victor paddled as hard as possible. The raft swung around like a deposit entering a toilet.

Suddenly in the rise and fall of the raft and the white and the black of the water and the spinning, Victor saw the fallacy in his earlier thinking. Now it was television channels appearing and disappearing as an angry father surfed reruns. Just below the churning, Pearl looked up, meeting his eyes. Victor, sweating profusely sliced into those waves for all he was worth. Pearl disappeared but Nona Ashby surfaced, her mouth still trying to extend the scream he had quieted. The two women faced one another and clasped hands. Victor realized in that moment – truly – there was no escape from what he'd done.

Back in Palm Coast, Florida, Detective Monroe had not given up trying to find the fugitive. It had been quite a summer. Victor's phone had been turned off, destroyed most probably. He hadn't been on social media since leaving his father's condo. After an initial possible sighting in North Carolina, the search had gone quiet. Detective Monroe went to interview the men who had worked with Victor. They didn't seem to have much to add.

Hoping to reach into their heads for something, anything, they might have unwittingly or unknowingly learned about Victor, Detective Monroe asked the men to describe a typical workday.

The three men were silent. One seemed to be thinking harder than the others. He shrugged an innocent memory.

"Victor showed up most mornings with a large Dunkin Donut coffee and two chocolate glazed donuts. That's what I remember."

That brought a different voice to the conversation. "We'd kid him about why he hadn't brought us some. He'd tell us to get our own or wait for Friday."

Detective Monroe was about to ask what that meant when the guy followed up.

"The big Boss, George, always brings donuts and coffee from Dunkin Donuts on Friday."

These harmless revelations seemed to relax the men.

Another worker recalled being at a bar after work with Victor. "He spent an awful lot of time studying the beer in his glass. Like he was trying to find something he dropped.

"Strange guy. That's all I know."

Detective Monroe prepared to leave.

The man remembered something else. "You know there was something else. My wife carries all these little bits of plastic on her keys. Kinda like coupons you swipe."

Detective Monroe wasn't really listening, it seemed like nothing here.

The man continued with his story. "Anyway I rode with Victor to a bar after work one time and noticed his keys had one of those little tags."

Detective Monroe picked up on that.

"My wife has a ton of tags." He rolled his head from side to side. "Victor, he only had one."

"Do you remember what that tag was?"

"Hell yes, I was reminded every morning."

"What tag was it?"

Thinking back to the old guy explaining the suspect he'd seen that night Detective Monroe nearly missed the clincher.

"It was a Dunkin Donut Tag."

Detective Monroe jotted it down. Probably meaningless. He thanked the men but left the work-site not having learned much.

It was late afternoon. He was on route 100 heading west. His mind was a muddle of information. He spotted a Dunkin Donut on his right and without thinking pulled into the shopping center that housed the business. He drove behind a series of businesses and found a parking spot. He got out, took his notes and walked into Dunkin Donut. Still not clear what was forming in his head he ordered a regular coffee with half the cream and a chocolate glazed donut. He'd be eating this here he said when asked. He took the tray and sat down. He took a sip, bit his donut and looked out the window at the traffic on route 100 heading who knew where. He looked through his notes. Victor was a ghost it seemed. The only thought that reached his mind was a simple factoid.

People are creatures of habit.

He went back over everything he had learned about Victor Thornton, which didn't seem to be much. Suddenly that little tag Victor carried on his key fob planted a seed in his mind. That tag and the fact that he showed up every morning with coffee and donuts from that business would indicate Victor might just be a creature of habit.

He took a sip of coffee and a bite of donut. Just as the donut mixed with the coffee and melted in his mouth his muddle provided a method to his madness. He glanced down at the tray. There it was staring right up at him. A paper insert promoting the product he was consuming.

Join Dunkin Donuts Online program and get free and discounted beverages and food. *Was it possible?*

Detective Earl Monroe sat back and enjoyed that cup of coffee and savored the taste of that donut. In fact he couldn't recall a more satisfying afternoon snack. When he finished he approached the manager.

CHAPTER THIRTY-NINE

September 6, 2017 began as a normal workday. Kids balked at going to school. A typical Wednesday hump day had arrived. Get through today though and it was all down-hill. Detective Monroe was excited on this Wednesday morning. He just might have his first big break in a different part of this case. He would be meeting with Franklin and Joel this afternoon. Apparently a former employer had been contacted by Bellamy. Franklin had a business address where the young man might be working soon.

In addition Detective Monroe also had a call into corporate headquarters of Dunkin Donut. He had laid out his request to a friendly voice. The young sounding female promised she would try to find out who he needed to speak with and get back to him within forty-eight hours. She had never had such a request but seemed eager to be part of a police investigation. Detective Monroe took that as a good sign the girl would follow through.

❖ ❖ ❖ ❖ ❖

I was back in school in a brand new grade. This year I was being completely mainstreamed whatever that means. I was told I'd sit near the front of the room where I could read the teacher's lips. I had a small laptop I used to type out questions and answers. I was also allowed to Google questions so I would not constantly be raising my hand. I was in full control of my education. I wasn't the only one in the room who was making strides I guess because when I looked across the room, my old friend Arnold sat, sporting glasses, a new haircut and clean clothing. Arnold was found to be capable and was thriving as well.

Still two years behind grade level but mainstreamed for the first time. I relaxed. *Yep it had been quite a summer and should be a good year.* At home I had my telescope and my friend Daniel. We continue to swim and study the stars, the Inter coastal waterway and my neighbors on both sides of the water from my room on the second floor. By the way I stopped migrating to my sister's room. I am nine years old after-all.

⸻ ● ⸺ ● ⸺ ● ⸺ ●⸻

Mom writes her blogs and tends to an herb garden she's planted. She is writing articles for various magazines. Her health has returned. She pores over eating habits of different cultures emulating and adding to recipes. Dad Sarah and I served as Guinea pigs.

⸻ ● ⸺ ● ⸺ ● ⸺ ●⸻

Dad seems happy. Whistling still, Mom wearing headphones. Sitting there reading lips at the dinner table I surmised the business is growing. Hailey is now in charge of all day to day activities. They still meet once a week at the office but Dad is working more and more from his home office, calling Betty when he needs something. His constant whistling drives Mom crazy but how do you criticize happiness? You don't, she decided and found this might be an opportunity to learn a new language. Her head phones are now spewing an introduction to Spanish.

Our family dinners are a sounding board for new ideas. Dad broached his latest idea last night. He started by taking inventory. Just like the nursery rhyme I closed my eyes to way back when Dad used his fingers to tick off our blessings.

"The house is finished, the company is thriving, you all seem happy." We all waited for that fourth finger to open and what would be revealed. "I have come to a decision. I want to do something different, at least part time. The finger remained in his palm. "My years of service in the military were good ones. I formed friendships with men that will last a lifetime." We sat there wondering where this was all headed.

"No, I am not going back into the military, he laughed." Our raised eyes begged the question, then what?

"I would like to serve this city though. I'm thinking maybe Law Enforcement." With that his finger opened and we were left to wonder what that would look like. I don't think Dad really knew himself.

• — ◆ •• ◆ •• — •

Dad called Sheriff Oliver Rodriguez. They ran through some possibilities and Dad was encouraged to start out by volunteering in a program called Citizens On Patrol COP the acronym. Next week he would do a drive around with the sheriff. Older law enforcement vehicles driven by retirees are put to use to give a visual presence around town. 'Another set of eyes,' the sheriff called it. "If this is something you take to, you are certainly still young enough to go through the academy."

• — ◆ •• ◆ •• — •

At 5pm. Detective Monroe pulled into the parking lot at Franklin's residence. He recognized Joel's truck. Franklin was standing on the balcony, his hat visible. He waved down and buzzed the detective in. Chicken wings and garden salads were on paper plates on the table. Detective Monroe's stomach growled. Sweet tea in a gallon jug had already given up a serving or two.

Franklin met him at the door, ushering him to the table he told the detective to fill his plate and join them on the covered porch overlooking the Intracoastal. As he filled his plate he looked through the glass doors. Breanna and Franklin were just sitting down. He remembered the lady with Joel who was just raising a glass. She was the manager at Cluck's Chicken Coop. He had not seen her since the funeral. Detective Monroe joined them and cleaned up a six pack of wings before the conversation turned serious. Breanna filled the time by asking about the crossword puzzle. Detective Monroe confessed he hadn't done much with it since their visit.

With the wings gone and the napkin laid down, agenda item number one reached the table.

Myrtle handed the detective a paper with the name and address of the company Bellamy had given her. Joel spoke up. "Do you think he knows something?"

"Well we have a little prodding material now don't we? Again this is an active investigation so I have to be careful in what I say but I will say he is a possible material witness in two murders. We do need to talk with him. There are also possible charges of obstruction of justice hanging over him. I'm hoping we can convince him that right now the truth might set him free."

Myrtle spoke up, she sounded angry. "In my estimation he's just a typical twenty-one year old. She sounded like a witness for the prosecution. "Bellamy doesn't take anything serious. His work, his life. He didn't actually commit the crime so he doesn't see how anything is going to stick to him." Then she became the voice of the prosecution. "Charge the little shit with an accessory to murder, that will get his attention. Let him stew. Let him find out what a lawyer costs. He's not living in the real world. Put him there." She squeezed Joel's hand. Joel squeezed back.

Detective Monroe nodded his head. "Seems like you have an opinion on all this Myrtle. Great wings by the way." Myrtle sighed, a million of the second chances she had given these kids over the years passed before her eyes. "Indeed I do Detective, indeed I do. And thank you about the wings. We try."

Detective Monroe rose and shook hands all around. "I am personally traveling to Texas. I don't trust anyone to do what they say they are going to do. I'll be in touch when I get back. Wish me luck."

Detective Monroe checked in at the Sheriff's office and found a message on his desk. A number to call at corporate headquarters for Dunkin Donuts and a time to call tomorrow morning. He left and, already fed, went back to his home. He lived alone. His house smelled like he lived alone. Not a bad smell but definitely a single guy lives here smell. The last visitors had been Franklin and Breanna. He looked at the kitchen table, the puzzle remained unfinished. Progress yes, but like this case still much to sort out. He turned on the classical music he loved and nodded off while seated in his favorite chair.

Darkness had just filled the room when he awoke and found his way to bed. He pulled the top sheet on an unmade bed up around his ears. A long day tomorrow.

———◆◆◆◆——

At four am the alarm went off. Victor lay there for a moment. He still wasn't sleeping well but the cool nights with his window open seemed to refresh him. He would have to say, Maine had been good for him. *No more raft trips though that rough water brought too many things to the surface.* He planned to live here. He hadn't experienced a winter but how bad could it be? It was September, Labor Day had come and gone.

Troy told him he'd find out about a Maine winter soon enough. "That will be a whole different kind of driving, Victor."

He rose, stretched his arms still lame from all that paddling, the raft, then the kayaking. He allowed the shower to soothe him.

Today he would be making his first out-of-state run. He still didn't have a car but was living on a side street in North Anson, just under a mile from his workplace.

Troy was already at his desk when Victor, traveling on foot, arrived. The two shook hands. "You ready to solo see the world from ten feet in the air Victor? Once you cross that Kittery Bridge with you in control it's a different beast."

It was too early for Victor to comment so he merely nodded. He was hankering a cup of coffee to go. Troy seemed to read his mind. "Tanya makes the coffee, she don't like the way I make it."

"That's ok I'll just get a cup in Madison."

"So you just do what you've been trained to do. Don't let the crazies get to you. I'm just a call away." Troy did a review.

"Stop only at areas that have truck parking available. That rig can keep you out of a lot of trouble. But if you don't plan ahead it can get you into a whole world of problems. Call me with any questions. We've gone over where you are picking up your load. Your log book is on the seat." He shook Victor's hand.

Victor spent a few minutes with the engine idling and mentally going over what he had learned. He left North Anson at 5:25 am. Twelve minutes later he pulled to the side of the street in downtown Madison. He crossed and entered Dunkin Donut. He was second in line. A girl who looked half-asleep, was alone and in charge. The girl seemed to be a quart low on the brew she was selling. She yawned into her hand. When the customer left, Victor stood up to the counter. He ordered a large coffee, black, and two chocolate coconut donuts. He handed the girl his plastic tag. He had to explain to the girl how that worked. He gave her a big smile when he found he would only be paying for one of the donuts. He walked back to his truck. Seated, he opened the sipping part of the lid allowing the burning liquid to cool. He headed south towards route. He would be picking up a load from the paper mill in Hinckley fifteen miles away.

—•—•—•—•—

Around this same time of morning Detective Monroe was entering Interstate 95 north towards Jacksonville. He too had a coffee going. He checked his watch, 6:03 am. He had to make a call to Dunkin Donut headquarters at 9:00 am. He should be well on his way west on route 10 by then. He had never been to Texas. With nothing clouding his mind he absently found a public news station that asked him to support their efforts to offer quality programming. 'And now the news.' The news from Texas still focused on the damage done to Houston by Hurricane Harvey three weeks earlier. Well he was headed to Dallas, thank his lucky stars. The news went on to mention a storm at sea that was beginning to grow, threatening the Caribbean Islands. A clear track and intensity not yet determined.

— ◆—◆—◆ —

Sarah and I and my friend Daniel were up getting ready for school. Dad and Mom were seated at the kitchen table holding hands. We rolled our eyes at one another. Teddi was reaching the end of her puppy stage. She signaled she had things to do and places to go. Me, and my brother from another mother, grabbed the leash from where it hung by the door. <u>My turn.</u>

"Have at it," mom dragged out, her hands busy. I read her lips and chuckled.

My sister Sarah kiddingly just had to ask, "Are you reading dad's fortune?" Mom turned serious. "In a way I guess I am Sarah. Your dad is about to start a new career as a volunteer deputy. I was just telling him to be careful."

Sarah looked at dad. "You're too nice to be a cop, dad. Our resource officer is just plain mean."

"Well they aren't all like that. You like Sheriff Rodriguez don't you?" Sarah nodded.

"You can't judge people until you have interacted with them. I know you already know that." Sarah nodded.

Mom broke the spell. "Let me whip you up my latest breakfast recipe, it's delicious."

Sarah was not sure about that, but she nodded once again. Daniel and I returned with Teddi. We missed the entire conversation.

———•••———

Franklin and Breanna were still in bed, but they weren't sleeping.

———•••———

Joel who was back staying with Myrtle was up and out the door. He had to be to work by six. He was pretty happy these days. The tic had disappeared and renewed hope started every day.

Myrtle was awake. She couldn't get those two girls off her mind. She studied the ceiling. Just let a spider try to spin a web, she'd fix em.

———•••———

Hailey was up and showered, she had let her new man spend the night. Two months in she was regretting it but not sure how to end it. The guy was nice enough and very attentive. But the only word that fit him was bland. Daniel seemed to have accepted him. No affection on either side but they tolerated one another. Daniel spent as much time with Bobby as possible these days. She glanced at her watch. He would just be getting up at the Whiting residence. She would pick him up from school. Anyway she could hear the man snoring in the bedroom so she wouldn't have to face him across the breakfast table. She dressed and quietly closed the door behind her. She sighed as she sat behind the wheel of her car facing the wall in the garage. *Was she asking for too much?* Shelves holding cardboard boxes of her life at different stages loomed accusingly. Each one dated and carrying a memory. From left to right she traced the years. Different emotions emanated from those boxes. *High School, 1994-98, lots to cheer about. College, 99-01 three great years. Marriage, 01-08, was supposed to last forever. Daniel, 2007 best thing I ever did. Divorce 2008, a box filled with lies.* There was room for one more box on that shelf. Hailey nodded and spoke to the windshield. "I'll be damned if that space is filled with another failure." Her eyes sparkled with emotion. "I'm telling him tonight."

CHAPTER FORTY

Myrtle opened Cluck's Chicken Coop at 10:30 per usual. Arriving at 8:00 am she found the night crew had done a shit job of cleaning. The glass doors had not been wiped clean, there were crumbs lingering around the tables and chairs. Streaks of dirt on the tile indicated the mop had not been rinsed and wrung out. And that was just the front of the house. She had entered through the back door and a single glance toward the working part of the kitchen beginning with the sink had told her all she needed to know. She went to the whiteboard and wrote in big letters, **Manager's meeting at 4pm.** Be There. Inside she was seething. *Where was a damn spider or a roach that needed crushing when you needed one?*

Somewhere between here and there Detective Monroe wasstopping for lunch. That single donut had dissolved hours ago. He had gotten what he wanted from Dunkin Donut Corporate and they would be putting an alert out for any use of Victor Thorntons rewards card. They couldn't go backward in time but as of noon today the use of the card would be noted. They gave Detective Monroe a case number and a number to check in with between the hours of 9:00 and 5Pm Monday thru Friday.

Somewhere between here and there Victor pulled into a truck stop. He had been driving since dawn and needed to stretch his legs. As the miles passed he did his best to free his mind from the terrible things he had done. His boss had checked in with him offering reassurance. He liked his new boss and didn't like deceiving him. He was the first adult male, past coaches included, who seemed to believe in him. *I am going to make this work.*

He stood at a urinal remembering that first conversation with his future boss. He entered the restaurant and devoured a burger and a shake. Re-entering his big rig he again studied the itinerary. He would stop in Virginia for the night and arrive in Florida sometime tomorrow. He wasn't excited about going back to Florida.

⸺•⸺•⸺•⸺

George met with the five other men and one woman who patrolled the county as part of the **C.O.P** program. Their past professions ran the gamut from law enforcement to business careers and a retired teacher. The one commonality they shared was graying, white, silver, or a sparse amount of hair. George felt like the kid on the block. He still had a full head of dark black hair. He sat at a rectangle table in a conference room at the Sheriff's department listening to the stories they had accumulated in their new roles. Stories; some tragic, some down-right belly laughing funny but most resulting from stupid decision making. Coffee fueled the stories. They all seemed eager to talk. They all felt like they were making a contribution. George left the group feeling he would learn much from these folks. He would ride with each one on separate days then get his own vintage former cruiser. No siren or lights just two good experienced eyes and a radio to call in anything that appeared hinky.

Franklin was feeling a bit uneasy. Now with Joel's problems seemingly settled, things were going too well. His whole life until recently had been Franklin against the world. His uncle had turned that around in time. And now Breanna was going to make the turn-around permanent. The two planned to be married on a date closest to the first time they met at that convenience store. Breanna said she wanted kids. Franklin couldn't even imagine having kids. He loved Jule's and Danni's son though. He watched Breanna getting ready for work from the bed they shared. She was humming some little ditty that had her moving her feet. He smiled to himself. *That girl does love to dance.* All the books he had devoured over the last few years promised nothing. Heroes and heroines, victims and bad guys, all trying to find this elusive happiness that he was experiencing in real time. Franklin silently thanked his uncle once more and moved to join Breanna in her dance, quieting any misgivings.

CHAPTER FORTY-ONE

Victor delivered his cargo to a warehouse in Jacksonville, Florida two full days after leaving Maine. He spent the night in a motel. His trailer was being reloaded for a delivery back in Virginia and then he'd pick up another load to the northeast.

Troy had kept in touch. He was working on one more load that Victor would need to pick up and deliver in southern Maine. If all went according to plan Victor would be back in North Anson on Friday. Troy offered a vehicle until Victor could afford one of his own. Victor was excited for the weekend.

He drove his truck back to the warehouse and backed up to a loaded trailer. It was 6:00 am. He was hitched and on the road with the paperwork necessary by 6:45. Before getting back onto Interstate Ninety-five north he pulled over when he saw a familiar sign. He had completed half his trip and was feeling pretty good about it. This morning he sprung for an egg and cheese bagel, a chocolate donut and a large coffee all to go. He had no more rewards in his account at the moment but swiping that little tag promised more freebies in the future.

❖ ❖ ❖ ❖ ❖

Detective Monroe was waking up with lots of possibilities in his head. Today he would be meeting with the company manager where Bellamy had applied. The local police were cooperating and one of the lone star state's finest would be there to help oversee the sting.

He shaved and showered and put on a collar shirt and blue jeans. While brushing his teeth he studied his face from different angles. He was thirty-five years old and still single. Why was that? He didn't have a hundred stories to tell of love and loss. Mostly it was about timing it seemed. Not one to go looking for love in all the wrong places or even the right places for that matter, time had simply passed. Lately though, meeting Franklin and Breanna and seeing how they seemed to complement one another without hovering he kinda wished he had a little of that in his life.

He closed the light, grabbed his bag and left thoughts of friendly companionship making their way down the drain along with the final rinse of toothpaste. He chuckled to himself. A final thought, and a head nod accompanying it, *if this trip works out I'll have a companion manacled in the back seat on my way back.*

———◆◆◆◆◆———

George began his first solo, **C**itizen **O**n **P**atrol shift with a coffee from Starbucks riding shotgun. He took the opportunity to explore streets and named sections of the city he'd never paid attention to beyond building a house here and there. New construction was springing up on nearly every street. He saw names on trucks he recognized from competing companies. He knew from Hailey, and Betty who handled the books, their company was thriving.

He saw trees being removed and lots being readied for future homes. He viewed future homes and businesses at every stage of the permitting process. Much had happened since Hurricane Matthew struck last October. Now every news cycle was predicting and speculating another storm was a possibility.

He recalled last October when every street was covered with debris that lay piled up for weeks. He thought back to how his own business had grown from that storm. Happy for the business but he didn't like the pain it had caused people.

He approached an intersection where not long ago a red light camera loomed over traffic. He had been caught twice himself. One fine he agreed with. That one had been early on. The next fine caught him off guard and he determined the time between the yellow light and the red had been shortened. Apparently enough of his fellow citizens had arrived at the same conclusion and most of the lights were gone.

He drove and stopped whenever his interest was piqued and he talked with people. Those who knew him expressed surprise that George emerged from a police cruiser, even one without lights on the roof. George heard plenty of opinions on a hundred different topics.

The possibility of another hurricane seemed to start every conversation. More than one person or group voiced several times and in the end it struck home.

"Why don't you run for Mayor, George, we'd support you. You are an honest man, we know that much." He was invited to join a weekly gathering at Dunkin Donut to solve the world's problems. Ten of us gather around an outside table weather permitting and discuss anything and everything." The man offering the invite even used a term for the group, we're an old bunch of 'ROMEO'S **R**etired **O**ld **M**en **E**ating **O**ut."

George listened and when he got back into his cruiser his eyes moved to study his tan face. *Yep laugh lines were appearing around his eyes and to the sides of his mouth. Had he retired? No just a change of focus he decided.* He'd learn this city, street by street and opinion by opinion and maybe, just maybe, he would throw his hat in the ring. In his mind, like framing a new construction, he began framing how he would approach Lane with this crazy idea. *There was to be a special election in November and the election of a new mayor was on the ballot. Again In his mind he had already hired his strongest advocate, Lane, to be his campaign manager. Heck she's already building a social network with her blogs. Yep maybe he would make a run for it.* By the time he was done ruminating he had arrived in his own driveway. He grabbed his hat and went to share his latest dream. Once more, mom Sarah and I would serve as a sounding board. Served up along with the latest healthy food choice was on the menu.

———◆———

Hailey, as gently as possible removed the recently added smells and snoring sounds from her life. The man left under protest but when she told Daniel, he showed maturity beyond his years. His only comment: "You can do better Mom." When she pressed her son on what he meant it was clear his friend Bobby was rubbing off on him.

"He was like one of those pasta salads someone kept bringing to Mr. Whiting's cookouts. Sarah always puts a scoop on my plate and I end up throwing it out cause it has no taste."

Hailey laughed right out loud and hugged her son.

———◆———

Bellamy woke to a morning of possibilities. He had received a call from the manager and was being invited in for an interview. His parent's home where he had been staying, feeling uninvited since arriving back in Texas, was quiet this morning. Every little squeak of his movements were magnified. It seemed the house as well as his parents were holding their breath. Three years ago they thought he was out of the house for good and suddenly he had landed back on their doorstep. His mother made him a hopeful breakfast of eggs, bacon and toast. Bellamy assured his parents that with employment he would be trying to get a roommate or two and find his own place.

So it was a morning of possibilities that found Bellamy pushing open the glass door to the future. It was 10: 55 am, a full five minutes early for an interview that he had been told would be brief.

The Grilling would go on well after noontime. The questions asked were not part of any normal job interview. Bellamy found the material he had studied briefly then discarded as mundane were not covered at all.

When Bellamy left the interview he was shaking his head in confusion and protesting the long ride back to Florida wearing handcuffs.

The Texas Ranger who sat in on the interrogation gave the states blessing on removing one of its citizens. "Go Florida Gators," he uttered, pumping his fist as Bellamy disappeared into the back seat.

Detective Monroe was feeling as good as Bellamy was feeling bad. A few miles into his return trip he spotted an afternoon coffee spot and was reminded of a call he needed to make. When he received word that Victor's Dunkin Donut online account had been tickled this morning, in Florida no less, he mimicked the fist pump the ranger had offered up. "Go Gators," he said to his rear-view mirror. He pulled off the road and sent a text. The normally loquacious Bellamy continued to feign sleep. Detective Monroe simply smiled and squeezed the steering wheel.

——•———•••—•———

George and Hailey met for lunch, they had a guest today, Joel. The company was thriving. Hailey was directing this meeting today, George here as support. Coffee and water was ordered for the table and when the waitress left, Hailey began. "Joel, you have been doing a great job and today we'd like to offer you even more responsibility."

Joel removed his silverware from the napkin and abstractly began arranging it on the table. He met Hailey's eyes. Then he looked to George. George wasn't talking.

Hailey chuckled, "George is about to go all political on us Joel, so I'm being asked to run the company. George doesn't want anybody raising a conflict of interest issue at any meetings so I would like your help. You have knowledge that I still need to gain. So what we're offering is one fifth of the company." Joel's eyes bugged open.

"George has arranged it so Lane and the two kids own three fifths." Joel looked like he wanted to say something. Hailey held up her hand. Hear me out. "I don't have any money for this and I'm pretty sure you don't either." She looked at her new benefactor and smiled. "George is offering our share of the company on a pay as you go basis. So much is deducted each week over a period of time. Are you interested?"

Joel was about to answer when the waitress returned with the coffee and water. She went to work taking the orders and again left the table.

"This is unexpected." Joel was choked up. "I thought I had blown any chances to ever run a company again, much less have ownership." Eyes glistening he looked to George. "As I told you when you hired me at my worst, I won't let you down." Joel wasn't finished. "As crazy as it may sound, even with all that's happened and with what's still up in the air, I'm happier than I have ever been. And a good measure of it is thanks to you George."

"Don't thank me Joel all I did was recognize talent going to waste and took advantage of it. By the way we have another storm brewing and it has us in mind once again. I would suggest you two plan ahead and buy as many blue tarps as you can get your hands on. Let the crews know they might be working a lot of overtime in the coming weeks."

Joel followed Hailey back to the office while George went back to studying his city and its citizens.

━ ◆━◆━◆ ━

Myrtle was head deep in a follow-up interview when Joel texted her with two pieces of good news, his new job title and news of Bellamy's capture. Myrtle paused in her interview to check the message. The interview ended abruptly when the applicant questioned why Myrtle could have a cell phone and be answering during business hours when she couldn't. Myrtle offered up an interview ending smile. Myrtle shook her head. "I'll call you with my decision but you might want to keep looking, I don't think we're hiring this week. Myrtle watched the oblivious girl leave the building thinking she would get a call. *Jesus what is wrong with people.* "Juan," she shouted to the back, "you want to pull out that pile of applicants, we need to start over."

In school my sister Sarah was starting for the Junior Varsity soccer team as a freshman while according to the reports my mother was getting from my teacher I had captivated my classmates in my first mainstream class. She told Mom with the technology available and my natural gifts my disability was not a disability at all. She wrote Mom that her other students were asking her to help them learn Sign.

Life continued to be good in the house that Jack built.

CHAPTER FORTY-TWO

Bellamy remained mostly quiet on the ride back to Florida. The interview that got him in the back seat came to mind. *Detective Monroe, and that damn living rerun of the old cable show he watched as a kid,* **Walker, Texas Ranger,** *yeah that was it. Bellamy acknowledged only what could be proven in a court of law. Yes he had worked for the security company. No he had no idea what had happened to a portion of the security tape that had gone missing. Yes everyone who had viewed the tapes had signed in and out. Try proving otherwise. And yet he still found himself in the back of this damn car with his hands joined together at the wrist. Did they know something? Had Victor's father said something after all? Did Victor do something to Pearl?*

As the man in the mirror continued to throw out little suggestions that barely registered, Bellamy continued to wool gather a dozen different scenarios that in total had him beginning to feel the pain associated with restricted movement. His mother often complained of sciatica. A numbing pain was working its way from his butt down his leg.

"Hey can we stop a minute so I can take a piss and stretch my legs."

The man in the mirror simply smiled as he appeared to glance down at his watch.

"One hand washes the other Bellamy, and so far your hands haven't reached the washroom. Best I can offer is we'll be stopping for the night unless you have something you want to tell me." He plopped a mint between his teeth clamped down lightly and finished with a question as the mint lay motionless between his teeth. "You know what a vise is, Bellamy?"

Bellamy clamped his own mouth shut and tried to shift his weight.

———•—•—•—•———

Five hundred miles away Victor was entering North Carolina. His butt was becoming uncomfortable. Unlike Bellamy, cuffed and strapped in the back seat of a detective's car, Victor could pull into a truck stop, stretch, relieve himself and get an early afternoon coffee. What he couldn't do, no matter how many miles he covered and leg stretches he performed, was escape the fact that he had killed two women. He entered the restroom and did his business. A row of mirrors refused to change the image of his tortured soul. As he passed each one he was silently accused. Back in the big rig the mundane roar of the engine became background white noise while a ribbon of black mimicked a VCR tape on a loop, unfiltered by commercials. Even as he sipped his bitter brew the man riding shotgun every step of the way poked and prodded him. Call him by any name: Guilt, regret, sorrow, blame, denial, in truth his name was conscience. Victor found he still had a conscience.

Tobias Thornton had no conscience but he did have connections. He knew people he could rely on to pass along information. Sometimes that information led to real estate deals, sometimes it was just that; information. Lately he had reached out for information of a different sort. Today he got a text from a friend in the sheriff's office, a deputy who moonlighted as a part-time real estate agent in Tobias's company.

*The security guy you mentioned is being returned from Texas for questioning, Just thought you might want to know.

Tobias canceled a showing and took the afternoon off. Back at his newly purchased one bedroom condo, Tobias shut the shades, poured a bourbon and snapped on the TV.

Commercials offering fixes for every malady known to man flashed by in succession. Tobias holding the remote in one hand and sipping with the other began flipping through his options.

— ·— ◆ — ◆ — ◆ — ·—

In the early evening hours Detective Monroe pulled off route and searched for a motel. They had been on the road since noontime. Bellamy in the back seat had closed down, either napping or feigning sleep. He pulled into a quiet looking little place that had two metal chairs beside each unit. Detective Monroe explained to the owner who he was, then registered using the department credit card.

When he returned, Bellamy was staring out the car window at him. He opened the door and unbuckled Bellamy from the seat belt leaving the cuffs in place. Bellamy in obvious distress nearly fell out of the vehicle.

The door to their room was directly in front of the unmarked cruiser. Detective Monroe managed to open the door, loosen Bellamy's dungarees and get him onto the toilet. He filled his cuffed hands with toilet paper. "You manage the rest, which ought to be interesting."

He left the bathroom door ajar. When Bellamy finally finished, he emerged trying to hold up his trousers from the back with his two cuffed hands. Detective Monroe was on his cell phone. When he finished his call he helped Bellamy buckle up his pants. Then he sat him on one of the double beds. "I hope you were able to wipe yourself properly Bellamy, those cuffs can be inconvenient don't you agree." Bellamy looked straight ahead, said nothing.

"Let me tell you a story Bellamy. It's about a guy who gets put into prison for a crime he didn't commit. He fluffed up a pillow on Bellamy's bed. "Lay back there, get comfortable." Detective Monroe walked between the two beds continuing with his story. "The man wasn't completely innocent Bellamy, what he was guilty of was being stupid. Too stupid to realize he was an accomplice in covering up a very serious crime."

Bellamy attempted to get comfortable. Detective Monroe fluffed up another pillow and placed it behind Bellamy's head.

"The pillows in jail are about one quarter as thick as this one Bellamy, and depending on the size of your cellmate you might actually get to use it." He let that sink in. "So, this guy not knowing the perils of prison keeps what he knows to himself and gets convicted of obstruction."

He waited a beat. "That's not the end of the story, that guy drew the short straw. He didn't get to use that pillow, Bellamy." Detective Monroe opened his eyes wide, "And that's the easy part of the story. The rest is just plain ugly if you get my meaning." Detective Monroe looked around for something to attach a short length of chain to. "I'm going to go get us a sandwich, Bellamy." I'm going to allow those cuffs to be in the front." Detective Monroe re-cuffed his prisoner and used the short chain to secure him. He placed him back on the bed and handed him the remote. "Oh by the way, that same guy who takes your pillow, he'll decide what you get to watch in the day room. So enjoy the moment Bellamy." He followed with one last offer. "If you would like to sit like a normal person in one of those chairs out front and watch the sun go down, eat that sandwich without all that metal in the way, just think about what I'm asking you to do.

Bellamy flipped through channels until he found an old episode of **Fresh Prince of Bel-Aire.** He had grown up watching reruns of a world he'd never experience. His own life was now being transported back to a future he would never have predicted for himself. He needed a lawyer. He needed a lawyer real bad.

Sheriff Rodriguez returned from a trip to Jacksonville. He had received a text from his detective on the road who was transporting a possible material witness back from Texas.

*Sheriff, our prime suspect, Victor Thornton bought coffee at a Dunkin Donut this morning in Jacksonville.

A second text followed. *He stopped again this afternoon in North Carolina. There might be a video in Jacksonville. Could you go there and secure that tape? It may go a long way in explaining what he's doing back in Florida. I'll be back tomorrow. Write down this address for that donut shop.

Sheriff Rodriguez looked to his right at the man accompanying him on this trip. George Whiting and the Sheriff had become good friends. George wasn't privy to all that the Sheriff was doing in that donut shop. On the way up they talked about their families, politics, and the good and bad going on in their new little city.

On the way back the Sheriff let George drive while he texted the detective. * The video shows not only the purchase of donuts and coffee but also Victor Thornton walking across the road to a big rig. The video does not reveal the company name on the cab of the truck.* The Sheriff turned to George, "I can't tell you much but I will say, I think we are closer to eliminating your employee as a possible suspect in that girl's death." George smiled, "Well that's good news."

CHAPTER FORTY-THREE

Back in Palm Coast Detective Monroe was having coffee and a celebratory doughnut with Sheriff Rodriguez.

The Sheriff raised his cup. "Good job bringing back that kid from Texas."

Detective Monroe raised his eyes in acknowledgment while biting into a raspberry filled donut.

"The District Attorney sees him as a strong part of any prosecution. They are charging him as an accessory to get him to talk. He's out on bail already but he won't be leaving town. So there's that."

The sheriff took a sip of his coffee. He then opened a manila folder containing still photos he had developed from the surveillance tape at the Jacksonville Dunkin Donut. Detective Monroe studied the photos, "So he's got a beard now."

Sheriff Rodriguez began moving through the stack. "We have a grainy photo of him crossing the road. Can't see a company logo on that truck. Now he's standing in line at the counter. That one is pretty clear. Now He's exiting again and finally getting back into his truck. Still can't make out a name on the truck or a license plate."

"Victor driving a big rig, who would have guessed? He bought coffee again in North Carolina but no surveillance tape there, broken camera I was told. It seems obvious he's heading back north to who knows where."

Sheriff Rodriguez sighed, "We are going to have put this on hold for a day or two though. Hurricane Irma will be on us in thirty six hours. This is a big one and even if it doesn't hit us full on, it's going to cause major flooding. We need to evacuate everyone along the beaches and along the Inter coastal. We are just getting the word out. We'll need to manage it." The Sheriff rose and looked out the window at the thickening clouds. "Victor will have to wait." ^

Hurricane Irma hit the smaller Caribbean Islands as a category five storm. It tore through Puerto Rico creating what would become a humanitarian crisis and devastated parts of the Florida Keys. As Irma moved north, coastal Flagler and C section of Palm Coast was again asked to evacuate. Schools closed.

—•—⬦—•—

This seemed like the perfect time, at least in in George Whiting's mind, to head north to Maine for a family vacation and local history lesson. Having been born in the state George thought it was time for his family to help him reexamine his roots.

The odyssey began with the family sitting around the kitchen table. This was a week before the city began herding people north out of the state but it was clear they would have to leave their new home.

"I have always wanted to revisit where I grew up. Let's go to Maine for a couple of weeks. I've been online and we can rent a cabin on a lake near my old hometown." The response was not as enthusiastic as George had hoped. George took a different tack. "Ok let's go hiking, whitewater rafting, kayaking, visit some famous landmarks, and eat lobster right off a boat."

My sister and I perked up our ears. "But what about school?"

"Let me deal with that. The schools will be closed for several days anyway so you won't miss that much." Dad began his sell job. "You need to know more about my family. My roots are there. Besides, it's the best time of year to be in Maine. You guys have never picked apples, you have never seen a whole forest change color.

Sarah rolled her eyes at me, we didn't jump off our chairs in support. Finally dad played the, daddy needs this card. "I am about to try to take on a huge responsibility in this city. I need to know I'm doing it for all the right reasons. Going back to where I grew up and reconnecting with my past will help me do that." Dad looked from me to Sarah. "So besides all the fun things we can do up there, do this for me."

Mom spoke for the first time. "Your father has worked for over twenty years to give us all we have. Let's go help him celebrate his roots."

I got what I needed when my family agreed Teddi could make the trip.

Sarah just wanted to please dad.

We flew into Maine landing in Portland, where we promptly rented an SUV. Dad said we weren't going to hurry to our destination on Embden Pond which was three hours north and west.

We first stopped in a town named Freeport. Dad began his history lesson which would last for the whole trip. Dad had us standing in front of a bunch of plaques and murals celebrating a famous outdoorsman L.L.Bean. The legacy of the man sold us a tent and sleeping bags and a couple of coolers. I got my first jackknife.

Dad explained that the cabin we were renting would be simply a jump off point for a series of day trips and an overnight here and there.

Maine had experienced a warm dry summer. The long term forecast was for more of the same. Dad received daily updates of what was happening in Florida from Hailey.

"Be glad you are gone George this is going to be a monster storm."

"If you need me back there for any reason when it's over, just let me know."

"We're all going to be hunkering down for a while. I sent the men home to take care of their families. I think we got this."

Dad closed his phone. We all looked up from our lobster feed. I was harvesting a row of kernels from his ear of corn, butter dripping from his fingers while Sarah looked at dad over a lobster claw. Teddi had run to the end of the wharf and was worrying the gulls who kept swooping down nearly within reach of the family's dinner. Dad watched mom and Sarah take turns yelling first at the gulls then at Teddi. He seemed to be chuckling to himself. His final words to his business partner echoed Hailey's words for a whole different reason, "I think we got this," he smiled and dug into his own crustacean.

We left Freeport driving north on Interstate. We found interstate 95 in Gardiner. Thirty miles north we exited the Interstate highway. Driving north on route the mighty Kennebec came into view. Dad began to whistle. I guess seeing that waterway relaxed him. He was almost home. He pulled over and after looking out over that ribbon of water for a few minutes he asked Sarah to join him in the front.

Mom seemed to know what was coming and joined me in the back seat. She smiled and ruffled my hair as she buckled her seat-belt. Here it comes, her smile was saying. "Listen up," began a history lesson. Mom delivered the salient points to me with Sign. By the time the town of Skowhegan appeared at the bottom of a long hill and the island where Benedict Arnold and his men rested on their way to Quebec, a century and a half earlier, Dad too decided to take a break.

The Island dairy Treat which was in fact on that very island, served up homemade ice cream and the opportunity to revisit some more of

Dad's history. With cones in hand we listened to Dad tell of some of his boyhood memories. Mom tried to keep me in the loop while managing to keep her cone from melting.

Teddi began heading towards the entrance to a swinging bridge that at the moment was creaking from a couple completing their trek across, the bridge moving, the cables creaking. Dad laughed as he told of daily having to cross that swinging bridge delivering the morning paper at 6am. "That bridge terrorized me when I was just a little older than you Bobby."

I give mom a lot of credit. Her ability to Sign and keep the emotion of the moment intact left me feeling like I wasn't missing a thing.

Dad told his story. "It's dark at six am up here except for in the summer. Well it wasn't summer. There were two old geezers who at least once a week came across that bridge at the same time I was trying to cross from this side." Dad walked us part way out onto the bridge then began moving his body up and down. The bridge began to sway. I had to grab Sarah to keep my balance. Teddi's mouth was moving as he was being bounced around like a rag doll, our usually quiet little dog yapping up a storm.

"They were probably harmless, but they scared the bejeezus out of me. Remember I was only twelve years old." He laughed out loud, "I got some of my football moves getting away from those two." Holding his arm out feinting left then right.

We laughed at our father. Then he pointed to where the old Junior High School used to be.

"My own father went to school there and from the stories he told me he was a bit of a wise guy. By the time I reached that grade this place was torn down, the grades had moved to a former high school." Mom and Dad went back to the picnic table but my sister and I wandered back and forth across that bridge with Teddi being thrown back and forth barking furiously at her tormentors.

We bought groceries at the Hannaford in Skowhegan, then drove north and west thru the town of Madison and Anson on our way to the camp we had rented on Embden Pond. Dad made sure we kids knew that the river we crossed in Madison and the one we followed to North Anson was the same river the swinging bridge spanned.

Without knowing it, in North Anson we passed with-in a quarter mile of the home where Victor Thornton was renting a room. Small World.

Franklin and Breanna decided to stay in their fourth floor condo during the storm though they did cover their windows. When deciding not to evacuate, they had prepared for the hurricane by buying candles, batteries, bottled water and non-perishables. Breanna brought plenty of wine. They planned on cooking on a propane grill if the power went out. The power went out. During those hours without power, the wind and rain whipping up the water in the Inter coastal, they read by flashlight and candle light. It was in those hours before the storm struck, the time the storm was upon them, and the day and a half without power that it became clear to the two they didn't need anyone else in their lives. This morning over coffee, which after-all had been the starting point of their relationship, Franklin and Breanna firmed up plans for a holiday wedding. Jules would serve as best man and Danni maid of honor. The beach is where they would exchange their vows then a reception in the restaurant and wine shop.

When the storm passed, Hailey and Joel, now running Georges' business, drove flooded streets in the two big Ford F250's. The storm had done most of its damage in areas along the Inter Coastal. South Central Avenue in Flagler 383 beach looked like a war zone. Already people were carrying out soggy furniture and ripping out floors and drywall. Hailey had her notebook out noting addresses. When she caught someone home she left a business card. In the western part of the county, the St. Johns River had flooded causing equal misery. She began to mentally tally how many crews the company could manage. She called George's cell.

"I'll get back as soon as I can to help. Put together as many crews as you need." George looked out the window at a peaceful body of water. He felt guilty, but only a little. Today the family would be kayaking on the mighty Kennebec.

— • — ● • • ● — • —

The city had some cleaning up to do but the Sheriff's office had done their job and so they were getting back to business. Sheriff Rodriguez and Detective Monroe sat at a table once more reviewing what they now knew regarding Victor Thornton.

"We haven't had a hit in the past few days. Not sure what that means. Maybe a layover. Maybe someone else is buying his coffee. Maybe he's figured out that he's leaving a trail. But I really doubt that."

Detective Monroe wiped the sugar from his mouth. He looked once more at the blown-up photo of Victor standing at the counter. "So what do we do now? We still don't know who he's driving for or exactly where he's headed.

"Well Detective, while you were driving back from Texas I was doing some thinking. And now that the storm has passed and you won't be fighting a northern flow of traffic we start with you driving up to North Carolina. As it turns out old Victor might be further north than we imagined. I got a call from George Whiting, he's not certain but thinks he might have seen Victor on a river up there. His wife got a picture. She'd send it but they got no signal where they are staying. George called from a land-line. He is going to bring it in when they return. So you might be heading north from the Carolina's to see the fall foliage. If he starts feeding his habit again and it's in Maine, he'll lead you back to his company headquarters. We'll let local authorities in that state help us pick him up."

Detective Monroe sighed, "Can I shower first?"

Bellamy had a lawyer-ed up. A public defender assigned. He was free but cautioned not to leave the state. Back in Palm Coast without a job and no car he was now staying on the open porch of his friend Treats house. Treat's Momma got the last word by moving him from the bedroom. He needed a job. Some of these nights were getting chilly. He borrowed money for bail from Treat's mother who was hoping her investment in Bellamy might once again reap a good bonus. But the move to the porch showed she was hedging her bet.

Bellamy had a lot on his mind. *He remembered well the revolver that accompanied the payment in the parking lot of Walmart. Should he try to contact Victor's father and assure him he would not name him? Was there more money to be had from this guy? Was he serious with that gun? Did the man even know he was back in town? Would Tobias Thornton help him pay for a good lawyer?*

After three days of riding a bicycle around the city not wanting to get his hands dirty cleaning up debris, he showed up at Cluck's Chicken Coop. Myrtle was working in the back, preparing for the day. The time was eight thirty am. Bellamy rang the buzzer at the employee entrance. Myrtle was alone in the building. When she pushed the back door open, a rush of air emerged from a large blower above the door. The violent burst of air designed to keep flies from entering the restaurant from the outside worked as advertised but also stood your hair straight up, like whoever was asking for entrance was a physical threat. Myrtle looked Bellamy straight in the eyes. She swallowed her tongue wondering if she was in trouble.

Bellamy gave her his infectious smile but seemed nervous, moving from foot to foot. His wise guy persona was still intact though.

"Hey Bellamy."

"Good morning Myrtle, love your hair."

Myrtle couldn't help but smile.

That seemed to relax Bellamy a bit. "Can I come in?" Inside with his back to the sink, he began, "Do you remember that call from a couple of weeks ago?"

Myrtle, wondering where this was going, smoothed her hair. "Of course. I faxed a positive recommendation. You didn't get that job?"

Bellamy wasn't sure how much to share but in the end partially opened up to Myrtle.

Myrtle studied this young man for a moment. *He didn't seem to be a bad kid. But confused, Oh yeah.* "Wow. I had no idea. So since you last worked for me you got to Texas, got a ride back here in a police car, spent three days in jail and may have to go to court as an accessory to murder. That's a lot Bellamy." Realizing he had made no connection whatsoever to her she reached out. "What do you need from me?"

"Bellamy pushed himself away from the sink. He stood up straight. "I trust you Myrtle. I know I screwed up." He wrung his hands. "So I need two things. Some advice and hopefully a job."

Myrtle took a deep breath. She thought of the hundred cop shows she had watched; *was she about to become a confidential informant again?*

She covered her nervousness by throwing Bellamy a life line. "You know me Bellamy, I'm all about second chances. So what's this advice you need?"

By nine thirty when the morning staff started arriving Myrtle knew much more than the authorities did about the who, the what, and the why of Bellamy's involvement in the murder that Joel had been accused of. Pieces still missing but the spigot had been turned on. "You can't tell anyone Myrtle, I need to find a real lawyer. Maybe they can tell me what to do. I need money for that.

Myrtle checked the schedule. "I can give you a shift tomorrow Bellamy, and three more, later in the week. I don't need to go over the ground rules, do I?"

"I'll be all knees and elbows Myrtle, I promise. I'll make this place shine. Those chickens won't have a thing to squawk about."

Myrtle chuckled in spite of herself. *That boy does have a way with words.*

With a handshake Bellamy exited the back, his final comment swallowed by the rush of the blower and the slamming of the steel door.

Myrtle sighed. Lots to absorb. But first she needed to open this damn business. She pasted on a smile.

—◦—◦◦—◦—

Tobias Thornton paced the floor, remote in hand. He had received information that Bellamy was back. He also knew where he was living. *What to do, what to do. Well one thing for sure no more nightly prayers, obviously the big man was leaving him to figure this out on his own. Could it be my delivery? He chuckled grimly.*

Tobias, with half a prayer still intact, decided to wait on any action. If Victor would just stay gone there would be no need to do anything. Tonight with a bourbon well iced, the remote warm to the touch, images flashing, a sound bar offering a staccato of disjointed sound bites, Tobias closed his eyes. Amid that assault on the senses came one more sound from a different source. Tobias didn't recognize the ringing at first. When the sound finally made it into his addled brain he opened his eyes. He tried to locate his cell phone which had found its way to the bathroom counter. The ringing stopped. He opened the phone but didn't recognize the number. There was a voicemail. 'I'll call back. Don't try to reach me.'

Tobias sat down on the toilet and played the message over and over. He drained his third bourbon and sucked greedily on the remaining ice as if trying to gather strength from it. In the living room the TV continued to blare. Tobias missed the ringing of his doorbell. Once more by the time the buzzing filtered through his liquored brain, the noise had ceased. He stumbled his way in the darkened room to the window. A figure was just disappearing from view. ^

Myrtle told Joel all that Bellamy had shared. Joel went to Franklin for advice. Franklin told Joel he would discuss it with the detective. In the end, like connecting pieces of one of Detective Monroe's jigsaw puzzles a pattern began to emerge.

CHAPTER FORTY-FOUR

There are twenty four hours in a day. Those twenty four hours include a time to work, a time to play and a time to rest. The aftermath of the storm offered a visual reminder that the resting part had been taking a hit. Picking up debris, raking, bagging, and putting it all out roadside, lots of sore muscles accompanied that first cup of coffee these days. And these were the fortunate ones.

Others who had suffered damage to their homes returned with takeout coffee, their own pots sitting idle in darkened kitchens. They stood on the street continuing to take inventory, trying to reach their Insurance Company while salvaging memories from the soggy mess.

The worst damage to homes in the county took place in Flagler Beach, partly from the intense rain as well as the storm surge from the InterCoastal. The western part of the county received extreme flooding from The St. Johns River. The city of Palm Coast, while littered with tree limbs and debris saw little damage to homes beyond a few roofs hit by falling trees.

— • — • — • — • —

Home from our vacation the kitchen table was again serving as the hub for the family. Hurricane Irma put a temporary stop to Dad's active pursuit of a career change. Our new home had not received any damage so he spent his mornings visiting those less fortunate in Flagler Beach. He bought boxes of coffee and doughnuts at one of the shops in Flagler beach. He put his campaigning for mayor on hold. Lane continued campaigning though, reaching out on his behalf with her blog and the feedback was encouraging.

Schools reopened. Today was Wednesday. I loved Wednesdays. In my mind two good things happen on Wednesdays. Science class runs a double class period and then in the afternoon physical education class is held. The afternoon was on my mind when I lifted the bowl to my lips and slurped the remaining liquid. I couldn't hear myself belch but I guess Mom did. She gave me the look. <u>Excuse yourself young man.</u>

<u>Sorry mom that new cereal is good.</u>

She gave me a big smile and shook her head at me.

<u>By the way guys, if you aren't busy this afternoon I am running a timed mile in gym class. We've been doing shorter distances for practice but today it's for real. I want to win fastest in my class.</u>

<u>So that's what all those sprints around the neighborhood have been about.</u>

My sister spoke up. "He's almost as fast as me Mom." "Well he comes by it naturally, your father was a really good athlete when he was younger." <u>Can you let Dad know?</u>

<u>We'll be there today to watch you.</u>

I smiled.

Mom smiled right back but her mind seemed to be someplace else. Even with my mind reading abilities I had no way of knowing she was mentally back on the river in Maine. And what they may or may not have seen. Mom had taken a picture and Dad had called Sheriff Rodriguez from Maine. He had delivered the photo as soon as we got home.

— • — • • • — • —

Bellamy, true to his word, was doing a good job at Cluck's Chicken Coop. The job was not paying enough for a lawyer though. As he parked his bike outside the Coop his thoughts turned to the only other place he might reach out to for money. He had not made contact with Mr. Thornton, but had left a voicemail. He had also rung his doorbell then became frightened and took off.

Lead detective, Errol Monroe had followed a lead that had gone cold since an initial contact from the suspect. Detective Monroe flew to North Carolina and rented a car. He hung around waiting for a call that Victor had used his rewards card. Nothing. He returned when the sheriff called him with information his back seat passenger, Bellamy had shared with her old boss at Cluck's Chicken Coop. That was agenda item number two for this morning's meeting.

More importantly George Whiting had possibly sighted Victor Thornton on a river in Maine. Detective Monroe nursed what was becoming a never ending cup of coffee while living a soap opera of a case. To his mind the photo clearly showed Victor Thornton in a kayak.

The construction company, THE HOUSE THAT JACK BUILT, was right out straight with rebuilds, remodels and roof replacements. What a late summer it had been. The city seemed ready for autumn to begin. Be careful what you wish for.

CHAPTER FORTY-FIVE

Historically November in Florida can be described as delicious. With hurricane season winding down, cooler evenings and mornings bring people outdoors. Windows are opened, the number of people populating the sidewalks for an evening stroll increase, and collectively the entire state takes a deep breath as it prepares for the holiday season.

Tuesday people in Flagler County will be going to the polls for a special election. On the ballot are two positions on the county school board that have become vacant, one county commissioner position, and the mayor for the city of Palm Coast. George Whiting got in the race late then put things on hold after Hurricane Irma but seemed to be making up ground. Lane had continued with her blog and if word of mouth could be trusted George Whiting just might pull this off.

While the headlines in both weekly papers, The Observer and The Tribune, focused on the up-coming election, holidays events, recent and future new construction, below the surface one bit of unfinished business remains. No one had been brought to justice in the murder of two young women.

━ ◦ ◦ ◦ ◦ ◦ ━

Victor was in the north when Hurricane Harvey hit Houston then Hurricane Irma struck Florida. His company made a business decision and had given their employees three weeks off with half pay. The company owner brought his employees together to make the announcement. "We do a lot of business in the south. When the dust settles from these storms we'll have six months of flat out over the top business for the company. When you come back, be prepared for long weeks and months. Spend some time with your families, you won't be seeing them much for a while."

Victor spent the weeks on the river. He kayaked every day. Easy paddling compared to a white water rafting trip but even in the gentle turning over of water he saw the flaw in his fabric. The weather was fabulous. Looking down into the cooling waters of the Kennebec River he could almost imagine just staying right here in this little town and starting over. In the next turn of the paddle he could not imagine being on the run for the rest of his life. *Yes he would go back and face the music. No, I'll just stay right here.* On his last day on the river Victor was lost in the mesmerizing flow of water and the glinting sun. He thought he was alone. Then he heard a dog bark. He looked up. The dog seemed to be barking at a group of ducks. He met the eyes of each family member. No conversation passed beyond a nod. *I must be hallucinating. Was that his boss from the construction company? I'm sure that's his kid. I know that dog for sure.* All the old nightmares returned at that moment. He nearly swamped his kayak as he blindly made his way to the shore. He sat in the shallows breathing deeply, dizzy and feeling as if he might pass out. When he left the river for the last time a decision had been made. He would go back and face an uncertain future. But at least maybe those girls would let him get some sleep. He felt better than he had in a year. So unbeknownst to his Employer, this morning would begin his last trip in a big rig. He fueled up with a coffee to go in Skowhegan, Maine. He hadn't tasted a good cup of coffee in a while. Maine had been good to him and he felt bad about leaving his boss in a lurch; he would at least let him know where he would leave the truck after delivering his last load.

— • —

Detective Monroe entered Cluck's Chicken Coop and asked the manager to send Bellamy to his table. He ordered a chicken sandwich and a soft drink. He filled his cup then walked to the furthest booth to sit down to wait for his order. Bellamy arrived with the detective's order on a tray and a cellophane wrapped chocolate chicken mint. He stood at the edge of the booth, body language shaping his words. "You wanted to see me? How did you even know I work here? Are you following me?"

The detective had to chuckle, "Sit down Bellamy I'll tell you all you need to know." The detective studied the wrapped sandwich. "Have you eaten Bellamy I'll buy your lunch if you're hungry? I hate to eat alone. I do way too much of that."

Bellamy sat. "I do love the wings here."

Detective Monroe smiled. "Well order some up and a soft drink too. Let's just talk Bellamy, maybe we can find a way out of this mess."

Five minutes into the sandwich and Bellamy's wings Detective Monroe got to the reason he was here this morning. "Information has reached my ears that you, Bellamy, are the one who destroyed the surveillance tape and that you were paid to do it."

Bellamy nearly choked on a wing. "That's a lie sir, I had nothing to do with erasing any tape."

"Why would someone come to me with something like that if it weren't true?"

What Detective Monroe was throwing at the wall hoping a little might stick was part of the story Bellamy had shared with his boss Myrtle Beech. The Detective was using a variation of that conversation to plant a seed with Bellamy. "Look Bellamy I don't believe it either but my bosses, they don't know you like I do. Hell we roomed together," he chuckled. "You got to give me something here. You do know more than you've been saying, right?"

Bellamy sucked on the bone of the last chicken wing. He studied the Detective. *How much of this was Netflix and how much of this was truth?*

"So you can't tell me who this someone that's accusing me is?"

"Doesn't work like that Bellamy. I'm giving you the opportunity to get ahead of this if it's not true. Otherwise you get to become part of a trial transcript. Someone is going down for conspiracy that much I can tell you. I'll tell you something else," he whispered, "The person who came forward is well respected in the community." That was another little nugget gleaned from Bellamy's revelation to Myrtle.

Bellamy wondered to himself if Mr. Thornton had decided to try to cut his losses. He tried to absorb all this. He needed to talk with him ASAP.

Suddenly those chicken bones seemed to draw his full attention. They sparked a memory of the one story he remembered as a kid, and that from the **Rocky the Flying Squirrel** animated version of **Hansel and Gretel.** He saw in those chicken bones Hansel sticking a bone out through those bars day after day keeping that half blind witch bitch from burning him alive. Was the detective trying to trick him? Seemed like maybe so. "Well thanks for the lunch Detective but I'll take my chances with what **I** know to be true."

Detective Monroe rose, studied the young man for a moment, shook Bellamy's hand and left. He sat in his car for a full five minutes jotting down what the plan would be from here. He had planted the seed. He called into the Sheriff's office and put the plan in motion. Just needed Bellamy to follow the plan.

When Bellamy's shift ended and he hopped on his bike he didn't see the unmarked vehicle that left the parking lot shortly after he did.

— · — ◆ — · — ◆ — · —

The new mayor of Palm Coast took his family out to dinner. Sarah and I insisted on wings. Mom studied the menu at Cluck's Chicken Coop, she supposed she could get the garden salad and a cup of water. For tonight she wouldn't force the kids to eat smart, let them have their wings, it was a celebration after all.

Myrtle was on duty and came to the table to congratulate dad on his victory. I had seen Myrtle at one of the cookouts and I liked her smile. She handed us both a chocolate chicken mint.

She also thanked dad for all he had done for Joel. "He's a new man since he went to work for you." Dad thanked her but insisted Joel had turned his own life around. "Certainly Myrtle you had more to do with it than I did."

"Well, anyway this meal is on the house." She handed back the credit card receipt dad had signed. Marked VOID.

Somewhere between Massachusetts and New York, Victor stood at a urinal emptying himself of one more trip down memory lane. He found himself- both on the road and at every stop-playing a game of mental **whack a mole.** One minute vowing to make restitution and in the next moment remembering the peacefulness of the river.

Back in his rig and still mentally wrist wrestling with himself an irate driver cut him off. Victor swerved and slammed on the brakes to avoid a collision. A blaring horn, and a black arm emerged from the window of the offending driver, one finger extended.

A different emotion arose in Victor; anger. Suddenly the black kid who in Victor's mind had started all this, morphed into the tailgater. The lies about Pearl flooded the cab, overtaking the feeling of guilt that was riding shotgun. In that moment Victor filled his emotional void with a new purpose, revenge. Victor squeezed the steering wheel. He shook his own arm at the windshield, picked up speed honked his horn, he swore, He accelerated further. *He'd knock this shit head right off the road.* Only a passing police car going the other way with lights flashing shocked Victor into easing off.

Sweating and shaken, he pulled into a breakdown lane and sat there breathing like he was going to have a heart attack. Clarity of his situation emerged with the slowing of his heart and Victor mad a decision. *Know what, none of this is my fault. Any way I play this I'll be spending the rest of my life in prison.* He took a series of deep breaths. His anger cooled. *And like trying to chase down that asshole driver all it guarantees is being caught.* The peacefulness of those days on the river refilled his head. He just needed to do what he was doing, don't break any laws, keep his nose clean. One other thing he decided, he was not going back to Maine. If that was his old Boss and his family he'd seen on the river and they had recognized Victor, they would be tracking him up there for sure.

He pulled into a truck stop. He had changed his mind again. His continued freedom was in his own hands. Standing at the urinal he found relief in his decision.

One thing that didn't change, his love of a good Dunkin Donut coffee.

Coffee in hand he headed for his truck. Not one to examine his surroundings, the new Victor looked around. Everyone was going about their business, not making eye contact. *Just stay cool Victor and find a new place to light.* I can do that.

A girl was hanging around just outside the building, looking lost. *Why not,* thought Victor. Having someone with him could help add camouflage. He asked the girl if she needed a ride. When she nodded, he offered to buy her a coffee. It was a very different sound that filled the cab when Victor pulled back onto Interstate 95 south.

•-•••-•

Back in Palm Coast the weather was delightful. Once again our family was taking nightly walks beneath the stars. We all wore headlights as dark-dark came earlier and earlier. Even little Teddi wore an Led light around her neck. My sister and I scuffed along trying not to step on cracks in the sidewalk that appeared every ten feet or so.

The two fit bit exercisers, well ahead passed the Condo building that was a crime scene so many months ago.

Mom asked dad what was happening with all that.

"Well after meeting with the Sheriff and the detective they have made contact with authorities in Maine. They are checking with all the long haul carriers, in the state of Maine."

Mom shuddered. "I still worry about Bobby having to testify if they ever catch him."

Dad sighed, "We'll cross that bridge when we come to it." He reached for Mom's hand.

Little Teddi remembering the parking lot where he nearly got kicked began barking at the memory.

— • • • • —

Four stories up Franklin and Breanna were putting together a crossword puzzle. Detective Monroe's hobby had sparked Breanna's interest. Franklin kidded he might be better at just making something appear rather than locating it from a pile. The windows were open and they heard a little dog yapping as it passed the building.

— • • • • —

In St. Augustine also in a condo building on the fourth floor Myrtle Beech and Joel were having a late dinner. Joel was cooking these days. He seemed intent on reinventing himself. Tonight he made Pizza dough from scratch. Myrtle loved being catered to, she sighed contentedly. ^

Back in Palm Coast Hailey took her son Daniel out for pizza.

Detective Monroe took himself out for pizza. He arrived at the door to Mezzaluna's, on the south side of the city at the same time Hailey and Daniel were about to enter. Detective Monroe opened the door for them and stood just behind as they waited for a table. A busy place. The hostess, a little frazzled, made the mistake of thinking the three were together. She grabbed three menus and without turning her head motioned them to follow. Hailey and Errol Monroe chuckled nervously but Daniel smirked and grabbed the detective's hand. "You can sit with us, right Mom?" ^ Bellamy, was out into this same night. He had located Mr. Thornton's Mercedes a week ago in the parking lot of his Real estate office. He remembered the passenger door panel from his first visit with the man in the WalMart parking lot on that rainy night. On the man's cell number he had left a message, tonight he wanted to speak to him. He rang the bell, this time he wouldn't run off.

Mr. Thornton opened the door holding a glass of liquor and ice. "I wondered if I might hear from you, Bellamy. A little birdie told me you were back in town. That was your voice on my cell message wasn't it? You didn't ring my doorbell and then run off did you? What is it you want from me?"

Bellamy made no attempt to go inside. "The cops are looking to jam me up about that tape. Somebody is saying I erased that tape." All this was making him breathless. He tried to calm himself. "I'm going to need a good lawyer, I'm going to need some money."

Mr. Thornton spoke reasonably, "I already gave you money Bellamy, remember. That didn't do me much good now, did it?"

"First off, I didn't come back here by choice. But now I got just two choices Mr. Thornton" Bellamy shook his head. "I get me a good lawyer, or I have to tell them all I know."

"Well that isn't a good idea Bellamy. Why don't we sit down and work something out."

As Bellamy entered and closed the door Bellamy watched Mr. Thornton move to a shelf. He relaxed a little when what sounded like ice clinked in a glass.

"Sit, Bellamy, sit." Mr. Thornton sat down beside him squeezing a whiskey tumbler in his right hand. He was barely able to keep the fury he was feeling out of his voice, but he managed. Both remained silent for a full minute.

Mr. Thornton broke the ice after sucking down a slug of bourbon. "I have to go check on a property tomorrow afternoon, suppose you meet me there. I don't keep money in the house. We'll work this out."

Tobias Thornton gave Bellamy the location, the directions and the time. When Bellamy complained that he would be riding all that way on his bike Mr. Thornton suggested a shortcut on a bike path through the woods. "You'll see the giant smokestack when you reach the end of the path. "Don't disappoint me again, Bellamy."

⸻ ❖ ⸻

A thousand miles north Victor pulled into a stop for big rigs. On a first name basis with the girl who replaced old doom and gloom in the passenger seat, Victor asked Nadine to go ahead and do whatever she needed to do then pick us up a coffee to go from Dunkin donut. "I'll get us a sandwich. You like Burger King?" The girl nodded her head. "I'll pick you up a Whopper and fries and meet you back at the truck." He handed the girl a twenty dollar bill and his keys with the Dunkin donut rewards card attached. The girl looked at him quizzically.

"I might have a free donut coming," he smiled. "Hand them the keys. They will swipe this little tab."

As the girl walked away Victor yelled after her, "Chocolate Coconut if they have it."

He watched as she disappeared into the travel mart his head filled with new possibilities. *Yup this new Victor, he was in full control.*

—————•—•—•—•—————

Detective Monroe was sitting on the toilet reading an issue of National Geographic when he heard a ping on his phone. A dated issue he had picked up as a give-away at the local library was attempting to define what constitutes Genius. Albert Einstein graced the cover. Detective Monroe finished his business and checked his phone. It seemed Victor Thornton was still buying coffee and donuts, this time in Virginia. *This guy is no genius. We should have nailed him by now.* He dialed the number in the message. An hour later the manager, having reviewed the tape, called back.

"It was a girl who swiped that rewards card. No male in the picture."

Detective Monroe went to his kitchen table and sat down. His cross word puzzle, still unfinished, allowed the polished glass surface covering the wooden table to shine through. He spent twenty minutes locating a single puzzle piece that completed a corner. He cocked his head first right then left. He Spoke to himself aloud, "Just got to stay with it detective." He checked his watch. Timing was everything it seemed. Just a week ago he met a lady and her son. Just happened. No rhyme nor reason but here he was checking his watch, counting the hours before he would be taking the lady and her son out to dinner. His last thought before closing the door behind him, *I wonder if Victor has found himself a lady. We need to find this guy before he hurts someone else.*

CHAPTER FORTY-SIX

Mayor George Whiting had a headache. This might have been the first honest to goodness headache he could remember. He sat in his office wondering what on God's green earth had possessed him to think he would be a good mayor. Simple yes and no answers after considering the alternatives had held him good stead as a businessman. What he was finding in the first month in office was every yes and no answer upset someone. Furthermore people were beginning to call his home with their concerns. Some wanted favors, some wanted attention, some wanted to vent. He had just come from a meeting where a gated community asked him to speak. *Stupid George thought they really wanted to talk about the new ten year plan for the city's growth.* He chuckled, though that made his head ache worse. "OOOH!" He held his head in his hands. *For a smart man George you got a lot to learn if governing is going to be a long term career choice.* He shook his head. That hurt as well.

An hour ago he had listened to complaints about traffic, the time between light changes, traffic patterns, speeders, how slowly the swale drains, the need for more street lights, need for the city to have its our own police department, better coordination of debris pick up after major storms, and with all that; taxes are too high.

After he had listened to an hour of this, George simply put his hand up. "Put your concerns in writing and sign your name and I will respond. Before I respond I will do my homework just like I ask my kids to do every night."

He made sure to make contact with every eye in the room. "So before you put that concern in writing I suggest you do your homework as well. You do that you'll answer a lot of your own questions and I think the number of letters and e-mail I get will dwindle down to something I can actually handle." There was a lot of disgruntled crowd noise that ended the meeting. George didn't wait around for the lunch he had been promised.

Now sitting on the second floor in his home office he looked out over the InterCoastal waterway. The headache had settled just behind his eyes. *Maybe he was hungry.* He breathed in, he breathed out. *His wife had taught him that.* Outside it was calm and peaceful, the winter sun warming the day into the low seventies. *Notice the beauty of the moment* his wife reminded him daily. He chuckled. That woman, my woman, had turned her quest for health into a mantra. He heard the Vacuum downstairs. He sat there reflecting on just how happy she had made him. The pain seemed to be easing. Two great kids both thriving and growing and contributing. This wonderful house, a successful company that gave him freedom to try new things. His headache disappeared as he replaced complaint with contentment. He walked down the stairs and pulled the plug on the vacuum. Lane looked to the cause of the power failure and was greeted by the 100 watt smile of the man she loved.

"Let's go get a late lunch, I didn't get fed at that meeting. On second thought, hold that thought." He took Lane's hand and began to climb the stairs.

◦•◦•◦•◦•◦

Tobias had still not heard from his son. He could only play the cards left in his hand. If Victor is ever brought back here to stand trial and that black kid testifies, it's over. Well today will take care of part of this problem. Tobias checked the time. He had lived in Palm Coast for the past twenty years. He had met some shady characters who found this little bit of paradise. He had sold some of them houses. He had employed some of them to rehab some of his properties. Some of them offered additional services. The doorbell rang. Why here was one of those characters now. He answered the door to a very distinctive Russian accent.

An hour later Tobias pulled into an abandoned parking lot well off the beaten track. An old cement plant chimney stood tall and silent.

Bellamy stood sweating from his bike ride, leaning against the 150 foot tall structure, his bike lying on the ground. From a fifty foot distance he watched an automobile he recognized pull in and park. He stared into the windshield. He could not make out the figure behind the tinted glass.

Half a minute passed before Tobias got out of his car quietly closing the door. He faced Bellamy wearing shorts and a tee shirt and open toed sandals. Not exactly killers clothes Bellamy decided and sighed in relief.

Tobias smiled big and waved an envelope that seemed thicker than the one he had passed Bellamy months ago. Bellamy made a decision to relax, his fight or flight gene calmed. He pushed away from the concrete and walked toward the hand that was being offered.

Tobias spoke, "Walk with me Bellamy, let's work this.

As this walk was unfolding, miles away a frenzied call had reached the Sheriff. "We lost him Sheriff, he crossed Belle Terre against traffic and disappeared along the walking trail." The deputy's voice grew more animated. "We turned into towncenter hoping to locate him. We're at the trail intersection now." The deputy's voice lowered as if Bellamy might hear him, "we have been here for twenty minutes but he hasn't appeared. We don't know if he headed back onto Belle Terre or is somewhere on the trail. We just don't know."

The sheriff was livid. He wanted to ask his deputies why they hadn't taken Royal Palm a much shorter, less circuitous, quicker route to that intersection.

George had told him when describing what the construction trade was like, it's fine as long as you double check every single job every day. *This job is a lot like that too I guess.*

In a quiet almost soothing voice that his men early on in his tenure had recognized as seething anger, he offered, "Have you considered he might have stayed on that trail, crossing Old Kings Road? You might want to ask for a patrol car to head to Colbert Lane and talk to anyone coming out of that end of the trail." The sheriff paused to collect himself. "Ask anyone if they saw a young black man riding a bike. If that pans out, call it in. In the meantime I'll get an officer on a motorbike onto the full length of that trail. As for you, don't leave that intersection."

The Sheriff turned to Detective Errol Monroe shaking his head in frustration, he explained what had happened. "We have been following him for a while now, he ever taken that trail before?"

Detective Errol Monroe shook his head. "He's never even been on that side of town that I know of. Either he's onto us and is trying to shake the tail or he's headed somewhere brand new. I don't see the kid being out for exercise."

"We'll keep someone in those areas, see if he re-emerges. Maybe the kid has found a new girlfriend."

"Let's hope that's what it is."

Tobias led Bellamy away from the cement plant. He pointed along the dry ground where seashells littered the area. He began telling Bellamy how this cement plant, stuck way out here, had once been a thriving industry. "Those sea shells were trucked in here by railroad car, ground up and mixed, then exited on those same railroad cars as cement to build cities all across this state and beyond."

Bellamy half listened. His mind wandering, antenna up, wondering where this was all headed; part of his brain looking for an escape route. They walked for five minutes or so. Mr. Thornton continued going on and on about the history surrounding these shells. Bellamy was getting nervous. This trail wasn't going to bring him anything but bad. He decided he needed to get out of here. He spotted a possible escape. He'd have to make his decision in the next twenty seconds or so.

Then Tobias abruptly stopped. He studied the fallen tree covering the path in front of him for a moment then turned back toward the smoke stack. He took the envelope from his back pocket and handed it to Bellamy. "Go ahead and count it Bellamy." Bellamy took a deep breath and relaxed once again.

As Bellamy counted the money Tobias continued his monologue.

"Nothing to see out here anymore," he waved toward the horizon, nothing stays the same Bellamy, this was just a brief history lesson."

The two made their way back the way they had come. Neither spoke. When Mr. Thornton's car came back into view a man was leaning against it. Bellamy did not see any other vehicle nearby. "History is a great teacher Bellamy if we'll just pay attention."

Bellamy, becoming uncomfortable began to look for an exit.

"Who is that guy Mr. Thornton?"

Mr. Thornton smiled, "Why I believe he's a History Teacher Bellamy."

Bellamy began to panic. "I haven't said anything Mr. Thornton and I don't plan to. I just need a good lawyer."

"Don't we all Bellamy," he sighed dropping his head slightly, "Don't we all."

— • • —

Cluck's Chicken Coop was busy this evening. Myrtle had the night off. In a booth in the back sat Joel, Franklin and Brianna. Myrtle was sitting with them getting ready to enjoy a casual meal. When an assistant manager approached and whispered to Myrtle, she rose. "I'll get back here as soon as I can. Go ahead and order and eat. One of my workers didn't call in, so we're short-handed. Once the rush is over I'll get back." Brianna volunteered to help but Myrtle wouldn't hear of it.

The threesome made small talk and laughed among themselves. Franklin did magic with straws and lids. They ordered and ate.

Behind the counter, Myrtle wasn't laughing; she was pissed. Bellamy was scheduled but hadn't called out or shown up.

The rush ended and she rejoined her friends. The food was gone, the table cleared. Myrtle tried to make light of the situation. "Franklin you don't have all those wings up your sleeve do you?" She sat down. The audience was at attention. "It was Bellamy who didn't show up or call. I'm a little surprised because he has been taking the job seriously since he came back." She shook her head, took Joel's hand, "I guess all second chances don't turn out as good as you have." Their eyes met. Joel nodded.

Franklin cleared his throat. "Can I order you up something, I could use a few more wings myself."

"Thank you Franklin, that would be nice."

— • • —

At a corner table in the same restaurant Detective Monroe was on his second date with Hailey and her son Daniel. Daniel picked the location and sat devouring his honey mustard covered boneless wing meal. He hadn't touched his fries but the celery sticks and the Blue cheese dip were quickly disappearing. He took a long slurp of his Dr. Pepper and smiled at the detective. "Isn't this just the best?" he patted his stomach and sat back contentedly.

Errol's eyes met Hailey's. Then he looked at the little boy who had innocently brought them together. "Yes Daniel, this might well be the best."

CHAPTER FORTY-SEVEN

Habits are hard to break. Tobias Thornton sat in the dark absorbing his second drink flipping through the channels in his head. *Well one show won't be repeating itself. Now to find his son and make sure he doesn't come back as a sequel.*

Before he left the scene Bellamy's bike had been placed in the trunk that had carried his Russian friend to the meeting. Through his back mirror he watched the two retracing the steps he had walked with Bellamy. The Russian had made plans to be picked up several miles from there. "Don't ask," Tobias had been admonished when the man accepted the assignment. His last communication with Bellamy had been prying the envelope from his hands and handing it to the Russian. The last sound he heard was Bellamy pleading his case as he walked away with a pistol pointing to his back.

Tobias poured himself a third congratulatory bourbon, then turned to the TV, flipping to find a favorite show; Dateline was just coming on. *How can people be so stupid?* But he watched stupid, week after week.

— ◆◆◆ —

Victor lay in the bunk of the cab. Nadine not yet committing to more than a ride, dozed in the passenger seat of the cab a light blanket pulled up over her shoulders.

So far so good, she told herself, *the man in the bunk had been a perfect gentleman.*

The miles had flown by and the conversation stayed light and playful. She stretched and felt the hard thing in her pocket against her thigh. Uncomfortable yes, but also comforting. She closed her eyes.

Nineteen years old but wise beyond her years, Nadine Packard had been in and out of trucks for three years now. She made her living out of sharing what she wished to offer, and taking what she wished to have. She had always liked math and though she didn't finish high school she was well educated in the ways of the world. One set of math terms she had learned stuck with her: (Greater than Less than.) The little pointers > and < seemed to enter nearly every decision she had made since she left home.

Right now huddled in a cheap blanket wondering what the man in the bunk behind her was thinking and planning she stroked the knife in her pocket bringing the knife's namesake to mind. In semi darkness in an overnight trucker rest stop, Nadine chuckled aloud. In the back, Victor, wide awake and trying to figure a line that might get the girl into his bunk, responded. "What you laughing about?"

Nadine took a long breath, "Oh just life I guess. The greater than and the less than. Didn't even know you but a little bit ago and now we're sharing a room; kinda." She laughed aloud.

"There's room for you back here if you feel you can trust me."

"'It's not a matter of trusting you Victor, it's about trusting myself. I don't want nobody getting hurt back there. Let's just sleep on it. We got a long day ahead of us tomorrow. We'll talk."

Victor was getting really good at keeping the big rig between the white lines, what he was really naive about was reading between them. An overhead rest stop light took that moment to burn out and victor was left totally in the dark.

When Victor awoke at first light Nadine wasn't in the passenger seat. Victor got out of his bunk and exited the cab, grabbing a towel. Maybe the girl was taking a shower herself. He returned to the smell of coffee and a bright smile covering Nadine's face, her hair still wet. She handed him a cup. "Thought you might need this. I heard you crying and talking in your sleep all night." She paused for effect, "By the way, who's Pearl?"

Sheriff Rodriguez had received a call from a fellow sheriff in Somerset County in the state of Maine. The owner of the trucking company Victor Thornton was apparently driving for had been reached. The owner was out of state at the moment visiting possible colleges with his wife and daughter. He would be back in his office in the morning.

Sheriff Rodriguez checked the time. *Early riser I'm betting,* he dialed.

"Troy Dunphy here, what can I move for you?"

"I'm Sheriff Rodriguez down here in Florida. We think a man we're trying to reach might be driving for you."

"Okay, do you have a name?"

"Victor Thornton." *Big kid maybe early twenties?*

"That sounds like Victor, what did he do?"

"We want to talk to him about two suspicious deaths involving young women."

Troy was speechless for a moment. He cleared his throat, "let me check the schedule, I've been out of town."

On the other end of the line Sheriff Rodriguez heard muttering and paper rustling. Troy came back onto the line.

"He's supposed to make a delivery in North Carolina today and then pick up a load and deliver it in Florida. He should be in Daytona Beach, Florida tomorrow night delivering the load." He paused checking his watch, "should be around 8pm or shortly after, to a metal fabrication business. They close at 9pm so he has to be there before that." Troy read off the name of the company and the address.

He had to throw in his thoughts on the matter because, well he was Troy and he had hired the kid. "He has done a good job for me. I hope you don't have to hurt him."

"Well, just don't let your feelings encourage a discussion with the man. He's wanted for possibly two murders. We will pick him up when he delivers that load. If anything changes on that delivery let me know immediately" "Yes sir I will." Troy hung up. He clasped his hands together. He sat back. *Wait till I tell my daughter the boy she has been bugging me about introducing her to is a stone cold killer.*

Troy's sister, his business partner, arrived.

"Make me a cup of coffee will you Tanya? And come in here and sit down. Have I got a story to tell you."

"So when do you think we'll be in North Carolina?" Victor, seemingly lost in thought, checked his watch, "I would say later this afternoon. I'll get unloaded and we can find a room, get a bite and maybe hit a bar or two. Gotta be early though. We'll be on the road by 5 am headed to Florida."

Nadine sat back saying nothing but absorbing it all. Victor had declined to talk about the nightmare the girl had overheard. Nadine heard what she heard however and was left feeling uncomfortable. Music choices and food had been the only topics since the day started.

"I'm thinking I'll head out when you make your delivery this afternoon. Maybe head west. I got some friends out there."

Victor frowned. "I thought you wanted to see Florida when it wasn't smoking hot."

"Yeah I did but a girl can change her mind, right?" "You've been pretty quiet. Something bothering you? You still thinking about that nightmare you heard?"

Nadine didn't answer. "Look it was nothing, I get emotional sometimes that's all. It's all good. Tell you what. I'll tell you anything you want to know over a beer tonight, fair enough?"

Nadine didn't have a comeback for that so she just nodded, "We'll see."

———————

Sheriff Rodriguez called in his detective. He poured the detective a cup of coffee. "Fix that the way you like it and sit down, our boy is soon to honor us with an appearance in Daytona Beach, we need to plan how we want to welcome him." The two touched cups.

———————

Franklin rose from his bed and stood in front of the bathroom mirror. The man looking back at him was happy. Two more days and he would be a married man looking in this same mirror. What would change? Nothing he decided. The two were already inseparable, beginning to finish one another's thoughts. Having spent time with Jule's dog, Roulx they decided the first together thing they would purchase was a puppy. If the dog made it through a year with them maybe they would try for a child. Franklin the jokester kidded he could just make the dog disappear if it didn't work out. Brianna thought maybe it might be better to take it to a shelter. The two were so playful with one another that even serious conversations remained light.

The mirror revealed the changes Franklin had gone through since meeting Brianna. His smile was wider, his eyes twinkled. He got up on his toes. *I think I just may be a little taller,* he stretched.

Brianna snuck up behind him, encircling his waist and squeezed. Franklin gasped and looking in the mirror saw his soon to be bride staring over his left shoulder. "I know the kind of dog I want, Franklin." Her eyes danced. "I want a mutt."

Franklin smiled to the mirror, "Because you fell in love with one?"

Brianna laughed out loud. "I hadn't thought of that. Maybe that's it." She nodded her head "Franklin my loveable mutt."

"Just know this mutt won't be leaving anytime soon." He turned and the two hugged.

Brianna took a deep breath and held up two fingers.

"Two days Franklin and we are one."

That afternoon Detective Monroe was sitting in Hailey's kitchen, the two talking quietly when Bobby rang the doorbell. Daniel rushed from his room to let his friend in. Bobby carrying his telescope in his metal case handed it to Daniel and with a quick wave of his hands disappeared into Daniel's room. The conversation between Hailey and Errol Monroe began again. "Peas in a pod those two."

Hailey having learned in their past two meetings (well one was a kind of a date) that Detective Monroe was the lead investigator of two murdered girls. Hailey had more than a passing interest.

"So Victor is still on the loose. You do know my boss's son, Bobby, that little boy who just walked through here, may have to testify if they get him back here."

"I'm afraid so, though we'll do all we can to prevent him having to do that."

"How is that going to happen?"

"I can't tell you much because it's an open investigation but I can tell you it should be wrapped up very soon. When we have him in hand I believe he'll plead for a lighter sentence. If he does, that boy won't have to take the stand."

— ◆ ◆ ◆ ◆ —

Sarah was playing in her last soccer game of the season. Since mid-season she had been on the varsity squad playing ever increasing minutes at a number of positions. It was

homecoming and there was to be a dance later in the evening. One of the parents thought it would be cool to ask the new Mayor to chaperone. George and Lane were in the bleachers, sitting with Sheriff Rodriguez and his wife.

"My daughter wants to go to this dance but she's not excited that her mother and I will be there. Is your daughter going Sheriff?"

The Sheriff looked to his wife for the answer. She nodded.

George spoke up. "Since our girls are best friends, how about you and your wife joining us as chaperones? That will take some of the pressure off me."

Lane looked at Margaret Rodriguez and smiled. "Let's go get a hot dog and let these two community leaders figure this all out. I don't think one hot dog will kill me."

When the two left, Sheriff Rodriguez brought George up to speed as much as he could without compromising the case. "We hope to have this wrapped up tomorrow night. A nice early Christmas present."

George nodded, "That would be nice. Lane is concerned for our son."

"Does the boy seem affected by all this?"

"Honestly I don't know. That kid goes a lot deeper than most adults and he lives in the stars so with him it's hard to say what's in his head at any given moment. Outwardly, I don't see any reason to worry but Mothers see things we men can't hope to. She's worrying, which worries me."

"Well let me ease one worry, I'll help you chaperone the dance."

The women reappeared carrying a hot dog for their spouses. George looked at his wife. He hadn't had any fast food in months. She smiled as she handed him the mustard, relish, and onion dressed, red hotdog. "Eat it slow George, you won't be seeing another till next season."

"I don't see any mustard on your face."

"I ended up sharing a pretzel with Margaret. I just couldn't pull the trigger."

The crowd noise brought them all to their feet. Sarah had been tripped near the opponent's goal and was now moving to the line to take a penalty shot. Margaret Rodriguez spoke up, "Wow that's putting some trust in a freshman. A penalty kick in a tie game in the last five minutes." She high-fived Lane.

Sarah, definitely a bit shorter than most of her teammates, seemed smaller still alone on that line. Sized didn't matter when she made contact with the ball. It jumped off her foot with a purpose and a direction, the goalie didn't even react. The other girls mobbed Sarah and the goal stood up for a 1-0 win. Sarah's first varsity goal.

Hours later the homecoming dance was a success. The daughters of the four chaperones danced with one another to a beat and lyrics that defied description. "Chalk tonight up to another piece of parenting. It's so loud you can't hear yourself think. Maybe Bobby's onto something." Lane mimicked Bobby by signing, <u>What did you just say?</u> George laughed.

— • — • — • —

In a bar in North Carolina it was as noisy as that dance in Palm Coast, FL. Victor and Nadine were drinking margaritas and munching on nachos.

During the afternoon, silence accompanied the roar of the engine. Victor felt like he was riding alone. He glanced at the seat beside him. Nadine had that little blanket pulled up to her ears and seemed asleep.

Nadine was not asleep, far from it, she was thinking with her eyes closed. The blanket warmed her thoughts and she tried to make sense of what she'd heard amidst the wailing and thrashing the night before. *The batch of I'm so sorrys leaving Victor's lips sounded a lot more guilt ridden than a simple break-up. Bad break-ups can get pretty messy but it had seemed much more than that. His eyes had gone all fishy looking when she had mentioned the girl's name. Why can't he tell me now if it's so innocent?* What she had heard and her own experience with men made her skeptical. *Leaving when we stop would probably be best. Maybe waiting till morning makes the most sense. I don't have a ride and it makes more sense to hike during daylight. If he's harmless and he doesn't bother me tonight maybe I could just get dropped off in Florida, I do have friends in Orlando. What to do, what to do?* As thoughts flitted through her mind she patted her pocket which seemed to settle things in her mind.

Now hours later in half-light, noise, and liquid courage Nadine decided to bring things to the surface. She cupped her hand so she could be heard, "Well we ain't gonna get any talking done in here, Victor." Victor didn't respond. She raised her voice, "We might just as well pick up some beer and head to that no-tell motel. I ain't hungry anyway after all those chips."

Victor heard the part about a motel and moved to the bar to settle up.

Nadine watched the back of this tall drink of water navigate among the tables. She was a little nervous but curious too. She again patted the folding knife she carried religiously. On more than one occasion that three inch blade had popped out and brought clarity to a situation. *Two things she knew: Not going to sleep with him. If things worked out she would continue to ride with him. One more thing she knew: She would cut him if she needed to.*

Victor, for all the harm he had done to women, in the ways of a woman, was an innocent. The two left the bar and found a package store. Nadine walked the beer case but kept one eye on Victor who was in quiet conversation with the clerk. The man handed him a small rectangular packet.

He hurriedly put it in his pocket. Nadine had to smile, *so old Victor intends to get his clock cleaned does he?* So one of the things she knew was already in play. She patted her front pocket. *Old Hiram here he might have his own thoughts on that.*

Just a touch brought back some really bad memories. *She named the knife after a step father who gave Nadine the knife when she was twelve when teaching her to fish. 'Got to cut the line if you get hung up.' Cut the hook out if you can't pull it out.' Need to learn to gut and clean a fish if you are going to be a true fisherman.' It all made sense to Nadine at the time. And it appeared the man was sincere.*

Just a year later though- Nadine was three inches taller and filling out- during another fishing trip- step father Hiram, fortified with cheap whiskey, was inspired to do a little more teaching.

He made the mistake of entering her little pup tent late in the night. Nadine woke to the sound of someone fumbling with the zipper on the tent closure. The smell of liquor breath reached her. She heard heavy breathing. They were in a campground with a half dozen other campers. Whoever it was, entered on hands and knees. No words were spoken. Nadine's heart raced. Her little fishing knife was warm under her pillow. She felt knees reach the bottom of her sleeping bag. A profile in silhouette, the light from a waning moon offering no identity. Sitting up suddenly Nadine turned on her flashlight, blinding the intruder. She gasped, it was her stepfather. Hiram reacted by shielding his eyes and hollering something she didn't catch. Nadine's little fishing knife, open for business, struck the first thing that reached her, his wrist. Hiram retreated as if snake bit; yelping. Not another single word passed between them. Hiram, still on his hands and knees, backed out the way he'd come.

Nothing was said in the morning, just a quick packing up and silent trip home. Nadine noted the blood on her sleeping bag and the bloody bandage on his wrist. She retreated to the back seat. Hiram's bloodshot eyes tracked her in the rear view mirror. Nadine met those eyes with defiance. That was their last fishing trip.

She tolerated the sullen glares and barely concealed anger for two years after that bandage had been removed from his wrist. Then she hit the road. She never did tell her mother. She was as much a bitch as he was a bastard. They deserved one another, she decided.

Nadine carried the twelve pack and her memories into the motel. She tore off a beer and another for Victor. She placed the rest in the bathroom sink and left the room to get some ice. When she returned Victor was already in the bed under the covers. Head propped up on two pillows, he was just draining his first beer.

Probably already wearing his protection, thought Nadine. She chuckled, "That was quick. You tired Victor?"

"Well there's only one little bitty chair in here. Thought we might as well get comfortable, we got to be on the road early." He winked and grinned.

Mmhm, men! Nadine dumped the ice over the beer in the sink and dragged that little bitty chair near the bed. She looked him dead in the eye. "Ok Victor, tell me about Pearl."

Victor stalled for time. He signaled his beer was empty. "Would you do me the pleasure?"

Nadine rose and unhooked a beer from the twelve pack. She returned to her chair and handed the beer to Victor.

Victor took an extended pull, sat down the can and began a long and fanciful tale of a wonderful relationship that had gone bad. He seemed inspired. The earlier margaritas and guzzled beer doing its magic even as his mouth moved; creating, embellishing, and lying, on and on.

Nadine thought of earlier back in that truck sneaking her own glances at Victor. One country song followed another, little nods and head movements told Nadine Victor was composing a sad country song on his mental typewriter. She could sense the gist of the lyrics, the type-overs, the whiteouts, the songs refrain. And now with beer moistened lips and tongue he was reading the lyrics he had composed just below the engine's roar, all inspired by a classic country station.

When he had finished, eyes as wet as a pure lie will allow, he looked directly at her for the first time since he had begun. "Pure truth, Nadine."

Nadine took a sip of her own beer, then toasted him, "Well Victor, you should get that song to Blake Shelton ASAP. Sure to be a hit." Nadine smiled, sighed, "Really doesn't matter what happened with you and Pearl, Victor," she sighed again, "I just wanted to see if you would be honest with me."

She rose, "I've heard this song before, if you don't mind I'll just sleep in the truck."

Victor, beginning to protest, was out of the bed in a flash, dropping his beer while trying to get his pants back on, not managing to hide that little latex attachment still clinging to his appendage, sputtering as he struggled, "Hey that was the truth."

Nadine pointed to the latex appendage still attached to a quickly shrinking idea, "Okay I'll take your word for it but I still want to sleep in the truck." She let that sink in. "I'll be gone in the morning." She turned away, "Mind if I take a couple of those beers?" In that moment Victor swarmed. He had her locked in his arms from behind. God he was strong. He began to squeeze.

—•——•••—•—•—

Errol Monroe was invited to spend the night in the guest room. Before lights out he played with the two boys and got to view the world through Bobby's telescope. Bobby and Daniel kept the telescope pointed to the stars.

Conspiratorially they winked at one another there was no reason for Detective Monroe to view their neighbors. Detective Monroe seemed nice and all but peeking into neighbors houses might be frowned upon.

Hailey was impressed with the calm demeanor Errol displayed with the boys. He had a great sense of humor and timing. He didn't force himself on the boys, he just let things happen naturally. He seemed content to let their own relationship form in the same way. As she pushed the button to close the garage door she glanced at that last empty space on the shelf. She locked the door from the inside for the night she couldn't remember when she had last felt so secure.

She turned out the light in the living room and the two kissed before going to the opposite ends of the house, their hands lingering, touching, wanting, both sighing audibly. Time enough for that they decided at the same moment. But both lay awake for a long time.

— · — ● — ● — ● — ● — · · —

Nadine couldn't get her breath. Victor continued squeezing, all the while blubbering and moaning into her neck; gibberish, nonsensical words and phrases. *She smelled the beer burning his breath, she smelled the margaritas, she smelled fear on herself, she heard the word sorry. A word repeated over and over last night.*

Instinctively now she knew what that sorry was all about. She managed to reach the hard thing in her pocket. Hiram appeared in her hand, Warm, comforting. Just need to get the damn thing open. Her lower forearms and wrists were free but she was beginning to see stars, no air reaching her lungs, time was running out. She stepped down hard onto Victor's foot. Barefoot, he reacted with a yell, momentarily letting up enough so that Nadine could turn slightly. She opened and drove the blade into Victor's thigh.

With a scream the cage door opened. Nadine turned, pulling out the blade and putting distance between herself and a now screaming, ranting, mad man. He glared, he winced in pain, calling her ugly names as she backed toward the door. But just as happened with her step father years ago no words left her own lips.

Outside, she embraced the night hiding behind the motel. Long pulls of air refilled her lungs. Her eyes gleamed with tears. She gathered herself, Hiram clutched in her hand still at the ready. Looking up, there were no visible stars. A naked tree in silhouette allowed leaky light from the street. Sounds of the night seemed amplified. Traffic was light yet she heard engine noises, a dog barking streets away, sirens filled the night but not coming in this direction.

Nadine hadn't been this scared for a long time, she shivered.

The smell of his panting beer breath clung to her clothing. She looked around furtively, she couldn't stay here.

Emerging from behind the building clinging to the shadows, the wind picked up, dead leaves moving across the pavement. Near the street riding that wind was a different smell. It reached her nostrils; a McDonald's smell, comfort food. Nadine felt her stomach rumble. She had to chuckle in spite of her fear. Apparently she was hungry. She followed her nose.

Back in the room Victor limped to the bathroom. There was no tub so he leaned on the sink that was filled with beer and ice. He was bleeding pretty good. He took a hand towel and ran it under the faucet then filled it with ice and pressed it to the wound. He was breathing heavily, spots in front of his eyes. He wanted to shower all this away but he was afraid he'd pass out. Muttering profanities, pain attached to each outburst, he limped back to the bed and sat down.

He looked at the towel pooling red. The bitch had cut into something that didn't appear was going to stop bleeding on its own. He weighed his options. *An emergency room,* "too many questions," he muttered aloud. *Call his boss.* He could say he'd been hurt on the job, He nodded. That's what he would do. He'd okay the medical attention needed. He rose and limped to the sink. *Right now he needed another beer.* Each step accompanied with a verbal gush of exertion, "THAT BITCH."

Nadine ate a late night breakfast at McDonald's. She replayed the last hour in her head. Sipping on a cup of coffee she zoned out. Eventually she fished her smartphone out of her bag. She turned it on. *Should she or shouldn't she? They would want her name, where they could find her. She sighed Endless questions. She had stabbed someone,* how would that be perceived? In the end she turned off her phone and wandered into the night. She began looking to where the big rigs parked overnight, maybe she could catch a ride. She patted her pocket, she felt better.

—•—•—•—

Victor called T&T trucking at six am. Troy was in his chair by the window already checking the day's pickups and deliveries. He was nursing a cup of Joe he had made and Tanya was right it tasted terrible. It was still dark and cold, only twenty-five degrees on the window thermometer. *Yep winter was coming.* He'd had to scrape a good measure of frost off his windshield earlier.

The phone rang. Troy sipped and grimaced. He studied the call-in number. He suddenly felt all that cold reach right through the window. He cleared his throat and took a deep breath. "Good morning Victor, you on the road to Florida?"

"Boss I hurt myself. I was stupidly trying to scrape some tar off the bumper with a jack knife and slipped and cut myself, bad."

"Have you had it attended to?"

"I don't have much money and no insurance."

Troy thought a minute. "Can you drive?"

"It's still seeping and my leg is pretty stiff, I think I need to see someone, get it stitched up."

"Well get a cab and get to a hospital. Have them fax me what they need to get you treated and I'll send them my policy information." Troy continued to think this through. He checked his watch. "You probably won't get that delivery to Florida before they close for the day. I'll make arrangements for a motel in Daytona Beach for the night. You can deliver tomorrow morning, they are open till noon I believe."

Victor sighed deeply. "Thanks boss, I won't forget how you've treated me."

"Just get that leg fixed. Everything else will take care of itself."

After ending that call Troy dialed up the Sheriff in Flagler County, Florida.

"Let me know what motel you set him up in and get a room number. We'll take it from there."

Victor was on the road by ten am. His leg was stiff and he had lost some blood. But after one transfusion and a dozen stitches inside and out he was assured with rest, he would be ok. Victor patted the baggie of pain pills he had been given from the hospital pharmacy. So far so good. He was pretty certain the girl hadn't called anyone. I'm long gone now anyway. The seat beside him held the blanket Nadine 438 had wrapped herself in. How could he be so wrong about her? He promised that blanket he was swearing off women. They can't be trusted, he decided.

On the sand in Flagler Beach Franklin was suggesting just the opposite. With Brianna's hand in his, he spoke of placing all his faith, love, hopes, and dreams in the hand he held. With Jule's as his Best Man, Danni the Maid of Honor, little Jake clutched a pillow with a ring pinned to it. The red setter, Roulx stood at attention, fighting the urge to chase the little birds flitting up and down the sand. As witnesses Myrtle and Joel holding hands, seemed to be planning their own future.

Victor left the Interstate in Daytona Beach shortly after midnight. He had been given the address for the motel and had punched it into his GPS. He saw the motel coming up on his left and turned into a large parking lot that served numerous businesses. Sitting behind the wheel he studied his surroundings. He spied what he was looking for, a lit Burger King sign. He'd leave his rig here over night and be gone before most of the businesses opened in the morning. The pain medication was wearing off and Victor's head was throbbing. He took two of the capsules and finished the bottled water he had nursed all day. His leg was super stiff from sitting behind the wheel for most of the past fourteen hours. He managed to get down from the cab and the sudden weight on his leg brought enough pain to bring tears to his eyes. He limped noticeably as he made his way across forty yards of pavement.

It was past midnight but the real darkness began where the parking lot and its meager lighting ended. As he headed for Burger King he needed to pass through a stretch of foliage that surrounded the restaurant which during the day allowed a brief respite from a relentless sun, complete with a park bench and a waste barrel.

At this hour, back here it was full on black. Victor reached that darkness. He would eventually remember seeing a cigarette glowing but nothing more. He never saw what or who hit him.

He was found in the early morning light by a Burger King employee who was going to empty yesterday's trash. He had no identification on his person when he was transported by ambulance to a local hospital. The Daytona police department called to investigate had no idea that two county sheriffs and a swat team were looking for this man. Like an Italian sandwich with too much oil, all the meat in this case simply slipped off the bread.

CHAPTER FORTY-EIGHT

The same morning Victor Thornton lay unconscious in Daytona Beach, Myrtle arrived early at Cluck's Chicken Coop to check in a rare weekend stock delivery. She parked her car and did a walk around the parking lot picking up debris. She opened the door to the concrete receptacle that held two dumpsters. She lifted the lid to the one that held trash. Just as she dropped the handful of paper and plastic a voice from behind startled her. She slammed down the lid. She involuntarily screamed and jumped back.

"Myrtle it's me, Bellamy!"

It was just past light at seven am but still semi dark in the concrete roofless building.

Myrtle squinted, "What the hell Bellamy, here you go scaring me again!"

"I'm sorry Myrtle I didn't know who else to come to." He was shaking, "someone tried to have me killed!" Myrtle, still shaking herself, responded, "Well we can't talk in a dumpster for god's sake, come on inside."

———— • — • — • ————

Sheriff Rodriguez was frustrated. His team and a full contingent of swat team members had staked out the motel all night long. Victor had not shown up. By five am he had woken the owner of the trucking company to ask if he had heard from his driver. By the time Troy located the truck on his GPS, Victor was long removed to the hospital.

The Sheriff also had the missing Bellamy on his mind. This case was unraveling before his eyes.

By noon time Saturday, sounds began to seep into Victor's unconsciousness. He heard voices but couldn't make out words. His head hurt but he had no idea what had happened. In his mind only the recollection of a glow and smell of a cigarette-then lights out. Right now he smelled the same antiseptic smells that accompanied his getting stitched up a day ago. His identification had been stolen but he didn't know that yet. His leg ached. He did remember what caused that pain. He grimaced.

Myrtle needed time to think. She immediately put Bellamy to work helping her put the frozen foods away. Her mind flitted from one possibility to another. One thing seemed clear, *Bellamy showed no signs of suspecting her of leaking any information.*

When the frozen chicken and boxes of cookie dough were put away, she spoke. "Leave the paper products till later, let's have a cup of coffee and talk." Sitting in her tiny office with the door closed cradling a steaming Styrofoam cup of black coffee, Bellamy took a deep breath. "Maybe I shouldn't tell anyone about this, maybe I should just get out of town." He covered his eyes with his hands.

Myrtle could hear the fear in his voice, "Bellamy, if someone is trying to kill you, you better tell the police." Bellamy shifted from one foot to the other; thinking. Then he nodded; decided. "Myrtle it's the father of that Victor guy, you know, Pearl's boyfriend. I had no idea at the time what had happened in that condo but I let him look at some tapes and he destroyed some of them."

"How were you involved?"

"I worked security for a company and when I wasn't walking the grounds I monitored surveillance cameras. Like I said, I let the man review some tapes. He destroyed some of them. I didn't know at the time he was covering up for his son."

"Ok, so that's all you did?"

Bellamy took another big old breath, "Well when the police got involved he paid me to leave the state. Then the cops found me and brought me back. He's afraid I might testify against him?"

"How do you know he wants to kill you?"

Bellamy began wringing his hands. "Because he left me in a parking lot with a guy holding a gun to my back." The memory of that had Bellamy closing his eyes.

Myrtle's eyes widened, "But you're still here Bellamy."

"Hmmph only because this guy walked me down the same path I had walked with Mr. Thornton earlier."

"I'm confused. You walked into the woods twice?" Bellamy sighed, "I know this sounds weird but first Mr. Thornton walked with me away from a cement chimney talking all history and shit. He carried an envelope he said was full of money. He promised me that envelope to disappear again. I was super nervous. I didn't know if I could trust him so I was all the time looking for a way out."

"OK." That was all Myrtle could muster.

"Well he handed me the money and I relaxed a little. But when we got back to his car there was another man there with a gun. Then Mr. Thornton left and this guy started walking me back along that same path. I begged the guy to let me go. He laughed and said, 'Just keep walking, you'll be gone soon enough.' I knew then I had one chance.

When I walked that path earlier, I was looking for a way out. This was before Mr. Thornton handed me the money. I was walking just ahead of him. We reached a point where a tree had fallen and some heavy branches kinda blocked the path. I had just decided to pull those branches back and let them hit him in the head. But it was then he told me to stop.

I turned and he gave me the envelope so I relaxed a little. I would have had to hold back those branches for Mr. Thornton to get through."

Bellamy was shaking as he remembered. "So with this guy behind me holding a gun I began jabbering as we neared that spot saying anything that came to mind. This guy was foreign, Russian maybe. Anyway I started mouthing anything I could think of to keep him from noticing what I was doing. He didn't notice. I grabbed the branches and pushed my way through then I ducked and let go of those branches. They struck him right in the face. He yelled and dropped the gun. I grabbed it."

"So you need to go to the sheriff Bellamy. Tell him what you told me."

Bellamy squirmed. His mouth twisted into a grimace, "It's not that simple Myrtle. I didn't just grab the gun." Myrtle's eyes widened.

Bellamy nodded. "I shot him Myrtle, then I ran."

"Did you kill him?"

"I don't know, I just ran."

"When did this happen?"

"A couple days ago. I've been hiding since. I spent last night in that concrete box out there."

"Tell you what, hang out in the office here. I'll close and lock the door. She checked her watch. 8:15. Let me think on this."

Tobias Thornton received a call. It was not a call he wanted to receive. The voice was Russian, the news was not good. When the call ended a ritual that usually dominated his evenings began in the early morning light. The TV lit up and a drink appeared in his hand along with the remote. For a man who could walk a client flawlessly through any real estate purchase or sale with every (t) crossed and (I) dotted, this situation had him pulling at his hair.

By late afternoon Victor was conscious. A detective entered his room. He pulled up a chair and smiled at Victor.

"Did you see who attacked you? We have some ideas from some of the surveillance cameras back there but obviously it was dark at the time. We're checking some of those ideas out. If you saw anything that might help pin things down. They must have taken your wallet, did you have any credit cards we might be able to flag?"

Victor suddenly realized this man had no idea who he was. He had no idea there was a nationwide search for him. Suddenly Victor was cheering for his assailant to stay gone. He cleared his throat. He held his head, he spoke slowly, "I was just going to get a burger and then it was lights out."

"So can you give me your name? Is there someone we can call?"

Victor shook his head, thinking as he lay there, "I'm not from here. I just hitched my way here yesterday. To be honest sir I'm homeless."

"Do you have a name at least?"

Victor never missed a beat. "I'd rather not say. I didn't leave home under the best of circumstances. I really don't want to involve anyone else."

The detective squirmed in his seat. "The nurse tells me you have a wound to your leg that has been treated recently. Care to tell me what happened?"

Victor smiled innocently; he was on a roll now. He paused and in that moment the story he had concocted for Nadine entered his head. Hoping for better results this time around he rattled out what he hoped could be believed. "Those homeless guys can be territorial" He chuckled which caused him to wince. "It was over a can of beans if you can believe it." The effort to talk seemed to tire him and his face whitened.

The detective rose, "Well you're not giving me much help here. Get some rest. Come Monday morning we may have some more information and you can bet my boss is going to want to find out more about you as well. So I'll be back."

Myrtle busied herself getting the restaurant ready to open. She made four big urns of iced tea, a batch of cookies and wiped down all the tables. All the while she was somewhere else in her head. What should she do? Was she harboring a criminal? No, she decided Bellamy was guilty of only one thing; young person stupidity. She needed to convince Bellamy to call the Sheriff's office for his own protection, that's what she needed to do.

Her assistant manager came to the front. "Hey Myrtle I need some days off, have you seen the vacation book? I couldn't find it in your office."

Myrtle was about to answer when she realized that office shouldn't be open. She rushed to the back. The door was indeed open and Bellamy was nowhere to be seen. The assistant manager looked at her oddly but Myrtle closed the office door behind her and dialed the number for the sheriff's office.

The law was already in the vicinity.

Detective Monroe was on his way to lunch. He had slept in after returning from the late night stakeout. He had promised the two boys a wing meal. Tired as he was, he wasn't about to miss the opportunity to be with Hailey. He had three passengers. Hailey was in the shotgun seat dialing up an easy listening station. In the back Danny and Bobby were silently taking turns twisting a Rubik's cube. One held a watch timing the other for twenty seconds, then counting the number of colored spaces lined up on each side. The boys were inseparable, moving between their respective homes.

Errol was just glad to have some movement in his life. He sighed contentedly gazing in the rear view mirror at the boys. When he returned his eyes to the road he saw a black kid to his right on the sidewalk.

The young man was moving quickly and left the sidewalk to enter the Walmart parking lot. The boy looked very familiar. His eyes widened. Errol had already passed the entrance to the mart so he took a quick right towards a Dollar Store. Their wing destination lay just ahead. When they turned left away from Clucks' Hailey noticed. She looked across at Errol. "I thought we were getting wings at Cluck's?"

"We were, I mean we are." Clucks was just fifty yards away. Errol stopped. He faced Hailey, "Look I think I just saw a suspect we've been trying to locate. You guys go on ahead, I'll join you shortly."

He let them out and headed back towards Walmart, about to sound the alarm to headquarters. Suddenly blue lights and sirens joined him in the parking lot. A half hour later he returned to Clucks. Bellamy was not to be found. If only the cruisers had arrived silently they might have surprised their reluctant witness. Hailey and the boys were polishing off their meals, wings for the boys and a salad for Hailey. Detective Monroe joined them. He was giving Hailey a shortened version of events when he sensed someone at his shoulder. It was Myrtle. Could I have a minute Detective I have some new information that could be important?

A few miles to the east, Tobias Thornton was packing a suitcase. His hired assassin told him over the phone he intended to finish the job. 'Just as soon as my arm heals.' Tobias had not been able to convince him to let it go. So now Tobias himself needed to go. Looking around at the comfort his years as a successful real estate agent and broker had netted him, Industry awards and plaques adorning shelves and cases, all thrown away for that ungrateful son of his. The blinds were drawn and the curtains pulled. When he snapped off the light the condo mirrored his own life, total darkness.

Detective Monroe and Myrtle moved away from the table but were visible to me. With what I had picked up at the table and now what Myrtle was telling the detective Errol, I read their lips. A witness named Bellamy, (I think I got the name right) was nearly killed. I read the name Victor as well. I realized for maybe the first time I might be in danger. I'd have to think about all this.

Later I told my father what I had heard at the restaurant. Dad immediately called the Sheriff.

Victor lay there thinking. About a lot of things. He was a fugitive. They had probably found his truck by now, if not it was just a matter of time. He had questions flooding his mind as well. Did that girl Nadine call the cops after-all? When he didn't show up for that delivery did his boss call the authorities? In the morning will that detective show back up and arrest him? He was sore all over. The nurse came in. Victor was really tired and he closed his eyes.

Bellamy had been just about to enter the grocery section at Walmart when he heard the sirens. He had no idea why the cops were coming here and he wasn't about to hang around and find out. He walked in the store to the garden section then slipped out that exit. He walked along a drainage canal that eventually got him back to a neighborhood.

He found an open garage and there was a nice looking ten speed hanging upside down from a hook just begging for an owner who would actually use it. Bellamy checked the air in the tires and nodded to himself, *Got wheels back, that's a start.*

------◆------

When George called the Sheriff he was told they already had that information and were trying to locate the witness now. The sheriff gave George a little inside information concerning the possible involvement of Victor's father.

"That's to be kept between you and me until we locate him and bring him in for questioning."

CHAPTER FORTY-NINE

Victor Dreamed. *He was no longer the big heavy lineman on his football team. He no longer did the grunt work so the hero could pick up a touchdown and get the girl in the end. Tonight he followed his old self and he was not placing a block in the line but rather was the running back who ends up on the dance floor with the prettiest girl in the room. Tonight he wore the crown as king of his class. The dream was going along nicely until three girls approached from the bleachers. It was dark. A spinning reflective mirror cast fleeting little bits of light on his jacket. He was still holding his date in his arms, her back to the approaching girls. The girls appeared to be smiling. One was holding something that caught a beam and glistened. The music stopped. Everyone was watching the king and queen in their first dance. Why would the music stop? The loudspeaker came on, **Victor Thornton** you are a then silence. The three girls finished the sentence as they came clearly into view, the lights coming slowly back on; **MURDERER!***

Victor awoke with a start but not before seeing the faces of three girls he had either killed or attempted to. Even awake he could still see the girls. And he remembered what was said. Two had said nothing after the word Murderer, (as if they were out of breath from the effort). The third girl though, she smiled and held up her knife. Nadine was having none of this hero stuff. She was the only one smiling. She began shouting, pointing her knife at him. Suddenly his old coach was there pointing a finger, then his father appeared with a whiskey in one hand and a remote in the other appearing bored and distracted. Troy Dunphy was standing there shaking his head looking very disappointed.

And there watching all this without even realizing he had set a good deal of it in motion was that black kid.

Victor was a ball of sweat. The room was quiet; it was still dark beyond the blinds. Victor slowly got out of bed testing his leg. His head hurt but he was able to function. None of this would have happened if that black kid had minded his business. Once more his mind filled then purged itself with one thought left dangling like an unnoticed booger; revenge. *If I don't have a future why should he,* was the thought that followed him out the door.

———————

Bellamy was sleeping on the porch. His friend's mother had received no money as of late. Last night she told him there was only one more door to the outdoors as she deposited a thin blanket onto the couch he was occupying. She pointed to a junk filled garage. 'That's where you'll be sleeping if I don't see some money soon. By the way, a detective was by here yesterday. It seems your presence is requested at the Sheriff's office. I covered for you Bellamy but that's the last time if I don't get my rent.'

Under dawn's early light after shivering through a night with a blanket that wouldn't keep a fart warm Bellamy packed up the little he owned. He raided the refrigerator for a cold piece of chicken, thought of his boss Myrtle Beech, and promised himself he would not be sleeping on a damn porch or in a damn garage tonight. As he reached his stolen bicycle an idea surfaced.

———————

In the end we are all creatures of habit.

———————

Victor now knew the lingo and some of the habits of big rig drivers. His thumb got him to a truck stop at destination Daytona. He counted his options. To his left was Route One, north or south. To his right was Interstate Ninety Five, again a north or south option. His recent nightmares troubled him. Some could be addressed, some couldn't. The two that could were his father, and that black kid. He knew how to find his father and he knew who could direct him to the black kid, Myrtle at Cluck's Chicken Coop.

Franklin and Breanna honeymooned on the garden island of Kuai. Never a drinker of hard liquor, the couple were enticed to try a local favorite at the Princeville resort where they were staying. Served with a native flower hugging the rim of the glass as if being nourished itself, the Mai Tais made them both instant believers. They toured the island visiting pineapple plantations, laid on the beach reading while sipping on their new favorite drink. They flew in a helicopter around, over and then into a volcano where Fantasy Island had been filmed. It was during this two week stay that Franklin broached the subject of having a child. Breanna as tan as a walnut and as happy as one person could be, readily agreed. He started the conversation by telling Brianna he didn't think they were dog people.

Breanna gazed out over a vast ocean. She breathed in the slightly salty air wafting onto their balcony, "Could we live here Franklin? I don't want to ever leave this Island."

Franklin had earlier received the answer that would allow him to honor his uncle Paul. If their future child was a girl a variation of the name Paul would work just fine.

"I'll open a local bank account tomorrow. Jule's will handle things from that end." He held up his glass, "Aloha Darling."

CHAPTER FIFTY

A storm was headed towards Flagler County. Dark clouds of emotion were already on the horizon. Others were building, coming from the south.

• — ▪ ◆ ▪ — •

Victor caught a ride to Palm Coast on the back of a Motor Trike. With the wind in his face riding up Route One he took a trip down memory lane. He never should have come. Here in the first place. His father certainly didn't want him around, even in the beginning. To his father he was just another channel to flip past. Nothing to watch here. A whole string of *shoulda, coulda, woulda,* moments flashed through his head as billboards touting one thing or another drew his attention briefly. Finally one more thought, *gonna.*

The man driving the bike was seventy five years old. Victor had offered up a sympathetic face when asking for a ride. The old man lived in the past. He remembered back when it was safe to stick out your thumb and travel all across this country. His late wife said he was just too trusting and this morning if she was looking down she would have said, 'I told you so.'

Victor remembered the Seminole Woods section of Palm Coast where he had placed his first victim. Secluded stretches that would aid him in making this ride his permanent. He directed the old guy to hang a right when the 457 sign for Seminole Woods appeared. It was a beautiful morning. The only clouds in the city were those hanging over the heads of a small circle of individuals who Victor felt had done him wrong. Victor had it in mind to clear the air. A mile and a half into the section Victor tapped the old man on the shoulder. "I need to take a piss," he fairly screamed into his ear. The old man with a gray beard flapping in his face when he turned his head, nodded. He eased his bike onto a grassy stretch just off the road. Victor waited till the man shut the engine down and got off his trike before stretching and climbing off himself, he looked around. Seclusion. Quiet.

"I think I'll join you in your endeavor, at my age every stop is an opportunity."

Victor had no idea what the man had said but nodded anyway.

The two walked to the edge of the woods just a stone's throw away. They faced away from one another and did their business. To make conversation the old man asked about Victor's limp. He hadn't noticed it in the parking lot when Victor begged for a ride.

"I was born with a limp."

"I'm sorry to hear that."

"Well old man that's why I'm going to need your ride."

"Excuse me."

"I got me some things I gotta do and I'm going to need your ride."

The old man bristled up. "I said I'd take you where you need to go but you can't have my bike."

"I'm over six feet and fifty years younger so this sounds like a silly argument to be having. I need your ride, you can hike a ride then turn me in. It won't matter by then anyway."

The old man dropped his head and nodded. "Do you mind if I get some of my stuff from my trunk?"

They walked back towards the bike. No one had passed.

The old man introduced himself. "Ashworth Cooper, here." He held out his hand. Victor took his hand and in that moment let down his guard. The old man reached into his trunk and came out with a jacket and his wallet. He opened it. "If you need some money I'm glad to help you out. Like I said before I'll drop you anywhere you need to go." "Sorry man but where I'm going is no place you want to be."

"Ok then let me get my cane and it's all yours." The old man brought the collapsible cane out and brought it to its full length. He stepped back as if leaving but then swung it at Victor's head. He caught just a piece of Victor's cheek laying it wide open.

Victor dove headlong into the old man's chest. He took the wind out of the old man and secured the cane. He struck just twice, viciously. The old man would never regain consciousness. Victor dragged him just inside the wood line. No second thoughts or guilt this time, just a reaffirmation of what victor saw as one more betrayal.

Still no one had passed by.

Victor found a towel in the trunk and wiped away the blood. He found a small first aid box that contained panty liners the old man used for god only knows what. Victor opened one and stuck it to his cheek. He put on the helmet the old man had been wearing and began his trip into Palm Coast. ^

Tobias Thornton had snuck back into Palm Coast to settle some business affairs. He had dyed his silver mane a dull black, grown a healthy beard, and wore sunglasses. His former office assistant didn't recognize him. One more bit of business and he would leave the country for good. He had signed what needed to be signed and was sitting in a rental car when his cell rang.

—••—◆—◆◆—◆—••—

The detectives in Daytona put two and two together, finally, and with red faces acknowledged they had let a killer get away. Detective Monroe listened once more to what failure to cross all the I's and T's ended up looking like.

Bellamy was living on the edges of the city. He took bike paths wherever he needed to go. He had had no luck in finding Tobias Thornton. He spent several nights camped out among the homeless on both sides of the city. He still had not heard of a body being found out near the old cement plant. So was he wanted as a state's witness involving the tapes or was he wanted for murder. One person would know.

Franklin called Myrtle and gave her the news. "If and when you and Joel tie the knot, you'll have to come to our little Island for your honeymoon. My treat. I might have a bit of more good news by the time you arrive."

Myrtle's next call was from Bellamy. "Can we meet Myrtle?"

"What's up Bellamy?"

"I need to leave the country. If I can get back to Texas I'm heading to Mexico. Can you lend me some money?"

"How much do you need?"

Money for a bus ticket and enough to get me over the border. Could you come up with $Five-hundred?

Myrtle was thinking of her next call even as she agreed.

Victor was going to visit Cluck's Chicken Coop on the other side of town but pulled into a shopping plaza just off route 100 when he saw side by side a phone store and a Dunkin Donut. Using some of the old man's cash he bought a cell phone and a data package. He then walked across the parking lot to Dunkin donut. He had plenty of cash but old habits are hard to break. He didn't have his fob but he gave them his old phone number and found that two more coffees and three donuts from now he would get a free hot beverage of his choice. He didn't notice the second look the man gave him when the number registered his account. He ordered a coffee and a chocolate glazed donut. He sat down at a table and dialed his father's cell.

Tobias hung up. He patted his pocket. Victor was back and seeking a meeting. He needed some money to get gone for good. Tobias had his own thoughts on that subject. ^

Joel insisted on going to any meeting with Bellamy.

"It's going to be in a public place Joel, I don't see any danger," Myrtle responded.

"There are two dead girls." He let that sit for a moment. "No Bellamy didn't do that but he's desperate. And he did tell you he shot someone."

"Detective Monroe is going to be hidden in my office and grab him as soon as he is settled in a booth."

"I still want to be there. Tell you what, I'll hide in the kitchen walk-in-cooler." Joel took her hand. "When this is over I'd like to take Franklin up on his offer." Myrtle smiled, liking that idea very much.

Detective Monroe was at home when Myrtle called. Hailey her son Daniel and friend Bobby were finally making some serious progress on that damn puzzle. Bobby was especially helpful when it came to locating pieces that didn't offer but the barest of shape or clue to where they fit. He watched Detective Monroe's mouth move. Things seemed to be coming to an end in all this drama. Maybe he wouldn't have to be involved after all. In a rare burst of exuberance Bobby spoke, using a metaphor for success that belied his years, "All the stars are lining up."

Hailey and Detective Monroe looked at the boy. Their eyes widened. It was the first time either had heard Bobby speak. Was he referring to the picture puzzle laid out before him or 463 did he mean something else? Bobby didn't follow up. He shyly put his head to the task of finding where this next piece fit.

Sheriff Rodriguez got a call from Dunkin Donut Corporate. Victor Thornton had made a purchase right here in Palm Coast. The red flag on his account had alerted the assistant manager who placed the order. This had happened just a half hour ago. Sheriff Rodriguez called Detective Monroe. Bellamy would have to wait. Sheriff Rodriguez called the Dunkin Donut on route 100 immediately. The assistant manager said the man was still at a table. He seemed to be waiting for someone.

"I'm on my way. I'll meet you there," said Detective Monroe. "There is a large parking lot behind the place. Don't bring the lights and sirens, we don't want to scare him away." On the way he tried to call Myrtle but the line was busy.

Bellamy parked his bike in the outdoor dumpster enclosure. He walked to the back door and rang the bell. One of the workers opened the door and a gust of fan-driven- air knocked the hat Bellamy was wearing to the floor. When he straightened, Myrtle was staring him in the face. She looked nervous. She checked her watch. Then she took a deep breath and smiled. "Come on in Bellamy, let me buy you a coke. Are you hungry?"

Victor checked the clock. He'd been here three quarters of an hour now. His father said he'd pick him up so they could go someplace to talk. He got up and began pacing. Would his own father set him up? The man behind the counter smiled nervously. "Can I warm that coffee for you?"

Victor was about to take the man up on the offer when the door burst open and a man he vaguely recognized, spoke. "Hello Victor, let's go somewhere to talk."

Mayor George Whiting and his wife and daughter were having a late lunch at Cluck's Chicken Coop.

Myrtle walked Bellamy to a booth nearby. She brought him a coke and sat down. Myrtle tried to make small talk; stalling. One of the staff told Myrtle she had a call. She excused herself.

When Detective Monroe finally got her on the line he was nearly to the Dunkin Donuts across town. 'I'll be there as soon as possible.' Did he need to send someone else immediately? Myrtle said she thought she could stall, "Bellamy seems to trust me."

"Give me a half hour." the detective hung up.

Myrtle went back to the booth. She gave Bellamy a reassuring pat on the shoulder. "Sorry about that. It was my boss. I asked him for a month's advance on my salary. And he's agreed. He'll overnight it he said." Myrtle gave him a big smile.

"Myrtle, I don't have that long. I need to be on a bus this afternoon. Can't you just take money from the safe and replace it tomorrow?"

"I can't do that Bellamy. That's not my money."

Bellamy began raising his voice. "You're the boss, you can do what you want."

Myrtle tried to quiet him. "Look if you need a place to stay tonight Bellamy you can stay with me. But I can't get that money until tomorrow."

Bellamy raised his voice even louder. "More of your shit rules Myrtle, Pearl bought into that hat and shirt shit but I don't. You could get me that money if you wanted to."

At the other table George Whiting turned his head. He saw Myrtle under verbal assault. Then he saw a young man take out a knife. Then he acted.

Bellamy was directing Myrtle to the registers. He wanted everything in them and then Myrtle was to empty the safe as well.

Myrtle was speechless and scared to death.

George walked directly towards Bellamy who was backing towards the counter keeping his eyes on the half dozen tables that were occupied. Nobody moved except George. Who began whistling. "Put that knife down son no one needs to get hurt here."

Bellamy glared at George. "Back off Jack off."

George continued to calmly walk slowly towards Bellamy who was now up against the front counter. George continued to whistle. Bellamy had Myrtle by the arm. Almost apologetically but still determined, he told Myrtle he was sorry but he needed the money now.

George was within arm's reach. He tried to make eye contact with Myrtle. He understood desperation when he saw it. He had to act. Bellamy continued to brandish the knife carving the air into circular pieces.

George stopped whistling. He opened his mouth to speak but in that moment Bellamy slashing recklessly, cut across his forearm. Blood appeared as if part of one of Franklin's magic tricks.

Myrtle screamed and twisted away from Bellamy. George stared at his arm. In that same moment Bellamy was driven forward by a body diving over the counter directly into his back. Bellamy collapsed on the tile, his knife folding under him. Joel hit his head when he landed and lay dazed.

Lane was already on the phone calling 911. Sarah was at her dad's side. George was bleeding heavily, trying to calm the chaos by whistling softly.

Myrtle was hollering for paper towels. Joel was still on the floor. Bellamy was screaming as he writhed on the floor holding his stomach, blood appearing on his hands.

The occupied tables emptied to their respective cars, shaken and ash colored.

—⋅—◆—◆◆⋅◆—◆—⋅—

It was a much quieter scene by the time Detective Monroe arrived at Cluck's Chicken Coop. Two ambulances and four patrol cars had responded. Bellamy was taken to the hospital under guard and George was taken to get stitched up, maybe needing a transfusion.

Myrtle was sitting in a booth with Joel. She seemed to be in shock. Joel was comforting her. Joel had a bandage on his head.

Detective Monroe joined them and dead panned a sheepish, "sorry I'm late."

Myrtle, resilient, came around.

Over chicken wings and soda Detective Monroe explained what happened at Dunkin Donuts.

"Victor was the reason I'm late. We got word he was in the donut shop on route 100. He had seen me in quite some time wearing a ball cap I just walked right in. When I saw that he was alone and appeared unarmed I invited him to talk with me. He recognized me then. He actually seemed relieved, melted really."

Detective Monroe nibbled on a wing and continued, "That should have been the end of the story, right? Not so fast."

Detective Monroe seemed to have picked up the ability to milk a good story from the old man who had described seeing Victor leave the vehicle in the yard across from his home. He had an attentive audience.

"Just as the door is closing behind us, much to my surprise, who should appear? The envelope please. "Victor's father shows up in disguise. I didn't recognize him, but Victor did."

When he saw his father Victor didn't flip channels he went right to an episode that just might make it to dateline.

"He greeted his father with, 'Hey Dad, nice hair.'"

"Then I recognized him as the man I interviewed on that rainy afternoon. His father had a gun but he was smart enough not to pull it.

"Father and son seemed to have nothing to say to one after an extended one liner from a disguised and obviously disgusted dad shook his head, mumbling 'Stupid Victor, stupid Victor, stupid Victor.'

So two criminals, captured on one donut." Detective Monroe studied Myrtle for a moment. "Are you sure you're ok Myrtle? You have been through a lot in helping with all this."

Myrtle took Joel's hand. "I'm ok. Joel is the one to thank.

If he hadn't insisted on being here when I spoke with Bellamy this could have all ended differently."

"I agree and I'll be letting the Sheriff know how you reacted, Joel."

Joel nodded. "I just hope George is ok, he was bleeding pretty badly.

"I'll be checking on him next. But I do have a few questions to tie things up. Myrtle, did Bellamy tell you why he needed the money?"

"He said he was going to Mexico."

"And when you said he'd need to wait for the money he pulled out a knife and threatened you?"

Myrtle nodded. "He was serious too. He was waving that knife like a crazy man."

"Ok, that's all I need for now. I'll call you to arrange a sit down where you can write all this out. That kid put himself in some serious doo-doo."

Lane and Sarah and Bobby surrounded George's bed. George was hooked up to a transfusion bag but was alert. "I'll be ok. No permanent damage. It's not my hammer arm." He grinned. Have you heard if that kid is going to make it?"

Lane took her husband's hand. "Leave it to you George to worry about someone else. Even someone who stabs you."

"I don't think he meant to hurt anyone when he got there. He just panicked. Check it out for me will you?"

Lane sighed and left the room. Bobby, who hadn't witnessed the drama, asked his dad for a blow by blow.

George pointed to his arm then to Sarah. "She can tell you better than me." And then to Sarah, "Don't exaggerate. I don't want Bobby thinking his father is some kind of hero."

CHAPTER FIFTY-ONE

A house rising from a wooded lot takes planning. The house that George Whiting built on an Inter Coastal lot in Palm Coast, Florida involved as many helpers as there are characters in the old nursery rhyme, **The House That Jack Built,** I so enjoyed as a child. Today most of those helpers are enjoying that barbecue Dad had promised.

Sarah and I spent the morning peeling potatoes and shucking corn. Teddi wasn't feeling the love so she made do with assaulting one of her play toys. Mom had a pot of beans baking while Dad and Joel were raising a tent. When I finished my assignment I went out to Join Dad. Hailey, my best friend Daniel, and the man she hopes will fill that final place on the shelf in her garage, Detective Errol Monroe arrived. I like him.

Much like those nursery rhyme characters, Dads workers and their families dribbled in. Dad made sure to greet each family as if they were the most important guest invited. Dad gave Myrtle a big hug when she arrived. Sheriff Rodriguez and his wife and daughter had never seen our house so Mom gave them the tour.

Hours later when most of the guests had gone the party moved indoors. Hailey and Detective Monroe, Myrtle and Joel, and we kids remained. All afternoon everyone had skirted the drama that we had witnessed and been involved in just a month ago.

The adults sat around the kitchen table, nursing a final beverage.

I invited Daniel and Sarah to my room to help me with my latest passion, Picture Puzzles.

At the kitchen table Detective Monroe was putting the finishing pieces in place as well. "Bellamy has pleaded guilty to attempted robbery of Cluck's Chicken Coop. We dropped the attempted murder charge and the obstruction charge in exchange for his testimony against Tobias Thornton." Detective Monroe took a sip of a good craft brown ale he had recently discovered.

Myrtle spoke up, "I'm more interested in what happens to Victor, he killed two young women."

"Victor won't be going to trial. I told you he seemed to melt when he realized he was caught. By the way he's admitted to the killing of an old man who he stole a motorcycle from. He has pled guilty to three counts of second degree murder. He will be in prison for at least the next forty- five years. Honestly I don't see him making it. For a big guy he's incredibly mentally weak. He'll never see the outside."

In my room as Sarah and I laid out the pieces, Daniel roamed my bookshelf. I had in my own way told him about my favorite bedtime story. He found the nursery rhyme book and asked if I thought my Mom and dad might read it to him just the way they had read it to me.

<u>Let's ask them.</u>

Sarah said she'd heard that story often enough so she remained hovering over the thousand pieces of what in its completed form would emerge as an observatory nestled up against a night sky filled with stars.

Daniel whispered to his mother, too shy to ask himself.

Mom and dad laughed but agreed.

And so around the kitchen table in the house that George built, our guests got the full treatment.

With Dad stretching his fingers Mom began, "THIS IS THE HOUSE THAT JACK BUILT."